Decision on Corregidor

Decision on Corregidor

A story of courage, determination and sorrow

Chuck Wullenjohn

iUniverse, Inc.
Bloomington

DECISION ON CORREGIDOR
A story of courage, determination and sorrow

iUniverse books may be ordered through booksellers or by contacting:

iUniverse
1663 Liberty Drive
Bloomington, IN 47403
www.iuniverse.com
1-800-Authors (1-800-288-4677)

ISBN: 978-1-4759-6238-3 (sc)
ISBN: 978-1-4759-6239-0 (ebk)

Printed in the United States of America

iUniverse rev. date: 01/28/2013

To Amanda

Contents

CHAPTER 1

TO TAKE A WIFE

Yuma, Arizona, November 1940

Ed gunned the engine and the plane swooped low, bare inches above a row of tall date palms, the rushing force of the crisp desert air slapping against the prickly fronds, causing them to snap back and forth in the winter air. Perched on gray weathered ladders propped against the slender trees, fruit pickers craned their heads up in surprise. It wasn't a common sight to see planes overhead at all, let alone one roaring over so low it forced their heads down. The aircraft flashed by in an instant and the workers shook their heads in disgust before resuming work amid a shower of leaves and twigs.

Laughing, Ed pointed the nose of the biplane into the sky and swooped away as he wriggled the wings back and forth. He liked living life on the edge, even when it had to be created.

Flying through the desert sky never failed to leave him refreshed and invigorated. The high altitude air was crisp and sweet, much cooler than the furnace-like temperatures typical most of the year in southwest Arizona. As he slowed into a lazy turn, he looked down on people walking the streets below. The sight was endlessly fascinating. Folks looked like insects and houses resembled flimsy toys amid cardboard cutout yards. Trains chugging out of town into the empty desert looked more appropriate to a fancy store window in a big city.

Today's flight was particularly eventful, for it was the plane's longest journey since Ed began working on it eight months before. It had once been an abandoned, ancient hulk and he had transformed it into a sleek, operational machine. Test flights around Tucson were one thing, but this was real and it made him swell with pride.

So far, the trip had been without incident. The plane's single engine sputtered and coughed now and then, but the noise smoothed out and disappeared each time. Minor problems like this were to be expected in a refurbished plane, Ed figured, and not worth worrying about. Simple turns of the wrench always seemed to set things right.

Besides, the flight had a more important purpose. The real goal was to visit Barbara, Ed's sweetheart for as long as he could remember. The question of marriage had been tumbling in his head for months, but the idea of making a permanent commitment, a decision that would set his future life in motion, for better or worse, had scared him away time and again. But now was different. A year of lonely life away at school had convinced him to pop the question . . . to ask for her hand in marriage. He planned to do it that afternoon.

He had wired ahead to tell her he was on the way, but sidestepped giving the real reason, for he wanted it to be a surprise. He wanted Barbara to think he was taking advantage of simple good fortune; that of being able to fly the 200 miles to and from Tucson in one afternoon. To Ed, catching a person unawares was almost always fun.

He smiled at the hearty joke that would make her happy. Just think . . . marriage . . . to Barbara! Since boyhood, it had always seemed the natural destination.

Ed set his jaw, tightened his grip on the throttle and descended toward an empty brown field behind a frame house on the edge of town, where Barbara lived with her parents and older brother. He couldn't miss it, perched on the end of the street as it was, with two giant Eucalyptus trees spreading over the front half of the house. These were two of the biggest trees he had ever seen.

After passing low over the trees and rolling to a bumpy landing, Ed leaped from the cockpit and sprinted toward the house. Before he was half-way, an excited voice called out, "Hey there, college man!" It was Barbara, rising from a wood rocking chair on the back porch. Her red lips curved into a seductive smile and her bright eyes twinkled as she leaned over the railing. She flung one end of a sunlit yellow scarf behind her shoulder and said, "You gonna stay put for a while so we can spend some time together?"

Beaming a wide grin, Ed leaped up the three worn wooden steps leading onto the porch. At the top, he paused for a split second to savor the sight of her freshly brushed honey-brown hair flowing over softly rounded shoulders. With thoughtful upturned brows and the light of passion in her eyes, Ed considered her as lovely as any woman had a right to be.

He approached and took her outstretched hands. Pulling her close, they kissed, but the excitement of the moment was too much. Ed stepped back. "I've gotta head back in a few hours," he said. "I need to be back by nightfall." Grinning, he jerked a finger back toward the plane. "What do you think of her?"

Barbara gave a quick glance at the biplane resting in the middle of the sun burnt field. "Your plane looks real nice," she said, "real nice."

"It took me near six months, working day and night," Ed said, pride in his voice. "It's a Lincoln Standard like Charles Lindbergh used to fly. I've been scrounging up parts all over. She's a real honey."

Barbara gave a gentle toss of her head. "You've accomplished quite a bit. But I hope you haven't ignored your schoolwork."

"Nah, I've been studying, too," he replied quickly. "But forget about that." Ed leaned toward Barbara and took her into his arms, clutching her waist and drawing her close. "We have serious business to discuss."

"Business?" Her fingers over his shoulders gripped tight. "What business?" Her heart thumped rapidly as she gazed into his eyes.

Ed laughed under his breath. "You know what business I'm talking about, Barbara," knowing full well she understood. "A little matter of a contract between us—a lifelong one. Legally, it's called a marriage contract. Just a formality, you know."

She gave out a breath and kissed him. He hungrily leaned forward, caressing her lips with his own as much as kissing them. They sunk into each other's arms for what seemed long minutes. On drawing back, their hearts pounded, breathless, and they stared into each other's eyes.

"Just a formality?" asked Barbara, playing with him, her voice a shade sharper. "I don't know that Mother will see it that way." She paused, the hint of a smile playing across her lips. "Considering we've had eyes for each other practically our whole lives, I guess it is sort of a formality, but marriage is a public act and I want everyone to know it. Call me old fashioned, but I want a big ceremony with everyone there."

Ed stepped back, chuckling. "Well, that's something I guess I can live with." He relaxed his arms, scratched behind an ear and fixed his gaze. "Let's set a date. How about the first weekend of next month? We can do it early and catch a train for the coast that evening. We'll get ourselves a compartment on the fancy part of the train and have one heck of a honeymoon in Los Angeles or maybe even San Francisco."

Barbara lifted eyebrows in delight. "Gee, I always wanted to see the Golden Gate Bridge and ride a cable car. I can't wait to tell Mom and Dad." She broke into a wide-open smile, sparkling with affection and delight. "They're out for awhile with my brother, but they'll be back any minute. Let's take that plane of yours out for a ride before they get home. Then we can tell them the news first thing." She grinned. "They'll like it."

"Okay," he replied, turning. "Let's get going. I want to show you what she can do."

"Just be careful," she cautioned, leaning over to plant a wet kiss on his lips. She circled arms around him and leaned close. They caressed, breathing into the hollow of each other's neck. "This is what it's going to be like forever and ever," she whispered, ever so softly. "Forever and ever." For them, the world had transformed into a perfect place; secure, like a warm cocoon.

* * *

The two crowded into the 1926 vintage aircraft and strapped themselves in. Ed started the engine, motored to the edge of the field and pointed the nose to the left of a line of tall trees in the far distance. Before gunning the engine, he took a deep breath, filling his lungs with the fresh scent of burning mesquite coming from a chimney over the hill. "It's good to be home, Barbara. You don't know how good it feels," he remarked while staring into the vast blue sky.

"This plane is pretty nice, Ed," observed Barbara as she ran a hand over the inside of the cockpit. Not equipped for extra passengers, she shared the wide pilot's seat with Ed, squeezing in to his left. "You did a good job, but we shouldn't be gone long. We have a lot to talk about with Mother and Father, let alone your parents."

"Yeah, I guess we have things to do." He drew on goggles, focused his gaze on the field and revved the engine, wrapping hands around the red-colored throttle. "We'll be back lickety-split." Barbara tightened the arm over his shoulder and pressed against the fuselage with the other. "Don't go too fast," she warned, a tinge of trepidation in her voice. "I want to get back in one piece."

"Don't worry," he said as the plane bumped along the field and rose into the air, a fresh breeze slipping by either side of the cockpit. "We're gonna have some fun up there."

The plane climbed, gaining altitude, and leveled off at a speed of about sixty miles per hour. Ed maintained that altitude and speed for the next five minutes, easing into gentle turns, offering a bird's eye view of metropolitan Yuma, Arizona, a town with a population of about four thousand.

"What do you think?" he asked. "Like it?"

Ill at ease at first, and uncomfortable amid the cramped quarters, Barbara's lips slowly spread into a smile. This was her first airplane ride and it took a few moments to become accustomed to it. "Wow, I think I could get used to this. You get quite a view from up here."

"Yeah, flying is great," remarked Ed. He banked to the left, still maintaining a level, easy course. While straightening out, he said,

"Tell you what. Let's go down lower, do a few barrel rolls and a figure eight, then we'll head on back to the house."

"Oh, no!" she snapped, "None of that stuff. All I want is a simple, relaxing ride. My stomach needs to be in shape when we touch down."

Ed scrunched up his mouth. Nothing could be more boring than flying level all the time. Acrobatics were the things that made piloting an airplane fun. Barbara's a typical woman, he shrugged; unwilling to take chances or do anything out of the ordinary. "Okay, no rolls or turns," he muttered, disappointment in his voice.

On the level, no nonsense course, Barbara craned her neck outside the open cockpit to take in the sights. The blue Colorado River meandered through the desert to the left, with downtown Yuma on the other, train tracks heading into the desert wilderness on either side of town. A steam locomotive pulling out of the train depot sent clouds of black smoke boiling into the air and Barbara could make out cars and trucks rolling along the highway. It was quite a sight for someone who had never before seen the earth from up above.

"What do you say we head on back?" called Ed. "I've got to save some fuel for the return trip."

Barbara gave a quick up and down movement of her head and Ed turned the plane around. Then he remembered the date grove and the harmless scare he had given the workers earlier. It might be fun to do it again.

"We're gonna make one slight detour," he said, grinning, as he revved the engine and dived toward the orchard. The plane screamed down and leveled off just above the trees, and the pickers again ducked as he approached. "Look at them!" he shouted as they blasted over the trees and shot over the end of the row. Ed put the plane into a steep bank to come around again. "One more time!" he shouted.

Barbara had gone rigid, white fingers digging into his leg. Ed glanced over and said, "Don't worry, honey. We're just having a little fun. Nobody'll get hurt."

Ed set the plane on a course back over the orchard, but on reaching the first tree, the engine sputtered and the plane dropped a few feet. He yanked back on the throttle with all his might, but it was too late; the plane's fixed landing gear collided with a heavy palm frond, causing the rear of the craft to buck upward. He tried to correct, but the left wing dipped down and a second frond slapped against it, jolting the light plane to the side.

Then things happened too fast. Another palm frond jumped up to be sliced through by the propeller, then another tangled itself around the propeller shaft. That was the end. The plane gave a sickening, screeching moan and crashed down among a row of trees, turning over two times, smashing into a stack of wooden crates, scattering dates and cuttings from the trees all over. Workers scrambled down ladders and ran toward the smoking wreckage.

They dragged out both bodies, but one was beyond help; they found Barbara crushed beneath the fuselage, staring upward, stone dead. The femoral artery in her upper leg had severed in the crash and most of her blood puddled the ground within five minutes. The owner of the date orchard, a friend of the family, squealed up in a truck and gently laid Ed in back and delivered him to the hospital, the only one in town, where a physician tended to his wounds. Before leaving the orchard, he covered Barbara with a dirty canvas tarp. One of the workers notified her parents and called a mortician.

Ed woke in his old room two days later, his left leg in a wooden splint and thick bandages covering the side of his face. His mother, seated in a rocking chair, saw him squirm beneath the blankets and put down her knitting. She leaned over.

"Son, can you hear me, son?"

"Mom?" he croaked, the room a hazy blur. "Where am I?"

"You're in bed, son, your own bed."

"In bed?" His mind whirling in confusion, he struggled to think of a reason why he would be lazing in bed. Last he remembered, he was flying over Yuma. The plane! He opened his eyes wide.

"Mom, where's Barbara?" he cried as loud as he was able. "Where's Barbara!"

"Settle down, son, don't get yourself excited," she said, placing a wet rag on his forehead. "We can talk about Barbara later. You go on back to sleep."

Ed's eyes, alert and wide, shot from side to side. "I gotta see her, Mom. We're getting married. Did she tell you?"

"No, son, she didn't. Now go back to sleep, please. Your body needs it."

Ed struggled for consciousness, but a wave of black confusion swept over him and he felt himself carried off, far from the desert. But a certain awareness of events in the room continued for a minute or two. It was silent for a moment, but then he heard voices speaking softly, almost in whispers.

"You didn't tell the boy, did you, Marion?" asked a male voice. He knew it was Dad.

"No, he's in no condition right now. How could I tell him Barbara is dead?" The voice faded away, followed by smothered sobs. His father tried to comfort her. "There, there, Marion, there's nothing any of us could have done. I'll tell him myself, in due time."

Inside Ed's subconscious, he wanted to speak out, to scream. Now he knew. But why her? Why not him? How could he go on? A sickening feeling of despair thudded down like a trap door and his mind went blank. How could he live with himself? Ed drifted into unconsciousness, not certain if he should allow himself to waken.

Chapter 2

Building a New Life

January 1941

Ed holed up in bed for days, flat on his back, right leg cradled in a pillow. He passed away the hours half-listening to the radio and leafing through magazines, the tragedy never far from his mind. What was he to do? How could he rebuild his life?

The question gnawed at his insides, picking and clawing, never letting up. How could he have allowed the accident to take place? He was a good pilot; a bit of a daredevil at times, but no more than his peers. And it had happened so fast! One moment Barbara sat smiling into the blue sky, her golden hair sparkling in the sun, looking toward the future. The next she was gone, her life ripped away like an autumn leaf swept up by a cruel wind and flung over a cliff.

Ed spent most of his waking hours fixated on the accident and the morning of the sixth day was no different. Roused from a fitful night's sleep by a neighbor's barking dog, he stared at the ceiling through moist eyes, motionless for ten minutes. Then he turned his head and slowly reached for the newspaper his mother had crept into his room to lay beside the bed early that morning. Rolling onto his side, he spread it out and scanned the front page, searching for something to take his mind off Barbara. Near the bottom, he spied an eyewitness report describing the air battles raging over Britain.

Fascinated by the aerial skirmishes raging thousands of feet above the earth, the pages of this ongoing saga had been turning for three months. World War II was more than a year old and Nazi Germany had won a series of lightning triumphs in continental Europe. Flushed with victory, she had taken on Britain, which seemed like an apple ready to fall from the tree. But it wasn't turning into the romp German leaders expected. British resistance to the Luftwaffe's attempts to bomb her into submission had been fierce.

Ed admired the stalwart gallantry of the British flyers, considering them modern gladiators, romantic and daring. He found their story remarkable, for they were fighting against tremendous odds. The issue over which side would emerge victorious had not yet been decided, though, seemingly, either the Germans or the British would have to break soon.

He licked his lips and looked for something else of equal interest. Not noticing anything on the front-page, he turned inside, rattling the paper, and spotted a headline on the next page that grabbed his attention. "Roosevelt touts U.S. as arsenal of democracy," it read. Ed reclined against the pillows piled against the headboard, propped up the newspaper and began to read.

The article detailed a speech President Roosevelt had given the previous day to a convention of businessmen in New York about the necessity for America to provide military aid to Britain during her hour of need.

"Let it be known, the United States is today's arsenal of democracy," he announced in stentorian tones to a packed house. "This year, American manufacturers will build tens of thousands of aircraft and other weapons of war. A sizeable proportion of these armaments will go to our friends and allies to aid in their fight against the forces of tyranny. Much, however, will remain here to replenish and build our own military might. No aggressor shall dare take on the United States."

Ed turned away and gazed out the window. So, the United States is building up its air force, he mused. That means the army'll be looking for pilots. They'll get the opportunity to lead the same heroic life as those Britishers in their Hurricane and Spitfire fighters. Might be worth keeping in mind, he thought.

But now was not the time. Things were starting to tumble inside his head and he felt tired. With a swipe of an outstretched hand, he knocked the newspaper to the floor and flopped back. Within minutes he dozed off, fast asleep.

Ten days passed, the slowest of his life, then one Wednesday morning his father walked in, rustled him out of bed and helped him down the stairs to the front parlor. After settling him into an easy chair and walking away, Ed, grim faced, stared out the window into the brown scrub brush desert, thinking back to the morning of Barbara's funeral. A concussion received during the accident had made it impossible for him to attend, but both his parents went and, afterward, the grim black hearse transporting her body to the cemetery passed in front of the house. Ed watched from his room. It rolled slowly by, followed by dozens of autos and horse drawn wagons carrying silent mourners. The image caused a cold shudder to course up his spine, making him feel isolated and hollow inside.

He dozed off afterward, waking when father's sedan crunched up the driveway and a second car squealed to a stop at the front curb. He perked up as he watched the door of the parked car open. Barbara's older brother, Hank, hopped out.

Ed had never liked or trusted him. A student who cared little about his studies, Hank had dropped out of high school in favor of working at a filling station pumping gas and repairing tires. Little more than nodding acquaintances, with few interests in common, neither spoke much to the other.

Standing on the curb, Hank wiped a nervous hand down the side of his trousers and waited for Ed's father to walk up and escort him inside. Ed sat ramrod straight as the door swung open and the two entered. Both removed their hats.

Ed's father, Marshall, approached and rubbed a finger along his mustache, uneasy at what he was about to do. He cleared his throat and began. "Ed," he said, "I've brought Hank along because he has something to get off his chest. His father and I talked it over and we've decided you two have to speak. You both need to get over what happened and it's best to start doing it now. If there's any trouble, I'll be here to stop it."

Wearing a stern expression, he looked into Hank's face, then shifted back to Ed. He continued. "It's been over two weeks since the accident, son. You're well enough for this."

He directed his next words to Hank. "Hank, I know this is a hard time," he said in a kind, caring manner, as if he were his own flesh and blood. "All of us hurt over what happened. But you've got anger inside, a hot-blooded, mean anger that's no good. I had it once myself, but I lost it forever back in the Great War. I got over it and so will you. It's time you started." He motioned with an arm. "All right," he snapped, stepping away. "Hank, you've got talking to do. Get on with it."

Lips drawn tight together, the muscles in Hank's neck bulged and a vein on the side of his forehead pulsed in and out. For a moment he stood in awkward silence, his heavy breathing echoing in the room. He had wanted this meeting, had begged both fathers to arrange it. But now that it was taking place, he found the words difficult to get out.

He waited a few seconds, ran a hand through his unruly black hair, and took two steps forward. His lips red and tight, he began to speak. "Hey," he stammered, shifting his weight from foot to foot.

"Hey," Ed answered in a low voice.

"How's the leg?"

"Not bad. Give it time and it'll heal."

"Yeah." Hank looked down at the floor and scrunched up his knit wool hat between his fingers. Wearing a cold, congested look, he opened his mouth and let out a long sigh. As the sound faded, the logjam in his head broke and his eyes grew wide.

"Ed, your leg's gonna heal, but what about Barbara?" His face grew red. "*What about her*?" His voice, which had been low, grew into a roar. Ed's mother walked in from the kitchen and leaned against the dining room table, her forehead wrinkled in concern. Marshall took a nervous step forward but did not intervene.

"Hank," Ed said in an even voice, "I'm sorry, truly sorry about what happened. Believe me, I'd give anything to have her back. Anything."

"Well, those are nice words, buddy-boy, but it's not possible, is it?" Hank's words were filled with sarcasm. "Soon, you'll be up walking around, doing whatever you want, but Barbara'll still be dead. Thinking about it makes me sick."

Hank lowered his hand and wiped a forearm over his eyes. Marshall put a comforting hand on Hank's shoulder but he shook it away. An awkward silence filled the room before Ed spoke in a pleading, nasally voice. "Look, Hank, me and Barbara were going to get married. We decided before we went on that airplane ride. Besides, you knew we were gonna get hitched someday."

Hank stepped forward. "Yeah, I figured it and tried to talk her out of it." He pointed an accusing finger. "You're a hothead, Ed. You take too many chances and expect others to follow along no matter what. You're the cause of this."

Ed ignored the stinging words and the accusation they contained. "The accident wasn't my fault. The fuel line clogged and the engine went out. There was nothing I could do."

"Yeah, there's always plenty of excuses, aren't there? You're good at that." Shaking his head, Hank moved back a few inches, his eyes darting about in frustration, his expression hard and resentful. He pointed a finger and wagged it up and down.

"You're no more than a stunt pilot fit for nothing better than a two bit, run down circus," he bellowed. "What happened is on your head. I tell you Ed, it's on your head!"

Ed and Hank stared at each other amid a ringing silence that threatened to explode like a volcano. A shadow of alarm touching his face, Marshall Bannon broke in. "I reckon that's enough," he declared in a voice of authority, stepping between the two boys. With stiff dignity, he turned and faced Hank. "All right, it's over. You said what you wanted. Leave it at that."

Fists clenched at his sides, anger pounding in his temple, Hank faced Marshall, his mouth tight and grim. After a moment, he nodded and strode to the door. Grasping the doorknob, he stopped and swung around, flashing a look of disdain before turning and continuing out. He climbed into his car, slammed the door and motored off.

Marshall heaved a sigh and flopped into a dark straight-backed chair beside the door. "I'm glad that's over," he mumbled. He sat for a moment, relieved, then rose up and shot his son a raking look of displeasure. "I don't know what to say, boy, I just don't know." He leaned forward and cradled his head in two palms as Marion walked over and placed a hand on his shoulder. She rubbed back and forth. Ed stared out the window, his face a mask of stone.

Several uncomfortable minutes passed and the antique wooden clock over the fireplace gonged the hour. Marshall looked up with a pained expression, as if studying the clock's face, and then shifted toward his son. "When will you take responsibility and begin thinking like an adult? Why did you ever fool around with learning how to fly? If you had stuck with your studies none of this would have happened."

Ed's mind swirled into a daze. Thoughts revolved as if in a whirlpool, only glimpses of familiar faces and fragments of language appearing. He wanted to speak out to justify what he had done, but no words were there. The whirlpool dissolved into a vast nothingness. It was as if his mind became blank. It took a minute before he could utter a reply.

"Dad, listen," he stammered. "Do you think I wanted it to happen? I asked Barbara to be my wife. We were going to be married."

"I know; you said that. Lots of times."

Ed shot up his hands. "Well, doesn't that mean anything? So I took her on an airplane ride . . . heck, most people would have to pay for that. It wasn't like I forced her; she *wanted* to go."

Marshall stiffened. He slipped a Meerschaum pipe from the left front pocket of his coat and pointed the stem at his son's chest. "You had no business flying airplanes. I sent you to school to make something of yourself, not to waste time in the sky."

"There's nothing wrong with airplanes, Dad. A couple years from now they'll be all over."

"That doesn't matter!" Marshall slammed a hand onto the surface of the table, causing a glass ashtray to crash to the polished wood floor. He bent forward to pick it up before resuming. "Look, son, flying is no good. It's too dangerous and keeps you away from what you should be doing. From now on, you're forbidden to fly. You go to school and study. That's all. No more flying."

Ed stared back and shook his head. Jutting out his lower lip, he shifted his gaze to Marion, who stood beside Marshall in silence, twisting the bottom of her apron into knots. She wouldn't get involved in this, Ed figured. The argument was between him and his father.

"Dad, I'm sorry. I'm sorry about what happened to Barbara and I'm sorry you have such a low opinion of flying." Angry and hurt over the events of the past two weeks, doing something drastic about his now barren life didn't seem so extreme. Ed straightened and flung a hand forward. "I'm quitting school," he scowled. "Since I can't afford another plane, I'll sign up for a hitch in the air corps. One tour should get me all the money I need."

He leaned back and stiffened his jaw in defiance. "What I do with my life from now on is my business and nobody elses. If I want to fly, I'll fly. Nobody can keep me cooped up on the ground."

Marshall narrowed his eyes into constricted slits. He took a long puff of smoldering tobacco, holding the smoke in his lungs before blowing it out through his nose. "Ed," he said in a low, measured voice, "you don't know what you're saying. Your mother and I scrimped and saved for years to put you through college. Schooling like that will give you a giant leg up on everyone else. You won't get stuck working on a railroad track gang, like me. You'll have opportunities I never had." He shoved the pipe back in his mouth and chewed on the stem.

Ed shook his head. "No, I can't do it that way, Dad. I'm not the same person as you. Gimme another week and my leg will have healed up enough to leave. I'll hitch a ride up to Phoenix and enlist."

"You have it all figured out, don't you?" Head resting against the back of the chair, Marshall spoke from the side of his mouth. "You think life is real simple." He paused for a moment while cradling fingers around the bowl of the pipe. "My advice is to forget the army. I can't think of a better way to waste your life. I was in it, so I know what I'm talking about."

Firm in the conviction of youth, Ed wasn't about to back off. "Dad, I can make my own decisions. I'll decide what's best. If I settle on the army air corps, it's final."

Marshall ignored the words, brushing them aside as so much chaff. "I've been telling you all your life about what I went through in the Great War. That war was fought for nothing more than the money-grubbers who control international finance and those dirty European countries that welched on their debts. I don't want my son involved in anything like that. I want better." His voice trailed off.

Ed leaned forward. "Dad, I know what you went through and what you think about war in general. But I need to forget about what happened and I can't go on ripping myself apart. My life's got to be different. Don't you understand?"

Marshall shook his head, his anger cooling, but still at a simmer. "But, the army." He paused for a moment, looking down, then bolted upright, his hackles rising. "You're better than the army, boy. It's not like you think it is. They'll send you to some base somewhere and forget about you. Mark my words, that's what they'll do."

He stared for a moment and then, all of a sudden, pushed his chair back against the wall, the chair scraping across the floor. He cast a sideways glance at Marion, bolted upright and moved toward the door, stopping and turning before reaching it. He waved a finger at Ed. "I gotta go outside and think. You ought to do some thinking yourself, boy. If you were younger I'd turn you over my knee. I don't like flying, I don't like pilots and I don't like what's going on overseas. If we get pulled into a war, every young pilot in the country will be called up and American boys'll be slaughtered again. You could be signing your death warrant, but you're too young to even know it."

With a disgusted expression, Marshall turned and stepped outside. He leaned forward and spit onto the trampled tan soil and then looked back over his shoulder and spoke through the open doorway in a loud voice. "Your mother and me have sacrificed for years and now you want to throw it away. Good God!"

So furious he could speak no more, Marshall walked away, clicking the door behind. Ed sat for a minute, listening to his father crunch across the gravel to a shade tree on the side of the house. As the footsteps faded, Marion moved forward and spoke.

"You'll listen to me, won't you, son? If you'll do it for anyone, you'll change your mind for me. You must!"

Ed looked up. "Mom, what do you mean, I must? I'm old enough to make my own decisions and I don't want to sit around in a classroom anymore. The army's sounding better all the time. If they'll let me fly, I'm signing on the dotted line."

Marion lowered her voice to a whisper. "Your father never told you everything that happened over in France. He told you some of the story, but never the whole thing."

Ed cocked his head back, surprised. "He didn't? What did he hold back?"

"War's a lot worse than you know, Eddy, a lot worse than you'd think from the men marching down the street on Armistice Day."

"Mom, I know that. I'm not stupid, you know. And don't call me 'Eddy'. I'm not a kid."

Marion grimaced with frustration. "Did he tell you about seeing his best friend's head blown off while he was standing next to him?"

Ed's eyes grew wide. "He saw that?"

"Yes, and plenty more. Blood spattered all over your father's chest when that man died." Silent, absorbing every word, Ed gazed at her. "After the war, he coughed and choked from mustard gas attacks for years, having to sleep sitting up in a chair lots of nights because of fluid in his lungs. That's why we moved here to the heat. Arizona's a lot better for lung conditions than Ohio."

"Gee, I didn't know that," Ed said in a whisper, looking down. "I thought we moved out here because he wanted to live on a ranch." He quieted for a moment as she patted the stiffened fingers of his hand. "I can see why he doesn't want me to enlist." He contemplated in silence for a moment before jerking his head up. "But if I join the air corps, I'll be flying way above the boys on the ground, where all the mud and poison gas is. I'll be fine."

Marion lifted a hand to her cheek. "Son, don't talk like that. You don't know what will happen. And why give up your schooling? You've already finished a whole year."

Ed's self-assurance had returned after wavering a few moments back. "Mom, I need to do something else. Barbara's always gonna be with me if I stay. I can't go through life living a memory."

Marion sat back, sensing she wasn't going to change his mind. Cupping a hand over her mouth, she fretted over what the future might bring. Ed quickly thrust out a hand, lacing her fingers with his own.

"I know this is right, Mom, so please understand. I'm not leaving for good. I'll write you and Dad every week and when my tour's up, I'll come back. I'll have enough money and flying experience to get a job anywhere. Until then, just be on my side. It'll work out."

He held her hand a moment longer and released it with a squeeze. The pillow under his leg had shifted and most hung over the side of the cushion. He reached forward to adjust it, but Marion quickly intervened.

"Let me do it, Eddy," she said, bending over. She gently lifted the leg and slid the pillow fully underneath. "There."

She gazed into his eyes, the quickest flicker of a smile appearing. "I liked Barbara," she said. "Always did. She would have made a fine wife."

"Yeah," replied Ed. "I miss her more than anyone."

"Folks all around town liked her. She even volunteered down at the hospital. She ever tell you that?'

"Yeah, she told me in a letter, but Mom, this is just making me feel worse." Ed lifted his eyes up to the window. "I'm the one who has to get used to being without her. It feels like everyone's trying to make me out to be a criminal or something."

Marion shook her head, hair gently swaying over the sides of her face. "Nobody's trying to do that, Eddy. What happened was an accident; everyone knows that. It's just that we miss Barbara."

"It's pretty clear where people think the blame lies. Dad thinks it, so does Hank and those people down at the date orchard. Everyone does."

"Folks are just upset. They liked Barbara. They like you, too."

Ed frowned. "I don't know, Mom. I have a feeling I'm not too popular hereabouts. I don't know that I'm so popular with me, either. To tell you the truth, I feel responsible. It's probably best for all concerned that I get out. The air corps'll be a good place. The sooner I leave this two-bit town the better."

Marion leaned back and closed her eyes. For the next thirty seconds her chest heaved and fingers dug into the armrests. Then she tilted her head toward Ed in a barely perceptible nod, straightened and rose up.

"No good will come of this," she muttered while walking into the kitchen. "Go ahead and do it; you're old enough, but you may live to regret it."

Behind, Ed listened from the easy chair, the clock again gonging as its hands reached the bottom of the hour. He shook his head in disgust. They're all against me, he muttered, even Mom and Dad. The sooner I get out of Arizona and into the air corps the better.

Chapter 3

Stationed in the Philippines

November 1941

In 1939, a mere twenty-one years after the conclusion of the "war to end all wars," the world again broke out in armed conflict. While European nations clashed and Japan gobbled huge chunks of China, America's leaders worked in frantic haste to rebuild the country's military might, for two decades of isolationism and neglect had caused America's strength to sharply decline to that of a third rate power. Steps to rearm began, but it took full national commitment, sacrifice and the time necessary to retool and focus the country's industrial might. The challenge was daunting and could not be accomplished overnight.

Ships were needed to service the nation's far flung outposts and, in early 1941, the Department of War pressed into service the luxury passenger liner *President Coolidge* for duty as a troop transport. In early November, it lay berthed at San Francisco's Fort Mason taking on a load of military personnel and cargo destined for the mysterious overseas destination of "PLUM." A guarded military codeword, only a few naval officers aboard knew the meaning.

Workers had fastened down gangplanks and a steady khaki-clad stream of men and cargo surged aboard from a huge weather-beaten redwood warehouse. Giant steam cranes worked overhead as sweethearts and families crowded against peeling gray rails lining the dock, waving handkerchiefs and dabbing eyes filled with moisture. Soldiers gathered along the port side of the ship, climbing lines and hanging from railings, waving and soaking in their last glimpses of home. A crisp fall day, white seagulls and other marine birds squawked and swooped up and down from the clouds, on the never-ending lookout for handouts or stray bits of food.

Ed, now wearing the shiny silver wings of an Army Air Corps pilot, huddled in a corner of the warehouse talking in low tones with his parents, who had come into town to see him off. He met them the day before at the Southern Pacific depot and, together, they rode cable cars, toured Chinatown and enjoyed a splendid seafood dinner at famous Fisherman's Wharf while watching workmen unload live crabs from colorful boats. Now the three had gathered against a rough plank wall, a respectful distance from a young soldier and his wife engaged in a passionate embrace.

"I'm glad you made it for my bon voyage," said Ed. "Seeing the sites of San Francisco together made a memory that'll last a long time." He flashed a quick smile. "And that was one heck of a seafood dinner last night. It was the first time I've raised my courage enough to down an oyster."

"Yeah, those ugly looking, slimy things," replied Marshall with a laugh, lifting his foot onto a rickety wood bench. "Aside from that, the food was terrific. I especially liked that sourdough bread. That's not something we get in Arizona."

He chuckled to himself before continuing. "You know, riding cable cars up and down hills through fog you could barely see through was something I'll never forget. The train ride out here was something your mother and I have never done before, either. We booked ourselves a compartment on a sleeping car and traveled in style; like rich folks." He smiled at his wife and took her hand.

Due to poor economic conditions during the depression, the Bannons hadn't traveled anywhere in years. Ever cautious about his job, Marshall refused to leave town, determined to be available whenever the railroad wanted him. He saw the railroad decrease its workforce by fifty percent and he watched proud men whither and pale as they walked away for the final time, knowing no other jobs were to be had.

Marshall gritted his teeth and refused to join them. He made it known that he would do anything for the railroad, from driving ties to scrubbing crusty dirt from oily locomotives—anything to stay employed. Over time, he developed a reputation in management circles as a steady, reliable worker who could always be counted on, no matter the day, no matter the time. That resulted in steady employment that got the family through hard economic times and sent his son to college.

His lips creased into a smile, a grateful Ed watched his parents, pleased to see them enjoying life together. They deserved it. His father was a self-taught gentleman, strong and taciturn, and together with mother was a complete man. As a boy who had become an adult, Ed realized the two made a fine couple.

As he watched his mother whisper into her husband's ear, Ed considered the woman who had raised him. Dark hair curling down to her neck, with only the slightest tinge of gray, she was at heart an Ohio farm girl who relocated to the state from West Virginia as a small child. The soil on her father's farm raised indifferent crops and, as a result, her life had been filled with one sacrifice after another, especially in the years after World War I. A steadfast, unwavering woman, she found comfort and order in the established rhythms of farm wives before her; baking bread each week, keeping chickens, putting up jams and vegetables, doing laundry every Thursday. Like her railroad worker husband, she had a capacity for hard work and a certain curiosity about the ways of the world.

Watching her only son depart the United States for somewhere far away was not easy. Marion dabbed at her eyes with a silk handkerchief, her expression a mixture of pride and sorrow. Ed remembered her breaking out in tears at momentous occasions like this throughout his life. She had even whimpered during his graduation ceremony in the high school auditorium three years before.

Proud of his parents, Ed looked back and forth in an attempt to stamp this moment in his mind. He wanted to store this mental photo right next to the one of Barbara. He thought hard for a moment, then perked up and grew serious. Time was short; the ship would soon edge away from the dock and head out to sea. That would be it. He placed hands on his narrow hips and coughed aloud. They glanced up, smiling.

He rubbed the back of a hand over his mouth and began. "Dad," he said, "I hope you and Mom don't hold it against me for joining the army. I'm sorry about what happened back home, but being a pilot is what I've always wanted. When I get out, I'll work for a private airline somewhere, maybe even in Arizona."

Marshall nodded, an arm around Marion's shoulder. She leaned against his strong frame. "Ed," he said, "you're our only son. Neither of us wanted you to enlist. It took a long time to get used to the idea." He raked his free hand through thick hair and cast a quick glance at his wife. "Truth be told, I wish one of us could have talked you out of it. But we've accepted your decision. You're a man; you're entitled. No matter what, we'll always be behind you." He winked at his wife. "Isn't that right, Marion?"

She stepped forward, leaving Marshall's comforting arm behind, and clasped her son's hand, cradling it in her own. "We love you, Eddy. Take care of yourself, no matter where this ship takes you." Trembling, she reached up and kissed his cheek.

Crossing arms, Marshall looked on, realizing only a few minutes remained before the final call to board. He intended to get something off his chest before then, for he wanted his son to leave with no false illusions about army life. He waited, nervous, while Marion and Ed hugged, taking the opportunity to draw a pipe from a pocket, tamp tobacco into the bowl and light it with a match.

When he finished the rather drawn out process, they had parted. Ed, wearing a pleased grin, looked up. This was Marshall's chance.

"Son," he said as gray, fragrant smoke curled up, "first off, I want to say I'm sorry for bringing Hank over that day. I figured I was doing the right thing, but I've thought about what happened ever since. There was no need for it and I apologize."

Ed chuckled in response. "Don't worry, Dad," he said. "I don't care what Hank thinks and never did. What happened was of no consequence. Flying's in my blood and I'd have joined the air corps anyhow."

Marshall breathed a sigh of relief. "Well, I'm glad to hear that. I worried that it had helped drive you into enlisting, which was the opposite of what I wanted."

"Naw," replied Ed with a smile, "that had nothing to do with it. I enlisted for lots of reasons. I wanted to fly, but I also wanted to forget about the accident. That hasn't happened yet, but I hope it will."

"I think I understand," replied Marshall in a low, drawn out tone. He studied his son's face for a long moment, drew the pipe from his mouth, gave it a quick glance, then thrust it back.

"Son, there's one more thing," he said, "I want to share some lessons I learned twenty-five years ago in France—in a stinking hell of trenches and craters." He sucked the pipe's stem and blew a thin stream of smoke out a corner of his mouth.

"Ed, the army in the field is different from the one you've been in; sleeping in nice beds each night and eating off clean plates. The army's the army and a soldier has to do whatever he's told, even if it doesn't make sense or he doesn't like it." He took the pipe from his mouth and jabbed it toward his son. "The army'll never change, but you might have to," he warned. "Things may not turn out like you expect."

Ed gave a gentle shake of his head. "Pilots are officers, Dad. It won't be so bad."

Marshall frowned. "Everyone's got to take orders from someone, from the lowest ranks to the highest. You gotta watch out for yourself. No one else will. The army's no democracy."

Ed chuckled. "Don't worry. I'll keep an eye out."

Frustrated, Marshall glanced down, for he didn't seem to be getting through. He took a deep breath and plowed on. "Look, son, I went through the Great War. I know what I'm talking about. Combat is full of uncertainties. Whether you're an officer or not, things you never imagined in your wildest dreams can happen. You gotta be prepared. You're a smart boy. Follow your instincts and use your own good sense."

"Don't worry, Dad," replied Ed, full of confidence. "I'll probably end up flying against the Japs someday, but I'll be fine. We trained on P-35 pursuits and we're getting spanking new P-40's overseas. Everyone tells me we can fly rings around the bamboo and rice paper contraptions the Japs fly."

Marshall narrowed his eyes and spoke with direct firmness. "Well, just don't fall into the trap of being overconfident. That can hurt you bad. Besides," he said, sliding the pipe back in his mouth, "I don't trust the government."

His bearing stiff and proud, Marshall reached forward and clapped Ed's shoulder. "Well, enough of that kind of talk. I guess I had my say." Just then, a steam whistle on the ship blew its deep-throated warning, signaling the last passengers to hurry aboard.

"Sounds like I gotta go," said Ed, in a voice containing a mixture of trepidation and self-confidence. He reached down for a brown leather satchel. "I'll write as often as I can."

Ed lifted the bag, feeling awkward, for the final goodbye was at hand. He shifted his weight from foot to foot. "Guess I better go," he said. "Jim Gatling's holding a spare bunk."

"You two've become good friends, haven't you?" asked Marion. "He's a married man, too. Where's he leaving his wife?"

"Yeah, Jim's a swell guy. His wife's name is Becky and he's leaving her near here in a town outside Hamilton Field—Novato."

A deep voice echoed through the warehouse. "Last call to board! Last call!"

Ed kissed his mother and threw an arm around Marshall's shoulder in a quick embrace. Then he turned on a heel and quick-stepped toward the gangplank. He stopped at the bottom, looking back in an expression mixed with confusion, pride and excitement. He waved, grabbed a side rail and continued up. Marshall and Marion exchanged sad glances as he vanished into a sea of soldiers and, hand in hand, strolled outside to the open dock, the smooth steel side of the giant passenger liner not more than twenty feet away.

Witnessing the departure hubbub carried Marshall back to 1917 when he went through a very similar experience in New Jersey on departing for France. He remembered as if it had happened yesterday. His entire family journeyed out by streetcar to line the dock. Everyone wore patriotic red, white and blue and he could still see them holding down their hats with one hand and waving with the other.

Every soldier on that ship overflowed with confidence and enthusiasm, including Marshall, believing the enemy would quake at their intimidating presence.

Boy, did we learn the hard, violent way, he thought with a shrug, for his regiment took heavy casualties during its stint in the trenches of the Western Front. He'd seen unimaginable things in that living nightmare, from men crippled for life, to others blown to bits. One afternoon a section of trench was hit by a sudden barrage of enemy artillery shells, burying dozens in what quickly became a pre-dug long grave. Remembering made the present scene even more poignant, causing his heart to pound with emotion.

The ship made ready to sail. Sailors pulled gangplanks aboard and three tugs nudged against its side to maneuver the unwieldy craft into the harbor. A cheer went up from the crowd, nearly drowning out the patriotic music of the thirty-member San Francisco Port of Embarkation band, playing from behind a portable white picket fence. Within minutes, the liner's powerful propellers churned through the blue-green water and she made her way out to sea beneath the Golden Gate Bridge, away from San Francisco and loved ones. The troops onboard had not been informed of the ship's destination, nor had they deduced it, only knowing they were on their way to "PLUM."

The ocean liner carried one thousand mostly enlisted soldiers and their equipment, and the passage proved uneventful and pleasant, with no duties and plenty of food. For the officers it was even better. Ed and Gatling, both second lieutenants, relaxed on narrow bunks in a private room, reading paperback novels, gazing at the stars at night, playing cards, and listening in on the conversations of other, more senior officers, who gathered each morning after breakfast for conversation in a wood-paneled, deep carpeted lounge in the center of the ship. Ed made a habit of attending the daily bull sessions, absorbing every word of men who were more knowledgeable and world-wise than he. The talks, though covering a wide variety of topics, always came back to the primary subject on everyone's mind—war in the Pacific.

"The Japanese would not be foolish enough to start a war with the United States," remarked a lieutenant colonel, a recent graduate of the Army War College. He spoke in a sharp, rapid-fire voice, with an accent that told everyone he hailed from Brooklyn. "They've got their hands full in China. At the very least, China has to be secure before they can turn their eyes this way." He leaned back, confident in his reasoning. "We're in a good position in the Pacific, overall."

Another man, a major, removed a pipe from his mouth and nodded in agreement. "It's true; they can't leave China at their backdoor while going to war with us. They have to contend with the British in Singapore, too." He tapped the bowl of the pipe against the palm of his hand over an ashtray, gray residue tumbling out. "Think about it. The Japanese are boxed in good and tight. Even if they wanted to launch a war, it would make little strategic sense."

A scholarly looking man with circular eyeglasses and premature gray hair at the side of the room shook his head. He spoke in a clipped, straightforward voice, as if addressing students in a lecture hall. "The British already have their hands full with the Germans," he said while straightening his glasses, "despite their fortifications in Singapore. Forget about the Brits. Forget about China, too. The United States is the only power capable of checking Japanese expansion in the Pacific. They aren't ready to make their move yet, but mark my words, it will happen—war between us and Japan."

One of the officers who spoke earlier turned and shook his head in disagreement. "You really think they'd go up against us? We've got the strongest military in the world," he said, thrusting a finger. "The Japanese aren't stupid. Our ships'll blast them out of the water and our planes'll control the skies, and they know it."

Ed enjoyed listening to these never-ending back-and-forth conversations, finding them fascinating, as well as educational.

International politics seemed almost an abstract concept back in Arizona and to be a participant on the world stage, to be part of something important, was a heady brew to a person reared in rural America. Having little else to occupy his mind, he absorbed every word.

Gatling listened in on some of the same discussions and maintained his firm conviction in the superiority of American arms. "Hogwash," he said dismissively at the end of one of the extended debates. "Any schoolboy knows we're stronger than the Japs."

But Ed wasn't so sure. Though he had but one year of active duty under his belt, the discussions seemed to prove that a reasonable case could be made for less optimistic points of view. Just about everyone aboard ship agreed that American power was unquestionable, but, for the first time, he harbored the slightest of reservations. Perhaps he had dismissed his father's warning too quickly.

Four days after leaving San Francisco the ship docked at Pearl Harbor, Hawaii, exchanged some cargo and people, and continued onward to Guam. Formed into a military convoy with a navy destroyer escort, the compact group of vessels plowed through empty seas, white wakes trailing behind. Sometimes he and Gatling moved onto the deck at night, the stars shining so brilliant and close in the black tropic sky that they felt as if they could reach out and touch them. The convoy crossed the International Date Line at some point, Ed never determined exactly where, and the date jumped ahead.

When the ship reached a point half way to Guam, the captain revealed their destination in a terse message broadcast on the ship's intercom. "PLUM" stood for the Philippine Islands, an acronym made from the first letters of three words: Philippines, Luzon, Manila. It had been a point of speculation, but now they knew for sure. "PLUM" was Manila, the "pearl of the Orient," on the largest island in the Philippine Island chain, Luzon.

After many more days of what had become a boring sailing routine, the vessel approached Manila Bay's Cavite Navy Yard. Ed stood on deck next to Gatling as the *President Coolidge* slowly steamed into the bay, passed through an expansive minefield and glided by the craggy outline of Corregidor, the well-known American Gibraltar of the Pacific. People said the island's fortifications were virtually impregnable; able to withstand a terrific pounding, with protected artillery that could punch huge holes in any vessel within range. They searched for gun emplacements facing the ship channel, but could make out only one or two, identified by gray concrete parapets facing the sea. As the ship plowed further into the bay, the damp, moldy odor of the jungle assaulted their senses, smelling something like rotted vegetables amid the damp humidity.

An army band played jaunty marching tunes as tugs nudged the ship into its berth and soldiers lined the decks, anxious to clamber off after the three-week passage. The delights awaiting them were many, for this was the mysterious Far East, the stuff of motion pictures and intrigue. They could make out tall palms, lush banana trees with wide green leaves and all manner of exotic, crisp vegetation. The ocean breeze carried with it new smells, both pungent and sweet.

"Here we are, finally," remarked Gatling as he gripped the railing as crews tied down gangplanks. He flipped up the bill of his baseball cap and took a deep breath. "It looked nice and green, inviting, from the sea, but wait until we see it close up. I hear Manila's a terrific place."

Ed broke into a wide grin. "I figure on liking it fine. A few months here sounds all right. It might even be fun."

CHAPTER 4

ASSIGNED TO IBA FIELD

Philippine Islands, late November 1941

The tropical climate struck soldiers in opposing ways; they either liked or hated it. Some considered the stifling, brutal heat insufferable. Near-constant humidity caused perspiration to bead on necks and clothes to cling to the body. The never ending high temperatures and the tangled, rugged jungle made some men count the days until they could leave for home.

Many, if not most, however, considered life in the Philippines not far from paradise. Tall swaying palms lined the boulevards, Manila's historic buildings dated back to the 1500's and vast expanses of sandy beach bordering the blue ocean made the collection of over two-dozen islands exotic and memorable. Best of all, the friendly Filipino people welcomed and respected Americans, helping make the Philippines a favorite duty location.

Soldiers could avail themselves of numerous pleasures. The far-flung archipelago, in which people spoke ten dialects, offered soldiers the benefit of what the army called "tropical routine," which meant the standard workday ended at noon. Because tropic heat made the afternoons swelter, the army granted everyone liberty, allowing soldiers to do as they pleased. That usually meant whiling away the hours in local bars, where drinks were cheap. American money went far in the Philippines and, as soldiers quickly discovered, local girls were abundant and very willing. Many, even the lowest enlisted, hired maids and valets to attend to their personal needs.

Assigned to quarters at Fort Stotsenberg, west of the main American bomber base at Clark Field, Ed and Gatling joined other officers occupying a wood frame house previously home for a family sent back to the states in July. They moved into a bedroom, but, after suffering through the first night's steaming heat, relocated their beds to the screened porch to take advantage of cool night breezes.

Within a short time they learned to appreciate the luxury of Philippine life. They hired servants at a few cents per day to keep up the house, maintain their uniforms and literally be at their beck and call. The servants did the laundry, made beds and washed dishes, polished shoes to a shiny gleam, prepared meals, and fetched tall, cool drinks whenever asked. Friendly and grateful, they seemed to want nothing more than to please their employers. The soldiers themselves spent hours swimming, playing golf, sightseeing, relaxing, or visiting local bars. The jungles, even near inhabited areas, teemed with delightful clusters of multi-colored birds, parrots, canaries and parakeets, all very much at home in the heavy vegetation.

After moving in, Ed and Gatling reported for duty at Interceptor Command headquarters at Nielson Field, a hubbub of activity due to the rapid expansion taking place. It had been a hot day and dark storm clouds gathering overhead threatened a heavy afternoon downpour, an almost daily occurrence, but causing grumbles and raising tempers nonetheless. A harried officer who could barely spare a few minutes announced in a clipped voice that their duty station would be Iba Field, thirty minutes flying time away.

Little more than a dirt runway adjacent to the South China Sea, Filipino laborers had carved Iba out of sharp-edged *cogon* grass growing freely in the area. The 3rd Pursuit Squadron and its new P-40E fighters were to operate from the field as interceptors for the next several weeks. In the process of being assembled and tested at Neilson Field, the planes would soon be ready.

"Your squadron commander's taken over the meeting room in the building behind us," he said. "Report to him Monday at 1000 for further instructions." Not paying them any further attention, he turned and stalked back to his desk, retrieved a cup of stale coffee and sat down to shuffle through a sheaf of papers.

"The army runs on paperwork," said Ed with a tone of disgust, taking Gatling's arm and pulling him away. "Let's get out of here."

They snapped a sloppy salute, turned and left the building. Gazing back and forth, they looked for a vehicle on which to hitch a ride back to Fort Stotsenberg. Getting the gift of four days off was a great opportunity, enabling them to visit Manila and sample the many delights she could offer. Manila wasn't called the "pearl of the Orient" for nothing.

Murky dark gray clouds roiling together overhead, the sky looked more threatening as each minute passed. An olive drab army truck pulled up a short distance away and they ran to it, hoping it was on its way to Stotsenberg. The driver nodded them aboard and they clambered into the back.

As they drove off, the downpour came, rattling on the canvas overhead and drenching those unfortunates caught in the open. The volume and velocity of the rain was terrific. Within half a minute, the roar was so loud they had to shout to be heard. It came down so hard that individual raindrops actually hurt when they hit bare heads or hands. Huge drops splashed up from the ground in a pale mist. The rainfall stopped after fifteen minutes, but not before drainage ditches had flooded over the surface of the road. By the time the truck turned into Fort Stotsenberg, their shoulders and upper arms were soaking wet.

"Iba Field's about a mile inland from the ocean, outside the town proper," explained Lieutenant Colonel Buck Skinner, 3rd Pursuit Squadron executive officer, to pilots assembled in a drab briefing room at Nielson Field, sprawled in chairs or leaning against the wall. Skinner was tall, skinny, almost completely bald, with deep-set eyes. A veteran of twenty-five years service, he was an experienced airman with a vinegary, gruff manner that brooked nonsense from no one.

He knew how to get things done and wanted them performed just that way.

"It's a new field," he said. "Facilities are fairly primitive, but we'll get first crack at any Japs coming our way."

A sharp crash sounded through the room as a folding chair toppled over, a soldier spilling to the floor. Raucous laughter erupted as the red faced victim got up and brushed himself off. "Sorry, sir," he stammered sheepishly.

Skinner glared at him, as if to say 'I'll deal with you later,' and continued. "I was talking about Iba Field. Once we get the planes out there, you pilots'll have to get on the ball familiarizing yourself with the new aircraft. The P-40E is one hot plane and you gotta know her inside and out."

Unconsciously, Ed and the other pilots nodded. They knew their performance would prove crucial to the defense of the Philippines and were determined to become masters of their craft.

"One other thing," Skinner continued. "There's a radar trailer at Iba that will give us early warning of enemy aircraft, which no other airfield has, so that's a big point in our favor. To my knowledge, it's the only operational radar set in the entire Philippines."

Ed swiveled toward Gatling and jabbed a forefinger into his rib cage. "The only operational radar?" he whispered in surprise.

"That's what the man said," replied Gatling. "Now shut up. He's still talking."

Ed shook his head and slumped low. "Only one radar set," he mumbled. "And I figured we'd have seven or eight."

Skinner's voice rose. "Remember this," he bellowed. "We're Americans and we have the best military in the world. There's no doubt our equipment is better than theirs. Colonel George and I have complete confidence in you."

Skinner scanned the faces in the room, leveling his gaze beneath thick eyebrows. "All right," he grumbled, screwing his mouth into a snarl. "Man your aircraft and let's go."

* * *

The eighteen planes of the 3rd Pursuit Squadron made Iba Field their own over the next two weeks, flying daily touch and go landings and missions far off the coast, hundreds of miles out over the South China Sea. They uncovered many mechanical problems with the P-40s, from machine guns that hadn't been bore sighted to engines that spewed oil all over the windshields.

Mechanics adjusted carburetors, cleaned fuel systems, replaced spark plugs and did much more to get the planes into fighting trim. Others set up machine guns behind sand bags among the trees to provide anti-aircraft defense and dug slit trenches alongside the runway, though the ground was soggy and muddy, with dirty water puddling the bottom of each trench.

Aircrews lived in canvas pyramid tents, but the usual tropical barracks, two stories with a veranda, was fast taking shape. At night, when aircraft were grounded, crews herded the P-40s together under floodlights to protect them from sabotage, a threat security forces took seriously.

Soldiers had covered the radar trailer, located at the end of the runway near the ocean, with camouflage netting to disguise it from the air. They had lowered it into the ground to provide side protection for the delicate instrument and stacked barrels full of dirt and sand alongside to provide additional cover.

Ammunition remained in short supply, however, and Skinner severely restricted gunnery practice. He allowed pilots to fire only a few short machine gun bursts into Laguna de Bay, a huge lake south of Nichols Field. Like the others, Ed's minimal gunnery training in California had consisted mostly of firing a few bursts at slicks in the ocean.

On December 6th, Colonel Harold George, senior pursuit officer, called together fighter pilots from all Luzon airfields for a meeting at Nichols Field. George had served in the air corps since 1917, had become an ace and won the Distinguished Flying Cross during World War I. He knew the rigors of combat first hand. An up-front man who didn't mince words or beat around the bush, the men respected him as a straight shooter.

The assembly took place in the humid dampness of a drafty, wood floored auditorium normally used for physical fitness programs and evening movies. As they gathered, the men talked to each other in low tones, an occasional laugh ringing out. Precisely at the appointed time, George walked onto the stage at the front of the auditorium in full dress uniform, looking solemn and determined. The room grew quiet as the men shot to attention. "Please, be seated, gentlemen," he said in a booming, commanding voice. He waited a moment while the sound of creaking chairs and shuffling feet died.

"Men," he said in a voice low enough they had to strain to hear, "tonight the United States of America is on the brink of war." He paused for a moment to let the words sink in. Everyone was quiet, staring forward. "Yes, war is on the horizon. An attack from Imperial Japanese forces can be expected at any hour."

George scrunched up his lips and looked through dead serious eyes at faces around the room. When he spoke, his words were somber and unhurried. "Gentlemen, we're about to enter into active combat. The British, the Australians, the Dutch—we'll all be in the war together, facing a common enemy."

As he continued, pausing often for maximum effect, George confirmed or quashed rumors that had floated around for weeks. Yes, he said, American and Filipino ground forces had moved out to beach defense positions throughout the Philippines and tens of thousands of Filipino draftees were in the process of undergoing training. No, Japanese civilians had not been rounded up and, yes, General MacArthur, commander of all army forces in the Far East, was closely following international developments. He had even coordinated defense plans with British forces in Singapore.

George admitted that Japanese planes had flown reconnaissance missions over the Philippines several times in November. "I warn everyone to be on their toes," he emphasized, pointing an index finger. "Don't be complacent, don't be overconfident. Just do your duty, as I know you will."

Colonel George gave the assemblage a final gaze, then turned and walked off. His presentation had lasted little more than five minutes. Skinner jumped up and dismissed the men. Some rose and walked to the doors; others remained, talking together in low tones. The air seemed somehow chilled, as if something was about to happen.

"I can't say I disagree with the Colonel, but I can't say I agree, either," said Gatling, who remained steadfast in his opinion that the superiority of American arms and the likelihood of diplomatic agreements would resolve international squabbles. "We're pretty dang ready and there's a lot more in the pipeline. There's nothing to be gloomy about."

Ed, on the other hand, had been struck by the openness of George's words and had grown thoughtful of American hopes. He remembered the lively debates on the transport and his father's cautionary words. Conventional wisdom maintained that the force of American arms would deter any adversary, but he wasn't so sure. Conventional wisdom wasn't always so wise.

"Maybe we aren't as ready as we think," he said. "Most of our pilots are fresh out of flight school. One guy I met today has logged barely fifteen hours in the cockpit of pursuit planes. That's nothing." His mood black, Ed cast his gaze down. "I never intended to enlist for a suicide mission."

Gatling looked back and snickered. "Ed, you take things too seriously," he said in a jovial voice, clapping his friend's shoulder. "And you believe everything you hear."

Ed felt his flesh color. "Colonel George knows what he's talking about. He was in the air corps before you and I were even born."

Unconcerned, Gatling gave a gentle outward flick of a hand. "I still think you worry too much." Just then they heard the impatient voice of Lieutenant Colonel Skinner shouting from the back of the room, telling them to get to their planes and return to Iba.

As they walked to the flight line, Gatling turned toward Ed. "What do you think of going into Manila tomorrow? I hear the B-17 boys are throwing a hell of a birthday bash for General Brereton. Probably'll last most of the night."

Ed answered as he walked. "Drunken revelry and debauchery has its place, but I don't figure now is the time. They can celebrate without me. Besides, Manila's too far away."

The two continued until reaching the parked planes of the squadron, all tethered securely to the ground. Ed leaned against his P-40's rudder and faced his friend. "I thought they were ordered to fly all the bombers to Mindanao to get out of range of Jap planes from Formosa. How can Brereton's men hold a party in Manila if they're six hundred miles away?"

"Because only half left for Mindanao, that's why," said Gatling. "The rest are waiting a day or two before leaving. They figure it's safe. Brereton and MacArthur must agree, otherwise they would have done something."

Disgusted, Ed's eyebrows shot up in disbelief. "My father was in the Great War and he warned me not to be overconfident. That's all I hear from people out here! If I believed half of it, we'd beat the Japs without a single loss if we went to war."

Gatling threw back his head and laughed. "You're a stubborn man, Ed Bannon." He reached into a back pocket for a billfold and withdrew a five-dollar bill. "Five bucks says there'll be no war at all." He waved it in the air. "Wanna take it?"

Ed glanced up. "Gatling, you can be a real jerk. Yeah, I'll take your bet and add five more that say the Japs'll attack within a week. You up for real action, big mouth?"

Gatling beamed. "Sure, sucker, I'll take that bet." The two shook and climbed aboard their P-40s, refueled and ready to depart. "Just don't forget, 'cause I won't."

Ed narrowed his gaze and shot a look back, shaking his head. "I still say you're a jerk, Gatling. And the Japs'll attack; you just wait." His words proved more accurate, and shocking, than Gatling or anyone else in the 3rd Pursuit Squadron later cared to think about.

Chapter 5

Damn the Torpedoes and Head for the Hills

December 8, 1941

Sun washed over a slumbering Iba Field on Monday, December 8, the early morning breeze barely disturbing the fronds of the highest palms bordering the field. Air crewmen soundly slept in their bunks, many groggy and hung over from a fresh load of beer driven out Sunday afternoon from Manila. The waters of the South China Sea glinted azure-blue in the sunlight. White sand on the narrow beaches of the Zambales coast sent heat waves shimmering as the coolness of night evaporated from the land.

First word of a Japanese attack on Pearl Harbor crackled over short wave radio shortly after 4 a.m., long before most were awake. Runners alerted gun crews and two fighters swooped into the night sky to patrol up and down the sparsely populated coast. The remaining crews were woken and sent up throughout the early morning, making sortie after sortie, but always chasing phantoms, first lunging toward one point, then to another, ceaselessly scanning the sky in search of the enemy.

At 8:45 a.m., operators spotted a large foreboding blip on the radar screen, indicating aircraft approaching over Lingayen Gulf. Senior officers interpreted it as an enemy flight headed toward

Clark Field, the major airfield on Luzon and home of the Far East Air Force's heavy bombers that had not retired to Mindanao. Iba's fighters, though some were half empty, received orders to scramble and intercept.

As the P-40s roared down the runway and clawed their way into the air, carrying a full load of ammunition for each of their six guns, soldiers manning machine guns on either side of the field looked on. Those left with nothing to do grabbed rifles, anything that would fire, and took cover, scanning the empty sky for dark spots that would grow into images of attacking aircraft.

Sixth in line to depart, Ed's P-40 rumbled down the earth runway into the sky, climbing upward, seeking the altitude he would need to attack the Japanese formation. Gatling, his wingman, followed behind, soaring higher until leveling off at ten thousand feet.

The eighteen fighters formed into three groups, but Ed and Gatling lost sight of the others while climbing through a cloudbank. The two scanned all around, but they had been ordered to minimize radio chatter and were unable to locate their companions.

Knowing the purpose of the mission, Ed motioned for Gatling to follow. Banking to the right, he roared off toward Lingayen Gulf, Gatling at his side. They arrived ten minutes later and fell into formation. Remaining aloft for some thirty minutes, swooping to one side of the gulf, then the other, the search proved fruitless. Perhaps they searched too low; perhaps the enemy had broken off to attack targets in the north.

"All pursuits low on fuel report back to Iba," ordered Skinner over the radio. "All others form up with me. We'll continue the search a while longer." Eight planes broke away and, wriggling their wings in farewell, headed back. Ed and Gatling remained behind.

Meanwhile, officers at the Interceptor Command at Neilson Field, trying to coordinate incoming threat information, were having a terrible time. Besieged with wild calls from coast watchers throughout the Philippines, they scratched their heads, not knowing who or what to believe. Panicky and exaggerated, most reports were incorrect. The number of incoming Japanese planes seemed to increase with each passing minute. Confused, many controllers shook their heads and rolled their eyes in wonder.

At 11:25 a.m., Iba's radar screen again came alive with blips, many more than earlier, more than they had ever seen before. An excited radar operator ran to the phone and called Neilson, which scrambled additional fighters and passed the information along to Clark Field.

For some reason, however, Clark's teletype and radio operators didn't respond. Some were at lunch; others later accused saboteurs of destroying the telegraph lines. In a panic, the pursuit control director at Neilson called over commercial telephone and passed the word to a lieutenant who answered the phone while on his way to the mess hall. He promised to pass the air raid warning to the base commander, but never did.

Within minutes, one hundred and eight Japanese Mitsubishi bombers escorted by eighty-four Zero fighters crossed over the coast and headed toward Clark Field, about half peeling away and heading toward Iba. As they approached, a few P-40s sat on the side of the runway being refueled in the tropical hush, pilots relaxing under the shade of the wings. Other P-40s circled low over the field in final approach formation, fuel tanks nearly empty. Despite the alert, peacetime routine had resumed; nobody expected an attack.

A rain of bombs suddenly caused the field to erupt. Great geysers of smoke and flame blossomed up and down the runway, the all-important radar trailer and its operators blasted into oblivion by some of the initial bursts. The control tower, from which airfield operations were directed, narrowly escaped a direct hit, but near misses caused it to slowly tip over and collapse. The unfinished barracks caught fire and fuel erupted in giant explosions of flame, smoke billowing into the sky.

The air raid siren wailed and ground crews dived into muddy slit trenches, others fired machine guns, rifles and pistols at the fast moving enemy aircraft. Grounded planes exploded as tracers ignited brimming fuel tanks.

As Ed made a lazy approach to the field, a sudden message from Gatling, in the plane behind, crackled over the radio. "Bandits overhead! Bandits!" He jerked up his head, grabbed the throttle and pulled back with all his might, veering the nose of the plane upward. He gunned the engine and sped forward, tracers from enemy fire flashing by his P-40. The plane gathered speed and zoomed off to the left, the enemy concentrating on demolishing the field rather than chasing a lone escapee.

Knowing he was low on fuel, Ed determined to knock down a few Japanese before being forced down. No enemy fighters followed, so he climbed over the ocean, slowly gaining altitude. As he reached two thousand feet, he pointed the nose of the P-40 inland and roared back.

His face paled with anger, Ed yearned for revenge. He twisted side-to-side, searching for close-by attackers, but they were far off, intent on putting the airfield out of commission. His fingers grew white on the throttle as he remembered that he had no idea where Gatling was or even if his friend remained alive.

As he approached Iba, he got his first glimpse of the wanton destruction below. Where the airfield should have been, the entire area now boiled with smoke, dust and flames. In the center, a huge column of greasy black smoke obliterated the sky, ugly red flames billowing upward. Ineffective, wild machine gun fire flew up from the ground.

He now flew directly over the field. The Japanese bombers had finished their gruesome job and had flown back toward Formosa, leaving Zero fighters to make devastating strafing runs up and down the field, making sure Iba could no longer be a menace. Ed spotted one completing a firing run about one thousand feet below and dove in for the kill.

Swooping down, he lined up the enemy plane in his gun sight and, for the first time, fired in anger. Three .50 caliber guns on each wing opened up, spitting their bullets in steady, angry streams. The surprised Zero fighter jumped sharply to the right, attempting to veer away. Ed's aim was accurate, but the guns fired wide of the mark, high and to the right. Though American luck had been poor that day, Ed's was the opposite, and the Zero flew directly into his line of fire. All of a sudden it exploded, bursting into an orange fireball.

"Got it!" Ed veered away and began climbing, excited, having accomplished exactly what his training had taught. Brimming with confidence, cool, collected, he continued to gain altitude, when two Zeros latched onto his tail one hundred yards behind, closing fast. They opened fire and he swerved sharply to the left. The P-40 shuddered as a burst of fire hit the left wing and swung into the fuselage, slamming into protective armor plate behind his seat.

Ed jerked the P-40 side to side, rolled over, turned, and looped, performing all the aerial acrobatics he knew, but the Zeros stayed with him, firing all the while, moving in closer and closer, narrowing the gap.

That Zero was no slouch of a plane, he told himself, perspiration beading on his forehead. Rice paper and bamboo indeed! Hell, the tenacious Zero could fly faster, climb more quickly and turn inside his curves, no matter what, sticking to him like flypaper. Didn't the army brass hats know? What were those idiots in military intelligence doing?

Then he remembered something he overheard Captain Ed Dyess of the 20th Pursuit Squadron say two nights before at Nichols Field: Never try to outmaneuver or get in a dogfight with a Zero. It's too maneuverable. The way to beat a Zero is to go into a steep dive and outrace it. The heavier P-40 will beat it every time.

That's what he did. Ed licked his dry lips and pushed the throttle wide open, gunning the engine and roaring for the ground. Wind shrieked over the windshield, whistled through the hole in his left wing and the green vegetation of earth flashed upward at horrifying speed. The fuselage shuddered and through his heavy flying boots he felt the rudder vibrate. He pulled out of the dive, corrected the rudder, and leveled off above the treetops near the ocean, some ten miles from Iba Field. Whipping around, he breathed out in relief. The Zeroes had fallen behind, unable to keep up with the superior diving capability of the P-40, one of its few advantages. They had turned tail and were heading back to Iba.

Ed broke into a wide grin. He had destroyed one enemy fighter and escaped from what looked like certain death. Filled with self-assurance, he turned the fighter back, but all of a sudden, the engine coughed and cut in and out. "My fuel!" he cried aloud.

The P-40's Allison engine continued to sputter, then stopped completely. Crestfallen, his eyes stony with anger, Ed swerved in his seat, taking quick glances out either side of the cockpit. On the left, the wide expanse of the ocean beckoned. The engine out, wind screeching through the hole in his wing, he glided toward the water. Trying to hold altitude, he gripped the throttle for all he was worth, attempting to remain level. But the fighter steadily dropped, the choppy surf coming at him at extraordinary speed. About to hit, he jerked back the mushy throttle with all his might, forcing the nose to rise a few inches, enabling the rear of the fuselage to make initial contact.

The P-40 smashed into the waves, spray flashing about, crashing to an abrupt, jolting stop. The jarring impact stunned Ed, causing him to stare forward in blank bewilderment, his mind reeling in confusion. But as the plane began to settle into the water, before it was too late, he came to his senses and bolted upright, releasing the straps that held him. He crawled from the cockpit onto the wing, first taking a nervous look around for sharks, kicked off his shoes and lowered himself into the water. Gasping at the cold temperature, he wiped a hand over his eyes to clear away the salt water and looked toward the glimmering shoreline, within swimming distance.

He started out. His right leg and shoulder throbbed with pain and forward progress was slow. About halfway, the weight of his waterlogged clothes began to drag him down and his arms flailed and slapped at the water, grasping for traction, using up his strength. Ed gasped for breath, heart pounding madly. Shivers of panic began shooting through his body.

An ocean swell rolled over, carrying him below the surface, then he popped back, spitting out a mouthful of the sickening, salty water. He continued to thrash, but slower now, his reserve of energy about used up. It felt like a hand had closed around his throat, ever tightening its grip.

Suddenly, fingers grabbed each shoulder. He found himself dragged upward and pulled along the ocean surface toward a native outrigger. Two Filipinos, one under each arm, maneuvered him to the side of the boat and placed his hands over the gunwales.

"Don't let go, friend," said one of the men who continued supporting his weight as the other climbed into the boat. Suddenly, Ed felt firm hands clasp each wrist and pull him aboard. He flopped to the bottom, exhausted, choking from the ordeal, his body in spasms. The other Filipino climbed in and, together, they paddled toward a group of bamboo huts set in a grove of palm trees, away from the beach.

Panting, his muscles taut and aching, Ed let out a sigh. He didn't know who these people were, but they had saved his life. He would now live to fight another day. He lay back, dog-tired, struggling to calm down.

The scales of war dramatically shifted that morning. American forces suffered a stunning defeat caused by bad luck, miscalculation and overconfidence. The Japanese attackers had turned Iba and Clark Fields into monstrous, grotesque wrecks. They had chopped the P-40s at Iba into unusable, ruined pieces, though mechanics later salvaged two by cannibalizing parts from the burned out skeletons of others. The early warning radar was destroyed and most of the airfield's contingent of men had fled inland in terror. The final word came down from Neilson Field later that day: Salvage what you can and abandon the field.

For the Far East Air Force, the day had been an unmitigated disaster. Nearly all the B-17 bombers at Clark Field had been destroyed on the ground, with only three able to again fly. America's fighter strength had been sliced in half and, within days, Japanese control of the air was undisputed. In the span of a few morning hours on the first day of war, America's hopes for holding the Philippines vanished.

Chapter 6

The Situation Deteriorates

December 1941

Privates Antonio Pilar and Ferdinand Cayab, Filipino soldiers on patrol along the deserted white beach, had been at it since before dawn. Walking back and forth in vain search of enemy activity, they had grown bored, the only diversion coming from peculiar rumbling explosions and plumes of fiery smoke over Iba Field, many miles away. Occasionally, a high-flying plane flitted overhead, no larger than a flyspeck, but they couldn't tell where it was headed or who was doing what to whom. Despite frequent glances, they continued their patrol.

Drafted into the Philippine army in October, Cayab and Pilar had found military life to be an everlasting string of shortages, disorganization and all manner of stumbling blocks. Extreme boredom was only one and they took it in stride. Neither had prior military experience and had received only the most rudimentary training.

The beach had been completely devoid of activity all morning and when they spied a lone American plane overhead hurtling toward the water, both jerked their eyes up. Fascinated, they tipped their hats back and watched it lose altitude and plunge into the waves one thousand yards away, sending up a huge spray of water before settling on the surface. Both scrutinized the cockpit, watching for some sort of movement indicating the pilot's survival. Moments went by before they breathed sighs of relief. The canopy slid back and a figure wobbled out onto the nearest wing and slipped into the water.

They knew the pilot would require rescue, for the waters of the South China Sea were more treacherous than they appeared. Hungry sharks on the lookout for meals infested the area. If injured, the pilot's prospects were even worse, for the smell of blood would attract the killers.

The Filipino soldiers sprang into action. They spotted a native *banca* pulled up onto the beach nearby and paddled out, reaching him just in time. He seemed in bad shape; about done in. They pulled him aboard and paddled for shore.

"There's a village just back of the beach," soothed Pilar as he looked down on the exhausted American flyer from the rear of the boat, continuing to paddle. "The people will take care of you and get you back to Iba." Ed could only grunt in response, sick and weakened by the ordeal.

It didn't take long to reach breakers along the shore. They jumped out and guided the *banca* onto the sand, tugging it above the surf line.

"You're safe now," said Pilar, smiling down on the American as Cayab lifted him.

Nodding his thanks, Ed rose and stepped out of the boat, supporting himself against Cayab. "Thanks for coming out," he whispered in a gravelly voice, his vacant eyes cast down. "I'd have gone down for good any minute."

The two grinned and led him back to the village, leaving him in the care of an elderly woman and her husband, who bade him to stretch out on a sleeping pad inside their woven *nipa* hut. Before returning to the beach to resume patrolling, the two soldiers bid Ed farewell.

"So long, yank," said Cayab as he swung a heavy 1903 vintage Springfield rifle over a shoulder. "Looks like Iba took a heavy hit this morning, but we'll beat the Japs yet."

Pilar nodded in agreement. "You yanks have many more planes. I believe in General MacArthur and I believe in America. The end will make us proud."

Smiling, the two waved and departed, whistling. Ed fell into a deep sleep that lasted the next two hours; a dreamless slumber that left him refreshed, but did not cure the many aches and pains in his joints. He woke to discover his clothes had been removed. He called out to the man and woman.

"Hey, I need my uniform," he shouted from inside the hut, hoping they could hear. "Please, my clothes."

The man walked in a moment later, smiling, holding the freshly laundered and neatly folded pants, shirt and socks. He placed them at the foot of the bed and walked out. Ed grabbed the clothes and slipped them on. While buttoning his shirt, the woman walked in. Her face was leathery and nut-brown, her shoulders slightly stooped. But her eyes sparkled and her wide lips held a certain welcoming radiance that caused one to relax and smile back.

"My husband, he no speak so good English," she said, placing a cup of cool water on a bamboo table just inside the door. "You sleep long time. You feel good now?"

Ed bowed and smiled. "I guess I needed some shut-eye, but I feel better. Thank you for taking me into your home."

The woman nodded in satisfaction. "Me make food," she said, motioning to a fire outside surrounded by a ring of smooth stones. "You go eat. Build strength."

Ed grinned and, nodding his thanks, descended the stairs from the raised hut and walked outside. Suspended over the campfire on an iron skewer roasted a whole chicken, the skin brown and crusty. Hot rice bubbled in a pot and a *baloot* had been placed in a rag nestled among the stones.

The woman followed Ed and dished up a plateful of hot rice, half the barbecued chicken and handed him the *baloot*. Ed sat on a rock and tore into the chicken and rice, not having eaten since early that morning. He left the *baloot* on the plate, not touching it.

The woman seemed annoyed, even hurt, by Ed's lack of interest in the *baloot*. To bestow one of the eggs on a guest was a great honor;

a grand distinction in Filipino eyes. But Ed had been warned about *baloots* before his first visit to Manila; they were fertilized eggs buried in the ground for weeks, foul smelling and unappealing to most Americans. Considered a Philippine delicacy, an abject refusal to eat such a gift amounted almost to an insult.

Ed spotted the disappointment in her eyes and knew what he had to do—force himself to eat the darned thing. He lifted it from the plate and held it up, smiling. Then he proceeded to peel and eat faster than he had ever eaten anything before in an attempt to swallow the *baloot* more rapidly than his brain could register the flavor.

It didn't work, for the strange, foul taste lingered in Ed's mouth for days, only dying later that week when he downed five Hershey chocolate bars and two glasses of Ovaltine in one sitting. But it pleased the woman and that's all he intended.

"You like *baloot*?" she asked, bending forward at the waist. "You eat fast."

Ed grinned, tossing the eggshells into the fire. "Yes, I like *baloot* very much. I'm honored that you gave it to me."

"Me happy." She backed toward a rock and relaxed against it, casually brushing a stray hair away from her eyes. She raised knees to her chest and clasped hands over them, her eyes bright with pleasure. "You good looking man. You have woman?"

Ed cast his eyes down and swung his head. "No," he said. "I once had a woman, but she died. There has been no one since."

The woman frowned, a shadow passing over her eyes. "How long ago this thing happen?"

"Oh, about a year ago. The months pass, but sometimes it seems like she's still around. My mind knows she isn't, but I wish it were so."

"All minds play tricks. You not different. I lost babies and young children, but had many more. You must not let one bad thing ruin life, especially a ghost. Life is filled with good things and bad. You young, but you will see."

For a long moment, Ed looked into her face, the hardships of a lifetime etched into her sharp, weather-beaten features. Yet her eyes shimmered with life and unquenchable warmth. He regarded her with somber curiosity, a sense of kindhearted respect welling inside.

She rose and approached Ed, placing hands aside his cheeks. "Like a fruit, your life will ripen in ways you cannot see," she said. "When you are old, like me, you will look back and give thanks." She stepped back, not removing her penetrating gaze. "But now you must drive the Japanese away. I know you will do this, for you are strong, like all Americans." She turned and walked away, leaving Ed behind staring at the back of her head.

He didn't know quite what to make of all this. He had fought an air battle, won a victory and crash landed in the ocean, all in one morning. Things had happened too fast, like film spit out of a movie projector in a theater and turning into a tangled heap. He scratched his head. This woman made him feel special. She welcomed him into her house, cleaned his clothes, shared a meal and asked nothing. Usually when good things happened or something went right, he chalked it up to dumb luck. But, for some reason, he felt there was more here.

He remembered the words of his father: "Don't believe everything you're told," he had said, referring to the army.

Ed resolved to stay on his guard. Maybe the bad luck the squadron experienced at Iba was a fluke and the Americans had been more successful elsewhere. But if that weren't the case, what would happen? He gritted his teeth. Keep your head, he reminded himself. Think for yourself. Be cautious.

Ed spent the next half hour sitting cross-legged next to the campfire whittling on a gnarly piece of wood, gazing at the peaceful blue sea, wondering when help would arrive. New P-40s would be welcome.

The woman walked back into the clearing with an armful of wood and tossed it onto the ground next to a stump. Picking up an ax, she prepared to split the firewood for use as kindling. Ed immediately rose to his feet.

"Splitting wood is the least I can do," he called out. Stepping toward the stump, he held out a hand. "Here, let me do it," he said.

"No, you rest. Get strength to fight Japanese."

Ed shook his head in a kindly manner. "Ma'am, I've spent half my life splitting wood. It's no bother at all." He reached forward and took the ax from her hand. She gave no resistance. "Don't worry," he said. "I can fight the Japs with one arm tied behind my back." The woman walked away, shaking her head.

Ed proceeded to split the wood against the stump, finishing in short order. Realizing it amounted only to a small supply, he walked into the jungle for more. He spent the next hour walking back and forth, tossing down wood and going back. Upon finishing, the supply had increased in size five or six times. It would be a small token of his gratitude.

A Filipino soldier passing through the village late that afternoon in a jeep offered to give Ed a lift to Iba Field, a forty-five minute drive away through thick jungle and wide grasslands. As they drove up, he scanned the airstrip, now a full-blown wreck. The huts next to the runway were destroyed, their canvas tents among the trees burned, pockmarked with machine gun fire or collapsed. Thin columns of wispy smoke still rose from the ruins of buildings. Jagged craters filled the runway and smoldering skeletons of aircraft lined the sides of the field. The control tower was a smashed shambles. Ed shook his head, depressed.

He bid his driver farewell and the man sped off, back toward the Filipino unit. Gazing at the unbelievable destruction, kicking away fragments of boards and disfigured pieces of blackened metal, Ed walked to the operations tent that had been moved back from the runway into the jungle, hidden beneath the sharp green foliage of a papaya tree. There an orderly told him that the airfield was being abandoned and all personnel were reporting to Neilson. When Ed started to ask a question, he waved him back to his superior, seated behind a table in the back corner of the tent.

Ed approached the operations officer, hunched down looking through official papers, and saluted, expecting to see Lieutenant Colonel Skinner. To his surprise, it was someone else—Major Karl Dohlman, the chain-smoking, pot-bellied blowhard who had been Ed's nemesis since flying school days back in Texas. He was a jowly, paperwork-oriented mid-westerner who spent most of his waking hours looking out for his own career. The two held a sense of mutual animosity.

Dohlman returned the salute, barely looking up. Ed glanced down at his watch and took a deep breath. "Where's Lieutenant Colonel Skinner?" he asked.

"Shot down," Dohlman replied without looking up. "I'm ops officer now."

Ed bit his lower lip and took a deep breath. "He was a good man—the squadron'll miss him."

Dohlman looked up through squinted, critical eyes. Several chilly moments passed before Ed again spoke. "Things look pretty bad around here. When are we leaving?"

"First thing in the morning," he muttered in reply, a half-smoked cigarette jutting from his lips. He moved in the chair and clasped hands over his ample stomach. Glancing down at Ed's leg, his eyes narrowed suspiciously. "What's with the leg, Bannon? If you're looking for sympathy after the mess we had today, forget it."

All of a sudden, anger rippled up Ed's spine. He gave Dohlman a black stare and replied in as reasonable voice as he could manage. "I'm simply reporting in, sir. I went down off the coast after getting a Nip fighter. My leg was knocked around in the crash." He flexed the knee. "I thought it might be hurt bad, but I guess it's okay."

"Well, we've got bigger problems than your bruised leg, haven't we?" Dohlman spoke in his usual brusque voice, drumming a foot under the table. Jutting a cigarette up from the corner of his mouth, a frown settled into his features. He moved a leather riding crop from one side of the desk to the other. Impressed by the towering image of General MacArthur who always seemed to carry one, he had taken up the habit. "Tell me what happened."

Ed scratched the back of his head while giving the details of his downing of a Zero and the crash.

Dohlman leaned back and nodded. He cleared his throat, eyebrows moving downward. "Did you get a good look at the pilots in those planes? I figure they had to be Germans or Italians. Japs aren't good enough to fly like that."

Ed's lower lip twitched a little. "No, sir, I didn't, but I wouldn't recommend making that kind of an assumption. Minimizing the ability of an enemy is dangerous. It can lead to big trouble."

Dohlman snorted. "Bannon, the army isn't paying you to think and doesn't care about your opinion. Your mission is to carry out the orders of people more qualified than you. I happen to know quite a bit about Japanese military capabilities, so keep your mouth shut."

"I know there are lots of opinions," retorted Ed, gesturing with his hands, "but . . ." Dohlman cut him off by snatching up the riding crop and slashing it through the air. "Enough, Bannon!"

Ed stopped in mid-sentence. "Okay, okay," he stammered.

"That's better," replied Dohlman, leaning back in his chair. He looked into Ed's face, waiting for the lesson to sink in. During times like these, he reflected, it is of paramount importance that superior officers maintain their authority. Inexperienced upstarts need to be slapped down.

After an appropriate period, he continued. "Okay, I'll ask you again, Lieutenant. Was the enemy face you saw in the cockpit white or yellow?"

Ed held back his temper, though his face flushed with frustrated anger. "It was a Jap plane," he blurted. "It was a Jap pilot."

Dohlman smirked. "But you don't really know, do you? That means my theory may yet prove correct." He leaned forward and sipped coffee from a mug, chuckling to himself. "Did you know that Japs suffer from night blindness?" He gave a toothy grin. "All we have to do is hit 'em after dark."

Dohlman chuckled again under his breath, then sat up ramrod straight and glared at Ed, who was scratching the back of his neck. "Okay, Lieutenant. I have one last question. After you crash-landed, how'd you get back?"

"Two Filipino soldiers fished me out of the water and another gave me a ride back. I'm lucky they were there."

Dohlman leaned forward and ruffled through a sheaf of papers, ashes from the dangling cigarette falling onto the desk. He knocked them away with the sweep of a hand. "Okay. Good for you. Anybody here at Iba look at that leg?"

"A Filipino lady did after I crashed. She has experience in this kind of thing. Said it was okay."

Dohlman looked up and gave a brutal, unfriendly stare. "Lieutenant Bannon, you mean you're taking the word of one of the natives? What the hell do they know? There might be something more serious involved." Wearing his sternest expression, his glare drilled into Ed's eyes. "Something happen to your brain out there?"

Ed met his icy gaze head on. "She knew what she was talking about. Seemed like a pretty smart old gal."

Disgusted, Dohlman ripped the cigarette from his mouth, crushing it between two fingers. "Bannon, report to a medic, now. Tell him to check your head as well as your leg." He looked him up and down, his mouth twisted in distaste. The visible line of a bulbous nerve throbbed on his forehead. "Get your gear ready after that, mister. It'll be awhile before you fly again. Dismissed."

Ed saluted and walked out, glad to be out of Dohlman's presence, a man he considered a, swaggering good-for-nothing. Anger simmered as a blizzard of thoughts filled his mind.

Like many Americans who held superior attitudes, Dohlman regarded Filipinos as children, judging them primitive and uneducated. But Ed wondered. Wasn't it such racist beliefs that led the United States to underestimate the military competence of an Asian nation, Japan, in the first place? When the Japanese Zero could out-fly and out-maneuver our best fighter? Those attitudes ignored reality in favor of ham-fisted, contrived stereotypes. Such shameful ignorance defied logic and made no military sense.

Shaking his head, he wandered across the field to his tent, finding it blown over, his belongings scattered. Bending forward, he gathered two jars of shaving cream, clothes, camera, a framed photo of Barbara, and the few paperback books he owned. Glancing over his shoulder at Gatling's green canvas cot, he could see that his friend had not returned. He would have to find out about that.

Trucks carrying the survivors of the Iba Field disaster pulled into Nielson after lunch the following day. A few mechanics remained behind to salvage what was left, but for all intents and purposes, the 3rd Pursuit Squadron was grounded.

Nielson Field's administrative offices were in a state of chaotic uproar, perspiring soldiers hurrying up and down hallways handling reams of paperwork, opening and slamming file cabinets and drawers, shouting back and forth. They worked around the clock amid jangling telephones, trying to ascertain where the Japanese would hit next, working to ready the defenses, trying to guess where the few American 3-inch anti-aircraft batteries should be located. A handful of planes based out of Nielson and those at nearby Nichols had flown to Clark Field, the feeling being that since Clark had already been attacked and Nichols and Nielson hadn't, they would be next.

The airmen of the 3rd Pursuit never received clear instructions of what to do, so they waited out each ensuing day hoping for reinforcements, helping out here and there, but mostly sitting around smoking cigarettes and drinking coffee. Japanese planes struck the airfields outside Manila, including Neilson, time after time, steadily diminishing what remained of America's fighter strength. Though watchful American anti-aircraft batteries opened fire on attacking formations, the antiquated guns fired 3-inch powder fuse ammunition that exploded at too low an altitude, allowing Japanese bombers to fly safely above.

Days before Christmas, his troops in headlong retreat, General MacArthur swallowed his pride. Though it galled him to do so, he scrapped his failed strategy and reverted to the battle plan he had discarded nine months before. Code-named "battle plan orange," it entailed withdrawing all forces into the Bataan Peninsula to hold out until help arrived.

The crucial snag was that MacArthur had ordered the huge stockpiles of food and supplies stored on Bataan and Manila to be dispersed throughout Luzon. There now wasn't time to move everything back, as Japanese forces were swiftly advancing.

Orders went out to forces in the field to delay the Japanese as long as possible, allowing quartermasters to stock Bataan with food, ammunition and supplies, everything necessary for a long siege. Officers and men worked round the clock, but found it an impossible task, a constant fight against the clock, a fight they could not win. They performed miracles of improvisation, building supply stocks from almost nothing, but time fast ran out.

Gatling finally showed up at Nielson Field the day before Christmas, bedraggled and thinner, after many days wandering around the jungle before being found by Filipinos and delivered to Manila. The pilots of the 3rd Pursuit Squadron were sitting together in a lounge that had not been destroyed, their feet up, dirty coffee cups and cigarette butts scattered all over. When Gatling appeared, it was like a ghost reappearing from the past. Ed and Gatling exulted upon seeing each other.

"Jim, I've been worrying about you for weeks!" exclaimed Ed as he shot up from a chair and pumped Gatling's arm up and down. "We gave you up for dead."

Gatling laughed. "If the Japs ever get me, it won't be that quick or easy." He took a swift look around the room. "How about a cup of coffee and a smoke, buddy?"

"You got it." Ed reached into his breast pocket, drew out a pack of cigarettes and handed it over. "Keep 'em," he said. "You deserve all you want. There's plenty more around."

Gatling tapped a cigarette from the pack and placed it between his lips, Ed lighting it with a Zippo lighter on which a jeweler had engraved his name next to Barbara's two years before. He cherished the lighter, keeping it close at hand, never loaning it out.

Ed watched as Gatling drew in his first breath and exhaled a cloud of gray smoke. He waited a moment, measuring him with a cool, appraising look, before asking, "Jim, how'd you go down? What happened?"

Frustrated, Gatling squinted, reflecting on the calamitous day. "The Japs jumped me right after I spotted them. I didn't have a chance to do anything." For a long moment, his eyes arched slowly back and forth. He looked up from beneath craggy eyebrows, a look of discomfort crossing his face. "They shot up my tail, turning it into shreds. Broken hydraulic lines sprayed fluid all over the cockpit." He took a quick cigarette puff and blew out the smoke. "I went down in the jungle miles from Iba and was out for a long time. I wandered around until some Filipinos found me."

"Were you hurt bad?" asked Ed, wondering why it had taken him so long to return to the squadron.

"When they found me, I was sitting next to a stream. I had been in and out for days. My P-40 turned upside down in the crash. It was a total wreck."

Ed nodded, took a long drag of a cigarette, and told his own story. "I went down in the ocean but got a Jap Zero first. Blew up right before my eyes. There's not much armor on those things."

"How many did we get over Iba?"

A fellow pilot, John Baxter, walked up and handed Gatling a mug of hot coffee, clapping his shoulder. Baxter had blond hair, freckles and seemed too young to be a pilot, but proved capable in his own boyish way. The three had hung around together since training days, mostly when going out on the town. In the states, Baxter always had to show bartenders his military identification to prove his age.

"They caught us with our pants down, Jim," Baxter explained. "Ed got the only one. We managed to put some holes in a few others, but that's all she wrote. What we accomplished added up to almost nothing."

Gatling reached down for another cigarette, lit it on Ed's Zippo and puffed out a wisp of chalky smoke, looking thoughtful. "I see," he said, drawing out the statement. Several moments passed as he stared through a window, his face a mask of stone, before he stirred and asked, "What's the word here? Every military installation I've seen has been bombed, including this one."

"Yeah, the Japs rule the skies," said Baxter, returning to the coffee pot to refill his own cup. He took a quick gulp and scrunched up his face. "The air corps has really been cut down to size. We don't go after their bombers anymore. Not near enough planes left." He raised his cup and took another gulp. "Ever want to fight in the infantry?"

Gatling swiveled toward Ed. "Infantry? What's he talking about?"

As Baxter returned to the corner of the room and picked up the comic book he had been reading, Ed, ill at ease over what he was about to say, lifted his dark eyebrows. "We're being reclassified as provisional infantry. We're gonna be issued rifles and all the other infantry gear tomorrow morning."

"Oh, geez," Gatling blurted, rolling his eyes. "Foot soldiers!" Snapping his head in astonishment, he added, "And that's what I joined the air corps to get out of."

"Well, it's only until we get more planes." Not knowing when that might be, Ed pulled his mouth into an awkward grin and shifted to a different subject. "Jim," he began, "you ought to write Becky and let her know you're okay. Better do it soon, because we've got orders to pull out of here, back to Bataan."

Gatling rubbed a hand through wiry black stubble on his chin, not having shaved in weeks. "That's one of the things I aim to do. I spent a lot of time in the jungle thinking about Becky. She's one helluva woman and I never appreciated her more than now. Suppose I'd better get to it. Don't want her to think I'm dead."

"There's paper over there," Ed said, pointing to a table on the far side of the room. "Lots of us are writing letters."

Gatling looked up for a moment, thoughtful, wondering where he would be one month from today. "After I tell her I'm alive, what else should I say?" he whispered, expecting no answer. "That we're knocking hell out of the Japs? Damn! We might as well be fighting them with spitballs." He grunted, blew out a puff of smoke, and walked away, shrugging his shoulders over and over, trying to form words in his mind.

Wearing a pained expression, Ed turned and sat, resting his feet atop an overturned gray government-issue trashcan. Gazing up at the ceiling, he studied the planks fitting close together, one after the other, peaking at the center. The roof protected them from the sun and kept out the rain. No leaks, no problems. A little prior planning and good workmanship was all that was needed. Would it be that way on Bataan? Would the American and Filipino forces streaming there be able to withstand a siege lasting who knows how long? Was help on the way?

Just then, a sharp explosion rumbled in the distance, sending a rocking tremble through the building and causing picture frames to rattle. Startled, he ran to a window and flung up the shade. Another enemy raid? Ed scanned the skies and saw nothing. No planes flitting through the clouds like mosquitoes, no strings of bombs, no chattering machine guns. Others ran out and stared up, rotating a full 360 degrees, outstretched palms shielding eyes from the brilliant sun. Nothing.

Turning toward the end of the runway, Ed saw more detonations occur, fireballs blossoming into the air. The explosions continued at regular intervals and he went back to his seat, deciding it was the Army blowing up ammunition dumps in order to prevent their falling into enemy hands. The alarm over, men filtered back, picking up coffee cups and resuming quiet conversations.

Ed reached for a sheet of paper on which he had begun a letter. It had been slow going, for he hadn't known what to say. He had completed little more than the first few words. Not having written home since the war began, feeling ashamed and awkward about the performance of the air corps, he didn't know whether to make his words cheerful or realistic, rosy or grim. It was tough misleading his parents in black and white. To the accompaniment of the racket outside, he readied a fountain pen and leaned over the paper. Words would come as he wrote.

December 24, 1941

Dear Mom and Dad:

Here it is, the day before Christmas, and I never imagined spending Christmas day in such a tropical paradise. We have all kinds of fruits like mangoes and papayas to eat whenever we want. I like it in the Philippines but look forward to returning home. I shot down my first Jap plane the other day and hope to get many more.

I'm at an airfield near Manila but the word is we'll move to a new base soon. It's being set up now and will be a good, safe one. We're expecting the arrival of a reinforcement convoy from the states any time. Once it gets here, we'll drive the Japs back into the sea.

Do you ever think of Barbara? I've been thinking of her a lot the past few weeks. I guess I wouldn't be here today if she was still alive. I miss her all the time. I keep busy, which keeps my mind off her, but it never works for long. I wonder how long people's hearts go on aching? When do they heal?

Well, Mom and Dad, I better finish this letter. I sure do miss the home cooking and wish I were in Yuma to share it with you. You will receive this letter long after the season, but I wish you a Merry Christmas. Did you listen to the Bing Crosby Christmas show on the radio this year? You always liked it. I remember listening with you. Those were good times.

I'll come home as soon as I can, but that won't be until after we've licked the Japs. All my love . . .

Your son,
Ed

CHAPTER 7

CHRISTMAS IN MANILA

December 25, 1941

Loneliness and homesickness were common maladies among Americans in the Philippines, for Christmas 1941 was unlike any before. The day offered little more than rumors about coming reinforcements, stories of advancing Japanese columns, air attacks, and the dismal face of defeat.

At Nielson Field, an armory was one of the few structures left untouched by Japanese flyers who bombed and strafed at will. Lined up outside, the airmen of the 3rd Pursuit Squadron entered a squad at a time. They shuffled beside a long string of tables in single file, soldiers handing each man a Model 1903 Springfield rifle, a khaki-colored canvas bandolier of ammunition, a fierce-looking bayonet inside a green scabbard, metal canteen and canvas cover, and a shovel.

The rifle barrels were filled with gooey yellow cosmolene, a jelly-like substance poured inside years earlier to protect against rust and corrosion. Enlisted soldiers had removed the majority of it earlier in the week with kerosene, but the crusty residue of the long-hardened jelly remained behind. Flopping down at tables covered with bottles of alcohol and buckets of hot water, the airmen sat down to give their rifles a thorough cleaning.

Sharing a work area of three planks extended between two wobbly crates, Ed Bannon and Jim Gatling exchanged few words for the first ten minutes, each immersed in private thoughts of Christmas and home. They thought of the mouth-watering smell of roast turkey, the laughter of happy people around a pine tree, carols wafting from a radio in the corner of the room, the delighted shouts of children opening gifts. But, like an artist painting a meticulous landscape, their thoughts, like a paintbrush, narrowed in on finer details, namely, women. For Ed it was Barbara, a memory still capable of triggering dull, aching pain. Gatling focused on his wife, Becky.

Lost in thought, both worked at a snail's pace, sometimes stopping entirely to stare in glassy eyed vacancy, seeing visions they could share with no one, sights only they could see. The rough warehouse setting, cold and drafty, was an incongruous one for Christmas day, one far removed from roaring oak fires and sleigh bells.

After a time, Ed shook his head and let out a gush of air, squinting at the commotion within the armory. He turned toward Gatling, just then quietly tugging a cleaning rod from the barrel of his Springfield.

"What a pain this is," Ed panted, reaching for a cigarette, giving himself a short two puff break before resuming. He inserted a two-inch square of white cotton fabric on the tip of a cleaning rod and dipped it in hot water. "Every time I run a cloth down the barrel it comes out with that stinking cosmolene on it," he spat out in a frustrated voice. "I don't know how long it'll take for this thing to get clean."

Gatling, shaken from his reverie, nodded. "These guns must have been in storage a long time. Years, probably."

Ed returned the briefest glance. "Jim, it's been decades. These guns came out of the crate wrapped in 1921 newspapers. What's that . . . twenty years ago? We weren't even born then."

Gatling chuckled. "Yeah, that's old, but it won't matter since most of us can't hit anything anyway. Hell, before today, I never even held a rifle." He lifted the Springfield and peered down the barrel. "Mine looks dang clean," he said, satisfaction in his voice. He lowered it and looked down with admiration. "I guess I'm ready for the firing range."

Ed had just placed his rifle flat on the table and was in the process of inserting a fresh square of cloth onto the cleaning rod. He flicked off the old cloth, yellow with cosmolene, and attached the new one.

"Gimme your gun," he said to Gatling. "We'll see how clean it is." Ed grabbed it and pumped the steel rod up and down the barrel. The square of fabric came out with blotches of oily yellow.

Ed held it up. "Your gun may look clean, my friend, but it's not as spotless as you think. Better keep at it."

Disappointed, Gatling peered at the rifle and glanced toward a soldier at the far end of the warehouse lounging behind a table chewing the stub of a cigar. "I don't suppose it'll pass inspection with that Master Sergeant over there, either. People have been handing rifles to him for the last half hour and he's passed every one back. Everybody's still here, cleaning away."

Ed crushed the butt of his cigarette into a cut down brass artillery shell casing serving as an ashtray. He placed a fresh cigarette in his mouth and lit it with the Zippo. After blowing out a breath of smoke, he observed, "This is our introduction to the real army. Soon we'll become invisible, one of tens of thousands of foot soldiers. Like it says in the old poem, 'ours is but to do or die.'"

Gatling looked up. "Don't forget, we're still officers. We won't be just one of tens of thousands of guys groveling around in the dirt with mud in their ears. They'll put us in charge of something. Besides, reinforcements are on the way and we'll be flying again soon enough."

Ed looked back through wistful eyes and smiled grimly. "I have a hunch we're going to be in for a lot. We don't even know what to expect. I want those reinforcements as much as you, but, until then, we're going to have to make do."

Gatling sucked in a deep breath of resignation. "Yeah, you're right." He remained silent for a moment, twisting his lips back and forth. "What do you say we get together with Baxter and the three of us go into Manila for some beer tonight? We'll be moving out in a day or two. It might be our last chance. Besides, it's Christmas and we need to kick up our heels a bit."

"Yeah, after spending the day cleaning rifles, beer sounds good. They better be icing down those San Miguel's now." Ed had learned that it was sometimes best to avoid thinking about things for a while and quaffing beer was one of the best ways he had found of doing it.

Gatling grabbed his rifle. "Let's get cleaning and get this over with. The faster we finish, the more time we'll have for the beer. The way I feel, that's a helluva lot more important."

The three returned to Nielson Field late that night, losing count of the number of bottles downed during what had turned into a raucous evening. They flopped into bunks without even taking off their clothes, sleeping the sleep of the dead until breakfast, when the noise and bustle of people rushing about filled the room they shared with many others.

"What're you fellas doing?" Ed asked, raising his head only slightly, a heavy weight somewhere in the back of his brain emitting a steady, grinding throb. "Show a little mercy, will 'ya?"

"You guys better get up," a shrill voice responded. "We've got orders to head out. Trucks are carrying us to the docks to catch a boat over to Bataan."

Ed raised himself up on an elbow. His mouth felt like it was filled with cotton wadding—the kind they used yesterday to clean the cosmoline. "We're moving today? I've still got things to do."

"Well, do what you gotta do, Ed, but you'd better get up," Lieutenant Bob Vaughan answered, looking down as he carried a stack of army green wool blankets. "There's still grub in the chow hall, but they've already started packing up. Time'll go by fast before we move out."

Ed dragged himself up and raised a hand to his head, feeling woozy after the antics of the previous night. He waited a half-minute before swinging his feet over the edge of the cot. After a couple more breaths, he decided to join the world. Opening and closing his eyes, he shouted at Gatling and Baxter. "Wake up, you two; it's time for breakfast."

Neither responded. Ed leaned across the narrow walkway and nudged Gatling's shoulder. "Wake up," he said, in a voice raised an octave.

Gatling slowly turned and opened a slit in his right eye. "I ain't hungry. Neither is Baxter. Leave us alone." He spoke in a low, gravelly voice, deep even for him.

"We're leaving for Bataan and we gotta get some food in our bellies. C'mon, let's go eat."

Gatling clamped the eye shut, with no intention of reopening it, and tugged the warm blanket over his head. From underneath, he muttered, "I said I ain't hungry. Go eat by yourself."

Ed shrugged, glanced at Baxter, also out to the world, and resigned himself to eating alone. He tugged on shoes, tucked in his shirt and walked outside toward the mess hall, a huge olive drab canvas tarp spread over the wreckage of their old dining facility, destroyed two weeks before. Ed grabbed a plate of cold scrambled eggs, cold fried ham, cold toast, and steaming hot coffee. Ah, coffee, he thought. That's what I need to get going. He balanced a cup on his plate and held a second in his hand.

Ed sat on an upturned crate amid others scraping up the last remnants of breakfast before heading out, the cooks and other members of the mess crew busy disassembling equipment and packing it into boxes. Neat stacks of crates stood outside, boxes of tinned salmon and corned beef, coffee, canned vegetables, sardines, condensed milk, preserved fruit, and much more. The food must be going to Bataan, too, he reckoned.

Reminiscing about his five weeks in the Philippines, his mind reeled at how different each had been and how their fortunes had plummeted. One month ago everyone talked big; certain American military strength was unquestionable, that any adversary could be easily crushed. One month ago he was a smug aviator; proud of his plane, proud of his flying prowess.

But the enemy had forced the Americans to pay heavily for taking it so lightly. The Japanese, flying their own planes, despite what Dohlman thought, ruled the skies and the Americans were incapable of even contesting it. No longer was he even a pilot. The war had amounted to one sorry screw-up after another.

And now the ultimate insult. Not only was the army ignominiously retreating, men from the air corps were now formed into infantry outfits, which, to some, was a fate worse than death.

Airmen had always considered themselves superior to foot soldiers. The air corps had a different mentality and method of doing things. Air corps soldiers were well-trained professionals who respected each other, skilled as aviators, mechanics, armorers, or other technical trades. They lived in rear areas and enjoyed regular meals of well-prepared hot food. They considered themselves a proud elite. But now the men of the air corps were being forced into the infantry; the god-awful, long suffering, earthbound infantry.

Ed shook his head, knowing he had come a long way, but not along a road he had envisioned or desired. Why had he joined in the first place? All he wanted to do was fly.

That afternoon, Ed sat next to the driver in the front seat of a truck, with Gatling and Baxter sprawled in back. The rest of the squadron had already left for the docks and they were last to depart.

The enlisted driver revved the engine, shifted the transmission into first and slowly started out. Ed turned slightly and asked if he was stopping for anyone else.

"No, sir, I'm not. Most everyone has left." He turned the wheel sharply to avoid chunks of concrete that had fallen from a nearby building. The truck swerved and continued on. "Orders are to destroy everything left behind."

"Everything?" Ed asked, as they passed the canvas awning of the mess hall. The neat stacks of canned food remained outside, untouched. "What about those rations?"

"We've got orders to destroy everything, sir. We probably have plenty of food on Bataan, so that stuff is staying behind. We'll burn it so the Japs can't use it."

Ed's eyes darkened like angry thunderclouds. "Stop the truck!" he barked, his voice sharp and piercing. The driver slammed down on the brakes and the truck screeched to a halt. "Back up to the mess tent," Ed ordered. "We're loading that food."

The driver flinched at his sharp tone. "But, sir," he said, swallowing hard, "we only have to get to the port. We don't have to worry about food. If the army needs it, the quartermasters'll get it."

Ed was in no mood to consider such talk. He had been listening to feeble explanations about why things weren't going right since the war began. People were always placing the blame on someone else; some helpless scapegoat who usually wasn't around to defend himself. But American forces were in a jam. It was time for men to take the initiative.

Ed did exactly that. Girding himself with resolve, he took charge. "We're bringing that food along," he said in a sharp, raking tone. "That's an order, soldier, so back up this truck and let's start humping crates."

"But, sir . . ." Ed shot him a cold look and reached down to his belt, unflapped a russet leather service holster and placed his hand on the hilt of a .45 caliber pistol. His voice taut with anger, he would not take 'no' for an answer. "I said back up this truck. Now!"

Without another word, the driver shoved the engine into gear and reversed direction toward the mess tent, screeching to a stop beside it. Ed fastened down the flap of the holster, knowing he had made his point. Besides, the pistol wasn't loaded. He opened the door and hopped out.

"C'mon, you guys," he said to Baxter and Gatling in as reasonable voice as he could muster. "Let's load these crates. We'll be glad once we get to Bataan. I'm not so sure things won't be slim over there."

Disbelieving, Gatling looked down, speaking in a thick, unsteady whisper. "Ed, my head is killing me. I haven't eaten, either. Show some consideration, will 'ya?"

"When we're done, we can open up a few of these boxes and have ourselves a feast on the way to the docks. What d'ya say?"

Gatling rose from the long bench and, groaning, lowered himself down. "C'mon, Baxter," he growled. "Let's load this stuff and get it over with. Let's make the man who shot down a Jap plane happy, even though there's bound to be plenty of food over there."

Ed grinned and the four began working, forming a line, stacking box after box in the truck. They finished in fifteen minutes, with only a couple crates of canned fruit broken on the ground. Ed picked up several cans, scrutinizing the colorful labels. "Hmmm," he said. "Libby's peaches and fruit cocktail. Sounds good. Let's all pick some up to eat on the way. Let's stop by the post exchange, too. Might be some candy bars sitting around we can liberate."

The driver, fully in the mood now, laughed as Ed mentioned the possibility of free candy. "Pile in, everyone," he called as he strolled back to the truck. "Next stop is the candy counter."

The men climbed in back and in a few minutes the truck pulled up to the post exchange, the doors hanging open, roof partially collapsed, a fat hole blown through one wall. They walked in and passed an open cash register at the front counter, its cash drawer empty. Clothes were strewn about, jars of shaving cream, loose socks, brown paper bags and assorted other items covering the floor. A grimy layer of oily dirt coated everything.

Baxter grabbed several jars of salted peanuts, a large metal container of potato chips and two boxes of candy. "Look, I got a box of Big Hunks and one of Baby Ruths," he said, his voice chuckling and hearty. "You guys get anything?"

"Yeah, I just found bottles of soda pop under a pile of clothes," said the driver, kneeling down. "They're warm, but still good. Want one?"

He picked up four bottles and offered one to each man, flipping off the caps with a pocketknife. As he approached Ed, his feet suddenly turned to clay and he hesitated, perplexed by the harsh words uttered to him by the strange officer who had made his point in such a threatening, belligerent way.

"I'll take one of those," Ed said, smiling, his face open and friendly. "Whatever flavor you have is fine."

Giving a brief nod, the soldier flipped off the cap and handed it over. He didn't know what to say, struggled to utter something, then came to rigid attention and snapped a salute. "The name's Buchman," he said. "Private First Class Mark Buchman."

Ed returned the salute in a casual manner. "Stand at ease, Mark," he said. "I apologize for acting like I was gonna pull my pistol back there. I guess you figured I was a lunatic."

Buchman's expression brightened as Ed continued. "You ought to know my gun wasn't loaded. I haven't loaded it a single time since war began."

"That's okay, sir, it's no big deal," replied Buchman in an apologetic tone. "It got me to go back for the food. I never once thought of taking anything before. It seems sort of like stealing and I was raised not to do that. But there ain't no sense leaving rations behind."

Ed downed the soda pop while Buchman spoke and nodded when he concluded, indicating he was ready for another by holding out the empty bottle. Buchman handed him a root beer, opened it, nodded and walked to the storage room at the rear of the store, on the look-out for more boxes of snacks.

Ed watched him disappear around a counter then walked outside to the truck. No one was rushing to leave and he felt no reason to hurry them. He climbed into the seat and leaned back, gulping down the lukewarm but welcome drink. While lowering the bottle, he spied a half-destroyed service station next door, most of the roof and half the building blown to smithereens. He hopped out and strolled over, taking a last swig of soda and tossing the empty bottle into the bushes.

The old gravity-feed gas pumps were still there, the canvas-reinforced rubber hoses lying askew on the pavement like frozen black snakes, as if they had been there for weeks. Wiping his mouth, he walked into the office as if he owned the place, broken glass and bits of ceiling littering the floor, and went straight to the glassed-in counter, spotting four unopened cases of chewing gum. He reached inside and pulled them out, stowing two under each arm. Each held 48 five-stick packs, two labeled "Blackjack" and the others "Beemans." He wore a grin, for he liked both flavors, and, besides, the price was right. Free. He knew Buchman would be appreciative when finding them on the seat behind the steering wheel.

* * *

Confused traffic moved to Bataan from every direction, clogging the main highway with all sorts of vehicles and cargo, from civilian buses and oxcarts to 155mm artillery pieces, M3 Stuart light tanks and long convoys of troops. A monumental traffic jam, backed up for miles, formed on the narrow road leading over two bridges crossing the unfordable Pampanga River. American anti-aircraft batteries established positions alongside the bridges to provide protection from Japanese air attacks, but activity in the sky was low. When enemy planes did pass over, it was only to fly somewhere else, and the anti-aircraft guns remained silent.

The traffic tie-up presented a golden opportunity to the Japanese that the general staff threw away due to a single-minded focus on capturing Manila. They considered the retreat nothing more than the disorganized flight of demoralized soldiers, to be easily mopped up later. It proved a major blunder, permitting tens of thousands of American and Filipino soldiers to pour into Bataan.

Arriving troops found the Bataan Peninsula an uninviting, inhospitable place, thick with dense jungle and steep ravines, fast turning into a snarling cauldron of confusion. Few facilities offering human comfort had been built and the trenches and fortifications that should have been laid out existed on paper alone. Within days, 15,000 American and 65,000 Filipino troops crammed onto the twenty-five mile long peninsula, with 11,000 more offshore in Manila Bay on Corregidor and several other fortified islands.

Though they launched a massive effort, the quantity of rations accumulated by quartermaster troops proved heartbreaking. Instead of the planned one hundred and eighty day supply, a thorough inventory turned up only enough canned meat and fish for fifty-nine days, forty days worth of canned milk, enough canned vegetables and flour for thirty-nine days, and rice enough for three weeks. MacArthur, however, estimated his forces would have to hold out for at least six months before help arrived. He immediately ordered rations cut in half.

Troops threw up an initial defense line across the peninsula between the villages of Abucay and Mauban, some twenty miles long, with the ancient volcano Mount Natib in the center. Engineers hacked three airfields out of the jungle, named Cabcaben, Bataan and Pilar, for use by the battered remnants of the Far East Air Force, which, as of Christmas day, numbered sixteen P-40's and four P-35's.

Over one hundred barges loaded with supplies anchored off Bataan and the supplies continued to be hustled ashore by work crews at night, while Japanese aviators slept. To prevent destruction of the precious cargo, the Americans towed them to the exact same positions before first light each morning, making the Japanese think they were forgotten derelicts. Many weeks passed before they caught on.

CHAPTER 8

SETTLING DOWN

Late December 1942

The band of four men missed the first trip of the inter-island steamer *Don Esteban* and lingered on the dock, exploring bomb blasted, abandoned buildings, on the watch for souvenirs; basically, killing time in wait for the next boat. Long lines of perspiring Filipino stevedores loaded barges with great quantities of foodstuffs and military supplies for use on Bataan.

Japanese planes crisscrossed the sky throughout the afternoon, dropping bombs or strafing knots of people in the dock area, with neither American planes nor anti-aircraft fire disputing their presence. The enemy made long, lazy bombing runs, laying deadly eggs with painstaking precision, a steady drumbeat of destruction that pounded docks, warehouses and cranes, and scattered workers.

Nearly all merchant ships had vacated the harbor weeks before, urged by authorities to depart when it became apparent no effective defense could be mounted. A few stragglers waited behind, one the *Corregidor*, an inter-island steamer charged with transporting artillery and munitions to American and Filipino troops in the southern Philippine Islands. Japanese planes swarmed over her while steaming out of the harbor, direct hits sending her to the bottom in minutes.

The four sailed aboard the *Don Esteban* that evening as the sky darkened behind broken pink clouds, a time when Japanese pilots winged home to celebrate their successes. The supply of food the Americans trucked from Neilson Field was carefully stacked on deck, no questions asked, and the half empty ship sailed away from Manila for the final time that day, her destination Mariveles, a small seaport village on the lower tip of the Bataan Peninsula.

As she pulled away, the four looked back at Manila receding behind, a sight which inspired and depressed at the same time. Declared an "open city" by MacArthur after consultation with civilian officials, confident residents believed the threat of Japanese attack had come to an end. Lights that had been blacked out for weeks twinkled in many windows, adding drama and beauty to the night skyline.

The voyage took place against the steady background thunder of demolitions exploding along the waterfront. Clouds of smoke boiled up, many of the fires smaller than earlier in the day as they burned themselves out, but others flared up as big as ever; violent torrents of orange and yellow in the fast fading daylight. The navy's fuel dump of more than a million gallons of oil and lubricants sent up blistering columns of smoke and flame, a conflagration that blazed for days.

The four watched for a time, glum looks on their faces, then separated, each going a different direction. Baxter and Buchman fell asleep against bulkheads on the far side of the deck while Ed rested on crossed arms atop a rail at the stern, watching the fiery plumes of Manila. Gatling meandered over to the crates of food, found a secluded seat and leaned back, staring at the night sky, so vast and unchanging. Brows furrowed in worry, he sat immobile, lost in contemplation, thinking of home, the fact that he'd never been able to fire even one shot at the enemy but, most of all, his wife, Becky.

As the ship neared the center of Manila Bay and the strapping outline of Corregidor Island loomed, Ed stepped away from the railing, wandered over and sat on a crate beside Gatling. "Wonder when we'll get back to Manila?" he asked in a tone intended to sound cheerful. He gazed at the black shore in the distance. "I don't expect conditions on Bataan to come close to what we had at Neilson."

Gatling ignored him, gazing up at bright stars making up constellations to which he had never paid attention. Against the dark sky, the stars stood out like lights on a Christmas tree. When he spoke, it was in a deep-timbered, controlled voice, flat and unemotional. "Who knows?" he replied. "We'll drive the Japs out of Manila soon as reinforcements get here, I expect."

"What if they don't come in time? Ever think about that?"

Gatling turned and twisted his mouth into a frown, icy anger flashing in his eyes. "Ed, do you think our country would leave us out here twisting in the wind? That's not what Americans do." He leaned back, his expression tight with strain. "They'll get here, even if it takes moving mountains. You'll see."

"Yeah, maybe you're right," a recalcitrant Ed muttered, taken aback by Gatling's rigid, perhaps wishful, attitude.

Several minutes of brittle silence ensued during which Ed thought about their situation. He fervently hoped reinforcements would come, but a nagging sensation hammered inside at the same time. The notion that the Japanese Empire had fielded an army and air force better than that of the United States was opposed to everything he had ever heard or been taught. It was a concept difficult to accept.

He shook his head, for the situation was truly confusing. Perhaps it's the nature of humans to think positive, to look at the bright, upbeat side of things; to believe rescuers will arrive, no matter how improbable. That would account for Gatling's attitude. But was there a basis of truth to it? Would the cavalry charge from nowhere just in time to avert disaster?

Ed sat alongside his friend, the two gazing into the heavens. Millions of years old, the stars had floated in the cosmos overseeing all of mankind's conflicts, even those in biblical times. If they could speak, perhaps they could shed some light on this crazy, topsy-turvy state of affairs. Another minute passed before he could manage a steady voice.

"Jim, this is a rough time. It's hard on everyone, including me." He leaned back. "But, I guess it's especially hard for you. You're thinking of Becky, right?"

Gatling, not wanting his emotions to show, hunched over, forearms resting on his thighs. "Yeah," he mumbled in a barely audible whisper.

"You worried?"

"Of course!" he replied in a voice congested with doubts and fears. "I don't know how things are back there. What if the Japs move their carriers off the California coast? They could hit Hamilton Field and that would put her in danger." He moved his shoulders in a shrug of anger. "I should have sent her back to her folks in Montana."

"Becky's a smart gal. She'll get out if she has to. Besides, if the Japs hit anything in California, it'll be the major port cities, like San Francisco or Los Angeles. They'll most likely go after our shipping. That'll give time for them to consolidate gains out here."

Gatling shifted slightly. "That makes sense, but you aren't in charge of the Jap navy and don't know what they'll do. Maybe they'll attack California, or even the Panama Canal, or maybe they'll just blast hell out of us right here. The air corps sure doesn't have a damn thing to say about it."

Ed reached into a front pocket for a cigarette, and then remembered the strict rules about lighting up. Given the clear air and blackness of the tropic night, even a glowing cigarette could give away a ship's position. A burly crewman warned when they came aboard that any man caught lighting up on deck would be tossed overboard, no questions asked. Given the shark infested waters, that was the same as a death sentence.

Ed slipped the pack back into his pocket and faced Gatling. "Why not write Becky a letter and tell her what you're thinking? There's no use sitting around stewing about something you can't do anything about."

"I'll have to mail it in Bataan and I don't know if it'll get out. What connection do we have to the states from there?"

"Well, I hear subs are still docking at Corregidor," said Ed, sitting up straight, wanting him to do it, to get the problem off his chest.

"Just go inside and write it. There'll be paper and an envelope around somewhere. We'll get it out from Corregidor."

His face closed as if guarding a secret, Gatling bolted upright. "Well, I suppose I might as well," he said while scratching his head. "We'll be on this tub for another hour anyway." He rose and walked away toward a hatch leading into the main cabin, the ship lurching up and down as it plowed through the choppy bay waters as fast as it could manage.

Ed rubbed his eyes as he watched him go, swallowing hard. He knew submarines were using Corregidor's north dock to offload supplies and evacuate personnel, but didn't know their intermittent schedule, or even if they devoted precious cargo space to hauling bags of mail. But just the act of writing would enable Gatling to get hold of himself.

From somewhere on the dark bay amid the chilly night, the throbbing chug-chug of another ship's engines could be heard. He turned and noticed a dark outline as it headed out toward the open sea, and freedom, should a Japanese patrol plane or lurking destroyer not spot it. For an instant, he felt tugging loneliness in his insides; the occupational disease of the nonprofessional soldier fighting a war far from home and loved ones.

Mariveles, a non-descript collection of wooden docks, tin-roofed bamboo buildings and native huts, bustled with activity as the *Don Esteban* approached. Only one road in town was paved, the cobblestone Highway 6 which wound its way twenty-five miles up the east side of the Bataan peninsula to Bagac, the far right of the American front line. A second road, this one little more than a widened jungle trail, led out of town along the west side of the peninsula toward the American left. Using bulldozers and scrapers, engineers were at work widening it.

About three miles from Corregidor Island, which stuck like a bone in the mouth of Manila Bay, Mariveles was the major communication hub connecting MacArthur's headquarters with the forces on Bataan.

Only as long as Bataan held could the island survive, and the forces on Corregidor well knew it. If Bataan fell, Japanese artillery would be able to blast them at point-blank range.

Assigned to Cabcaben Field, Ed caught a ride in a civilian sedan commandeered by the military during the retreat from Manila, leaving the others behind to keep an eye on the food. He returned with an empty army truck a short time later and they stacked everything inside and roared back to the airfield, stowing it in an empty bamboo shack. Many of their 3rd Pursuit Squadron companions had already arrived, though others had traveled by truck and were tangled in traffic somewhere on the upper part of the peninsula.

Cabcaben Field was little more than a widened roadway that required aircraft attempting to land to approach low over Manila Bay. Planes taking off had to climb quickly to avoid crashing over steep hills into the water. About a half dozen planes were resting under trees alongside the strip, eventually to be dispersed among the three airfields yet to become operational. Also constructed nearby was one of two hospitals on Bataan, General Hospital Number Two, mostly consisting of beds spread under trees in the jungle.

Once they settled in, the four men were assigned to the construction of protective revetments for B-17 bombers due to fly in from Mindanao. They went to work with relish, intending to make the bomber revetments the safest ones the world had ever seen.

"We don't want the Japs to spot our planes from the sky, so be careful!" shouted Gatling to the operator of an idling bulldozer as he prepared to scoop out a place for a revetment. "Don't run hell for leather over everything!"

The sweating driver nodded impatiently and revved the engine, dropping the angled blade before him, scraping the surface of the ground and pushing dirt off to the side. "I know what I'm doing, Mack," he shouted as the bulldozer jerked forward. Gatling couldn't make out his words due to the wracking cacophony of noise.

He exchanged glances with Ed. "Best round up some Filipinos and get'em to making camouflage," he said. "There's rice and cane fields around and, from overhead, we need to fit into the landscape, all natural-like."

"Okay, Jim," replied Ed. "We'll get to it. You're the boss on this project."

Working with a Filipino work gang, excited to be doing something concrete, they built revetments at the edge of the cane field. Though the B-17 bombers never flew in, several of the revetments were used to protect smaller aircraft and other equipment. When they moved planes inside, they covered the revetments with nets of chicken wire in which stalks of fresh, green cane stuck out. In front of each plane a row of bamboo tubes also held green cane stalks. From the air, the unspoiled cane field illusion was perfect.

The airstrip itself was packed earth, with no asphalt or concrete pavement. Huge clouds of blowing dust plagued operations, with flights sometimes curtailed. Due to the lack of aircraft, the airfield commander ordered the few remaining P-40s and P-35s to fly only reconnaissance missions, usually lasting no more than thirty minutes.

Japanese bombers attacked the Bataan airfields regularly, digging great circular holes in the runways with bombs; the damage repaired as soon as they left. Most attacks came each morning with the characteristic punctuality shown by the Japanese. Sometimes American aircraft roared in from the clouds to pick off the attackers, surprise actions that often left Japanese aircraft flaming toward the ground. But they also hit back, sometimes sending American fighters spinning out of control. It was an unsustainable exchange rate, for while the Japanese could replace their aircraft, the Americans could not. The defenders were finally forced to operate under standing orders to avoid aerial combat and to engage the enemy only when absolutely necessary.

Many more pilots and aircrews were available than planes and, until reinforcements flew in or evacuations took place, top officers knew they were needed on the ground. Infantry training became the order of the day, despite its unpopularity. For the last days of December and the first weeks of January 1942, the men charged up and down hills and fired their rifles on a shooting range set up a safe distance from camp.

On the whole, the men of the 3rd Pursuit Squadron were willing pupils, albeit awkward with the new gear. For most of early January they went on forced marches through rough terrain, learned the manual of arms, and patrolled beaches in search of signs of Japanese activity. Bivouacked in a canyon near Cabcaben Field, they had plenty of land for practice.

Their motley collection of equipment came from all sorts of places, some of which they preferred not talking about. This included four old navy Lewis .30-caliber machine guns and six air corps .50-caliber machine guns taken from the wings of wrecked P-40s and placed on homemade bamboo mounts, as well as a few Browning automatic rifles.

They carried the Lewis machine guns by looping a leather sling over the shoulder, requiring the user to hold it steady while firing with an asbestos glove-covered hand. The new infantry outfit was issued two boxes of hand grenades but, as they were to find out, many failed to explode due to rusted detonators. The grenades had been manufactured twenty-three years before.

The squadron appeared well fixed for food, but it quickly became evident that a major supply problem had developed. Within days, quartermaster officials ordered all units to turn in food supplies and go on half rations. The value of the canned food Ed had so obstinately brought from Neilson Field rose into the stratosphere overnight. Dohlman ordered the crates transferred into a more secure, padlocked building, and, to keep the quartermasters off their backs, ordered that five crates be turned in. The balance, dozens of cases of beef, fish, canned milk, fruits and vegetables, and lots more, formed the squadron's reserve, to be horded and husbanded judiciously until the end of the campaign.

CHAPTER 9

MacArthur visits Bataan

January 10, 1942

Four days after word of the ration reduction, Ed stood in formation on the airstrip, staring into the sky, thinking of home and family while thick clouds of gritty brown dust swirled about. With one dozen others, he waited to welcome a "very important visitor" to the field . . . who they all knew would be General Douglas MacArthur. He was to arrive by patrol boat for an inspection tour of defenses on the Bataan Peninsula, his first, and last, visit to Bataan.

As Ed stood, impatiently twisting his neck and blinking his eyes against the swirling dust, Gatling, standing next to him, nudged his elbow. "Hey, Ed," he whispered in an annoyed tone, "think MacArthur's bringing good news? I'm ready to listen."

Ed, looking straight ahead, spoke from the side of his mouth. "I dunno. Scuttlebutt says there're planes flying in soon from a carrier, but I don't know whether to believe it."

"Probably just another story," Gatling replied. "Too many rumors don't come true around here."

Silence enveloped the two for a few minutes, the low tones of other whispered conversations and the irritating wind whipping across the airstrip hanging in the background. Daily rumors of reinforcements "just over the horizon" had battered everyone, turning each day into an emotional roller coaster. The high hopes generated by yesterday's wishful chatter led to despondency the next.

Gatling let out a loud harrumph. "I've never been able to figure out MacArthur. He's supposed to be a genius, but why he let our planes get caught helpless the first day is beyond me. That 'genius' let our airfields become death traps."

"Yeah," Ed replied, continuing to stare forward. "Our bombers could've hit Jap air bases on Formosa when word of the Pearl Harbor attack first came through. Formosa's only three hours away. The Nip planes that thumped us were based there. Why we didn't blast 'em, God only knows."

"I think it's because MacArthur's more gutless than he lets on. This past fall, he told everyone who would listen, even the top brass back in Washington, that we were ready for war in the Philippines. He had a lot of confidence in nothing. He's no genius in my book."

Ed glanced at his friend. "Jim, we both have a pretty low opinion of MacArthur, but who cares what we think? You can say at least one good thing about him—he got us to Bataan when we could've been left high and dry in Manila. Besides, maybe help will come through; who knows?"

Gatling looked back. "Well, I don't like uppity people who think they're better than everyone else. MacArthur considers himself as an earth-bound version of God. The man's a nut."

The rumble of motor vehicles crunching over the dirt road leading to the airfield mounted. Ed gave a quick smile and snapped his gaze forward. "Well, you're gonna have to put up with MacArthur personal," he said. "He's here."

Gatling raised himself to his tallest position, knowing it wasn't everyday that the commander of all U.S. army forces in the Far East visited. He craned his neck to the left, seeing clouds of brown dust boil upward from four cars turning off the road onto the strip, carrying MacArthur and his staff. Unlike the soldiers in Ed's group clothed in soiled, rumpled khaki uniforms that hadn't seen soap and water in weeks, the visitors wore immaculate uniforms, with neat neckties and smartly pressed pants.

"Take a look at those pretty boys," whispered Gatling as they climbed out of their vehicles. "It's hot as hell but MacArthur's wearing a jacket. The man's been holed up in Corregidor tunnels too long."

Ed chuckled. "He does look a bit out of place. Maybe he thinks the Japs are taking the day off."

MacArthur, a pair of dark sunglasses perched on his craggy nose, stopped and gazed at the formation. His broad, hawk-like face stiffened as heavy eyebrows drew together. He looked them over, one end of the line to the other, then nodded and walked toward Colonel Harold George, saluting at the front of the formation. Snapping a return salute and extending a hand, MacArthur greeted him warmly.

"It's good to see you, Harold," said MacArthur. In his eyes, George had performed well and was fast shaping into one of the few air corps officers for whom he had any respect. He blamed Brereton for the poor performance of the air corps during the opening days of war and had shipped him off to Australia. George, he believed, was a different cut of man. "The strip has shaped up well, I see," he observed.

"Yes, sir, it has. Welcome to Cabcaben Field, General."

MacArthur smiled. "Your men are doing a fine job with the remaining planes. But more are coming, I assure you."

George gave a quick nod. "That's good to hear, sir." The two men, their hands still clasped together, drew apart. "General MacArthur, with your permission, sir, I'd like to introduce you to some of my key officers. All are doing an excellent job and deserve recognition."

"I'll be glad to, Harold," said MacArthur, nodding. With George and several others in tow, he walked along the line of waiting officers and talked briefly with each. Standing before Ed, he asked where he was from, to which Ed replied Yuma, Arizona.

"You must speak Spanish, then," smiled MacArthur, knowing Yuma's location near the Mexican border. He had passed through the town numerous times when riding passenger trains coast to coast, always taking time to stretch his legs at the Yuma depot as thirsty steam locomotives took on water.

"I don't know much Spanish, sir. Only a smattering," Ed replied. "I'm really nothing more than a simple country boy—riding and roping and all that."

MacArthur grinned and clapped his shoulder. "A true western American. Well, just keep up the good work, son. You'll be back riding and roping as soon as we lick the Japs and win this war."

"Yes, sir," replied Ed, an eyebrow raised in amusement as MacArthur sidled to the left to face Gatling.

"And what's your name, Lieutenant?" he asked, peering into his eyes.

"Jim Gatling, sir; 3rd Pursuit Squadron, now provisional infantry."

"Where's your hometown?"

"San Jose, California, sir."

"Ah, yes. In the midst of Santa Clara Valley—the valley of heart's delight, as they say. So you've now become a ground pounder?"

"Yes, sir. But I've been spending my spare time repairing a Loening OA-1 biplane in a revetment near here. A group of us dug it out of a rice paddy and are rebuilding it."

"That's good to hear, son," said MacArthur, sliding a corncob pipe in his mouth. "Anything that flies is useful."

MacArthur continued down the line and then strode to the front of the formation to address the men. Although fifty-nine years old, he brimmed with confidence, bearing an almost regal demeanor. He removed his sunglasses and wiped them with a handkerchief, taking his time before replacing them, allowing anticipation to build. He intended for his remarks to boost sagging morale, to generate optimism and enthusiasm about the victory to come.

"Men, the situation here on Bataan is shaping up nicely," he began, chin jutting out. "Japanese forces are attacking the front lines but we're driving them back. We have ample supplies and can hold out for many months; until relief arrives from the states."

MacArthur raised the pipe to his lips and puffed the smoldering tobacco, blowing out a thin stream of gray smoke. "Airstrips are currently under construction in Mindanao which we expect to be used by aircraft flying up from Australia. Heavy bombers will strike the enemy and new pursuits flying from Bataan will retake the skies. Enemy control of the air is only temporary, let me assure you. Soon the air will be black with clouds of our own planes. Within a few months we'll break out of these lines in a major counteroffensive to retake Manila."

He held the bowl of the pipe and pointed with the stem as he spoke, his eyes burning with intensity. "Your resistance thus far has fired the imagination of the American people. They're inspired, truly inspired by what you're accomplishing here. You must continue to fight, knowing your country, the entire free world and God is behind you."

Stirred by his hopeful words, the enthusiastic officers shouted and cheered. Grinning, MacArthur turned toward Colonel George. He considered his formal remarks concluded, but the enthusiastic response moved him to reconsider. He reached behind and slipped a leather wallet from his back pocket, pulled out a bill, and thrust it over his head, waving it back and forth.

"Does anyone here want to bet me fifty dollars that we won't be back in Manila by Easter?"

The men shuffled their feet, cast sideways glances at each other, but even though doubters were scattered about, none dared challenge MacArthur. He continued waving the bill for a few seconds then, satisfied, for there were no takers, slipped it back inside the wallet and turned to George. "Let's have a word," he said.

The two walked off to a camouflaged bunker situated in thick jungle astride the runway, where it couldn't be sighted from the air. Bamboo poles, palm trunks, and hardwood planks overlaid with sandbags provided protection from all but direct hits. His staff huddled outside as the two senior officers, along with MacArthur's chief-of-staff, Major General Richard Sutherland, met in private. They walked out moments later, MacArthur stepping into a Ford sedan and motoring away with the short convoy.

Lieutenant Colonel Dohlman, dismissed the formation and Ed and Gatling walked away together. Gatling elbowed his friend as they strolled toward the OA-1 biplane, well hidden among the trees. "You big liar," he joshed. "What were you talking about, telling MacArthur you're a 'country boy' who did nothing but ride and rope? Why didn't you tell him you went to college? You ain't no country boy. You probably don't even know how to rope."

Grinning, Ed let out a chuckle. "Because he doesn't need to know, that's why." He walked on for a moment and then continued. "Some people puff their chests out when they go to college, but I don't. Besides, I don't trust MacArthur."

"Well, he sure had some nice words," said Gatling. "Wonder if any of 'em are true?"

"I don't know," replied Ed. "Maybe there's a kernel in there somewhere, but he's sure a good one for waving the flag. The man's a helluva speaker."

"What about going back to Manila? Think it'll happen?"

Ed didn't answer for a moment. He continued walking forward and grunted a response. "I don't know. Depends on whether you believe MacArthur and his big talk, I suppose."

Inside, both held doubts. The forces on Bataan were in grave trouble, that they knew—not enough supplies, few planes, no navy, too much unreliable equipment, and not enough trained men. The vast majority of the raw Philippine army, the bulk of the defending force, had been called up in the weeks leading up to the war or right after it broke out. Until they gained experience, many Filipino units were little more than armed mobs.

"Well, just watch yourself," warned Gatling, taking on a somber tone. "Playing around with what you say to generals can come back to bite you. Best play it straight."

Ed reached for his companion's sleeve and yanked him to a stop, peering into his face. "Look, Jim, we've been buddies since Hamilton Field. We've been through a lot together, so we can give one another the straight dope, right?"

Gatling nodded, not saying a word. Ed continued. "Playing it conservative, too cautious—that's what lost us half our air force the first day of war. Waiting and then being caught flat-footed was pure stupidity. We agree on that."

Gatling's forehead furrowed into a frown. "Yeah, we agree, but we're stuck here, plain and simple. You want to get back to Arizona and I want to go home to Becky, but being we're on Bataan, we can't go anywhere."

Ed stared back. "I was leading to that. We've gotta be resourceful, you and me, or we aren't gonna make it. I mean, look at what the general said—that we have ample supplies. If that's so, why did he cut our rations in half? Why did the quartermasters confiscate everyone's extra food? Because things aren't as rosy as McArthur makes them out, that's why. We can't swallow baloney like this. You gotta look out for number one out here."

Gatling nodded. "Well, you were the one who got the food here from Neilson. You must have something on the ball," he said with a grin. "We'll stick together and make out okay."

"Yeah, let's you and me watch out for each other," Ed replied, caught up in the seriousness of the moment. "Sooner or later we'll be thrown into action. The odds for two guys working as a team are a lot better than every man for himself."

Ed angled in the direction of the revetment storing the OA-1 aircraft. "Let's take a look at that plane of yours. Maybe you fellas are making it into a better plane than it used to be." Gatling grinned and followed.

They approached the blue and yellow OA-1, an ungainly open cockpit aircraft in use since 1925. With a cruising speed of ninety miles per hour, easy pickings for roving enemy fighters, it would be able to fly only at night when the skies were largely safe. Gatling and a crew of mechanics worked on it each evening, scattering greasy engine parts and tools over tables and benches.

Gatling flung open the engine cowling and glanced inside. "How's she running?" asked Ed, leaning forward, hands in his pockets.

"We've taken the carburetor apart and straightened the propeller, which was a bent up mess. Right now we're cleaning mud out of the engine," replied Gatling as he leaned over the inverted liberty engine that powered the craft. "It's slow work, but we've almost got it finished. This thing will purr like a kitten soon."

"Another plane will amount to a substantial increase in the size of our air corps," Ed remarked in a sarcastic voice. "You know, there's a name for salvaged planes like this. They're called the 'bamboo fleet.'"

Gatling looked up. "Well, it doesn't matter what people call it as long as it works," he said. "We're putting this thing together with spit, chewing gum and bamboo anyway." His lips ruffled into a wide smile. "You know, though, another plane'll come in real handy."

"Gonna work on it this afternoon?"

Gatling had again turned toward the engine, reaching into its greasy innards to feel a rubber hose, grunting his response. "Yeah," he said. "Might be able to fly her in a few weeks."

Ed stepped back from the plane. "Well, then, I'll get going. I'm off to camp to see what kind of chow they're serving up tonight. See you later."

He turned and walked along a winding path descending into a narrow ravine leading to the provisional infantry's mess hall, a bamboo-shaded structure dug into a steep hillside. It was nothing like the spacious mess tent they had enjoyed at Iba Field before the war, with waiters and fresh flowers, but it was becoming more like home as time passed. Just yesterday, one of the men affixed the dried horns of a carabao above the entrance. War trophies were displayed on the walls: a Japanese flag, several helmets, a rifle, an officer's samurai sword, and a thumb-tacked December 18th edition of the Manila Herald. Giant letters plastered on the front page reported the repulse of a major Japanese invasion convoy near Manila. The headline never failed to generate derisive laughs, for though reported as genuine fact, even corroborated by McArthur's press office, the event was pure fiction.

Baxter and Master Sergeant John Evans sat across from each other in the mess hall, talking and smoking cigarettes. Ed walked up and slid beside Evans.

"Hi, guys," he said as his boots scraped across hard-packed earth beneath the table. "Heard about our visitor?"

They replied in unison, eyes wide with excitement. "Yeah, we sure did."

Evans, crushing the butt of his cigarette into an empty C-ration can, tossed back a thick crop of jet black hair and spoke in a lively, excited voice. "The news sounds real good, just real good. Help is on the way and we're gonna take back Manila. I can't wait to be sleeping between soft sheets again. Manila Hotel here we come!"

Baxter slapped the table with the flat of a hand. "We've built a dozen revetments alongside the runway, I don't know how many, but this news'll sure buck up spirits," he enthused in a bubbly, high-pitched voice. "Everyone'll work harder knowing help is on the way."

Ed's mouth widened into an awkward smile and he rubbed an ear. "You guys sure sound confident. Are you going on what MacArthur said or did you hear the same thing somewhere else? We've all heard enough rumors to strangle a cat."

Baxter shook his head and pointed a rolled up comic book at Ed. He waved it back and forth. "Nope, we heard it from the navy, too, down in Mariveles. They're betting two to one that planes'll be here inside twenty-four hours."

Ed lowered his head and remembered the past. "We've heard rumors from the navy before. Remember what that chaplain said? Then we heard stories from Corregidor. None of 'em came true—we're still here."

"Yeah, but Ed, this is solid!" His voice taut with excitement, Baxter jolted upright, full of good spirits and eager to share them. "There's a mile long convoy on its way carrying everything we need," he said while waving the comic book. "The army hasn't written us off—this is proof positive!"

Ed sat back and pondered the situation, eyebrows slanted into a frown. "I sure want to believe it, but what proof are you talking about? All I hear is words." he drawled. "To me, it comes down to the same old thing—I'll believe there's reinforcements on the way when I see 'em coming."

Baxter wrinkled his nose. "Ed, you're a tough nut to crack. But you'll become a believer soon enough."

A smile found its way through Ed's uncertainty. "Well, I hope I'm wrong—for all our sakes." He shrugged his shoulders and took a quick look toward the kitchen, sniffing to catch a smell that might identify the evening meal. "I hate to ask, boys, but do you know what we're having for dinner?"

Both scowled, rolling their eyes, for they knew the quartermaster-issued, reduced supper would consist of the same thing it had for each of the past five nights; unappetizing plain boiled rice, canned tomatoes, and two thin slices of canned corned beef. "Same boring, tasteless garbage," Evans said in a low voice. "I can't hardly look at a plate of canned tomatoes and corned beef straight. A little variety, and bigger servings, would be nice. I come for dinner hungry and leave hungry."

Ed checked his wristwatch and rose up. "Well, that won't be the case for long." He turned on a heel and took several long steps toward the door. Scoffing at them, he swerved around, winked an eye and said, "Reinforcements are coming, remember?" The two men cast a quick glance at each other as he gave the thumbs up signal, grinned and continued out.

Despite Ed's outward skepticism, it was almost beyond his comprehension that the American people would do nothing while tens of thousands of troops withered on the vine. As he wandered back to his tent, flung aside the canvas opening and stepped inside, he thought back to a fundamental belief he had held since his youngest days: Americans are a "can do" people who always come to the aid of their countrymen.

Ed sat on the edge of his cot and stared out the tent's entrance, wiping away perspiration beading his forehead. The afternoon had turned hot and humid, with a dearth of dark clouds that would deliver a downpour to cool things down for a short while. Without letup or mercy, the sun's rays beat down. Little activity seemed apparent anywhere in camp, as people had retreated to the relative coolness beneath shade trees to make the hours pass.

He took a deep breath, twisted around and reached for the framed photograph of Barbara resting atop a wooden crate. It was scarred and battered, for he had carried it from one duty station to another since joining the army. He stared at it for a long moment then scrunched up his lips and leaned back flat on the cot. Gazing at the ceiling of the tent, the photograph resting against his chest, Ed's eyes closed and he fell asleep, the warm memory of their moments together filling his mind.

Chapter 10

Action at Longoskawayan Point

January 1942

Training and patrolling filled the next weeks. Other than daily bombing and strafing raids by vicious Japanese Zeros zooming down from the clouds, no enemy contact occurred. The long-awaited reinforcement convoy never sailed into Manila Bay, to everyone's chagrin, but hopeful soldiers continued ascending high ridges each evening in desperate search for any sign of what had once seemed a certainty.

The misgivings Ed expressed to others about the rumors were public show, for he wanted them to be true as much as anyone. When the talk turned out false, he felt the same hurting disappointment, the same despair. The sourness in his stomach caused a nauseating, sinking anguish that left him bereft and desolate. Sometimes he sat alone for hours or wandered through the jungle in forlorn solitude.

As the days grew into weeks, the ties binding the provisional infantrymen with their squadron buddies who continued to fly frayed and declined; Ed found his visits to Cabcaben Field growing farther apart. Even Gatling, who once spent most of his spare time working on the Loening OA-1, lost interest. His non-flying status and disgust at being exiled from the squadron over which he once exuded zealous pride, had proven a bitter pill.

On the front, increasing Japanese pressure and one battering attack after another forced American and Filipino troops to fall back eight miles to a second, shorter line. This new position stretched fourteen miles across the peninsula through fierce, mountainous terrain. The withdrawal progressed as well as could be expected, despite confusion among many of the retreating troops, the loss of some vehicles, supplies and artillery, and numerous traffic tie-ups. The Japanese resumed their attacks a few days later but made no headway against the feisty defenders who intended to retreat no more.

Japanese occupied Manila

In a foul mood, a beet red General Masaharu Homma, commanding officer of the Japanese forces, fumed at the once triumphant campaign that had stalled. High-level military officials in Tokyo were whispering critical remarks about his competency, unkind comments that threatened to ruin his career.

In the series of attacks throughout the Pacific that began December 7th, only in the Philippines had allied forces successfully resisted the Japanese juggernaut. Right now, the two opponents on Bataan faced each other in a position of basic stalemate. The stubborn American and Filipino resistance had fast become an embarrassment and the military staff in Tokyo wanted the operation over, once and for all. "Intolerable," Homma bristled.

In mid-January, he called a conference among top Japanese army leaders in Manila. They tossed ideas back and forth, one officer suggesting they starve the defenders into submission. Homma slammed a fist onto the table and shot up in anger. "No!" he shouted. "That is a position of weakness that will go on for months. I will not allow it! We must defeat them on the battlefield."

Bristling with rage, Homma shot his eyes back and forth and slipped back into his chair. After a moment he raised a cup of green tea to his lips, then, after taking a sip, looked down at the pencil sketch he was drawing of an oil painting he planned to begin soon. An accomplished artist and author of poetry, the hobby helped keep his mind clear. As he studied his work, he thought back to the repeated amphibious attacks launched by Japanese forces behind British lines in Malaya that had collapsed their defenses. He wondered if perhaps the same tactical maneuver might be effective on Bataan.

He made an immediate decision. Setting down the porcelain cup, he held up a hand to signal an end of discussion. He scanned the hardened faces around the table and began. "I have decided," he proclaimed in a clipped voice. "We will launch an attack on the soft American underbelly near Mariveles. By severing the road used to supply their left flank, we will force the defense to give way. The result will be victory with honor."

Confident of success, Homma pounded one fist into the other as he barked orders. His subordinate commanders rose to attention and bowed, voicing no objections.

On the night of January 22nd, assault forces stood ready. Japanese troops clambered aboard landing craft in high spirits for the journey through the South China Sea along Bataan's mountainous west coast. At first, conditions were encouraging, with cloud cover providing excellent concealment, but soon they encountered strong tides, pitch-black skies and rough, raging seas. The invasion barges rocked back and forth, plowing through choppy ocean swells that sent waves of cold water scudding into each boat, drenching the men huddling together for warmth. Many emptied their stomachs over the side, miserable. As they neared the lower portion of the peninsula, the lack of detailed maps hindered their ability to pinpoint the correct landing zones, as the dense foliage rolling down to the sea made one area look like another. Confusion and hesitation resulted.

Then another problem arose, of more immediate danger. American torpedo boats on routine patrol spotted them several miles offshore. Twin .50 caliber machine guns raked the Japanese boats with deadly fire, pouring out streams of angry bullets. Lieutenant John Bulkeley, torpedo boat squadron commander, leaped aboard one barge before it went down, taking two prisoners and capturing a dispatch case full of army documents.

A motley collection of grounded sailors led by Commander Francis Bridgett scrambled to confront them on the beaches, with more forces to come, including the provisional infantry battalion. Word of the attack crackled over Cabcaben Field's radio around 10 a.m. and a motorcycle runner carried orders to the provisional infantry camp one-half mile away. As the runner arrived, the men sat under huge hardwood trees leisurely cleaning rifles after a morning of target practice. Knowing the humid afternoon temperature would reach ninety-five degrees, even in the jungle's gloomy shade, the shooting had been scheduled early to minimize physical activity during the hottest hours of the day.

"All right, you guys," hollered Ed as he scanned the message. "We're moving out. Finish quick and get your gear. This is the real thing. We leave in ten minutes."

The men exchanged glances, knowing the moment of truth had arrived. Drills, target shooting and marching had ended. Everything became quiet; no one spoke, no one asked questions, for they had been expecting it sooner or later. Within minutes, trucks pulled up and the backs banged open. The men rolled their blankets, checked the operation of their weapons, filed over and climbed inside, ready to motor through Mariveles to the West Road to confront the threat, to meet the enemy face to face.

Like much of Bataan, nature had plagued the Japanese landing area at Longoskawayan Point with harsh, almost impenetrable jungle filled with tall, dense bamboo. Huge hardwood trees grew up to seventy feet in height, from which luxuriant tropical vines and creepers extended down, mingling with smaller plants. Thick underbrush restricted visibility, often to no more than ten or fifteen feet.

Ed lay flattened in a rocky depression crammed with dead leaves and sticks, the enemy somewhere before him within a thick screen of vegetation. Other American airmen spread out for a hundred yards on either side. He fingered his Springfield rifle, brushing the blackened metal guard around the trigger and the fine-grained oiled wood under the barrel. Every once in awhile shots barked out, punctuated by the staccato rattling of machine guns and the boom of an exploding mortar shell or hand grenade.

Though he occasionally popped up for a quick look, to his front he could see nothing. Sweat coated his skin, thick and heavy as grease. It plastered his shirt and the back of his trousers to his body.

Enemy soldiers might be waiting, drawing beads from safe hiding places, preparing to drop the Americans in their tracks when they tried to advance. Not that he would know, of course. There seemed no *way* to know. Not playing your cards right, even guessing wrong, could mean instant death. Though the temperature was sweltering, Ed's body registered cold. All over, his skin tingled and itched.

While wiping perspiration from his brow, he thought of the grim life of an infantryman that had become his lot. His father had warned him about this back in Yuma, describing his own 1918 wartime experiences in grisly detail. The slaughter that took place amid battlefields of churned mud and grisly ruins had turned him into a committed pacifist who attended rallies, wrote letters to politicians and took part in demonstrations. Whether those beliefs were right or wrong was of no matter. The point was that Marshall Bannon had faced the horror of warfare first hand, head on and with guts.

Ed wondered: Had his father ever lost his fear, even grown used to the nerve-wracking uncertainties of battle? He shook his head. How could *anybody* get used to it? Today was Ed's first and already he loathed it. He squeezed down even further, almost frozen, his belly as low to the ground as that of a rattlesnake, waiting for something to happen; something positive, almost anything. Hands sticky with sweat, he swallowed and licked his lips over and over.

As happened so often during bad times, Ed's thoughts turned to memories of Barbara. A dreamy look overtook his features. He thought back to a hazy time, years before the war, when his father accepted a railroad job across the state at Fort Seward, where the family lived in an antique boxcar provided by the Southern Pacific. An isolated, rocky spot amid barren desert foothills, fierce winds gusted through each afternoon, lonely and powerful, rearranging the desert's fine brown layer of sandy dust and dried weeds. When the economic depression cost his friend Barbara's father his job and home, a victim of a failed bank that took along his life savings, Barbara moved in with the Bannon family.

Two rambunctious ten year olds bent on having fun, Ed and Barbara had plenty of time on their hands, with entertainment their chief concern. A pet goat, detested by his mother for getting into everything, became a trusted playmate, chasing them around the small community and giving bareback rides. They watched slimy tadpoles grow into adults in a nearby cattle reservoir. The two furiously waved to passing trains, from which crews often threw pieces of hard candy. Hoboes sometimes wandered by and mother always gave them food in exchange for chopping wood, and they were friendly to the youngsters, without fail.

Each weekend the family drove into town for supplies or to watch a movie, and, one time, father spent ten of his hard earned dollars to purchase a used bicycle. A man from the Western Auto store came by in his truck to deliver it, bringing terrific pleasure to the two children who rode it, whooping and hollering, up and down nearby country roads, all unpaved.

Those were delightful times, Ed thought, an unconscious smile flickering on his face. They were years that weren't easy for mother and father who had to scrape for everything, but he and Barbara never knew it, for their fantasy world seemed secure and unchanging. Their stomachs were full, the bus picked them up each day to bring them to school, and life in the boxcar seemed somehow exciting, as if filled with mystery.

By the time Barbara's father found a job in Yuma and came to fetch his daughter, their friendship had blossomed. Initially heartbroken, Ed rejoiced two months later when his father received a promotion and returned the family to Yuma. Within weeks, they were ensconced in a new house, with Ed having a room of his own at the top of the stairs . . . the room in which he recuperated after Barbara's death.

As Ed lay in the jungle, the thought of Barbara seemed very real; an actual breathing presence he felt he could touch. He reached down to his right breast pocket and slipped out the engraved Zippo lighter, clutching it in a palm. Without looking down he rocked it back and forth, sensually aware of its smooth gold finish, its weight. As he did, a .30 caliber machine gun off to the left began firing, shaking him back to reality. A steady stream of bullets crashed into bushes and trees across the way.

It was a long, protracted moment of firing, and though he stared, he could see nothing other than bullets ripping into the underbrush. Then it stopped. A long period of silence ensued, the only sounds the muffled, regular coughs of a mortar off to the far right, firing about every thirty or forty seconds. A gentle breeze whistled through the trees and rivers of perspiration rose up in Ed's hair. He tipped back his steel helmet and wiped his forehead with a sleeve, quickly sliding it back above his eyes.

He reached down and felt the bulge in his chest shirt pocket to make sure the Zippo hadn't slipped out. The touch was reassuring and made him feel better. Ed raised himself up and focused his attention on the trees to his immediate front, scanning up and down, looking for enemy snipers who might have lashed themselves amid the foliage, on the lookout for easy targets. Japanese soldiers could be anywhere or everywhere.

The two sides seemed in a state of fundamental stalemate; the Japanese couldn't move forward to sever the road, but neither could the Americans drive them into the sea. Most defenders lay on their bellies flat on the ground, able to mount a static defense, but little more. They required some sort of spark to get them to begin pushing back the enemy.

That spark came as Jim Gatling ran up, bending over, avoiding making himself too much of a target. He flopped down beside Ed, panting. "Ed," he said, breathing in and out. He turned away for a moment and cleared his raspy throat. "The colonel says you're supposed to go on the offensive."

Ed scrutinized his face, eyes growing wide. "Me?" he replied, raising his voice in surprise. "There's only five or six men within twenty yards of here." He tipped his helmet back with the rifle's muzzle.

"Dohlman's sending up a platoon to help out. He's going to clear the way with a mortar barrage."

"And when's all this supposed to happen?"

Gatling shrugged. "Maybe ten, fifteen minutes."

"If Dohlman's so smart, why doesn't he do it himself?" Ed grimaced, bending down in frustration. He looked sullen and angry. "We don't even know what's out there. Could be a hundred Japs just waiting for us to do something stupid. Dohlman's been out to get me ever since I made a fool out of him in Texas. Looks like he found a way to do it."

"Dohlman, Schollman, Ed. It don't matter. He told you, er us, to do it. We can't just stay here."

"You mean you're coming, too?"

Gatling broke into a wide grin. "Yeah, me too. Dohlman doesn't think much of me, either," he said, pointing a thumb toward his chest.

"Okay," replied Ed. "When's that mortar coming?"

"Should be here before the men. They're coming up from the rear, making one hell of a racket. The mortar's shifting over from the right. Not too far away."

"Okay, we wait." Ed rose up above ground level until only his helmet and eyes showed and scanned back and forth. He gazed into a jungle that appeared calm, but held hidden, unseen dangers. Isolated shots had echoed up and down the line all morning as the Americans fired into the trees at moving figures, those figures almost always turning out to be harmless monkeys. Nobody had taken count, but there were now a dozen or two dead or wounded monkeys out there.

Too bad, thought Ed. This was their jungle, their home, but today those monkeys were yapping and playing in the exact wrong place. Japanese snipers lurked in the same trees, there was no doubt of that, for a couple Americans had been hit. But he had no personal intention of wasting rounds on harmless apes. He hunkered down and focused his attention, studying the trees as much as possible, looking twice at any movement or sway of a leaf; squinting, watching, scrutinizing. He had yet to fire his rifle even once.

Several false alarms came and went before he saw something—a disturbance high up in a tree, an inkling of a movement. He raised his Springfield, hoping it wasn't another chimp, took aim and squinted through the sights. So far, their infantry training had proven pretty much worthless in preparing them for the actual experience of combat, but maybe he could put the target practice to good use. His accuracy wasn't bad. On the range, he either hit the center of the target or close to it every time. He chuckled, remembering his lie to MacArthur—maybe he *was* a country boy at heart.

He studied the tree, motionless. After a time, he spotted another flicker in the same place, maybe a flash coming from a shaft of sunlight hitting against something shiny, like a belt buckle or canteen, maybe a rifle barrel. Ed snugged the rifle against his shoulder and sucked in his breath. He wanted nothing to disturb his aim.

He sighted carefully, then . . . crack! The gun barked and slammed back. Ed lowered it and clicked the bolt back, ejecting the used cartridge and replacing it in the firing chamber with a fresh bullet. Moving fast, he raised it up and took aim. Crack! Suddenly, the leaves shook and a body slumped down, a rifle clattering to the ground. Lowering the Springfield, Ed could now make out the enemy soldier, clearly visible, leaves sticking out from all over; his belt, pockets, buttonholes, helmet.

He hung frozen now, gently swaying, lifeless. Ed felt a sense of pride well up, for he had exacted his first enemy blood since the first day of war. Getting one with a rifle wasn't what he planned on when leaving home, but it felt good, nonetheless. Hitting back after taking it for weeks created a warm inner glow. He rested the rifle on the edge of the depression and lowered himself down, gazing toward Gatling through slanted eyes.

"Why don't you go on back and hurry that platoon up here. We've got work to do."

* * *

The platoon soon slogged into Ed's position, twenty Filipinos from the Philippine army's 33rd division, soldiers who had been collecting supplies in Mariveles and shanghaied into action by American officers. Unhappy to be detached from the men they normally fought alongside to assist a group of unknowns, they wanted to get the job over and done with so they could head back.

The crew of a Stokes trench mortar that had been lobbing shells at the Japanese for the last quarter hour received orders to support the attack. Only eight rounds of mortar ammunition remained when they lugged the heavy weapon into position.

A shallow, narrow ditch emerged from the ground ten yards forward of the trail to Ed's left and ran to the right of the machine gun emplacement in the trees, ending about twenty yards short. Four men had made a run for the ditch earlier that afternoon, but none had been successful. Two ran forward a few yards and fell back, another was cut down by enemy fire and the fourth made it most of the way, but spun to the ground, hit by enemy bullets. He now lay prostrate and helpless inside the ditch, moaning and calling for help. His body now obstructed the advance, for if someone could get to the ditch, he would be exposed to hostile fire when crawling over the wounded soldier.

Ed and Gatling moved back a few yards into a clump of bushes, removed their helmets, and spoke back and forth for several minutes, gesturing with their hands and pointing toward the trees. Then both slapped on headgear and returned.

Ed beckoned the sergeant in charge of the platoon to come over. "Do you understand English?" he asked. The sergeant nodded crisply and replied, "Yes, sir, I do."

"What's your name?"

The sergeant came to attention. "1st Sergeant Vicente Pena, sir, 33rd Division."

"Sergeant Pena," said Ed, "we're going to get that man out of the ditch and wipe out that Jap machine gun in the trees over there." He pointed across the road to the left. "See it?" he asked.

"Yes, sir, I know where it is," replied the sergeant. "Tell us what to do and we'll do it."

"All right. Have your men spread out behind that long log off to the right, but close enough to attack together. When I give the order, you fire to attract Jap attention your way. Make 'em think you're about to attack."

Sergeant Pena nodded in understanding and snapped a respectful salute. Crouching forward, he relayed the orders to his men in Tagalog. His platoon ran across the trail and spread out behind the log, lying amid bright green vines and bushy weeds. Crouching, eyes darting side to side, they waited for the action to begin. While the platoon settled in, Gatling ran off to the left, beyond an American machine gun.

Ed watched the action, pleased to see the crispness of the platoon moving into position. He turned and shouted an order to the mortar crew. "Prepare to fire three rounds."

They lifted the piece off the ground and pointed it in the direction of the enemy machine gun nest, adjusting controls to set the range and deflection. Setting them was an educated guess, for with only three rounds, they wouldn't have the luxury of adjusting aim between rounds to assure accuracy.

Soon, all was ready. Ed waved his hand and the attack began. Booms filled the air and the steady rat-a-tat-tat of the heavy machine gun on the left echoed through the jungle. The first mortar round flew up hopefully and crashed down through the forest cover, but nothing happened. A dud. The latter two exploded, albeit outside the tree line, not harming the machine gun. The platoon lying behind the log fired rifles, yelled and waved their hands, and lifted helmets off their heads, trying to attract enemy fire. Several rose up, fired their Enfield rifles and flopped down. Four soldiers threw out smoke grenades, as if to disguise an advance. All the grenades operated as designed, spewing out noxious clouds of billowy gray chemical smoke.

The ruse worked. The Japanese machine gun turned sharply toward the men, hammering the log with a long string of bullets and, while it did, Gatling scampered toward the ditch from the far left like a madman. With all his might, he heaved the wounded soldier across his shoulders and ran back, returning unharmed. The enemy machine gun swerved back too late, firing a burst behind him into a hillock he had just crested. A cheer erupted from the Americans and Filipinos, jubilant that one of their own had been saved.

The American firing ended and Japanese return fire died out and, within seconds, quiet crept back. The vaporous strands of dull smoke emitted by the grenades hugged the uneven surface of the ground and gradually dissipated.

Excited, the pungent odor of acrid gunpowder permeating the air, Ed ran toward Sergeant Pena and told him to relay additional orders. He nodded and Ed began speaking, lethal calmness in his eyes. "I need two volunteers." He waited a moment, clenching and unclenching his right hand as the sergeant translated to his men. "Those volunteers will crawl through the ditch and blow that machine gun nest off the face of the earth."

Sixteen hands flashed up. Ed smiled and tilted toward Pena. "Sergeant Pena, they're your men—pick the ones that can do the job." The sergeant gave a brisk nod and pointed toward two men, about halfway down the log. Ed motioned them back into the trees on the far side of the trail and joined them beneath a gangly flowering bush. "Empty your musette bags," he told them. "You'll be carrying grenades instead." They unslung the canvas bags from their shoulders and spread the contents on the matted jungle growth, mostly personal items, and replaced them with six grenades apiece.

"I'm counting on you two," Ed said, the sergeant again translating. "You're very brave and I know you'll do it."

With a nod, the two crossed the trail, crouched for a moment and crawled out toward the ditch, squeezing down as low as possible to avert attention. Creeping through vegetation, moving at a cautious, measured pace to avoid causing leaves to crackle, they took their own sweet time. As the ditch neared, the man in front stopped and pulled a grenade out of his pouch. Removing the pin to activate it, he kept a finger pressed against the lever to make sure it wouldn't go off. As he crawled on, the grenade's pin rested between his teeth in case he needed to reinsert it.

Coming to the ditch, he slithered down into the muck and began making his way through the shallow trench, the second man following behind. The rest of the platoon kept up a steady covering fire from behind the log, forcing the Japanese to keep their heads down. Every once in awhile the Japanese machine gun replied, but only in short bursts, for the ammunition supply was not inexhaustible. They needed to conserve it, for they had only what they had been able to carry on their backs from the invasion barges.

As the two volunteers neared the end of the ditch where it became level with the surrounding ground, they knew they would have to make a run for the nearest tree, about ten yards away. The man in front licked his lips and turned back to his comrade, crawling up behind. His forehead creased with worry. Did the Japanese know they were there, waiting for them to come out into the open? The second man, confidence on his face, winked. "Go on. You can do it," he whispered. "Lead the way." The first man hesitated a moment, then smiled back.

He took two deep breaths, thrust out his chin and sprang up. With a burst of speed he high stepped across the clearing, racing to the protective, wide trunk of the nearest tree. The Japanese, startled to see the nearby Filipino, opened fire, but not before he reached safety, diving head first behind the tree.

Instantly he rose to his knees, shook his head back and forth, and swiveled back, hoping to see his friend about to join him. But shock met his eyes. Japanese fire had cut him in two before he had even reached the half-way mark. A pool of bright red blood dribbled into a pool next to his body, a spent smoke grenade issuing wispy tendrils that lightly streaked the air overhead.

Rage overtook him, his anger reaching the level of scalding fury. That man had been his friend. His final words were that he should lead the way. So be it. He crossed himself with the sign of the cross, closed his eyes and bowed for a moment, then looked up. Taking a grenade from the bag, he dashed toward a tree to the right and cocked back to throw it as far as he could.

"This is for my friend!" he cried as the grenade left his hand, his voice stabbing the air. When he reached the second tree, he rocked back on his heels and tossed another.

The second grenade landed just where he wanted, inside the machine gun nest next to open boxes containing spare ammunition. It rolled back and forth, hissing and fizzing. A panicky Japanese soldier dove for it and knocked it with the tips of his fingers under an ammunition box. He looked up, fearing it would explode any second, and scrambled outside over the rocks and logs that ringed the position. Motivated by rash terror, two others followed. Americans and Filipinos along the trail took immediate advantage of the easy targets and opened fire, killing the helpless men.

For a moment, it seemed the grenade wasn't going to explode, that it was another dud. Then, all of a sudden, flame and smoke rocketed up and the earth quaked with a shattering roar. Stones, leaves, bits of wood and other debris rained down for twenty seconds.

Clenching a .45 in his right fist, the Filipino dashed forward and zigzagged his way to the destroyed enemy position. Making his way up the slope, he grabbed another grenade and tossed it inside. It went off instantly, smoke and flame belching upward. "Those Japs are being tortured in hell now," he mumbled.

At the sight of the explosion, the platoon of Philippine soldiers at the trail jumped over the log and ran forward, their boots crunching through the jungle underbrush, no longer caring about the noise. Bayonets fixed, gleaming silvery in the filtered light, they hopped over the ditch and continued on.

The soldier who had thrown the grenades cast a cold, brooding glance toward them, but decided not to wait, to enter the Japanese position himself. Gingerly, he stepped inside over jumbled logs and rocks. Bodies lay scattered about, their uniforms smoking in numerous places from the fiery explosion. A severed arm, scarlet blood dripping onto the torn ground, rested against an upturned crate. He kicked the arm aside and stepped toward the first body, the man's eyes locked in an empty stare. Without making an expression, the Filipino coolly aimed the pistol between the man's eyes.

Crack! The gun recoiled upward. He walked to the second and did the same, then the third and fourth. By then the rest of the platoon had come up. They stood outside the machine gun nest and stared.

"Live Japs will shoot you in the back." he hollered while firing a second round into a lifeless body. "I've seen it. Make sure they're dead!"

The men kicked at bodies littering the ground, but found no survivors. All had been hit more than once. Out of ammunition, the soldier within the machine gun nest dropped the pistol and flopped down on a rock, burying his face in his hands.

"Antonio was my best friend!" he wailed. "We were like brothers." He leaned forward in anguish, clenched fingers pressing into his face, as his comrades stepped inside.

Some of the dead Japanese soldiers carried green canvas bags over their shoulders and the Filipinos ripped them off, rifling through them in search of food. They found a few rice balls, some tinned fish, but little else. One walked over to the Filipino soldier who had originally secured the machine gun nest, spread out a bit of fish on a battered tin plate, and offered to share it.

"You eat," he said, touching a grimy hand to his shoulder. "Many more Japanese up ahead. We get them."

The man looked up, accepting the smoked fish. Tears reddened his eyes and streaked his cheeks, and he waited a moment before speaking, first tipping back his helmet with the quick swipe of a finger. "The sun will go behind the mountains soon," he growled. "We go now."

He turned to watch Sergeant Pena stepping into the position. Straightening his helmet, he stood and faced his superior. "Where you lead, we will follow," he stammered, his face hard with resolve. "The Japanese come, the Japanese die."

Pena placed a hand on his shoulder and looked down, sympathy in his eyes. "We will go forward, but we must wait for orders. You sit here and rest. Orders will come." He looked over his shoulder toward the trail and spotted Ed staring at him, helmet dangling from a hand at his side. Pena waved and Ed waved back. The fight would continue.

Chapter 11

Mopping up

Late January 1942

Ed came up to Sergeant Pena minutes later, the two conferring in low tones behind dust covered bushes lining the upper slope of a ravine. Buoyed by success, both felt ready to move against the main Japanese line. They discussed plans back and forth before settling on a general advance from the trail up to a new line anchored on the captured enemy position.

The two motioned their hands forward and, all along the line, men sprang from their hiding places and charged forward, exchanging shots with Japanese snipers. A few Japanese scrambled down from their camouflaged perches in alarm and ran through the brush back toward their own lines; the Americans shot them down like jackrabbits. The defenders advanced about fifty yards until face to face with the enemy main line before hunkering down behind rocks and brush, scraping out shallow pits and pointing their rifles toward the Japanese.

They pushed against the line several times over the next several hours, but intense fire drove them back each time. The battle-hardened Filipinos broke through once and established a toehold amid the Japanese defenses, but the inexperienced Americans could provide little support, and they fell back. By nightfall, fighting died down and it seemed an end had descended on the day.

The soldiers had burned up nearly their entire supply of ammunition that afternoon and had begun dipping into reserve stocks. Ed sent runners back requesting more, but ordnance personnel responded that it would not come up until morning. This news caused Lieutenant Colonel Dohlman, just then visiting the American line, to go into a red-faced rage, cursing loudly at everyone. "How're we supposed to win this war with idiots like this in our own ranks?" he cried, stamping up and down. Finally, higher officers heard his complaints and two truckloads of fresh ammunition pulled up at midnight.

In good spirits, Ed nodded toward Gatling, the two sharing a hole. "That proves even Dohlman has a few intelligent brain cells." Gatling chuckled and aimed his Springfield over a fallen log, searching for targets, but the well-camouflaged Japanese jungle fighters had vanished in the dense, dark foliage.

The Japanese had lost ground, but were far from defeated and refused to leave matters as they stood—they began exerting steady, painful pressure on the Filipino and American line. Skilled at night engagements, a time at which Americans preferred relaxing in their foxholes, they crept over steep-fingered, wooded slopes to the left of the American line and infiltrated into the rear. The Americans, most of whom were drowsy or asleep, fired wildly into the blackness at noises and flashes of light. With no training in night combat, their response was uncoordinated and deadly—to each other. The Japanese quickly advanced, forcing them to retreat in disarray back to the trail.

The enemy had turned the tables. They again held the forward machine gun nest and had forced the sweat-stained Bataan defenders back to the same position as earlier that day. Japanese machine gun and mortar fire kept everyone low and honest throughout the night, turning the situation into a stalemate.

Officers in army headquarters, wishing to eliminate the Japanese threat, decided to call upon heavy artillery on Corregidor to soften them up the next morning. Artillery officers had made meticulous mathematic calculations and determined that, at maximum elevation, Longoskawayan Point would be within range of Corregidor's heavy guns, thus allowing the cannon crews to fire their first rounds of the war.

The point-detonated projectiles to be used were huge. Weighing 670 lbs. apiece, deadly within a bursting radius of five hundred yards, eight huge ten-ton mortars mounted in deep concrete pits would do the honors.

Dohlman sent word of the upcoming barrage to Ed and the other commanders and everyone moved back a safe distance. The twelve-inch mortars would be firing at maximum range and, like all long-range artillery fire, wouldn't zero in on the target until adjustments took place between rounds. A safety zone to allow for errant rounds was standard procedure.

The shoot began at 11 a.m. on January 26th as the first projectile exploded out of Corregidor's Battery Geary, then a second and a third. Ed watched from a branch high up a leafy banyan tree atop a ridge, offering a panoramic field of view. Within minutes, the shells began impacting with huge, fiery explosions that sent enormous clouds of smoke and debris swirling upward, hanging in the air.

Steadying himself against the tree's gnarly trunk, Ed stood in awe, transfixed at the spectacle. It seemed as if God himself was hurling down giant hammer blows of fire and thunder.

"Holy Mother of God," he mumbled as shells hurtled from the sky, sounding like freight trains as they flew over. "There won't be a twig left standing when this ends." A grim, somber look overtook his features as he watched projectile after projectile explode in fiery balls of anger.

Ed viewed the fall of the first eight rounds, then shinnied down the tree and approached Gatling, leaning against the trunk eating a tin of sardines. "You wouldn't believe what it looks like," he said, excitement in his voice. "It must be a living hell for the Japs."

Gatling casually looked up and tipped his helmet back. "Yeah, I heard it," he said. "Gives me a chance to get some food."

"That's all you ever think about." Ed rolled his head back and laughed, for the sight of the exploding shells gave him a giddy feeling of hope that the Japanese would soon be either dead or ready to surrender.

Gatling replied as he held a spoon before his mouth. "Say, Ed, I was reading the wrapper on this tin of sardines and it says it was packed in Monterey, California. That's just down the road from where I grew up."

"If it was just down the road, it's a good thing you didn't wind up smelling like those things. Sardines stink to high heaven."

Chewing a mouthful of the small fish, Gatling chuckled. "Smell or no smell, I like 'em. Just wish I had some crackers alongside. They're better that way."

"Well, hurry and finish up," Ed said. "We need to move forward soon as the firing ends; while the Japs are in shock."

Gatling tipped the can sideways, scooped out the last morsels and drank the salty oil that remained. After tossing it away and wiping his mouth, he said, "All right, let's go."

The two men roused twenty others resting nearby and advanced toward the trail. Crouching, they moved through the long ditch toward the machine gun nest the Japanese had recaptured the night before. Pausing behind trees to catch a quick glimpse, the first men could see it had been abandoned. No one remained inside.

"Come on," the soldier leading the way, Corporal Jeremy Ashton, a sharp-featured farm boy from Nebraska, shouted as he leaped forward. "We got'em on the run!"

He jumped into the machine gun nest, pointing his Springfield in all directions, the rest of the Americans following many yards behind. His initial judgment was correct; the Japanese had indeed pulled back. The position now lay empty other than scattered ration tins, empty boxes, spent ammunition casings, and other assorted debris.

Attempting to grab food lying around before the others arrived, Ashton reached down for a long, narrow tin of preserved fish and a small pouch containing dried vegetables. He stuffed them inside a canvas gasmask pouch slung over a shoulder from which he had removed the useless gasmask long ago and reached down for another, an oblong tin of sardines near an empty ammunition box.

As his fingers closed around the shiny can and lifted it away, a sharp snap followed by an almost immediate explosion occurred. The resounding roar shook the ground and he violently flew back, stone dead, his chest ripped wide open.

Japanese soldiers had attached a string to the bottom of the can before retreating, connecting it to the trigger of a hand grenade set ready to go off. Unwittingly, Ashton had pulled the pin from the grenade, causing it to explode. He now lay dead, the front of his body a mass of torn flesh and glimmering crimson blood. As others stepped into the position, they looked down and contorted their faces. One turned away and retched.

Though the heavy mortar attack devastated much of the Japanese defense line and caused a few to jump over steep cliffs at the edge of the sea in terror, they were far from finished off. The motley American force of airmen, sailors and shanghaied Filipinos made a little headway, then stalled. The Japanese even attempted a counterattack that night, though the Americans had grown wise and stayed alert, beating off the assault.

Another try with the artillery took place the following morning. At 7 a.m., every piece the Americans could bring to bear opened up. This included 75mm howitzers, two 81mm mortars fired by Marines transferred over from Corregidor, a battery of 2.95-inch pack howitzers, and the massive twelve-inch mortars. The Japanese took a terrific pounding, with many casualties, but again weathered the steel storm.

It became obvious to American commanders that airmen and sailor amateurs were encountering real problems handling well-trained Japanese infantry regulars. Early that afternoon, they ordered two infantry battalions of crack Philippine Scouts into the area, one of which, about five hundred strong, made its way to Longoskawayan Point. The Scouts arrived at dusk, Gatling first spotting them.

"Here come men who know what they're doing," he shouted from behind a mass of jungle creepers, not much beyond the captured machine gun position. "Now we'll see some real action."

The Scouts, Philippine soldiers formed into an elite unit of the regular U.S. Army, were well trained and equipped infantrymen who knew their jobs. Part of the crack Philippine Division, the Scouts were regarded in military circles as tough, professional fighters. After hopping down from their vehicles and spreading out, they made thorough preparations, digging in machine guns and mortars and arranging for artillery support before grabbing a few hours sleep. Next morning at first light, they launched an assault that made steady progress after another artillery barrage, pushing the Japanese back six hundred yards to the lower third of the peninsula.

Accurate fire from local field artillery batteries and the giant mortars on Corregidor was supplemented by the 185-foot minesweeper *USS Quail*, standing offshore sniping with three-inchers at Japanese troops cowering in caves above the sea. The ship sent nearly one hundred high explosive rounds into every cave and clump of vegetation in sight.

Ed sprawled on a smooth-sided slab of limestone alongside Gatling and Baxter on the slope of Mount Pucot as mortar shells fell on the point. The enormous twelve-inch projectiles impacted with terrible violence, the force of the blasts denuding huge areas of jungle and instantly killing anyone nearby. Ravines once choked with shrubs six to nine feet tall, nearly impassable for people without the laborious task of cutting trails with machete knives, were now clear and spacious. The *Quail* darted back and forth, its guns blossoming puffs of smoke as targets came into view. Khaki uniformed Scouts moved forward, routing the Japanese from their positions. Opposing fire dwindled and became less accurate, the enemy stunned by fire that came from all around.

"Those Scouts know their job," observed Baxter, transfixed at the panorama before him. "It's hard to believe any Japs are still alive."

Waiting a few seconds while he craned his neck to follow the flight of a twelve-inch projectile arcing above, Ed answered after it exploded in a mammoth ball of flame. "Remember what happened a couple days ago when the mortars first fired? I don't know how they did it, but the Japs lived through that, too. They're tough."

"That may be, but we're doing them a favor by sending them to Buddha or whoever it is they worship," said Gatling, a sharpened twig dangling from his mouth. "Those Jap devils are condemned no matter how you look at it—fast from an artillery blast or slow from a bayonet in the gut. They can't be rescued or reinforced." He leaned forward and adjusted his position, trying to get more comfortable. "Their goose is cooked."

Ed blinked, continuing to look forward, not quite accustomed to the barbarity of warfare. He didn't like the Japanese, didn't feel sorry about anything that might happen to them, but there were civilized rules about warfare that somehow seemed relevant.

He knew battlefield atrocities took place, for he had seen a few such instances himself. He once came across prisoners of the Japanese brutally bayoneted to death against trees, hands tied behind their backs. He heard stories of men hanged from palm trees between the lines or wrapped in barbed wire until bleeding to death. Atrocities like these had caused his beliefs to change a good deal and, like others, he felt a deep, powerful thirst for revenge. But still, he couldn't help harboring a glimmer of sorrow for helpless men being blasted to bits from overhead.

The mortar fire came to an end, but the 75mm field pieces and the guns aboard the *Quail* continued pounding away. The Philippine Scouts fired their rifles and machine guns all across Longoskawayan Point, infiltrating behind enemy positions, sometimes rushing head on, almost always victorious.

Every so often, Ed spotted clusters of Scouts at the edges of blasted jungle where vegetation had been torn away. Few Japanese would surrender or allow themselves to be taken prisoner, he knew, for based on his experience they would either fight to the death or commit suicide. He had already observed several leap off cliffs to the rocky coast rather than face capture.

The three watched for twenty minutes, the rest of the men in the squadron either spread out on the ground resting amid grass or sitting up watching events below. Some munched on double portions of rice, tomatoes and canned salmon delivered by truck a short while before. Most were in a bit of a state of shock from their first infantry battle, an experience their training hadn't prepared them for, though they couldn't put their finger on what could have been done differently. Maybe it was just impossible to transform an airman into a trained infantryman in the span of a few short weeks.

Ed and his men remained on Mount Pucot for the remainder of the day and advanced onto the point early the next morning. Their mission was to mop up enemy troops, but few remained, huddled within caves facing the sea on the tip of the point, a problem that could only be solved from the water. Sailors in Mariveles came up with a solution in short order by converting a forty-foot motor launch into a "Mickey Mouse battleship" by adding armor plate, a 37mm light field piece, two .50 caliber machine guns and sandbags around the gas tank. The launch bobbed in the blue-green water off Longoskawayan Point, destroying the caves at point blank range, the gunners taking their own good time.

A few Japanese ripped off their uniforms, ran across crumbling ledges and dived into the cold ocean water, trying to swim to some imagined place of safety. Exultant Scouts fired machine guns and rifles into the surf, killing scores. Gatling spotted one enemy soldier dart from a cave out into the water and commented to the man nearest him, "It's a hell of a long way to Japan." He dropped to one knee and began firing, the bullets zinging into the water all around the swimming soldier, flailing and kicking with all his might while the little geysers erupted.

After watching the inaccurate fire, Ed patted Gatling on the shoulder and said, "Let me have a try." He dropped to a prone position, wrapped the sling around his arm, took careful aim and commenced a slow, deliberate, deadly fire. Spouts of red foam marked the strike of the bullets, blood spreading on the surface of the water. He stopped firing and looked up. "Take time with your shots, Jim, and stay as steady as you can. It always works for me."

Gatling rose to his feet, dark eyebrows slanted into a frown. His eyes, however, glinted with admiration. He appreciated nice shooting. Ed rose, grunted, and the two continued moving up the peninsula, searching for more targets. They fired a few more shots, but within a short time no resistance remained. The few remaining enemy soldiers were rounded up and marched off.

The airmen received orders to return to Mount Pucot that afternoon and remained there for several days, amid talk that they might be sent off to fight at one of the other Japanese invasion points. But more experienced, well-trained men were needed and the green airmen were ordered back to Cabcaben. They set out on foot, but after a few miles came across empty buses motoring in that direction. They motioned the buses to the side of the road and clambered aboard, glad to be done with fighting and marching.

Ed, wedged next to Gatling, nudged him on the shoulder and gushed, "Jim, I wish we could get us some of that San Miguel beer. A six-pack or two for every man here would be about right."

Gatling grinned and drew close, not wanting others to hear. "I don't have enough for everyone, but it'll be enough for me, you and Baxter," he whispered in a gravelly voice. "I got a bottle of rum off one of those sailor boys. It'll help us celebrate."

Ed's mouth spread into a smile. He had no idea how Gatling had "acquired" a bottle of liquor. "Jim, you're a good man," he declared. "A damn good man."

Commander Francis Bridget, who led the sailors that fought alongside the airmen, was so pleased by the performance of the Philippine Scouts that he dug into naval food stocks and presented them two truckloads of canned fruits, vegetables, salmon, meats, soups, and jam. Each succeeding Sunday a navy truck protected by armed guards delivered cigarettes, bottles of liquor and a five-gallon can of frozen ice cream fresh-churned aboard the submarine tender *USS Canopus*. Needless to say, the Scouts wore smiles as they departed Longoskawayan Point.

Chapter 12

Slow Starvation

February 1942

The successful fight brought about days of delirious self-congratulation and merriment. After two months of never-ending pounding from the air and steady retreat on the ground, the Bataan defenders had beaten the Japanese. Even the remaining P-40s of the Far East Air Force provided welcome support, bombing and strafing Japanese reinforcements off the Bataan coast, exacting a fearsome toll, sending dozens of vulnerable barges brimming with soldiers and supplies to the bottom of the South China Sea. More than that, American and Filipino losses had been light, with nearly every Japanese soldier ashore killed or wounded.

The provisional infantry battalion returned to its camp near Cabcaben Field and, as the days turned into weeks, elation resulting from the triumph declined, replaced by sober realism. Sure, a battle had been won and the Japanese driven off. But the inadequate supply system remained, with ration and medicine stocks growing smaller by the day. Men tightened belts, muscles withered, stamina declined, and morale dropped.

Meals had been reduced to two skimpy offerings per day, one in the early morning and the other in the evening, always when the sun hung below the horizon. Cooks prepared food over open fires, which meant they had to keep a constant lookout for Japanese planes, which searched for plumes of smoke.

Rice had become the staple of the Bataan diet, which American soldiers, accustomed to meat, potatoes, bread and gravy, dismissed as a poor substitute. Consisting mostly of starch and a few vitamins, the nutritional value of the rice was minimal, and without seasonings or other additions, it had little flavor. Much was of low quality, infested with worms or weevils. The diet proved monotonous, never satisfying and a constant and never-ending topic of conversation.

On the outskirts of camp, small groups congregated during the hottest hours of the day to swap rumors, complain and reminisce, even if the stories had been told many times before. One afternoon in mid-February, Ed and Gatling sat with a number of others in the shade of a huge old *belote* tree with green and gray mottled bark that provided welcome relief from the fierce sun. As they talked, Baxter stormed up and threw himself against a buttress of the giant tree.

"I just saw our rice ration brought into the mess tent," he announced as he mopped a river of sweat streaming down the back of his neck. "The rice is filled with worms. It's disgusting." He rolled his eyes and ripped off his hat.

Gatling, who had been scratching at the ground with a stick, glanced up. "Great, just great. Crappy rice is just what we need." He shook his head in resignation, but was well aware of the score. "Well, we're gonna eat it anyway. It isn't like we got a choice in the matter. Anyhow, there's a hell of a lot of things worse than wormy rice. When folks are hungry they'll eat about anything, and that's where we're at these days."

"I'm with you, brother," said Staff Sergeant Joe Torres, an aircraft mechanic who hadn't been near anything that flies in weeks. Black grease stained the legs of his khaki pants, a permanent reminder of his real job. "Rice is one of those weird foods. Some say it's the best chow in the whole world. Rice has no flavor of its own and is improved by practically anything you add to it. It's bland as all hell. No other food can make that claim."

Laughter erupted. As it died, Baxter leaned back and observed, "I don't know about rice having no flavor." He paused to spit at a large insect walking along the ground, but missed, off to the right. The black insect veered sharply and continued on as if nothing had happened. “To me, rice sort of tastes like wallpaper paste. Maybe it’s just the lousy rice we get, but all it amounts to is a space-filler in the stomach. Once I leave Bataan I don’t plan on looking at a grain of it ever again. If anyone serves it, I’ll throw it in their face.”

Master Sergeant Evans nodded in agreement. “Yeah, the rice stinks, but so does everything else. When you think about it, wormy rice is sort of a blessing in disguise. Worms are full of protein, and we never get enough of that.” He scanned the faces under the shade of the tree. “I’ll eat whatever’s served up. If anybody else doesn’t want their rice, I’ll eat that, too. Just hand it over.”

A light chuckle rumbled through the group. Smiling, Ed faced Evans and said, “People’ll complain, but there won’t be any leftovers and nobody’s going to give their rice away. We’re all too hungry for that. The plates’ll be clean.”

Evans snorted. “Still, I stand ready to accommodate anyone who doesn’t want their rice,” he replied, jerking a thumb toward his chest. “It’s a service I’m offering today.”

“Okay, Evans, you want everyone’s rice,” said Ed. “It’ll be a miracle if you get any. Like I said, everyone’s too hungry.”

Evans straightened. “Well, I’m gonna sweeten the deal, Lieutenant. I’ll trade two cigarettes, no,” he decided, “make it *four* cigarettes to anyone for their rice tonight. Any takers?”

Evans crossed arms over his chest and waited, the men glancing at each other, not because they liked the idea of wormy rice, but because they needed food to fill their bellies. But four cigarettes made a tempting bargain, for only one or two were issued per man, per day. For inveterate smokers who smoked through a pack or more each day before the war, the forced abstinence was especially hard.

“I’ll take you up on that,” said a desperate voice from the back. “Cigarettes settle my stomach more than rice. Rice and worms sound lousy anyway.”

“All right!” exclaimed an enthused Evans. He snapped his head forward. “You got a deal. Four cigarettes for your spoonful of rice, and that means the whole thing. I get it all.”

"Yeah, you get it all, jerk face. Just hand over your cigarettes, and I don't mean ones that are bent or torn. They better be good, or no deal."

"They'll be good," replied Evans. "I'll bring'em to dinner. You have your rice ready to hand over."

Ed slapped dust off his filthy pants and raised his voice. "All right, all right! Let's talk about something else. If you want to make deals, do it somewhere else."

Silence ensued for a few moments. Some adjusted their positions, a few slapped at flies or mosquitoes. There were a few oaths. Then Gatling sat up in anticipation. "Ed," he said, twisting around. "Everybody knows you and Dohlman don't get along. How about telling us what happened between you two?"

Ed, reclining against a large root, shook his head. "Our problems are between the two of us. I don't think anyone else would be interested."

"Oh, we're interested," remarked Gatling. "The feud goes back a long way, too. Tell us all the details and don't leave anything out."

"Well, okay," said Ed. "I guess we have the time." He raised his knees up and held a baseball cap between them. "It all started at Kelly Field back in Texas. I was a cadet pilot and he was operations officer. I had completed most of my flight training when he tried to wash me out."

"What'd you do?" asked Master Sergeant Evans. "Put a scorpion in his bunk?"

Ed chuckled. "No, it was nothing like that. He tried to kick me out for something I didn't do."

"Whadda'ya mean? Explain." Evans leaned forward expectantly.

Ed nodded. "I spent one morning practicing my landings before turning the plane over to the mechanics and heading to class. Right after lunch I received orders to report to his office."

"What'd he want?" asked Gatling.

"He said my flying days were over. Pointing a finger, he claimed I knew what I'd done and didn't want any explanations. I asked what he was talking about, but he wouldn't say. He just kicked me out. I went back to class, but this had come out of the clear blue sky. The afternoon was miserable."

The men nodded. "So, what did you do?" asked Gatling.

"After class I went straight to the operations hut to get the straight dope. Apparently, the crew chief reported that the propeller of my plane was cracked and that the landing gear had a cornstalk wedged into it. Dohlman figured this meant I had set down somewhere off the field and didn't report it."

"I charged into Dohlman's office and argued, but he wouldn't budge. We finally went over to one of the hangers and inspected the plane. There was a tiny crack in the propeller, but that could have been caused by plenty of other students training on the same plane. The corn stalk turned out to be a weed from the airstrip. The upshot was that Dohlman had to eat crow in front of everyone. Other students spoke up and he ended up being transferred out. It was a big embarrassment and Dohlman blamed me for causing it. He's hated me ever since."

"Hrrmph. So that's it," said Gatling. "You embarrassed him and he's trying to get back at you. Is that why he never returned you to flight duty?"

"Yeah, it had something to do with it. That and the lack of aircraft, that is."

Just then, three twin-engine planes with meatball insignias on their wings zoomed overhead, just above the top of the trees, buzzing toward Cabcaben Field at high speed on another afternoon bombing run. Machine guns surrounding the field opened up, but within seconds, bombs rained down and the planes banked over Manila Bay and flew away, unharmed.

The cratered runway would again require a series of repairs, but within sixty minutes, the dozers, graders and other heavy repair vehicles would return to the safety of their camouflaged revetments and the airfield would again be declared operational. Air raids had become a daily occurrence and nothing more than standard routine, like idle chatter among the men.

* * *

Ed sat across from Gatling at breakfast eating bowls of steamed rice saturated with tan colored evaporated milk from the stock brought in from Neilson Field. Nothing accompanied the rice other than a few prunes and a half slice of bread, baked in giant ovens within canyon walls near Mariveles. Cooks baked thousands of loaves each day, but as flour supplies ran short, fewer and fewer loaves reached fighting units.

They spooned the rice amid the growing morning humidity, their shirts already beginning to stick to their backs. All of a sudden, Ed jerked up. "It's been darn quiet lately and I bet you and me can get the okay from Dohlman to go hunting for food supplies," he announced while holding a spoonful of rice midway between the bowl and his mouth. "The squadron needs rations and maybe we can get some."

"Yeah," Gatling nodded. "Rice doesn't stick to your stomach long. After an hour goes by I'm as hungry as when I came in." Gatling reached forward and grabbed a can of evaporated milk in the center of the table and poured a stream of the thick liquid into his bowl, stirring it with a spoon. "At least we have milk once in awhile, but most other units don't. It's not a good situation."

Ed fixed his gaze on Gatling. "Well, finish up and let's go find Dohlman. The earlier we start out the better."

"But Dohlman hates you. Why would he give us the okay to go gallivanting around the countryside?"

Ed shot a withering stare. "Because it's worth the try, that's why. We either do something or do nothing. I choose the former." Gatling shrugged and resumed eating.

A short while later, the two found Dohlman lounging in the headquarters tent, playing dominoes with his enlisted orderly on a table lashed together from bamboo stalks. Photographs of women striking suggestive poses clipped from magazines had been tacked up around the room. Annoyed, Dohlman looked up as they entered. "What do you two want?" he grumbled, peering over reading glasses perched on the bridge of his nose. "Up to no good of some kind, I'm sure."

"Good morning, sir," they said in unison, coming to attention. "We came to ask for your okay on something," announced Ed.

"Well, go ahead," Dohlman replied with a wave of a hand. "I'm winning right now and I want to get back to the game."

"Sir," Ed said, stepping forward. "We want to go into Mariveles to scrounge up some food. The rations are getting darn thin around here. Something's got to be done."

Dohlman lowered an eyelid. "And what do you propose? If there was more food, don't you think the quartermaster corps would issue it?"

"They probably would, sir, but we might be able to scare up something on our own. Informally, you might say. You know, without going through proper channels."

Dohlman straightened. "You aren't talking about stealing, are you? If it is, the answer is 'no.'"

Ed shook his head. "No, sir, we're not planning on stealing food," he said with disgust. His respect for Dohlman was practically non-existent. If the army during World War I had been filled with more men like him, Ed figured the allies would have lost. He took in a deep breath. "We're just gonna see if any rations are available. If there's a way to get some, we won't steal it, but we'll get it one way or another. Probably buy it."

Dohlman, no stranger to the hollow pangs of hunger, had dropped ten pounds since Christmas. If there were a chance of obtaining food, he'd not stand in the way. "All right," he grumbled, "you two have my permission, but only for two days. Be back Sunday afternoon. And remember you're officers. Shoddy ones, but officers nonetheless."

Ed tipped his head forward, keeping his temper in check. "That's fine, sir. We'll be back." He whipped around, shot a quick glimpse at Gatling and turned back. "We're gonna get going. See you in two days."

"One more thing," muttered Dohlman as he flicked away a spotted brown insect crawling up the table leg. "You two latch on to any food, call for a truck. It'll carry back anything you get. I doubt you'll come up with much, but what the hell."

Snapping a quick salute, the two about faced and walked out. As they followed a dusty footpath toward their tents, they exchanged knowing glances and slowly shook their heads, feeling similar emotions about the quality of their leader. At least they wouldn't have to look at him for two days.

Ed and Gatling spent the remainder of the day trudging from one supply dump to another, always getting the same response—no food to spare. They begged, they cajoled, they argued and offered money under the table, but nothing worked. The supply dumps were well guarded and military police stationed along the east road watching for illicit traffic seemed to make the effort all but impossible.

As they approached Mariveles from the west late that Saturday afternoon as evening shadows began to grow long, the road crossed over a series of steep washboard-like hills cutting through thick, intimidating jungle. As they plodded along the edge of the road, trucks kicked thick dust clouds into the air as they slowed and shifted into low to power up an uphill grade.

His face streaked with a congealed mixture of dirt and salty perspiration, Ed coughed as he worked his way through the brown haze. "At least the dust is keeping the mosquitoes away," he shouted to Gatling, his knees working up and down. He turned toward the string of vehicles and noted its slow rate of speed. "Look, those trucks are going about as fast as we are."

Gatling snatched a quick glance and continued walking, then had an idea. He motioned Ed away from the road into the jungle and hunched down on one knee. Wiping his forehead, he winked an eye.

"I got me an idea, Ed, and I think it's good." He built up a load of dusty moisture in his mouth and spit it out. Reaching toward the canteen hanging from his web belt, he raised it and took a deep drink. Shaking his head, he said, "It's been one hell of a day."

Hands on his knees, Ed leaned forward, breathing in and out. "Yeah, it has been. Pretty darn futile." He paused a moment before asking, "So, what's your idea?"

Gatling perked up, swiping at a shock of unruly hair hanging down over his forehead. "This'll make the day better." Squinting, he glanced to each side and lowered his voice. "Those trucks are having to slow way down to make it up this hill." His eyes bored in. "You saw it for yourself. If we wait until dark, one of us can hop right into the back of one of those trucks and toss out a crate or two. Might get some food that way."

Ed looked back, scrunched up his mouth and shook his head. "I don't know. I don't like the idea of stealing. Everybody's rations have been cut." He didn't like the idea of agreeing with Dohlman, but this time he did.

"But Ed, we're in the far rear now. Everybody knows the quartermasters eat better than anyone else. And what about the guys on Corregidor? They're eating better yet. It's not right. We're only getting our fair share."

"Yeah, we've all heard the same stories. Maybe they're true, maybe they're not. Everyone blames someone else; that's human nature."

Gatling rolled his head and neck back and forth, trying to recover from the frustration of the day. With a shrug, he said, "Look, I'll be the one who hops into the back of the truck. I'll toss a couple crates off, then we'll hide it in the jungle and come back tomorrow. I say it's worth a try. How about it?"

Ed formed his lips into a tight line, struggling over what to do. The idea had merit, for it could possibly result in some food. That's what they were here for and these behind-the-line rear enders would never miss it. Dohlman would never find out. But still, stealing is stealing. There's no way around it.

"Sorry, Jim, I can't go along Believe me, I want food as much as you, but I won't stoop to the level of a common thief. Things aren't that far gone yet." He rose up and fixed eyes on his friend. "Come on, let's hitch a ride into Mariveles. There's a few more places we can check."

With a forlorn shrug, Gatling reluctantly followed Ed out of the jungle onto the road. Waving to the driver of an oncoming jeep, they hopped aboard as it slowed and speeded off toward Mariveles. Maybe they could get something off the docks. Fish, rusty cans, anything.

The two men scratched their heads in disappointment on reaching the Mariveles docks, for the entire area seemed a bastion of inactivity. Motor vessels carrying personnel and key items of equipment between Corregidor and the mainland stopped and sped away, but it was otherwise quiet. Far off to the left, about three hundred yards from shore, rested the deserted hulk of the *USS Canopus*, a submarine tender Japanese aircraft had sunk after Christmas. The ship lay tipped over, her cranes askew, ragged streams of brown rust growing on her starboard side. As night fell, the two flopped onto a low row of empty wood crates lining the side of the longest pier, discouraged, tired and hungry.

"We may as well head back to Cabcaben," sighed Gatling. "We aren't doing any good back here."

Ed studied the ground between his feet. "Yeah, we probably used up more calories walking around than we got from anything we ate. We're worse off now than when we started."

The two slouched down, tired and dejected, their shoulders hunched forward. The day had been a series of one disappointing rebuff after another. A few guards were sympathetic, one even sharing his meal, but the end always came out the same. No food.

Wearing a vacant look, Ed stared out into the wide bay, not really seeing anything, his mind immersed in the struggle for food and its meaning to the future. All of a sudden, a civilian sedan pulled up ten yards away and a group of sailors piled out, laughing and joking with one another. Ed and Gatling looked up and watched them approach the pier, wondering what they were so happy about. The first three walked by without a glance, but one in the second group, a pot bellied chief petty officer who looked like he'd served in the navy since the days of sailing ships, nodded as he approached.

"How's it going, you two?" he asked in a friendly voice. "I don't recollect seeing you before."

Ed raised himself a little and responded. "We aren't stationed here. We're from up around Cabcaben Field. We're looking for food."

The sailor veered over, stopped and looked down. "Have any luck?"

Ed shook his head. "Nope. Not a thing."

"Things are tightening up all around. What unit you guys in?"

"We're from the 3rd Pursuit Squadron. Our planes were all shot down, so we're fighting as infantry. We were out on Longoskawayan Point a few weeks ago."

"You don't say? Some of my boys were there, too." The chief petty officer smiled and thrust out a gnarled hand. "The name's Borden; Master Chief Borden."

Ed rose, clasped the extended hand and the two shook. "Nice to meet you, master chief," he said in a friendly voice. "You wouldn't know where we could get a little food, would you?"

Borden smiled and turned. "Hang on for a second." He raised himself up a few inches and spotted a lieutenant commander who had shared the sedan with them. Borden waved a hand to attract his attention, but he was locked in conversation and didn't look up.

Annoyed, Borden took in a deep breath and gave off a high-pitched whistle through two fingers. The officer immediately broke off the discussion and stepped over. Amused, Ed and Gatling exchanged glances. This navy master chief obviously carried clout.

"Sir," Borden said, facing the officer, "these two've been hunting rations all day and didn't have any luck. How about if we feed'em dinner and let'em spend the night?"

The officer shrugged and mumbled, "Bring 'em along. Two more makes no difference." He turned and ambled away.

Borden smirked behind his back. "Well, there you go. You heard the man. Fall in for the best grub you've had since Christmas."

Ed and Gatling rose up wondering where exactly they were going. Who were these sailors, anyhow? "Where we off to—Corregidor?" asked Ed.

Setting a smart pace, Borden replied without looking back. "We're off the *USS Canopus*. We work aboard the ship at night and sleep all day. We get plenty of food, too, including ice cream."

"Ice cream?" bellowed Gatling. "Where in heaven's name do you get that?"

Everyone coming aboard reacted the same way. He answered with quiet patience. "We have an ice cream freezer on the ship and make our own. We have toppings for it, too. Chocolate, butterscotch, you name it."

Bewildered, not quite ready to accept the good fortune coming his way, Ed muttered a question. "How is it you have so much food? Besides, I thought the *Canopus* was sunk. It looks like a wreck."

Borden chuckled. "That's what we want the Nips to think. At first, we tried to camouflage the ship to keep planes away, but it didn't work. We left the *Canopus* like this to make'em think it was sunk and abandoned. But we've kept her running the whole time. They don't have any idea what's going on."

Incredulous, Ed continued. "But why do you have so much food? Aren't you on half rations like everyone else?"

"The navy isn't the same as the army," he explained. "We're on half rations, but we make sure it's a *good* half ration, with plenty of variety. The navy does what's right for itself—army be damned."

"Well, where'd you get all the food? We couldn't get a scrap for ourselves today, no matter where we looked."

Borden stopped walking and leaned against the dock's railing, facing the two aviators. The railing was splintered and worn, holed numerous times by strafing enemy fighters. He cocked an eye and said, "The *Canopus* is a submarine tender, which means we carry machine tools to repair about anything you can think of. We carry enough food to stock a dozen submarines with enough for months. Since there ain't no subs hereabouts, the food's ours for the taking."

He shuffled to the far end of the dock and clambered down a ladder to the pitching deck of a tied up civilian whaleboat. He called up, "Watch your step, you two. We don't like fishing landlubbers out of the water."

Ed and Gatling descended the ladder, the deck dipping up and down to the rhythm of the waves, and sat next to Borden on a long wooden bench going the length of the boat. "You guys eat a lot of rice?" asked Ed, fearing the answer.

"We have some, but we eat lots of other things. Last night they served up baked ham, candied yams and fruit cocktail. For breakfast we usually have powdered eggs, bacon or sausage and toast. Real coffee, too."

"Oh, brother," the two airmen said in unison, exchanging wide-eyed glances.

"You mean we're going to get real food?" asked Gatling, salivating at the thought.

"Yep. I don't know what we're having tonight, but it's bound to be a helluva lot better than the slop the army serves up. I can promise you rice won't be the main thing."

Ed leaned back, content, hoping the wait would be short. As the whaleboat shoved off and gathered speed, a fresh breeze rushed against his face, cool and refreshing, a reminder of when he first taxied an open cockpit biplane into the wind. No swarms of blood-sucking mosquitoes, no sensation of roasting in a relentless sun; true exhilaration.

The back of his head reclined against the padded side of the speeding boat, he turned toward Gatling. "Looks like this trip won't turn out to be the complete disaster it was starting to feel like." He rubbed his hands together. "I can't wait for that meal. It's almost like all the Sunday dinners I had back home wrapped into one."

"Yeah, I'm hungry enough to eat a horse," answered Gatling. "I'll even eat a little rice if I have to."

"That's big of you." Ed paused as a foamy wave slapped the side of the boat, sending salt spray over his legs. He didn't care. "I hope they serve up mashed potatoes, though. Potatoes have been on my mind for weeks." Gatling smiled.

Side by side, the two sat as the boat sped along, looking into the heavens. Ed's mind shot back to when they crossed Manila Bay on the *Don Esteban* after Christmas. The same stars gleamed against the black nighttime tableau, their pearly incandescence just as dazzling.

For the first time in days, he allowed a sliver of confidence to well up; perhaps things weren't as bad as they seemed. Bataan was a big place, with tens of thousands of well-armed, determined troops. True, food was in short supply and the Americans could not boast of much of an air force, but artillery was another matter. There was a plentiful supply of 75mm and 155mm field artillery on Bataan and, though he had never gazed upon them, Corregidor bristled with guns. And those giant mortars! They had wreaked havoc on Japanese troops at Longoskawayan Point.

"Corregidor's a real fortress. Impregnable," he mumbled beneath the roar of the whaleboat's motor, feeling smug. The reality of holding out until reinforcements pulled into Manila Bay suddenly didn't seem so far fetched.

For a moment, he closed his eyes. The only thing that could make the evening better would be to have his one true love, Barbara, leaning on his shoulder, cuddling in his arms. No matter how much he yearned for it, though, he knew it was the stuff of dreams and a hurtful one at that.

Memories of Barbara clogged his mind, only slightly diminished by the passage of time. Though he remembered her several times each day, at least now the steady downward spiral in which the army seemed trapped had changed. Maybe reinforcements *were* on the way to reverse the situation.

Thoughts of eventual victory were comforting, thoughts he should take the time to relish and enjoy. Just do it, he said to himself. Forget the war for a moment, relax. You can do that at least until getting to the *Canopus*, right?

CHAPTER 13

MOVING OUT

March 1942

The meal proved filling, memorable and a darn good time. They wolfed down two steaming slices of roast beef apiece, mashed potatoes and brown gravy, fresh baked rolls, and canned peas. Glasses of chalky powdered non-fat dry milk, despite their low opinion after sampling it for the first time aboard the *President Coolidge* somewhere in the Pacific, tasted cool and refreshing. They gulped down two each; their first glasses of milk of any kind in six weeks.

But the crowning glory came afterward when sailors shared their cigarettes and everyone stretched back and lit up, the gray smoke curling upward, swirling around the ceiling. Before the cigarettes had burned even half down, cooks walked in and set a bowlful of vanilla ice cream in front of each man, dripping with chocolate syrup and nuts. Their eyes grew wide at just seeing it. They had put up with weeks of dust, heat, sweat, wearing the same filthy uniforms, and steadily growing hungrier, never expecting to see something like this again until much later in the war.

After slurping down three spoonfuls, Ed turned toward Master Chief Borden and wagged his head. "You told us about having ice cream, but eating it is something else. Marvelous! Ice cream is like something from the deep dark past. I knew I'd have it again, but

Bataan never seemed like the place to get it. You swabbies really know how to live."

Borden snickered. "Yeah, we've got the Nips fooled. They think the *Canopus* is sunk and we aim for them to go on thinking right that way."

"I hope they do." Ed savored more heaping bites before speaking again. He looked up and asked, "What else goes on here the Japs know nothing about?"

"We do all kinds of machine shop work for you fellas on Bataan. Just last week I sharpened scalpels for doctors up in Hospital Number Two and then made a bunch more because they don't have enough. Basically, when there's machine shop work to get done, we're the blacksmith shop hereabouts."

Ed moved in his chair. "How does your workload compare to back in December before the rest of the navy skedaddled?"

"We're busier than ever. This ship really hums at night."

Ed finished the ice cream in four more bites and turned in his chair, drawing it across the deck close to Borden. He lowered his voice to just above a whisper. "Look," he said, "I've got some money and I'll hand some of it over if you've got food to spare. What d'ya say?'

Borden's gaze remained fixed on Ed, unmoving. "How much you looking to spend?"

"I have ten bucks with me. What can I get for it?"

"Well, we can spare some tomato juice. Want it?"

"Tomato juice, huh? We haven't got any of that. How many cans will ten dollars buy?"

"It'll get you a case. That's twenty-four 12 ounce cans."

Ed sat back. "Done," he snapped. "We'll take it."

Borden nodded. "Not so fast. Let's see the money first."

Ed stretched out his legs and reached into the depths of a trouser pocket. After rummaging around, he pulled out a discolored cloth bag secured with cotton drawstrings. He opened the sack and took out ten shiny silver dollar coins, clicking them together in his hand. Borden leaned forward.

"Silver dollars," he exclaimed, raising his voice a little. "That's better than paper money. You got yourself a deal."

Just then, another sailor entered the room, snatched off his cap, and walked over to Borden and whispered in his ear. He immediately stood, straightened his shoulders and cleared his throat. "Duty calls, gentlemen," he said as he stubbed out his cigarette in an ashtray. "I've gotta get to the metal shop. But don't worry, you'll get your juice." He turned toward the sailor and told him to show Ed and Gatling to their accommodations for the night. "We'll wake you up before first light and put you on a boat back to shore." Borden winked and walked out.

Ed and Gatling slept in hammocks that night, finding them a great deal more uncomfortable than sleeping on the ground. Each spent sleepless hours twisting and turning in search of a comfortable position, not finally drifting off until well after midnight. The ensuing hours sped by, for before they knew it, a man with a flashlight was shaking them, saying they needed to get dressed. They slipped on their dirty uniforms and reported to the whaleboat, bobbing up and down next to the *Canopus*.

The sailor handed them each a scrambled egg sandwich and told them about two burlap-covered boxes Master Chief Borden had placed on the boat.

"He's giving you two cases of tomato juice," said the sailor with a toothy smile. "He's got the duty and has to stay on board, but you're supposed to give me the money. I'll pass it along."

"Two cases, wow! The deal was only for one, but I'm not complaining," said Ed. "That juice is the only thing we're bringing back to camp." He reached into his pocket, pulled out the coins and handed them over.

The sailor thrust them into a pocket and passed over a canvas sack as Ed stepped into the whaleboat. "The Master Chief told me to give you this, too."

Ed looked up, curiosity on his face. "Yeah? What is it?"

"Two bottles of whiskey. He says you two look like you can use a belt."

Ed laughed as he reached over and took the sack. "Well, it has been awhile." He took two steps back and handed the sack to Gatling, taking more care of the liquor than he did of himself. Gatling cradled it in his arms and raised a bottle to examine the label.

"Scotch," he said with a smile. "Good stuff, too. Johnny Walker Black Label." He leaned forward and planted a kiss on it.

"Tell Borden we're indebted," said Ed to the sailor. "That scotch whiskey won't last long." As the crew of the whaleboat cast off and motored toward shore, the two men waved at the ship. It had been a worthwhile journey after all.

Upon reaching the dock, they stacked the crates of tomato juice on the pier and walked off in search of a phone. A jeep pulled up some forty-five minutes later and they were soon loaded up and on their way back to Cabcaben.

"What're you figuring to do with the scotch?" asked Gatling, sitting next to Ed in back as the jeep bounced along. "Seeing as it was your money, I suppose you're the one who gets to choose."

"Well, I'm not telling Dohlman about it, I can tell you that. It's none of that dope's business."

"So, what're you gonna do?"

Ed relaxed. This was a nice decision to make. One not dealing with war or death. Pure pleasure. "One is for you and me, and we can cut Baxter in on it, too."

"Okay, that sounds good, but what about Buchman? He's been supplying us with chewing gum for weeks. Seems like we owe him something."

"I wasn't forgetting. We can cut him in, but that's the limit. Four guys. The bottle'll be spread too thin with more."

Gatling gave a quick forward nod. "Okay, that's one bottle. What about the other?"

Ed had already thought about it and was ready with an answer. “You know those bull sessions we have under the tree? Let’s share it with everyone. Everybody can have a swig.”

The jeep fast approached Cabcaben, the infantry camp a short distance over a rise to the right. “Just keep the two bottles quiet,” said Ed. “We won’t keep ’em around long, but it’s our secret.”

“Okay,” replied Gatling. “I can almost taste that scotch now. Waiting’ll be tough, but wait I will.”

Life had developed into almost a routine. They ate meals twice a day, scrounged for extra food in the jungle and bathed in nearby streams. Shortages grew more acute by the week. Hungry men grew hungrier. Tents, bedding, mosquito nets, all dwindled in quantity. Uniforms grew tattered, underwear wore through, socks fell apart, and shoes rotted and disintegrated. Lack of cigarettes sapped morale. Fabric machine gun belts frayed and tore from heavy use.

While it lasted, quartermasters issued fresh meat at regular intervals, usually every third day. Most often the meat came from slaughtered *carabao*, which, since there was no refrigeration, had to be cut up and issued as fast as possible. Later, when the *carabao* supply was exhausted, quartermasters slaughtered the two hundred and fifty horses and forty-eight pack mules of the 26th Cavalry and added it to the menu in a last gasp attempt to keep protein in the diet.

Like all soldiers on Bataan, the provisional infantry supplemented the meager diet by arranging hunting expeditions into the jungle in search of meat, shooting scrawny wild chickens, slithering snakes, native hogs, and ugly iguanas. Just about anything that moved was fair game. Once in awhile they managed to bring down a stray *carabao*, a huge animal that spent much of each day wallowing in mud holes to combat the high heat and swarms of flies.

Other days they fished in the ocean or in freshwater streams, being most successful when stunning schools of fish with hand grenades. The underwater explosions drove fish to the surface, where all the hungry men had to do was scoop them up. Baxter observed it was the best use of hand grenades they had come up with, since they had proven so unreliable in battle.

For Ed, desert-bred in Arizona, along with others from rural areas, living off the land was a natural thing to do during these desperate times. As he explained to Gatling one steamy afternoon, "If an animal eats a plant, humans generally can, too. But be careful," he warned. "If something tastes bitter, it's probably poisonous."

The men discovered that the inside of male palm trees resembled the flavor of cabbage. They ate huge elephant ears, the floppy green leaves of a common jungle plant, and mangoes and cashews that grew on trees. They gathered tiny fresh-water shrimp from creeks splashing down from the mountains. They stretched thin soup by adding roots or grass. Some even ate worms and grasshoppers, scrunching their eyes while swallowing, having never imagined they'd one day be forced to eat like this.

By mid-February, a lull had descended. Japanese commander Homma ordered his forces to break off action and pull back, adapting an attitude of extreme passivity. They patrolled between the lines, sniped at American reconnaissance patrols and launched air attacks, but large-scale offensives came to an end. Instead, Japanese forces secured their hold on the rest of the Philippine Islands, tightened the blockade of Manila Bay and awaited reinforcements.

The Bataan defenses had proven surprisingly tough. The Japanese developed particular respect for defending artillery batteries, which rained shells upon them and caused heavy damage on too many occasions. To make matters worse, many Japanese troops had taken ill from tropical diseases such as malaria, beriberi and dysentery, reducing fighting strength even further. Some 13,000 Japanese soldiers on Bataan were placed in hospitals as non-battle casualties.

One morning, after a skimpy breakfast of three canned prunes, two spoonfuls of rice and a slice of canned ham, Ed, Gatling and Baxter gathered in a clearing atop a fallen log beside the Coast Road near Cabcaben Field. Each day's weather seemed a repeat of the day before, humid and warm with an afternoon downpour, and the sector had been quiet for weeks. They had become restless for something to do. Ed and Gatling had made plans to do something major about it, but hadn't found the right time to break the news to Baxter, who was not included.

A native Filipino man had wandered through camp several times the past week selling a thin stew made from jungle vegetables and mysterious, stringy meat, the origin of which no one could identify. He claimed it came from small animals captured with snares in the jungle, but it was unlike any dark meat they had eaten before. It had become a sizzling discussion topic and they proposed to find out that morning once and for all.

"Let's go," bellowed an impatient Ed after sitting around making small talk for five minutes. He hopped off the log and led the way to a narrow trail cutting through jungle underbrush where the man always appeared with the soup. The sun rose quickly and the thick air clung to their skin, sweat soaking through their shirts. No one carried a rifle, though Gatling's pistol swung inside a leather holster affixed to his belt. All three sported steel helmets and canteens of cool water dipped from a creek they crossed over.

Ed called for a rest after thirty minutes of hiking through steep ravines and hillsides. "There's no sense hurrying," he announced while dropping down on a smooth boulder at the base of a tree. "What are we gonna do once we find the guy, anyway? All we'll do is buy some soup."

Tipping his helmet back, Gatling answered, "That alone is a good enough reason. I spend most of my waking hours thinking of food. If it led to a full stomach, I'd walk across a whole mountain range."

Ed chuckled and stared down at a long serpentine line of army ants crawling over the ground carrying burdens of freshly hewn bits of green leaves. The ants never stopped, never wavered, acting as if under the central control of a ruling force that dictated and dominated their every action. Just like those crazy Nazi's in Germany, he smiled.

"I've never seen more insects in my life than I've seen around here," he observed aloud. "There were plenty of ants in Arizona, but nothing like this. These are twice as big as the ones back home."

As Ed watched the ants on their never ending journey, Baxter unscrewed the top of his canteen and took a gulp, letting some of the water dribble down his chin, which had been dripping with sweat. "You know, I heard some news last night that'll interest you two." He wiped his chin on a sleeve.

"What is it?" asked Gatling, turning.

Baxter's face took on a sardonic grin. "I hear General Homma has committed suicide," he said with relish. "He lost face among the Jap higher-ups because he failed to beat us. I figure reinforcements gotta be on the way, now."

Ed, listening with quiet curiosity, shook his head. "Yeah, I heard that story, too. It isn't exactly new. Where'd you hear it?"

"Lieutenant Colonel Dohlman told me outside headquarters. He said it to a whole group of us. Must be true."

Ed let out a disbelieving grunt. "You'd be smart if you didn't put much stock in it. Look at the guy you got it from—Dohlman. When he tells you something, take it with a great big fat grain of salt."

Baxter cast a quick glimpse at Ed. Ignoring the warning, he leaned forward and cocked his head. "Yeah, but I haven't told you the best part. Homma's suicide took place in the exact same apartment General MacArthur used at the Manila Hotel before the war. Is that poetic justice or what?"

Ed's eyes grew wide. "The same room? How would we know that?"

"Because of Filipino informants. Manila's crawling with people feeding us information."

Ed shook his head, fed up with this loose talk. "That sounds too neat and tidy to be believable. I mean, the same room? Come on . . ."

Baxter leaned forward to wipe away a clump of brown mud adhering to a trouser leg. "Well, I'm not saying it's an absolute fact; I'm just telling you what I heard. Dohlman believed it."

Ed squinted and raised his voice. "I told you what I think of him. Why he's a lieutenant colonel is one of those unexplainable freaks of nature." Twisting to the side, he faced Gatling. "What do you figure, Jim. What about Homma?"

Gatling wore a blank, depressed look and took his time before answering. He hadn't talked much since breakfast. "Sounds like the same old crapola," he whispered, the words coming out slow as molasses. "But it doesn't make much difference. The Japs are out there," he said, waving a hand over a shoulder, "and we're here. Who cares which Jap is in charge? Only two things will happen: we're either gonna die or be taken prisoner."

"What?" exclaimed Baxter, taken aback. He firmly believed MacArthur's optimistic promises and religiously listened to *The Voice of Freedom* each evening, an army radio broadcast beamed from Corregidor known for its thick propaganda. He naively swallowed the stories broadcasters told of new fighters and bombers on their way from Australia.

Baxter whirled around, his face suddenly red. "Ed, tell that friend of yours he's off base!" he spat.

While Ed's opinion had evolved into a more realistic, less hopeful one than Baxter's, he, too, had been taken by surprise. He gazed at Gatling. Most of the time, he found Gatling to be an optimistic, good-natured fellow, not given to wide emotional swings. The two friends had discussed the situation between themselves many times, deciding the unlikely chance of outside aid declined by the day, but their words had been private. But now, even if not meaning to, he had revived the gloomy topic, one better not to bring up in front of Baxter, a first-rate pilot but an immature boy.

Ed addressed Gatling in a soft murmur, as if someone had punched him in the stomach. "Gatling," he said, "keep that trap of yours shut. Sometimes you say things no one wants to hear."

"Yeah," said Baxter, pointing a wobbly finger. "We'll hold the Japs on Bataan until help comes, which'll be soon."

Gatling's eyes bored in. "Rumors of reinforcements have proven false time after time. President Roosevelt talks on the radio about increases in production next year and the year after that." He sat ramrod straight and sneered. "We don't need help in the future; we need it now. My opinion is that America has given up on the Philippines. We're cooked."

Ed shot to his feet and straightened his helmet, wearing a stern visage. "All right," he barked in a loud, grating voice. "Cut the talk. It doesn't matter one way or the other. We're here to hunt for that soup man, not argue. Come on, let's go."

They found him a short while later in a secluded clearing, humming as he sliced weird-looking greens and roots with an old machete knife atop a flat piece of wood. A black clay pot bubbled over an open fire some ten feet behind. Next to it, dangling from a rope suspended between two low branches, lay a sight that caused the breath to catch in their throats.

Before them hanged what looked to be a skinned, beheaded human baby, with tiny feet and hands, crimson blood dripping from its open neck onto the ground. Baxter screwed up his face, bent at the waist and heaved the contents of his stomach onto a nearby bush.

The Filipino man heard the loud retching and looked up, grasping fingers around the machete. "Who there?" he called. "Who there?"

Red-faced, hands on his hips, Ed stepped forward and pointed at the dangling figure, his expression a marble effigy of contempt. "What's your explanation for that?" Drawing a pistol, Gatling walked up behind.

The man shot a quick glance back at the creature and, shuddering before the two intruders, took a deep swallow. He dropped the machete onto the cutting board. "That nothing," he stammered. "Only meat for soup."

Ed advanced a step, his mouth dipping into an even deeper frown, hands bunched into fists. "You're making soup out of human babies?" He took a heavy, rasping breath. "You blood-sucking, baby killing murderer!"

Gatling released the safety on his gun, the metallic click echoing in the clearing. "No!" the man cried. "No, No!" Gatling raised the pistol and pointed it. "That not people meat—it monkey!" he shrieked, as he threw arms over his face and crumpled to the ground, scared out of his wits.

The two Americans stared at the creature and then looked at each other in wide-eyed astonishment, shaking their heads. Gatling lowered the pistol and slid it back into its holster. While running the back of a hand over his forehead, Ed whispered, "That monkey sure looks like a baby." He remained silent for a moment, thinking about almost shooting a man for skinning an animal. "My God," he called aloud, "I figured we were looking at a skinned human being!"

"Yeah, I did too," Gatling muttered, eyes affixed on the sight. Behind, Baxter wandered up, wiping his mouth on a sleeve. Transfixed, he stared at the creature.

The man looked up. "I show you, I show you monkey," he stammered, speaking in rapid-fire bursts. "This no baby; you see monkey."

Flashing a toothy grin, he got up and retreated back to the animal and held out one of its paws. It was long and lanky; the ends of each finger covered with brown, hairy skin near the fingernails. The man held them out, wagging his head up and down. "It monkey, it monkey," he repeated over and over. Then he released the arm and let it flop down, giving the monkey a spin around and reaching for the stub of the tail. He had chopped it off, but an inch remained. "You see; it monkey, it monkey."

Ed blew out a disgusted breath. "Yeah," he said, "okay, okay. It's a monkey." He retreated to the edge of the trail some yards away and flopped onto an old log. He removed his helmet and ran a hand through greasy, matted hair. This war must be driving me nuts, he thought to himself. Maybe it's affecting everyone the same way.

His companions, also breathing heavily, sat alongside. Gatling reached for a long stick extending from the side of the log and snapped it off. Reaching into a front pocket, he pulled out a pocketknife and began whittling, shaving off long pieces of green bark. Thoughtfully, he gazed into the leafy trees of the thick forest.

The Filipino man crouched over the pot simmering on the campfire. "I give soup," he called, gesturing with his hands. "It free.

I no charge." He reached for a ladle and dipped it inside, stirring the contents. "It smell good!" He gave a big grin.

The three Americans shot unenthusiastic glances at each other and Ed nodded, knowing what to say. "We don't want anything to do with that soup. We're going to rest up a minute then head out of here."

Sadness in his eyes, the man looked up. "But soup good. Monkey make good soup."

Ed rose. "Maybe so," he said, slapping on his helmet, "but that monkey looks too close to a person for us. We're not cannibals."

He promptly led the way out of the clearing and back to camp, not pausing to rest. That was enough adventure for one day.

They passed the afternoon relaxing on cots behind mosquito nets, reading old letters, magazines or dog-eared paperback novels passed from one man to another. As the sun grew red and began dipping behind the hills, shadows growing longer and the horizon turning pink, the regular group of men gathered, Ed and Baxter among the first to arrive. They sat a couple feet away from each other against a giant root, their feet stretched straight out. They always looked forward to evening, not just for the second meal of the day, but because the air cooled as night approached.

Leaning back, Ed lifted his eyes, a look of tired sadness settling on his features. He fidgeted in silence, pondering the possibility that he might never again see the states. Becoming a prisoner of the Japanese was almost unthinkable.

He glanced at Baxter and cleared his throat. "Look, John, I didn't tell you about something me and Gatling cooked up. I guess now's the time."

"What's that?"

"Officers are needed in Filipino units along the front and we volunteered. That means me and Gatling are leaving Cabcaben."

"Huh," Baxter grunted. He delayed a few seconds then asked, "Why do you want to leave? Conditions are better here than up close to the Japs. We get more food in a rear area, too."

Ed shrugged. "That's so, but we haven't done anything since six weeks ago back at Longoskawayan. We want to get into the war. We're tired of sitting around doing nothing but patrolling empty beach and wandering around the jungle scrounging for food."

Baxter nodded and clasped his rough hands together. "Did you have to go through Lieutenant Colonel Dohlman to arrange the transfer? He's not the type to do favors for people, let alone you two."

"No, we arranged it through headquarters at Cabcaben. Dohlman didn't know until it was set. He got all red and complained, but it didn't matter. I despise that no good bum and am glad to be out of his sight for good."

Baxter scrunched up his mouth and leaned back. A look of tiredness swept over his features. "Well, I wish you luck, buddy." He liked Ed, viewing him somewhat as a big brother, and disliked the prospect of his leaving.

He thought for a moment and came to a realization. When the reinforcement convoy arrived, he'd be flying planes again while Ed and Gatling would be stuck in a Filipino infantry outfit. The joke would be on them. He chuckled inside and perked up.

"Well, maybe you'll be able to kick some Jap butt up there," Baxter remarked. "When're you leaving?"

"In the next day or two," he replied. "We're reporting to the 41st division of the Philippine Army. We're getting promotions, too. Soon I'll be Captain Bannon. Gatling's moving up to 1st lieutenant."

"We'll miss you two back here, but think of this. From Cabcaben we'll see the reinforcement convoy steaming into the bay long before you ever do." Baxter grinned, but just then a Japanese Zero roared over, its machine guns hammering at groups of men caught in the open. The two edged toward the trunk of the tree and ducked behind one of the large roots. In a moment, the Zero gunned its engine and sped off, its attention now on Cabcaben Field.

Out in Manila Bay the deep throated, echoing blasts of artillery rang out as Corregidor's largest caliber guns opened up on a suspected enemy position in the Pico de Loro hills across the bay. Japanese artillery had moved into the wooded area several weeks before to fire at Forts Frank and Drum, American harbor defense fortifications located on small islands at the bay's mouth. The inaccurate fire caused little damage, but the annoying challenge could not go unanswered. Batteries on all four of the Manila Bay forts fired daily, hoping they might knock out the Japanese guns with a lucky hit.

The American counter-battery fire was hampered by the difficulty of locating the enemy guns, which took every precaution: employing skillful camouflage, firing in the morning when bright sunrays blinded observers and sending up false smoke rings at various locations when the guns fired. American gunners and spotters estimated the best they could, sometimes getting hits, sometimes not. And so the unequal struggle went on.

Corregidor Island

Several military vehicles slowly wound away from Malinta Tunnel toward Corregidor's blasted north dock, the island's water transportation hub, still operational despite repeated attacks. Dodging shell holes and uprooted trees, the vehicles pulled to a stop just short of the dock, next to a bombed out wood frame building once used as an office by military police. Pieces of blackened wood and broken red roof tiles littered the ground and General Douglas MacArthur kicked at one as he hopped out of the sedan, not waiting for an aide to swing open the door. The tile skidded away and clanked into a pile of others against the asphalt street's concave curb. Major General Jonathon Wainright, who would assume overall command as soon as MacArthur departed, quietly edged out of the car behind.

"Well, Jonathon," said MacArthur, as he gazed into the dark night sky toward the Bataan Peninsula, "as soon as I get to Australia I'll lead a force back into the Philippines and relieve as much pressure against you I can. I'll get the supply ships moving, too. I plan to turn this situation around very soon."

Wainright, standing beside his superior in respectful silence, nodded. "I know you will, General. I know you will."

"Keep the flag flying; I'll be back." For a moment, MacArthur stood motionless against the sky, dimly silhouetted against shell explosions lighting up the night over Bataan. His craggy face stood out sharply, his mind far away, worrying about the troops, but also about the long, dangerous trip ahead. He remained for what seemed a long time, but actually amounted to no more than a minute. "I'll get back with as much as I can, as fast as I can," he mumbled.

Tied up at the end of the dock bobbed four patrol torpedo boats under the command of flamboyant Lieutenant John Bulkeley, who had led the vessels that exacted first blood at Longoskawayan Point. The engines burbled as twenty-two passengers clambered aboard. The manifest included MacArthur's wife, their young son and his Chinese nurse, seventeen members of his personal staff, and a few elderly officers who were not standing up well, mentally or physically, to the rigors of the campaign.

As the final rays of sun dipped below the horizon, MacArthur exchanged a last round of handshakes with the senior officers remaining behind and climbed into Bulkeley's boat, his wife and son resting on a mattress below. Crewmen cast lines away and each boat slowly idled out into the night. Two hours later they cleared the minefields blocking the mouth of Manila Bay and sped south.

President Franklin Roosevelt had ordered MacArthur to leave Corregidor, knowing surrender was inevitable. Though he protested at first, refusing to obey, MacArthur relented. He consoled himself with the thought that his personal efforts would speed blockade runners, send bombers over Manila and launch a diversionary campaign to relieve pressure on the Bataan defenders.

His escape to Mindanao and plane trip to Australia took ten days of hard travel. When he stepped foot on Australian soil, however, he was stunned to discover American forces there so weak that reinforcing the Philippines or doing anything concrete to resolve the situation out of the question.

Though those left behind on Bataan and Corregidor prayed he would use his tremendous influence to send aid, nothing resulted. Within days, most Americans and many Filipinos accepted his departure for what it was; a token of doom. No help was coming from any source.

The architect of the Bataan failure, the army commander who had squandered the supplies and medicines so necessary to his army's sustenance in a series of unrealistic, bungled decisions, reached his haven of safety in Australia. For MacArthur's abandoned, beleaguered forces, death or capture had become their certain fate.

CHAPTER 14

THE BATTLE LULL CONTINUES

Yuma, Arizona, March 19, 1942

The Yuma morning dawned with a dazzling bright sun foreshadowing a hot day, unseasonably warm for March. Ed's father, Marshall, hoed weeds in the garden behind the house; a crop of tomatoes, green beans, corn, and radishes that reached enormous proportions each year in Yuma's rich soil, fertilized for eons by annual flooding of the Colorado River.

The railroad had sent him away to Dome Valley the previous three days to repair washed out culverts beneath the gravel roadbed, work that required him to spend two nights in a beat up maintenance of way car. It had turned into a bigger job than expected and, with war pressures on the railroad, the work crew needed to set things right. This was his single day off before having to return.

Marshall enjoyed working in the garden, regarding it as a sanctuary from the strain of the outside work world and the brown monotony of the desert. He liked turning over rich, brown soil and watching tiny seeds grow into thriving plants, heavy with produce. By mid-summer, when Southwest Arizona's sweltering heat approached its zenith, he was always disappointed to see his treasured vegetable plants wither and die.

The Bannon parents had received no mail from Ed since the day war broke out, a source of constant and ever-mounting worry. They knew he was in the Philippines, but it was almost as if their son had become a jackrabbit who disappeared down a hole and never stuck his head out again. As promised when sailing from San Francisco, Ed wrote home regularly during the final weeks of peace. Then the letters stopped. Why? Their son had vanished into one of the most dangerous areas of the world and they had only newspaper and radio reports to go on.

As Marshall Bannon chopped away at weeds growing amid his precious vegetables, threatening to steal nutrients and choke their sunlight, his mind wandered far away, to a world of blood, explosions, shouts, moans, and the never ending rat-a-tat-tat chatter of machine guns. To the World War I battlefields of France.

He remembered the ugly, torn combat zones all to well. Those scenes had seared themselves into his mind. Life in the trenches was one tension-filled minute after another, with little romance or glory. Rats were underfoot constantly, with the perpetual smell of gunpowder, death and putrification.

Then there was his best friend, Jacob. They had spent the early months of the war together, but, late one evening while on patrol between the lines, Jacob's head nearly exploded from the well-aimed bullet of a concealed sniper. In tears, Marshall threw down his rifle to cradle the lifeless body in his arms while others in the patrol fired wildly, one side of his own face and chest covered with blood, gelatinous pink goo and bits of bone. Heedless of the gore, Marshall rocked Jacob's body back and forth in horror, but there was nothing to be done.

He never recovered from that shock. Many times he had tried to erase the memory, but it remained to haunt his dreams. Warfare, he came to believe, was nothing more than folly and inhumanity taken to its highest degree. It certainly involved no virtue or decency. When he returned home, he was happy to throw off the uniform and join the ranks of the nation's pacifists.

Marshall reacted with revulsion when Ed told him of his interest in enlisting in the army. He had warned his son to stay out, but the words had fallen on deaf ears. Enamored with the romance of flying and seeking solace from the loss of Barbara, he had gone ahead.

But what does a father do? When a child is young, the problems tend to be small also, easily remedied. But what about when that child grows into an adult and makes a poor decision? As a father, do you put your foot down and forbid it? Even if it's for the best?

Frozen in mid-step, Marshall's heart swelled with longing as he dropped the wood handled hoe and looked up. What kind of father had he turned out to be? He snapped off his hat and ran fingers through the thinning gray hair, wondering why his son had chosen to defy him.

Just then the rusting screen door slammed and his wife's delighted voice rang out. "A letter, a letter from Eddy!" She ran toward him, waving it overhead, her loose yellow print housedress flowing behind. "Honey, he must be alive!"

Marshall Bannon dropped the hat as astonishment siphoned blood from his face. He froze for a moment then bolted toward his wife, meeting her halfway to the house. He ripped the letter from her hand and held it before his eyes, trembling with eagerness. "Manila, Philippine Islands. That's where he wrote it," he exclaimed, tearing it open. "I'll, I'll read it out loud, Marion."

In eager anticipation, he rubbed a hand across his mouth and slipped the letter from the envelope. With a rattle, he unfolded the lone page. Quickly scanning it, his eyes suddenly darkened with pain and his shoulders drooped. A moment passed before he mumbled in a dismayed voice, "Marion, he wrote this back on Christmas Eve." He glanced up, a worried look on his face. "That's, what, three months ago? My God, we still don't know if he's alive."

His face a stony mask, he sucked in a deep breath, looking at her in desperation. Their eyes locked and then he looked down at the letter and read the first words. "Dear Mom and Dad." His voice broke and he turned away to cough, wetness building in his eyes.

Marion reached forward and gathered him in the loving protectiveness of her arms, resting her head against his shoulder. "Just wait a minute, dear. Wait until you're ready."

The two caressed in the open yard, their bodies clasped together as one. Marshall kept his face turned away, not wanting his wife to see her husband, a hardened railroad worker capable of pounding steel spikes for hours, with tears streaking down his cheeks. He bit his lower lip to control the sobs racking his insides, but his body heaved and trembled, and she knew.

It must have been five minutes that they remained there, neither speaking. Marshall finally broke the silence with a heavy sigh. "Marion, let's go sit under the shade tree," he squeaked, barely above a whisper, fatigue settled in pockets under his eyes.

She brushed a silent kiss across his forehead and, hand in hand, they walked to a bench and sat next to each other. Marshall slumped forward, clutching the letter on his lap. Marion, leaning against his shoulder, clasped her slender hands together and cast her eyes toward the ground.

He cleared his throat and read the letter aloud, then read it again. "It's a nice letter," said Marion as he finished the second reading. "Sounds like life in the tropics agrees with him."

Marshall looked up into the branches of the tree, remembering when Ed built a tree house there as a young boy. His first attempt resulted in a rickety structure that looked like it would fall in the first big wind, but Marshall pitched in and they rebuilt it together. The boy spent an untold number of hours up there until growing out of it. Though the tree house was long gone, a few boards remained, nailed to the tree with rusty nails.

"Yeah, maybe life in the Philippines isn't so bad," he mused. All of a sudden, he swiveled toward his wife. "And did you hear how he got himself a Nip plane? That's my boy!" he said, pride in his voice.

Just to receive the letter, to hear from their only child and to know he was alive on Christmas brought comfort, but a great deal of time had passed since then. Why had it taken so long for it to reach home? Could they expect another letter?

Inwardly, each shuddered at another prospect. Could they expect a telegram from the War Department informing them in cold, bureaucratic language that he had been killed?

At least the reasons for this war were better than the last. The Japanese started this one with a sneak attack that had killed thousands. Even Marshall's antiwar feelings had undergone a transformation. "They'll pay, they'll pay," he pledged aloud as he clenched and unclenched his hand over and over.

Passenger and freight traffic on the railroad had picked up dramatically in the first months of 1942 and Marshall resolved to do his utmost to ensure the tracks remained up to the task. From crack streamliners like the *Golden State* and the *Sunset Limited* that carried the captains of industry, to troop trains and the lowest status mud spattered local freights, he vowed that no obstacles or slow track would be encountered in his territory.

Bataan Peninsula, Philippines

Standing before his desk, Ed and Gatling asked Lieutenant Colonel Dohlman if one of the unit's vehicles could be spared to give them a ride to the 41st Division. Enmeshed in paperwork, he continued writing for a moment and then slowly looked up, his lips twisting into a cynical smile. "We're not in the business of running a taxi service," he snapped. "Or didn't you screw-ups know? Get your own ride." Exchanging sideways glances, by mutual consent they turned on their heels and walked away. They did not bother to salute or say another word.

A civilian bus commandeered by the military came by a short time later, its top sliced off to allow passengers to jump out fast in case of an air attack. Half empty, the driver stopped amid a cloud of dust and they clambered aboard, throwing their equipment onto an empty seat. Soon they were motoring out of the lowlands surrounding Cabcaben, over hogbacks up rocky hills bordered by thick jungle. Looking to the right, they could see the island of Corregidor, the "Rock," jutting out of the blue water of Manila Bay, foggy haze tempering the brilliance of the early morning sunlight.

The lack of a roof made the bus appear odd, ungainly, but the forward motion of the vehicle created a fresh breeze that made the ride more comfortable than they had anticipated. Gusts of wind rattling through the jungle also helped, drying the perspiration caused by the growing humidity. On the bay the wind was even stronger, making the defiant American flag mounted on Corregidor's highest point flutter straight out. Though more than three miles away, it was a sight that made them feel proud. Each wore an approving smile.

The bus continued on the Coast Road toward the front for nearly an hour, three times turning off under the safety of a large tree to avoid enemy observation planes. Two observers wearing dark glasses posted at the front of the bus kept a careful watch overhead, yelling a warning to the driver whenever a flyspeck appeared in the sky.

The bus drew to a halt at the intersection of Trail 19, a rough dirt road cut through virgin jungle to connect with troops manning the center of the defense line. The driver motioned for everyone to get off, as this was as far as he intended to go. Waving in thanks, Ed and Gatling threw on their gear and waited as the bus backed up with a loud grinding sound and motored back to Mariveles. Most of the other passengers veered away on Trail 19.

Miles from their destination, they began walking along the Coast Road, hoping another vehicle would pass. Broken dark clouds seemed to be massing over the peninsula, threatening another rainstorm, and they hoped to avoid getting drenched. After walking less than two hundred yards, they happened upon a battered green army ambulance sporting a large red cross, stopped beside the road between trees offering a solid canopy of leaves and vines. The crunching barks of nearby 155mm artillery, the sound of which had been muffled in Cabcaben, echoed throughout the area.

"Hey there!" Gatling hollered as they approached the stalled vehicle, its hood open.

The driver, leaning over a small campfire behind the vehicle, looked up in surprise. He had driven a wooden stick through the backbone of a ten-inch skinned iguana and was in the process of roasting it over smoldering pieces of brushwood. He leaned the stick holding the lizard against a stone and stood. "You two are just who I was waiting for," he blurted. "I've been here for near two hours."

"What's the trouble?" asked Gatling.

"Battery's dead," he replied. "I stopped when I spotted a Jap plane and the dang thing stalled. It refused to start again, but if you give me a shove, the engine might start up on its own."

Ed trudged up behind Gatling and removed his hat, wiping rivulets of perspiration from his neck. "You've been here two hours and nobody'd help? There've been plenty of men walking up and down this road."

The driver's eyes shifted from one man to the other in embarrassment. "To tell you the truth, I wasn't here most of the time. I went off into the woods looking for something to eat. Found two green mangoes, which I ate right off the tree, and this lizard. You're welcome to have some."

Gatling had walked up to the fire and was in the process of inspecting the dead reptile. "How'd you kill this thing?" he asked. "Iguanas are hard to catch." He paused for a moment before adding, "By the way, what's your name?"

"It's Stew," he replied. "As for getting the iguana, it was a lucky shot. I've always missed when I shot at those things before, but this time I blew its head off. Can't explain it."

"Huh," Gatling grunted. "So, you want us to give you a push?"

"You two get me started and I'll give you a ride wherever you're going. What d'ya say?"

"You got a deal," said Gatling, taking off his gear and throwing it into the back of the ambulance. "We'll get you started, then you come back and get us."

"Okay," replied Stew, "but let's eat the iguana first. It's ready." The three men knelt by the fire and tore it apart, deciding the taste of lizard resembled that of chicken. In a couple minutes they polished it off. Stew raised up and walked toward the ambulance. "I'll put the transmission in gear and you two shove. Sing out when you're ready."

The two positioned themselves behind the vehicle and placed their hands against the bumper, digging their toes into the ground. "We're ready," shouted Gatling. "Start her up."

Ed and Gatling put their backs into it, shoving with all their might. The ambulance jolted and sputtered, and as it moved forward, the engine kicked into gear and began an encouraging rumble that settled into a purr. Out of breath, leaning over and panting, neither watched the ambulance move ahead under its own power, as two months of half rations had sapped their strength.

It motored a short distance forward, then Stew, as agreed, spun the steering wheel around and returned. "C'mon," he said, pulling up. "You can rest inside." He leaned over and pushed open the passenger-side door with outstretched fingers.

Relieved, Ed and Gatling climbed in. "Whew," grunted Gatling as he slid to the center of the worn out seat. The leather was ripped and torn, with metal springs sticking out in numerous places. "We're going up to the 41st Philippine Division. That anywhere near?"

Stew nodded, swiveled the steering wheel and revved the engine. "Yeah, it's just up ahead," he replied, a tiny bone from the tail of the iguana wedged against the inside of his lower lip. He turned and spit it out the driver's side window jammed halfway down. "Hang on. I'll get you there, but we're gonna make tracks on the way."

Stew ducked his head low, squinted and surveyed the road ahead, noting they would be driving straight into the sun. "One of you better stand on the running board and keep a lookout for Jap planes. Sing out, loud, if you see anything."

"I'll do it," said Ed, no longer out of breath. He opened the door and stepped outside, grabbing firm handholds. "Okay, let's go," he said through the open window.

The two passengers held on as best they could as the ambulance careened up the road, traveling as fast as Stew could safely manage. There was little traffic at this hour, as most vehicle movement took place at night; Japanese planes placed special emphasis on shooting up daytime motor traffic. The ambulance bounced up and down, jostling the passengers and shoving them to one side or the other.

"Aren't you going a mite fast?" gasped a grim Gatling as he propped himself against a door. Stew pulled one corner of his mouth into a thin smile as a sharp curve appeared ahead. "I'm supposed to pick up a couple idiot officers and bring them back to Hospital Number Two. Why they can't wait until night, I don't know. They're probably dimwit behind-the-line heroes who got themselves scratched." Staring through wide eyes, Gatling nodded as the ambulance continued on.

Stew kept his mouth clamped in a straight line as he speeded along, a never-ending stream of dust blowing in through the open windows. Ed said little due to the clouds of dust and fast rate of speed, but also because of the seriousness of his job. One mistake and they would be chopped to pieces by machine gun fire. He had slipped on dark sunglasses to shield his eyes from the dazzling glare of the sun that peeked through the growing gray overcast.

All of a sudden, he spotted something that looked suspicious. As if from out of the sun, a black speck hurtled down in a direct line toward the vehicle. As he squinted, holding his breath, the speck grew larger, second by second, and its wings grew in size.

"Jap plane! Jap plane!" he shouted. "Get out!"

Stew jammed his foot against the brake pedal and the ambulance squealed to a dusty halt. The men piled out, sprinting for the cover of trees lining the road. As they reached safety, a stream of bullets sliced up the road, sending up little geysers of dust, tearing into the ambulance.

"Crimoney!" Ed yelled, reaching for his .45. He got off a quick round, but the Zero zipped by and was long out of range by the time he fired. The others raised their heads and drifted from behind the bushes. Stew walked out to examine the riddled ambulance and counted ten holes.

Ed cast a grim sideways glance at Gatling. "God, that was close," he gasped.

Gatling yelled to Stew, just then kneeling before the front bumper examining the path of one of the .50 caliber slugs. "Will she still run?"

Stew looked up and grinned. "She never stopped running," he said. "It's still purring like a kitten."

Ed and Gatling prepared to get inside, but Stew stopped them with a wave of a hand. "I'm heading back from here. I was gonna let you off around the bend anyway. My driving today is over, no matter what anybody says."

"Yeah, but where's the 41st?" Ed asked. "Next to the road?"

"No, the headquarters of the 41st is back of those hills off to the right. There's a trail cutting off just around the bend." He jabbed a finger to the right, indicating the direction they would have to travel on foot. "It isn't far."

The two exchanged looks of relief. "Well, that was one helluva trip," Ed said, whipping off his hat and shaking his mane of thick brown hair. His mouth quirked with humor. "I don't figure I'll be riding on ambulances much in the future. That is, if I have a choice about it."

Stew smiled. "Well, I told you I'd have to go like hell," he said. "We shouldn't even have been out here this time of day."

Ed shrugged. "Well, we're obliged for the lift. Just be careful going back."

A half-smile crossed Stew's face. "Don't worry, I will. I've had enough excitement today to last a lifetime. I'll go back aways and wait for a convoy to come along. I can't drive and watch out for planes at the same time."

The two pulled out their gear and waved. Stew gunned the engine and steered the vehicle back into the road, curling up a tan cloud of dust. The two watched him disappear around a curve.

Ed grimaced. "He better be careful," he said. "That dust is a dead giveaway to the Japs."

"Speaking of going, we better split, too," observed Gatling, who had slung his blanket, mosquito net, rifle, and other gear over a shoulder. "I don't want to lug this stuff around a second more than I have to. Let's go."

Ed slung on his equipment and set off. They cut off at the path and found it wide enough for a single man. The jungle choked either side of the trail with shrubs six to nine feet tall, hiding them from aerial observation. They trudged over a low ridge and came across a fast moving river the trail followed before wandering into a verdant side valley cut by two small streams.

In this bucolic setting nestled the headquarters of the Philippine army's 41st Infantry Division. A neat bamboo bridge spanned one creek, well-camouflaged bamboo and banana leaf huts blended into the hillside and huts clustered along the stream banks, taking full advantage of the heavy overhead foliage. A place of great natural beauty, the area seemed cool and secure.

The 41st Division, a reserve outfit called to active duty in the fall of 1941, consisted of three infantry battalions and an artillery regiment that had been thrown into battle after three weeks of inadequate training. The artillery regiment didn't take delivery of its guns until war broke out and fired only five training rounds before going into action. Roughly handled during the campaign's opening weeks, the men of the division had since developed into tough combat veterans who could fight toe-to-toe with the enemy. American officers and enlisted experts assigned to each battalion provided training and advice. Brigadier General Vicente Lim, an American of part Chinese ancestry and the first Filipino to graduate from West Point, commanded the division.

Ed and Gatling sauntered into camp, first bending over the stream to splash water in their faces, and stopped a passing soldier to ask directions to General Lim's headquarters. He jerked a thumb over a shoulder, toward a long row of huts backed against a rocky vine shrouded slope. They ascended the stairs of the last hut in line, the largest, set their equipment down and addressed an orderly, who told them to enter the inner office. Lim greeted them with tea and, after several minutes of polite small talk, instructed them to report to the 33rd battalion as advisors.

Though the Filipino soldiers were about as prepared for a Japanese assault as they could be, long months of inadequate rations and lack of vitamins had done great damage to their fighting ability and morale. A crushing blow came when word spread of MacArthur's departure, which seemed like a skipper deserting a sinking ship. Even they, the loyal Filipinos, now feared the campaign's outcome. Japanese reinforcements, planes, tanks, artillery, and troops, had been streaming into the Philippines for weeks, much sent from Malaya where Japanese forces had outmaneuvered and outfought a numerically superior British force in Singapore. The situation for the 41st Division, as for everyone on Bataan, had grown bleak indeed.

Chapter 15

The Inevitable Occurs

April 1942

The two Americans threw themselves into their new jobs with wholehearted abandon, seeing little of each other while acquainting themselves with life on the front. They inspected the forward defenses the first day, finding them well thought out and constructed. The Filipinos had built extensive barbed wire entanglements, driven sharpened bamboo stakes into the ground in pits along likely lanes of attack, and laid out an almost solid palisade of sharpened six-foot bamboo poles along the entire front.

Artillery had carefully registered on terrain features up and down the line, ready to blast apart concentrations of enemy troops as they massed or approached. Machine guns were assigned fields of fire, bamboo patches and tangled brush had been cleared, and defenses were camouflaged to blend in with the natural terrain. Trenches zigzagged up and down the line, with strong points taking full advantage of hills, gullies and streambeds. Communication trenches linked everyone and automatic weapons poked from well-concealed bunkers. Advance outposts a quarter mile toward the enemy were prepared to give ample warning of advancing troops.

The defenses appeared impressive at first glance, but a serious liability marred the effort and worsened each day. It was the men's pitiful physical condition. It had declined to the point that some openly questioned whether an effective defense could be mounted at all.

Soldiers were down to one thousand calories per day, a level barely sufficient to sustain life without physical activity. Many had lost weight down to two thirds of normal. The daily ration had declined so badly that many could hold their day's food in the palm of a hand. Huge numbers were sick with malaria and nearly everyone suffered from dysentery. Quinine was gone and no other medicines to combat malaria were available. Many soldiers, discouraged and listless, could do nothing more than sit in foxholes and point their rifles in the direction of the enemy.

Ed inspected the defenses with Captain Arturo Dominguez, a former schoolteacher who had fought alongside the Americans throughout the war. As they maneuvered up a gully toward the outpost line, keeping under cover, Ed asked about minefields laid by the Filipinos, knowing stockpiles of landmines were inadequate.

"We've buried about two hundred box mines put together from wood crates containing dynamite," Dominguez explained. "The division lost most of its mines in the retreat back in January. Come on," he said. "I'll show you one."

Behind a screen of bushes, the two edged out of the gully, coming across a group of five men amid low brush assembling box mines prior to placing them in the ground. The wooden boxes were about nine inches square, set to explode under a weight of five hundred pounds. Dynamite had been placed inside at engineering depots and flashlight batteries to detonate the explosive were inserted just before placing each box in the ground.

"These are anti-tank, not anti-personnel mines," said Dominguez. "We place them in open areas tanks might cross."

Ed nodded in approval. "That's good," he said. "But what about enemy troops?"

Dominguez explained. "We have a few anti-personnel mines, but we've done a lot on our own. We've dug punji pits, made booby traps out of grenades and cleared huge areas of bamboo for good fields of fire. And don't forget we have a double apron of barbed wire out there. That, and our small arms fire, should hold them." He flashed a quick smile and moved a few inches back. "Let's move up to the outpost line."

Enemy activity had been increasing throughout the latter half of March in the form of frequent artillery duels and repeated bombing and strafing attacks. At the beginning of April, the Japanese launched a sausage-shaped World War I-style observation balloon to monitor movements along the Filipino-American line. Observers suspended in a basket below the balloon spied on defense works through telescopes, methodically pinpointing strong points and watching for artillery fire.

"I haven't seen a balloon like that before," commented Ed as he pushed back the brim of his steel helmet after reaching the forward edge of the outpost line. He crouched behind a blackened stump and studied the balloon, safely tethered to the ground within Japanese lines. "A P-40 ought to shoot that thing down."

"It wouldn't get through," said Dominguez. "Jap planes are always flying around when it's up."

"Still, that's what an air corps is for." Ed didn't know it, but the Far East Air Force had shrunken to two planes; one P-40 and one P-35, both tired and riddled with patched-up holes. They had been reduced to flying mostly at night to Cebu or one of the outlying islands to bring in crucial medical supplies. A mission aimed against the well-protected balloon would most likely be a one way, suicide affair; a loss the air corps could not afford. The loss of a single plane would be catastrophic.

As they surveyed the terrain between them and the Japanese, four Filipino soldiers walked along a trail behind the lip of a ridge, about fifty yards to the rear, toward a camouflaged machine gun. Coming out from the concealment of several mammoth trees, the whine of incoming artillery shells made them scramble for cover. They dove behind a fallen log as three shells burst in rapid succession where they had just been. As smoke and dust died away, they raised their heads and cast worried glances at each other, for observers on the balloon had spotted them and called in the fire. They delayed a few minutes before crawling on, hugging the ground and moving with great caution.

Ed, having viewed the affair, twisted toward Dominguez, a shadow of alarm touching his face. "The Japs must have moved up one helluva supply of ammunition to waste three shells on four men. We better watch out." He shook his head and turned away.

Dominguez shuddered and drew in a sharp breath. Events like this warned of an attack. He had painted Ed a confident picture of the Filipino ability to turn back the Japanese. When the time came, would they be able to do it?

It was Good Friday, April 3rd. The sun rose early and bright, its glinting rays hot and glaring. Ed and Gatling got up from their cots and walked to a brook to wash sleep out of their eyes, exchanging few words at that early hour. Both were disturbed by the events of the previous day, as the Japanese pushed the outpost line back with heavy losses. Enemy forces now sat poised in attack positions, ready to strike.

The two wandered to regimental headquarters where they found officers clustered around a table enjoying cups of rice coffee. Handed mugs, they found the concoction warming, though it barely resembled coffee. They began to look forward to breakfast, a meal to consist of the usual thin rice gruel, known as *lugao*.

About 8:30, they heard shelling off in the distance. It grew in tempo, the crash of exploding shells growing closer and closer by the minute. Nearby artillery batteries fired in response, but had to cease-fire moments later when an accurate cascade of enemy shells came back. Japanese gunners aimed at all the likely Filipino strong points and, with balloon observation, began to lay deadly, precise fire. Before smoke obscured the view, American observers on the peaks of nearby hills counted nineteen batteries of artillery and ten batteries of mortars, for a total of one hundred and ninety-six guns arrayed against the 41st Division.

Through sheer courage, the Filipino gunners maintained a moderate rate of return fire, but the effect on the famished crews was grim. Jumping into foxholes when Japanese fire crashed in, then running back to get off a few rounds in return, hour after hour, exhausted the gunners. Bamboo thickets caught fire and sent clouds of black smoke rolling over the pieces, collecting among trees, causing men to cough and hack, their eyes swelling with burning tears.

Concentrated on a narrow portion of the line, shells began showering down faster than anyone could count. American veterans of World War I said it was worse than anything they had ever received from the Germans. By mid-afternoon, the volume and intensity of the fire had completely staggered the defenders, producing a literal bedlam amid the high tropic heat.

The barrage uprooted trees forty to seventy feet high. Swollen, stinking bodies lay scattered along the line. One man, a runner from a forward unit, commented in the command bunker that the stench was so bad that he was almost thankful there was nothing to eat. The clamor, concussion and emotional exhaustion produced by the fearful hours of waiting drew the last physical reserves from the Filipino rifleman cowering in their foxholes.

"Where's our artillery?" shouted Gatling as reports poured in from the front lines. "We need counter-battery fire!"

Ed grabbed a telephone and made contact with the 31st artillery, armed with towed 75mm pieces. Securely ensconced in dug-in, camouflaged positions, Japanese observers had been unable to pinpoint their precise location. Major Alfonso Arellano, artillery officer at the fire direction center, picked up the phone. The thudding of artillery explosions provided a backdrop to his words.

"What's going on over there?" shouted Ed over the telephone line. "Why aren't you guys firing back?"

Arellano held the telephone close, hollering his response. "We're shooting like hell whenever we can, but when planes fly over, we have to cease-fire," he replied. "Standing orders are for us to take cover whenever enemy aircraft are overhead."

Ed frowned in frustration. The standing orders to cease fire when enemy aircraft flew overhead had been issued in January. If it had not been strictly enforced, the artillery would have been destroyed long ago. Knowing this, Ed cupped hands around the receiver and lowered his voice to a calmer, more reasonable tone. "How bad is it?"

"Jap planes have been hovering around all day. Whenever we fire, they swoop down and lay a few eggs. We can't do much of anything."

Ed blew out a breath of air and his expression grew hard. "The battalion commander wants you to do what you can. We need your artillery fire, so take chances if you have to." He quietly set the telephone receiver back in its cradle.

Nimble Zero fighters and two engine bombers ranged up and down the line, strafing troop concentrations and dropping over sixty tons of bombs on the 41st Division by the close of the day. Giving particular attention to the artillery, fragmentation bombs slashed through gun positions, driving crews to cover, cutting telephone wires running to forward observers. Anti-aircraft fire from a 3-inch gun proved ineffective and gunners watched in frustration as enemy planes flew serenely overhead, just above its maximum range. The gun was soon put out of commission for good.

Over the course of the day, the Japanese fire shattered the fighting effectiveness of the 41st Division. Red dust and choking gray-black smoke boiled upward, raging infernos sending flames high into the sky. Wounded men roasted to death, screaming. Formerly well-concealed works now lay exposed and vulnerable.

"Two of our three regiments are pulling back," shouted Dominguez as the cacophony of explosions continued. "Many have thrown down their guns!"

Trails leading to the rear filled with hopelessly shell-shocked soldiers, the ever-growing tide hurrying along at a frantic pace, exhausted and defeated. Whenever an officer tried to stop and reorganize the fleeing men, he was met with blank stares and a babble of frightened voices.

The next day proved worse. The Japanese, estimating before the attack that several weeks of hard fighting would be required to break through the well-prepared line, took heart and advanced the schedule. They resumed their devastating artillery and air barrage, sending more defenders stampeding to the rear. All attempts to rally the men proved futile and they rushed south as fast as they could, the retreat rapidly turning into a rout.

Tanks of the Japanese 7th Tank Regiment cut behind the defenses, crushing men in the trenches and shooting at everything in sight, including the wounded. Without antitank guns and with the box mines destroyed during the barrage, defending forces were helpless. Rifle and machine gun fire bounced off the armored skins of the light tanks. They roamed freely and with contempt, creating panic and confusion.

Word came to evacuate the command post and pull back early in the morning, just after sunrise, long after the situation had become untenable. Soon, the officers were busy packing papers and clothing. Ed, stuffing personal items into a musette bag, looked out to see a band of men streaming along the road next to the command post. He got up and ran toward the trail, stopping next to a dust-covered green bush.

"What's going on?" he shouted while waving his hands. The men barely glanced up, looks of wild bewilderment in their eyes; jostling and shoving like a herd of uncontrollable sheep. "You've got to stop! Form up here and we'll move back together, as soldiers."

But the mob didn't slow. If anything, it began moving faster, the men wanting nothing more to do with combat. Some shouted that they were searching for the nearest hospital or were going back to Mariveles for rice. Some mumbled unintelligible words. The tangle had turned into a stampede; leaderless, intent on fleeing from an enemy firing at any sound, taking few prisoners.

"I said *stop*!" hollered Ed as he stepped onto the trail and drew his .45. "Stop right here!"

Nothing happened. The terrified mob continued its unmanageable surge. Ed swept their eyes and, in desperation, moved to the center of the trail and aimed the pistol into the air, firing once, then again. Gazing around, his eyes met with grief. The pace slackened not a bit. He raised his pistol and fired a third time.

One of the Filipinos, looking askance at the foolish American blocking the way, raised the rock-hard stock of his Springfield rifle and slammed it into his head. "Damn Yankee fool," he muttered while continuing down the trail, breaking his stride for only a moment.

An array of hundreds of multicolored stars exploded in Ed's eyes. His legs buckled, the shuffling feet dividing as the cattle herd of starved, diseased men poured alongside. Within minutes the group passed, leaving behind the shape of a man lying crumpled in the dirt, unconscious and forlorn. The nearby command post had been evacuated, the communication gear smashed and scattered, crumpled papers littering the floor. Not far away, the rattle of small arms fire and the metallic clank of tanks moving through the underbrush, pushing over small trees, reverberated in the morning light.

But one man remained behind, moving about gingerly, darting from one concealed position to another, avoiding movement that might attract attention. It was Jim Gatling, searching for his friend who had disappeared in the span of an instant. One moment, Ed kneeled over his blanket scrambling to gather his belongings; the next he had vanished. What happened? The two had spent the war together and neither would leave without the other. He had to be somewhere nearby.

Chapter 16

Retreat and Return

April 5, 1942

The Japanese had the defenders on the run. Gatling could clearly hear excited back and forth yelling through the bushes, the exchange of shots with random isolated Filipinos, explosions from tossed grenades, blood curdling screams; the last vestiges of resistance. Time was running out. Ed had to be somewhere around here.

Gatling nervously swiveled his head, studying the rolling, forested terrain. The enemy was advancing by the minute and the thought gnawed at him, for he knew they would arrive in no time. He gulped and wiped his brow.

Japanese artillery pieces continued their fire, but the projectiles now screamed overhead into the rear. The rattle of small arms fire up ahead died down as the few remaining Filipinos threw up their hands in surrender.

Forehead creased with worry, he crouched against the sandbagged wall of the abandoned command post. He shot a quick glimpse inside, seeing rats nosing through rubbish, then twisted to the left, cocking an ear toward the enemy, gauging their approach. He gulped again and stepped back.

Licking his lips, he gazed to the left, slightly downhill, toward the wide trail used for transporting supplies into the command post area. The trail was now almost empty, except for scattered stragglers limping to the rear. He watched for a moment and saw one step over something. He ran a few feet toward the trail for a closer look. It was a human body, all, right, maybe Ed. Gatling rose to full height and sprinted down the hill.

He found his friend lying in the trail, covered with fine dust kicked up by the fleeing men. He had taken a stiff blow to the side of the head, a giant red lump growing in size, but with no visible blood. Crouching, he lifted Ed's head and cradled it in a hand. Reaching down, he unscrewed the cap of his canteen and splashed water into his face. "Ed," he whispered, "Ed."

No response. He leaned forward and emptied the canteen onto his forehead, flung it aside, and spread the water with his fingers. "Eddie boy," he said in a louder voice.

Ed remained unconscious, gently breathing in and out. Gatling swallowed, feeling a tingle of fear rise up, knowing the Japanese were dangerously close. He could almost make out their individual voices. Rising up, he spotted a row of bushes move back and forth, men flickering behind. It was either head to the rear now or throw up his hands in surrender. In a split second, Gatling decided. He leaned forward, threw Ed's body over a shoulder, and ran down the trail, abandoning his rifle and canteen.

Jagged and uneven, a loose mixture of rocks and dirt, the trail slanted downhill to a stream tumbling through a narrow ravine choked with vegetation. Tendrils of long, thin vines hung down gray-streaked limestone canyon walls, large white flowers studding the upper portion of the north face where they could absorb the slanting rays of the afternoon sun. Gatling stopped at the stream at the bottom of the ravine, shallow and wide at that point, varying between six and eighteen inches deep and some twenty feet across. Distraught Filipino soldiers wearing khaki uniforms caked with mud sat on boulders or lay on the ground, their spirits broken.

"Can one of you guys give me a little help?" asked a frustrated Gatling as he turned to each side. "I've got to get this man to an aid station."

A few narrowed their eyes and looked up, but most didn't move. No one spoke.

"Please," he begged. His pleading voice raised an octave. "Just help me up the other side of the canyon. The Japs are coming."

One of them tossed down his rifle and rose up. Chin set in a stubborn line, he stepped forward. "All right, Lieutenant," he said in a half reluctant voice. The man walked over to Gatling and grabbed Ed's feet. "Let's go. You carry his head and I'll take his feet." Gatling grunted and waded out into the stream, the Filipino behind.

The Filipino soldier was much shorter than Gatling, by about eight inches. Scraggly, uncombed black hair covered his head, he hadn't shaved in days, and scraggly whiskers colored the sides of his brown face and chin.

The two trudged through the cold stream, swirling up dark mud, not caring about their soaked leather boots. On reaching the far side, they refused to pause, following the trail up hill and finally cresting the ravine. They set Ed down in the shade of a gargantuan hundred-foot tree, the sweet smell of frangipani tingeing the air. Both were winded by the climb and had to rest.

They crouched in the shade and took deep breaths, giving their bodies time to settle down. Ed slumbered, unconscious, the welt on his head as big as ever.

"You have a first aid kit?" asked the Filipino soldier. Gatling nodded as he reached into a canvas pouch on his belt. "I'll bandage up that head," he continued.

Gatling handed over a rolled up white bandage and a tiny glass jar of brown jelly-like ointment, and leaned back against the tree trunk. Edging over, the Filipino leaned over Ed, studying his head for broken skin.

"I don't see any breaks and that's good," he grunted. He smeared ointment from the jar onto the welt, put on a thick cotton dressing and wound a bandage around his head.

"There, that'll hold him," he muttered while backing away. He turned toward Gatling. "Let's get going."

"What do you mean?" Gatling asked in surprise. "I thought you were only going to the top of this hill."

"No, I changed my mind. I don't want to be captured by the Japs. If you'll let me, I'll come."

Gatling's tight expression relaxed into a grin. "Yeah," he replied, "you sure are welcome. Damn welcome."

The two jury-rigged a stretcher from two poles, blankets they found tossed beside the trail and ropes, then picked up their burden and resumed walking south, passing discarded rifles, helmets and other military gear scattered about. They paused for a breather every fifteen minutes, eventually veering toward the Coast Road, the same one Ed and Gatling had taken the week before. It was now jammed with vehicles and disorganized, frantic men, all fleeing the onrushing Japanese hoard.

Zero fighters screamed up and down the road several times each hour, scattering everyone behind vegetation and hilly ground to the sides while they strafed and bombed. They always got results, too; men unlucky enough to be caught in the open or within a vehicle. The injured stuffed inside ambulances and trucks were helpless, unable to dash outside in a split second, sitting ducks for the Japanese planes. They screamed and cried in agony as vehicles exploded, were riddled with machine gun fire or caught fire and burned.

The sight was horrific. A shaken Gatling gazed at the scene of mass confusion, flames shooting up, ammunition exploding, blood and body parts scattered willy-nilly. He let out a low groan and fat tears welled up in the corners of his eyes. "Oh, my good Lord!" he gasped in a choked voice. "I can't take Ed out there." A glazed look of despair spreading over his face, he turned toward his Filipino companion. "What are we gonna do?"

The Filipino soldier, also struck by the sight, answered in a clear, unwavering voice. "Let's you and me bring him back into the trees and let him rest in the shade. We all can use some shut-eye. We'll wait until nightfall when it's safe."

Gatling nodded, stunned. He had no ideas of his own. They lifted Ed off the ground and carried him into the jungle, stretching him out on a blanket. He was mumbling now, his utterances a jumble of incoherent pieces of sentences, but he seemed to be coming around. The two sat at his side and looked at each other.

"I never asked your name," said Gatling, reaching for a moist stick nestled among the weeds, soaked through like everything else. "Mine's Jim Gatling."

The Filipino nodded. Dark, proud eyes looked out from his sun-toughened, pockmarked face. "I'm Sergeant Armando Leuterio of the 43rd Regiment of the 41st Division. At your service, sir."

Gatling slipped a pocketknife from his front pocket and began whittling, shaving off smooth slivers of green bark. He had whittled for years, particularly when nervous or upset, always finding it calming. That's what he needed now—to settle down.

"Sergeant Leuterio," he said, concentrating on his work. "You speak pretty good English, so I guess I can talk straight. You figure to come along wherever we end up? If the Japs aren't stopped on Bataan, we might go all the way to Corregidor. You can come if you want. You've earned it."

"Yes," Leuterio nodded, "if you permit me, I will come." He glanced at Ed, who showed more signs of coming around. His eyes were open and his vacant gaze seemed to be clearing. Leuterio was pleased. "Captain," he said, "you're among friends."

Unable to focus, Ed blinked and rubbed fingers across his forehead. "Where am I?" he mumbled in a gravelly voice. "Do I know you?"

Gatling leaned forward and blurted, "Eddie boy, it's me, Jim Gatling." He was all smiles. "Sergeant Leuterio here helped carry you back. We're on the Coast Road now, waiting for nightfall."

Deep lines of concentration formed on Ed's brow. "What happened? Why'd you need to carry me?"

Leuterio answered. "You got hit on the head, sir. You were out for many hours."

"How'd I get hit?"

Leuterio glanced toward Gatling, who proceeded to answer. "I don't know how. I found you on the trail beneath our command post and hightailed it out of there. The Japs were right behind."

"Oh," muttered Ed, his memory hazy. He did, however, feel a rumbling sensation in his stomach, the hollow pang of hunger that had become a sad but normal part of everyday life. "You guys got anything to eat?"

Gatling flinched and shook his head. "Nope, haven't got a thing."

Leuterio reached into a canvas bag and pulled out a can of corned beef hash and another of diced tomatoes. He tossed them onto the blanket.

"Where'd you get those?" asked Gatling in surprise. "I haven't seen corned beef hash since February."

Leuterio grinned. "I found them on the trail. Must have been dropped. God is watching out for us."

"Yeah, well, bad luck for whoever lost it and good luck for us." Gatling shot up and began gathering sticks for a fire, intending to heat everything in a metal canteen cup. As he worked, gray clouds gathered overhead, darkening the sky. Muted light filtered through the thick jungle canopy. Soon, tremendous thunderclaps boomed in the heavens and raindrops pelted down, transforming the torn up road into a jumbled quagmire and drawing the three companions close together under a rubber poncho. As water dripped down, puddling in low depressions among shallow roots, the three ate their lukewarm rations, getting a bit of nutritious food into their stomachs in preparation for an unknown future.

Ed was now fully awake and aware of their plight, though a sharp, throbbing headache pounded away. As water dropping from the leaves slowed, he pulled off the poncho and gazed out, his eyes darting about the clearing. Deep jungle, closely packed vegetation of all colors surrounded the little group. A cacophony of sputtering engines and other noises on the road rumbled in the distance, muffled into background dullness by the curtain of jungle.

As he stared into the dampness, an annoying feeling gnawed at his mind. Perhaps the persistent throbbing had set him on edge or maybe it was the memory of something more fundamental, like losing his temper. All of a sudden, he remembered exactly what he had done.

Firing into the air in the midst of a headlong retreat was stupid, pure and simple. It showed little knowledge of the psychology of starving men on the verge of panic. What he had done was humiliating. Those were brave soldiers who had performed as well as they could—Ed Bannon was the one who hadn't measured up.

He drew his eyelids tight. Why did he do these things? Why did he try to inject himself where he wasn't wanted, losing self-control in the process? Unconsciously, he shook his head. He thought for a moment and remembered something from his Yuma days. Old timers would say if you fell from a horse, the best course of action was to get back on. He nodded. Perhaps heading back to fight the Japanese would be the right thing to do. Maybe this would put his mind at ease.

He tugged off the poncho and flung it away. Leuterio and Gatling, who had been dozing, woke up, startled. Ed shot them a penetrating stare. "You boys ready to head back?" he asked, his voice low but forceful, as if he wanted no argument. Both Leuterio and Gatling blinked in bewilderment.

A moment passed before Gatling responded. "The 41st Division is gone, evaporated. There's no use going back. Our line collapsed. It was a rout back there."

Ed narrowed his gaze. "I don't mean for us to go back to the same place," he said in a harsh, raw voice. "The 41st probably fell back a ways to set up another line. We'll join 'em there."

Taken aback, as he was responsible for saving Ed's life, Gatling hesitated a moment. Ed seemed to be showing no gratitude and was trying to push them into something hopelessly unrealistic. Anger rising, he pointed the sharp end of his whittled stick and spoke in a sharp voice. "Ed, listen. Everyone retreated into the jungle in total panic. We evacuated the command post and there was no plan to do anything. How can you set up an orderly line of defense under those conditions?"

Ed's face went grim. "There have to be men left. Besides, if we run out on the division we'd be nothing better than deserters."

"We aren't running out on anybody. There *is* no division."

Frowning, they exchanged glances for a long moment and looked away. Ed turned toward Leuterio. "Sergeant Leuterio, you're neutral in this. What do you think we should do?"

Leuterio scratched his head, uncomfortable at having to make a recommendation to two officers he barely knew. "Well," he said, "if there's anyone left in the 41st they're bound to be in bad shape. The Japs took the fight out of them." He gazed into their faces and added, "That's what happens when you starve men for three months."

"Okay, so most retreated," Ed said in a fit of temper. "Do we join what's left or do we fall back ourselves? We can retreat as far as Cabcaben, but everyone'll know what happened. You can figure what they'll think."

Gatling exploded. "Ed, you're putting Leuterio on the spot. Leave him alone." He waved the stick back and forth. "You're acting like a jerk, buddy boy. We're the ones who saved you from the Japs. You were good as dead back there. If we had left you, the Japs would have done you in with a bayonet."

Ed gulped in some air and stretched his legs, allowing himself a moment to think. "I'm obliged for that." With a pang, he bit into his lower lip until it throbbed like his pulse. He realized he was again being pushy and unreasonable. Kind of like what Hank, Barbara's brother, told him in Arizona after the accident. A fiery temper was something he had struggled with since youth.

Ed lowered his voice, ridding it of its steely edge. "Jim, this army needs to hold the Japs somewhere. Dang it, we need to fight them!"

His defenses beginning to subside, Gatling spoke severely, but in a quieter tone. "You make me damn mad sometimes," he blustered. "We're in this war together and all three of us should decide. Not one pushy guy who thinks he can boss everyone around. Hell," he said, gesturing toward Leuterio, "when you think about it, he's probably the best qualified infantryman here. But I still think the three of us should make up our minds together."

Ed took a deep breath. "Okay," he stammered in a matter-of-fact voice that sounded tired. "I'm sorry. I guess I talked too fast. Maybe I'm not even thinking straight. You two deserve better." He touched the side of his head and winced. "Tell you what. You two talk and figure something out. I don't even need to be involved. You know what I think. I'll go along with whatever you decide."

Leuterio and Gatling exchanged glances. Neither relished going back, for each remembered the pandemonium all too well. But withdrawing all the way to Cabcaben seemed out of the question. Allowing the Japanese to advance that far down the peninsula would mean the battle was over. They conversed in low tones, then Gatling nodded and turned.

"This is what we do," he announced. "Tonight we go south on the Coast Road a mile or so, then cut off. We'll join whatever defense line we come across. It could be the remnants of the 41st, that's the direction they were heading, or it could be some other unit. It doesn't matter. That sound okay?"

Ed shrugged. "I told you I'd do whatever you decided." He straightened. "So we leave at nightfall?"

Gatling nodded without speaking. Another hour or two of daylight remained. He leaned back against the the tree and closed his eyes, intending to catch a little more shut-eye. Leuterio patted Ed on the leg and said, "You sleep, too, Captain. You will soon need all your strength."

Ed gave a quick up and down movement of his head, but before closing his eyes, looked into the Filipino's face. He asked in a quiet voice, "Sergeant Leuterio, what was it like up front before you retreated? How bad was it?"

Leuterio, pictures of the disaster sharp-etched in his memory, rubbed a hand over stubble on his chin before answering. "It was terrible, sir, worse than anything before." He spoke in a low, wooden voice, eyes fixed straight ahead. "At first, we sat in our holes not thinking much about it, waiting for the shelling to stop. When the Jap artillery switched to incendiary shells, dry leaves and bamboo burst into flame and a few men even lit cigarettes on burning wood. It was a change from the monotony of the last month; we took it kind of light at first, but it kept getting worse."

Leuterio breathed rapidly as the images poured in. "The heat grew and grew, and everything began burning. Flames surrounded us and everyone started jumping out of foxholes. It was a choice between roasting to death or taking your chances. We fell back, but everywhere we went, shells rained down, killing more and more. It was no use to fight. Everyone was demoralized; the men, the officers. We all ran."

Leuterio sat silent for a moment and then turned to Ed, raw hurt glittering in his dark eyes. "Captain, I saw death take friends I had lived with since last year. I saw good men scattered into bits, arms and legs flying into trees; buddies sliced in half, blood spurting in all directions. All of us were starving and sick; we had reached our limit and could do no more."

His eyes remained on Ed for a moment, then he calmed and dropped hands to his side. His chest heaved up and down. "If I can fight the Japanese again, I will. I have seen what they do. The Japs are cruel and show no mercy."

He brought his legs up to his chin and leaned forward, deep in thought. A big drop of water splashed onto the back of his head, but he ignored it. After thirty seconds, he spoke in a low, rumbling voice. "We'll be moving tonight. Sleep while you can."

Impressed by Leuterio's heartfelt description of the one-sided battle, out of respect, Ed gave a quick nod but didn't move, refusing to speak. It became so quiet, the electric silence of the jungle seemed almost alive, as if it had become a living, breathing presence. He reflected on Leuterio's words, weighing them in his mind, and watched the Filipino lay back and lace fingers behind his head. But soon, Ed's stomach rumbled and his thoughts turned to more immediate concerns.

He wished for more food. Two cans among three hungry men meant nobody got enough. His empty stomach growled and his head continued to ache. His entire body seemed wracked by overall weakness. He reached up, running fingers against the gauze bandage wrapped around his head. No blood, but it felt tender. Sighing, he needed some sleep.

Crossing arms, he closed his eyes and tried to think of something far away, something pleasant to take his mind off this terrible place, this disgusting situation. He thought back to the good times he had with Barbara. How long had it been?

He couldn't remember. Having spent three months on Bataan, those days seemed in another lifetime; a fuzzy one at that. But those years were the best of his life.

Ed focused on those times, concentrating hard. He closed his eyes and imagined the scent of her hair. Barbara's face felt very near and, for a moment or two, her breath tickled his neck and he saw lips widen into a beautiful, seductive smile. Soon his mind glazed over and fingers relaxed at his side. He breathed softly in and out, fast asleep. Even after all this time, Barbara could still work her magic.

Chapter 17

Heading South

April 6, 1942

They headed to the road as the red ball of the sun drooped behind craggy ridgelines that shielded them from the high-spirited Japanese forces that had made significant gains that day. Besides shattering the 41st Division, they had stormed up the rugged, jungle-covered slope of Mount Samat, the highest point on the Filipino-American line, driving defenders away and planting the Rising Sun flag on its crest. The volcanic peak had offered observers an excellent location from which to identify Japanese targets and view the fall of artillery shells. Loss of the strategic high ground amounted to a severe kick in the teeth.

On the road, mobs of troops streamed rearward, joined by new groups pouring out of the jungle. Most were demoralized by the long campaign and the unstoppable, brutal attack. Men trudging south with bowed heads crowded the road, men who had tasted defeat and feared that the biting tang would linger long into the future.

The tiny band of three broke away after walking about two miles, angling east toward the center of the peninsula. As they disappeared into the jungle, other marchers barely looked up, figuring they had given up and were seeking shelter.

As the three curved around a copse of thick palms surrounded by bushes bristling with thorns, Leuterio, leading the way, warned, "Keep a sharp watch. If we surprise friendly troops, they might figure us for Japs." He ducked under a vine and pushed on, the other two nodding as they followed.

They trudged through the night, attempting to make as little noise as possible amid the silence of the jungle. Stopping at intervals for short breaks, they took a longer rest around 2 a.m. that would have been for a meal, had there been one to serve. Leuterio, always a man who rose to the occasion, dug down deep into a canvas pouch and produced a sack of dried coconut; enough for a small handful apiece. They dined in the jungle darkness, not daring to build a fire. After ninety minutes of light sleep, they slung on their gear and continued on, not stopping for several more hours.

As darkness faded into somber gray with the coming of sunrise, the landscape grew lighter by the minute. Rose-colored fingers of sunlight peered over the horizon, spectacular with pearl-gray clouds, and morning dawned with the faintest hint of damp fog hanging low on the land.

All of a sudden, Leuterio flung up a hand and motioned them to the side of the trail behind a thick flowering bush. Peering through leaves, they watched four Filipino soldiers maneuvering a 37mm antitank gun atop a short rise not far away; the first indication of resistance they had witnessed since yesterday morning. The gun pointed over a wide clearing toward an opening in the jungle, obviously where they expected enemy forces. A couple dozen others, they couldn't see how many, hacked away with entrenching tools at the stony surface atop steep rises on either side of the gun, making little headway in the hard earth. The entire ridge was punctuated with stunted trees and low underbrush.

"They can use a hand," commented Ed as he shaded his eyes. "They better get under cover by daybreak before a Jap plane spots them on that hill."

"Yes, sir," replied Leuterio, "but we better let them know we're here first."

Nodding, Gatling suggested, "Let's all three of us go out in the clear with rifles over our heads. We can yell out that we're Americans."

"Sounds good," nodded Ed. "Let's go."

The three walked into the open, yelling and waving rifles over their heads. Soldiers looked down and several scrambled for their rifles, but a husky voice yelled, "Don't fire; they're Americans!" They ascended the hill and joined the soldiers hacking away on top. Lieutenant Dominguez, in command, walked over.

"Well, I'll be," he said in surprise. "If it isn't Captain Bannon and Lieutenant Gatling. We had pretty much given you two up for dead."

They were as surprised as Dominguez. "We didn't figure we'd ever see you again, either," exclaimed Ed. He liked Dominguez, a man with a good sense of humor who, unlike Lieutenant Colonel Dohlman and too many other officers he had seen, demonstrated a passionate caring for his troops. Ed extended a warm hand to the exhausted-looking figure clothed in torn, mud spattered khakis. "Nice to see you again," he said.

Dominguez, who had caught only a few hours sleep over the past three days, shook his hand, as well as Gatling's. Turning to Leuterio he said, "And what's your name? I don't believe we've met."

"Sergeant Armando Leuterio, reporting for duty," he replied, snapping to attention. "I'm from the 43rd Regiment, but I don't know where any of them are."

"Just fall in with us, friend. You're welcome here." Dominguez turned to Ed. "How'd you know we were here?"

Ed shook his head. "We didn't. We just came this way figuring someone would be setting up some sort of defense. Whoever it was, we planned to join in."

Dominguez smiled. "Well, we need men," he said with a sweep of the arm. "We only have twenty-three. We can use more."

"That's all?" Ed exclaimed, tipping his helmet back. "You won't be able to hold out long. Is there a line further back?"

"Sort of. A line is being surveyed a mile or so to the rear, but there have been many desertions. Our orders are to hold the Japs as long as we can."

"I see," stated Ed in a low voice while, at the same time, casting a furtive sideways glance at Gatling. "What do you want us to do?"

Dominguez swiveled on his heel to judge the progress on the hill. The men were widely scattered, though it was difficult to make some of them out within the underbrush. He turned back and faced Ed. "Just dig in where you can. This is a rocky, hard surface, but do your best."

He paused for a moment, watching the antitank gun crew cut branches from a tree and set them on either side of the gun's muzzle. Dominguez smiled. "We hope to surprise a few tanks with that thing." He took a step back. "Good luck, my friends."

Dominguez walked away toward the antitank gun, leaving the small group clustered on the brow of the hill. "Well, where do we set up?" asked Leuterio, looking at Ed.

Ed twisted as he scanned the surroundings. "Looks like men are needed right here. Let's move up a bit and dig in."

Gatling and Leuterio nodded and walked a few feet forward, angling to the right between two trees. The view was about one hundred yards to the immediate front, making it a good position. A trail wide enough for vehicles wound through the jungle on the far side of the clearing toward a gap on the right side of the hill, at which the Japanese would most likely center their attack. The Filipinos had concentrated most of their firepower in that area.

The immediate problem was the surface of the hill. It was hard packed, baked earth, almost flat except for outcroppings of dark gray limestone. Soldiers who had steadily chopped away with entrenching tools and bayonets for fifteen minutes were down only a few inches. Most had given up and were piling rocks into makeshift parapets.

The three newcomers found a six-inch depression filled with leaves between overhanging bushes, which all agreed was about the best they could hope for. The streaked limestone in front of the depression slanted down so steep that an enemy would have to use a ladder or cut places to wedge their feet. That, and the panoramic view, made it ideal.

"Let's get in and get comfortable," said Gatling as he stood at the edge of the depression dropping his gear onto the ground. "Maybe we can scrounge up something for breakfast."

Leuterio leaned his rifle against a tree and began looking for boulders to maneuver in front of the hole. "We better get things ready first, sir," he said as he worked. "The Japs may come sooner than we expect."

Gatling grunted. "I'll help with the rocks, don't worry. I'm gonna clean this stuff out of the hole first."

Ed and Leuterio found a number of bowling ball-sized stones nearby, skidding and rolling them in front of the position while Gatling scraped out leaves and other debris. They worked for about thirty minutes when two soldiers, each carrying a ration can, came up from the rear where they had prepared food over a campfire within the forest. Lieutenant Dominguez called out that breakfast was now being served.

"Wow, food!" enthused Gatling as he stood at the edge of the hole, his face covered with dirt and perspiration. "It's about time we had a meal."

They threw down whatever they had in their hands and ran to the two soldiers, who, smiling, were ladling three scoops of warm rice covered with watery salmon gravy onto plates. The gravy for all twenty-six men was made from three cans of salmon, all that remained in the cook's larder.

"Whatever happened to bacon and eggs?" grumbled Gatling as he waited in line. "What about hotcakes and hash brown potatoes?"

Ed chuckled. "Platefuls of everything are waiting inside the cargo holds of that mythical mile long convoy." He gazed at the food with a bland half-smile. "Rice and gravy are better than nothing, I guess, but it sure doesn't fill a belly."

The three men filled their mess kits and walked back to their hole and sat on the side, slumped over, mechanically eating their meager meal. No conversation ensued; the only sound the metallic clicking of forks striking against metal plates as they gazed across the clearing. The orange-colored slanting early morning sun shined against the jungle screen, making it contrast sharply with the lighter color of the gently waving meadow grass.

"The Japs don't know we're here," said Gatling as he slurped a spoonful of watery gravy, absent minded, expecting no response. "That's a point in our favor."

Ed and Leuterio continued eating small forkfuls, attempting to make the meal last as long as possible. After a couple minutes, Leuterio looked up and spoke. "The Japs'll be here soon. We better get ready."

"Keep your shirt on, Armando," said Ed, stirring the food on his plate. "Take your time eating. It may be a long while before you get another chance at a hot meal."

Leuterio sniffed, unwilling to take chances. He gave the Japanese credit as persistent fighters, never giving up, always pushing at the American-Filipino line. Shaking his head, he gobbled the remainder of his rice and climbed into the hole, pushing his rifle through an opening in the rock barricade, studying the jungle for signs of the enemy. The two Americans continued eating.

After a few minutes they wiped off their plates and walked to the back of the hole and squirmed in, joining Leuterio. About everyone was doing the same, with light chatter and laughs emerging from the widely scattered holes. Now there was nothing to do but wait. As the sun climbed on its axis, the pleasant clean warmth of morning burned away and became a palpable, searing presence that caused sweat to build and soak through the backs of their shirts.

After surveying the jungle for some ten minutes, Gatling mopped perspiration off his forehead with an old handkerchief and spoke to Ed in a low, solemn voice. "Ed, I've been thinking about this for a long time, though I don't like saying it."

"What's that?" asked Ed, practicing his aim by sighting his rifle at various points along the edge of the jungle.

"I know I've said it before, but it's been eating at me. It's that we've been abandoned, pure and simple. MacArthur promised reinforcements we never got; supplies didn't get through; no planes came to replace the ones shot down, and the nation left us out here to die. Why? I never thought our country would do this." He heaved a sigh. "I'm not the kind of guy that gives up easy and I've always hated sunshine patriots, but I sure never believed this could happen. Not to Americans, anyway."

Ed turned toward his friend. "My father warned me back in Arizona," he said. "He told me the government could be cold and heartless when it wanted to. It all boils down to international politics."

"International politics? We're Americans here; you think helping us would come first. Not stupid treaties with other countries."

Ed shrugged. "It's not like I agree with it, but you heard the president's speech on the radio a few weeks ago like I did. They're sending reinforcements to the British before they send them to the Pacific." He twisted his mouth and turned to the side to spit before continuing. "Can you believe it? We're saving British before American lives." He paused a moment. "It's a crazy world and a crazy war. Maybe we just don't know how bad things are everywhere else. Being sent to the Philippines put you and me in the wrong place at the wrong time."

"Well, it makes me ashamed," Gatling said with a frown. "Here we are, the most powerful nation in the world, and we let this happen. Our military is standing by doing nothing while we starve."

"I'm sure the army and navy are doing something," replied Ed. "They'd help if they could. Maybe the attack at Pearl Harbor did more damage than we know."

"You're a bighearted guy, Ed, giving them the benefit of the doubt, but face the facts; we're here, they're there, and they've left us to die. It makes me sick. I'll never see Becky again at this rate."

Ed shot Gatling a glance. "Now, don't talk like that. You'll see her again. We'll make it to Corregidor and hold out until summer, when reinforcements are bound to get through. We'll be safe there." Ed didn't believe his own words, but they sounded nice.

Gatling continued staring off through glazed eyes, his mouth tight and grim. "Yeah, sure. If that's true, why did the army get MacArthur out of here and leave us? That was one helluva thing. The army saves his butt and leaves ours in the wringer. Old 'Dugout Doug' will probably see out the rest of the war, but if I could get my hands on the man, I'd strangle him."

"I know," Ed said, his expression stilled and serious. "You haven't thought much of MacArthur for months. Remember when we saw him at Cabcaben Field? He sure talked big. Made it sound like help was around the corner." Ed paused and added, "But neither of us believed him, remember?"

"Yeah, we had our doubts, even then." Gatling laid down his gun and took a long swig from his canteen. He glanced up, wiped the handkerchief over the back of his neck and watched a hawk fly lazy circles in the clear sky. "I've been thinking about another thing, Ed." He paused for a moment, his expression hard and touched by sadness. "Holding up the Japs for long with only twenty-six men is a complete fantasy. Once they knock out the antitank gun they'll be able to pound the hell out of us. They'll kill everyone."

"I figure it that way, too. Maybe we can retreat into the jungle before the end."

Gatling's voice trailed off and his gaze shifted slightly upward, in a distracted sort of way. Ed faced him and peered into his eyes. He could see a strange light shining deep within them. "What is it you're getting at, anyway? There's something else . . . spill it."

"Well, Ed, it's this. If you, me and Leuterio get out with our skins, I want to go back to the Coast Road and head south. Let's catch a boat over to Corregidor." Gatling leaned forward. "Ed, this is it. When it's over, we go to Corregidor. That's the best thing. Agreed?"

Ed nodded. "Agreed," he said. "It looks like Bataan's getting ready to fall, anyhow. Besides, you came to this hill because of me. I suppose it's your turn now."

"Good," replied Gatling. He paused and gazed at a flock of white birds flying in the same direction as the hawk, rolling the tip of his tongue along the inside of his mouth. "I think we'll have to keep an eye out for military police, though," he said in an absent-minded way. "They've probably thrown up a cordon around Mariveles to keep people from hijacking boats."

Ed's mouth curved into a friendly smile.

"Yeah, they probably have, but let's take one problem at a time. Right now we have Jap infantry to worry about. Let's be ready."

* * *

The Filipinos and Americans spent all morning hunkered down so as to not attract the attention of Japanese observation planes and dive-bombers that became numerous in full daylight. The first Japanese ground troops, scouts from a larger body following behind, appeared shortly before noon, advancing slowly up the trail into the clearing, zigzagging tree to tree.

As they approached the hill, not aware of the danger, Filipino soldiers jumped out from behind bushes, grabbed them and quietly slit their throats. The Japanese soldiers, not expecting resistance, went down like limp rags. Wiping blood from their knives, the Filipinos dragged the bodies into the underbrush and tossed them where they couldn't be seen. Then silence resumed.

A short while later the metallic clank of metal tracks sounded and a large column of men and vehicles crowded the trail, two light tanks leading the way. As they passed beyond the edge of the jungle, the column stopped and one of the tanks and two squads of Japanese soldiers advanced.

Lieutenant Dominguez, wishing to disguise the position as long as possible, knew he could wait only moments, as the antitank gun would have to fire or risk discovery. As he watched the tank approach through field glasses, clanking ever closer, he shouted the order. "Fire!"

The gun barked and sent a high velocity projectile screaming toward the oncoming tank. It smashed through light armor plate just below the turret and exploded in a giant ball of flame. Shaken, the Japanese soldiers dropped to the ground and began firing wildly, the Filipinos and Americans opening up. The machine gun from the second Japanese tank began hammering at the hill followed by the boom of its main gun aimed at a machine gun nest set up above the road.

The high explosive shell burst on the slope of the hill off to the right, making a loud explosion but hurting no one. The Filipino gunners operating a water-cooled .30 caliber machine gun coolly aimed at a row of Japanese soldiers advancing from the woods, mowing them down like a scythe through stalks of corn. Firing short bursts to keep the barrel from overheating, they worked over the entire edge of the clearing, flinging back men firing from behind bushes and trees. Alarmed, many Japanese melted into the jungle, while others stayed where they were and continued pecking away with their small arms. Already, dozens had been killed or wounded.

"We're committed, so make your shots count!" shouted Ed as he squeezed off a round at a man kneeling behind a tree. Leuterio and Gatling barely heard him, as they madly worked the bolts of their own rifles and thrust in fresh clips of cartridges. The antitank gun boomed again, this time striking a glancing blow against the second tank's turret, the round ricocheting into a truck loaded with spare ammunition, igniting an impressive shower of fireworks and blasts that lasted for several minutes.

Japanese mortars, ignoring the confusion caused by the exploding truck, opened up on the hill, thumping explosions blossoming up and down as gunners fine tuned their aim. A few minutes later, satisfied that the rounds were on target, they fired for effect, forcing the defenders to dive for cover. The shells crashed down and made a great roaring murk of smoke and dust and flickering flames of bright red and orange. A short time later, Japanese dive-bombers appeared, making careful, accurate runs, dropping a combination of fragmentation and phosphorous bombs.

The planes did their utmost to obliterate resistance. The hill rocked and heaved from the bursts of bombs and mortar shells. Fragments hit the rocks and splattered pieces of steel all over the surface of the hill. The very trees seemed to writhe in agony, big limbs crashed down or, half severed, swayed back and forth. Many were killed or wounded within minutes.

A low flying Zero made a slow strafing run toward the machine gun, knocking up puffs of dust from the ground as .50 caliber rounds pummeled everyone within the position, punching holes in the gun's water jacket and igniting ammunition in the ready box. An exploding mortar projectile wiped out the crew operating the antitank gun and an incoming tank round peeled back the gun's protective steel shield like a piece of paper, putting it out of action for good. Phosphorous bombs ignited fires in trees and brush all over the hill, turning it into a nightmare.

Though the defenders kept firing, the position quickly became untenable. Japanese aircraft strafed and dropped bombs relentlessly, and the mortar fire proved ceaseless. Lieutenant Dominguez, before he went down with a burning shell fragment in the leg, barked orders to abandon the hill. He knew it was the only thing left to do; stay and be slaughtered or run and, perhaps, fight another day.

Covered with grime and darkened from gunpowder, their rifle barrels heated to the point of almost jamming, Ed, Gatling and Leuterio exchanged understanding glances and edged out of the depression toward the back slope of the hill, in the direction of the Coast Road. Soon they disappeared into dense undergrowth, crunching away on a carpet of dead leaves, leaving behind men flinging up their hands in surrender, throwing themselves upon the mercy of the Japanese.

But the victors had no time for prisoners. Their mission was to aggressively pursue the enemy and bring the campaign to a rapid close, ahead of schedule, if possible. The Japanese mortars ceased fire and troops advanced up the hill, pausing only a few minutes before moving beyond toward other defensive works. Prisoners could be such a bother and Japanese troops on the point of the spear could not afford the luxury of detaching men to act as guards. Quick bayonet thrusts were so much more expedient.

The little band reached the Coast Road late that afternoon, the cacophony of traffic different from the night before, for a good reason: this portion of the road was now in enemy hands. Japanese troops and equipment crowded it from side-to-side, surging forward as fast as possible to maintain pressure on the crumbling defense. Armored vehicles, trucks, sedans, marching columns of well armed, well fed troops moved toward the front, knowing they had the enemy on the run. Complete victory was in their grasp. They could almost smell it.

"Now what do we do?" whispered an uneasy Ed as the three men peered at the procession from high up a mountain ridge. "The Japs beat us to the road."

Inches away, Gatling released the branch he had pulled aside. "I don't know," he said. "I suppose we can parallel the road, but the tangle of jungle will make it miserable. It'll be slow going."

Ed sat back and ran fingers through his hair. The bandage around his head remained, but was now a tattered, soiled mess. "Well, we can go back to the trail, look for friendly forces and head back with them."

"No, the trail's out," said Gatling. "I'm not going back. It's gotta be something else." He swiveled toward Leuterio, who had remained silent. "You know your way around here better than we do. What do you think?"

Leuterio shook his head. "The road is no good and neither is the trail, which leads straight into the Japs. There must be another way." He licked his lips and peered down at the Japanese. He watched for a short time and then lifted his eyes toward the coast and gazed out at the blue water of Manila Bay. He came up with an idea. "If we can get across the road we can head toward the shore and go back that way. There are no enemy forces there."

Both Ed and Gatling spread the bushes aside to look. "Yeah, it makes sense," muttered Ed, "and it's not too far away."

Gatling said, while still staring, "How are we supposed to cross the road? You think the Japs'll just let us?" He shook his head and backed away. "Doesn't seem too practical unless we can think of a safe way across."

Ed faced him. "Jim, you remember where that plane shot up the ambulance we were riding a week or so ago? The road took a bunch of sharp curves around there. If we find those curves, we can wait until there's a break in the action and run right across. They'll never see us."

Gatling leaned back on his elbows, considering the idea. "Any idea how far away those curves are?"

Leuterio answered. "Not far. I know this road. Only a half mile or so."

Gatling shrugged. "Okay, it's worth a shot. Let's go."

"There's not much daylight left," instructed Leuterio as he picked up his rifle. "Follow me." Hunched forward, he angled out of the clearing.

The three members of the band sat on rocks at the edge of a circular cove, dangling feet in the clear, cold water of Manila Bay. Thick trees, roots and vines prevented observation on three sides and a canopy of leaves stretched overhead, making their temporary haven snug and secure.

Crossing the road had proven surprisingly easy. Japanese traffic thinned out a great deal as darkness fell and they crossed long before even reaching the curves, taking advantage of lengthy gaps in the passing parade. The seashore wasn't much farther beyond and they headed right for it, down a precipitous ravine filled with a jumble of boulders and fallen trees.

Rations were now out of the question, for none remained. Each felt lethargic and weak, in the last stage of exhaustion. Now that they had reached safety, the idea of following the zigzag coast down the peninsula to Mariveles seemed a monolithic, unworkable undertaking, discouraging even to think about.

Gentle bayside waves licked the narrow beach, carrying with it a fresh salt tang that spoke of free lands unsullied by battle just out of reach. A half moon sat low on the horizon, glowing yellow and orange, and stars beamed down like a billion flashlights. It was pleasant after the travails of the day. They leaned back and spread their toes apart, quietly kicking the water, savoring the protective, quiet atmosphere.

But they could not help themselves. Within minutes, each succumbed to a tidal wave of exhaustion. Eyes sagged and they drifted off while gazing out over the placid bay. A few hours of sleep before setting off wouldn't matter.

CHAPTER 18

JOINING GARRISON CORREGIDOR

April 7-8, 1942

The three slept through the night, dead to the world. The dark nighttime hours passed in languid silence, a light, salt-scented breeze from the ocean and the gentle waves offering soothing accompaniment. They had discussed taking turns standing guard, but talk was as far as it got, as the need for sleep took over.

Early next morning, well before dawn, Ed woke with a start, hearing the metallic throb of an engine out in the water. A tangle of thick vegetation concealed the cove, but he was not of a mind to take chances. He ran to the edge of the water and crouched behind a boulder, staring out to sea.

"Jim, Armando!" he shouted in a loud whisper over his shoulder. "Wake up!" Neither responded, each asleep in the sand with his head in the crook of an arm. The chug-chug of the engine grew louder and they slept as if drugged, out to the world. He crawled back as fast as he could and roughly shook each man. "Wake up! There's a Jap boat out there!"

Startled, they looked up, eyes unfocussed and brains filled with cobwebs. Without thinking, they grabbed their gear and slid behind rocks. Low to the ground, the three watched through wide-open eyes as the throbbing sound came closer. It seemed just outside the cove.

As the boat's prow came into view, the apprehensive men flattened themselves, almost burrowing into the sand. The vessel was quite a bit farther out then they had earlier thought, but the clear night air made it sound like it was right on top of them. It was a two-level craft with twin funnels, a cannon mounted on the bow and machine guns manned and pointing out along the sides. It was moving slowly, probably to make the least amount of noise.

As it glided by, they noticed a flag atop a mast above the forward section of the vessel. The wind had died, however, and they couldn't make it out. But a moment later it freshened and the flag lifted away, billowing in the wind. It was red, white and blue . . . American!

Ed gasped and shot up. Waving hands and shouting, he ran into the bay. He waved his rifle overhead and splashed water into the air, but the boat took no notice and stayed on course.

Gatling and Leuterio rose up and deliriously hollered, waving their arms side to side. As the boat continued, not seeing them, they scrambled along the left side of the cove to the open beach beyond. By the time they got there, the craft had passed and was sailing away. Gatling took a chance and fired his Springfield into the air. Boom! Boom! Boom! Gunners manning the cannon at the rear of the craft trained binoculars in their direction. Others pointed a searchlight and, seeing they were Americans, swung around to pick them up. Ed, wading through the cove, joined the others.

"We're saved!" he said as he trudged onto the beach, boots and pants soaking wet. "We're gonna make it out of this godforsaken hell hole!"

Gatling and Leuterio stared with fixed, grateful eyes as the craft approached. Sailors lined the side and they exchanged waves. "Thank God, thank God," Gatling mumbled over and over.

The boat stopped and lowered a thirty-foot launch that sped toward them. Sailors had mounted a .30 caliber machine gun at the prow and one man maintained a careful watch of the beach while approaching.

"Ahoy there!" a voice from the launch shouted as the small band ran into waist deep water waving their helmets. "Climb aboard when we get closer. We'll swing around first."

The three men handed there rifles to sailors extending their hands over the side and were lifted off their feet and pulled in. Puffing from exertion and excitement, they gazed at their saviors, unable to speak at first. Ed coughed out water he had swallowed and wiped the back of a hand over rough stubble on his chin.

"I was getting to the point of thinking we weren't gonna make it out," he said while leaning against a gunwale. "You guys sure came along at the right time."

"We're glad we spotted you," said a man holding a Thompson sub-machine gun as they sped toward the ship. "We almost passed right by."

Another sailor spit into the water before speaking. "It's a good thing we were looking."

Caught off guard, Ed's voice rose in surprise. "You were looking? How'd you know we were there? *We* didn't even know where we were."

The sailor's mouth twitched with amusement. "Well, we weren't exactly looking for you three. We picked up two dozen men not far from here earlier tonight. They were surrounded by Japs and about done in, so we've been keeping an eye out. You were damn lucky."

"I think this is our last trip this far up the coast, too" said another. "This is all Jap territory now and we can do more good somewhere else."

Gatling grunted. "What's the name of your ship?" he asked as the launch slowed for its final approach.

"We're the *USS Mindanao*," said the sailor manning the machine gun. He swung it into the air and bent down to pick up a heaving line. "The *Mindanao's* a river gunboat. We were stationed in China before the war."

He threw the line up to a waiting sailor and the three soldiers climbed a rope ladder, aided by hands that hooked under their shoulders as they neared the deck. The sailors could barely disguise looks of amazement as they came aboard. They were absolutely filthy, covered with caked mud and powder stains, wearing tattered, torn uniforms, their bodies thin and emaciated. They didn't look like fighting men, but appearances can deceive, for they were. Each had even refused to leave his rifle behind.

A spry young lieutenant in a spotless uniform walked up moments later and addressed them. "You men hungry?" The three nodded, looking something like ravenous wolves. "Follow me. Our cooks have laid on the best grub around. You can have all you want."

The eighty sailors on the ship, well fed by Bataan standards, felt deep sympathy for the men they rescued, sharing clothes, providing food and offering their bunks. But the two dozen soldiers picked up earlier that night were in even worse condition than Ed's band. Surrounded by Japanese and pushed to the edge of the water, one of them had flagged down the passing *USS Mindanao* from a rowboat. When the launch arrived with a rescue party, the sailors found many of the stranded men suffering from acute malaria. Many could not even get out of their foxholes without assistance. It was quite an eye-opener for sailors who had never experienced and didn't quite understand how bad conditions were on Bataan.

The gunboat pulled beside Corregidor about mid-morning, an island separated from Bataan by only three miles but far removed from the deadly struggle. Though frequent bombing attacks and random shelling had taken place, the artillery batteries on Corregidor and the surrounding smaller islands were intact and in good order, with even more artillery pieces positioned and ready than before the war.

Ed and the others had eaten a voracious meal of beef stew and biscuits in the ship's galley, stuffing down several helpings apiece. After, they were shown to the crew quarters where they washed and slept atop mattresses for the first time in months. They drifted off as soon as their heads hit the pillows, not rousing until the rumble of the vessel's eight hundred and fifty horsepower engine throttled down as it neared the island. Line handlers tossed thick lines to men on Corregidor's north dock and the ship idled as passengers disembarked and walked the short distance to the mouth of Malinta Tunnel, where they were given hot coffee and ordered to report to the hospital.

"Where's the hospital?" asked Gatling, downing the coffee in one continuous gulp. Around him, clean-uniformed men streamed back and forth amid neat, tidy surroundings. The normalcy sure felt good.

A corporal jerked a thumb over his shoulder. "It's back in the tunnel," he said. "The hospital lateral cuts off to the right from the main tunnel about fifty yards back. You'll see it."

Gatling shook his head. "No, I'm not going in there. I feel fine and morning sunshine is just the ticket. I'll stay here."

A gruff redheaded sergeant, chewing an unlit cigar, looked up. "Sir, all evacuees gotta report to the hospital straight away. Them's orders. No choice about it."

Gatling's face lost a little color. He turned toward Ed. "Ed," he said in a lowered voice, "I don't like tunnels. I'm no coward, you know that, but I can't stand being cooped up underground." He cast a quick glance at the sergeant and turned back. "Can't you talk to him?"

Ed nodded and took a step forward. "Look," he said, glaring at the sergeant. "This man has been through hell over on Bataan. Give him a break, will 'ya? So what if he doesn't go to the hospital? Nobody'll know."

The sergeant removed the cigar from his mouth and looked up, responding in an even voice. "Sorry, sir, I'd like to oblige, but I gotta obey orders. If he doesn't go, we gotta throw him in the stockade. There's been a lot of disease carried over from Bataan and that's what the docs are looking for. Nothing personal."

Ed shrugged and faced Gatling. "Sounds reasonable to me. Guess we gotta go." He turned and walked toward the tunnel entrance. "Stay next to me," he said. Gatling grimaced and followed, hating every minute.

* * *

Prepared to handle one thousand patients at a time, Corregidor's well stocked hospital had been relocated in the campaign's early days from above ground into a lateral off the main tunnel. With reinforced concrete walls and overhead arches, Malinta Tunnel provided secure bombproof protection.

Hospital orderlies had stacked bunks three beds deep along each wall and piled boxes of supplies six feet tall in spaces between. Bare incandescent light bulbs hung down from the ceilings and huge blowers sucked out stale air and replaced it with fresh air several times each day. Though the tunnels shook when explosions occurred on the surface, sending down showers of fine dust from the ceiling, medical conditions were much better than on Bataan.

The band of men descended into the depths of the tunnel, threading their way through the plethora of crates and men, and found the entrance to the hospital. They stopped at a desk behind which a young enlisted orderly sat. He quirked an eyebrow and gave them a quick up and down look. "Let me guess, you just came over from Bataan," he observed with a thin-lipped smile. He leaned back and shouted over a shoulder, "We got more customers from Bataan."

A nurse in a starched khaki uniform walked out, her face stern and businesslike. "All right, you men," she instructed in a brusque tone. "Take seats on the bench and we'll see you in order."

Ed, staring at the nurse, jabbed Gatling's ribcage. "Look at her. That's the first woman we've seen since December." Mesmerized, he gazed as if photographing her with his eyes. A queer feeling welled up he hadn't felt in years. He plopped down on the bench, not taking his eyes off her until she walked behind an opaque cloth screen with the first patient.

"Ain't that something?" he mused. "We should have come to Corregidor a long time ago."

Gatling chuckled, forgetting he was deep underground. "You're a free man, Ed, but I'm not. I've got a woman waiting back in California." He chuckled again. "But it sure doesn't hurt to look."

The three sat at the end of the bench, behind the soldiers the *Mindanao* rescued who were in such bad physical condition. After about an hour, the nurse came out from behind the screen and motioned to Ed, indicating his turn. He got up and sauntered toward her, leaving his rifle and helmet behind.

"Sit up on the table," she ordered as he circled behind the screen. She aided him with a hand under the shoulder as he climbed up. "When's the last time you had any quinine?'

"Uh, I think it was about a month ago, but I can't remember," he replied, scratching his head.

"I'm giving you an inoculation, then. Roll up your sleeve, Captain. Either arm." The nurse wiped a spot on his upper arm with an alcohol swab, dropped it in a bowl, and reached for a glass syringe. She held it over a white ceramic bowl and squirted a stream of fluid out through the needle to ensure the absence of air bubbles. "Here I go," she said, leaning forward.

Struck by her closeness, Ed paid little attention to what she was doing, enthralled by her dainty, feminine movements. As the silvery needle neared, he blanched. "I don't like shots," he stammered.

She glanced up and smiled. "Don't worry, hon, it feels about like a mosquito bite." Ed clamped his eyes and scrunched up his nose. She gave the inoculation and dropped the used syringe on a cloth covered metal table. "There, that wasn't so bad, was it?" she said while patting his shoulder. "I'm sure you went through a lot worse on Bataan."

Ed was still stunned, not from the shot, so much, but from her presence. "Yeah, I guess," he replied, his brow high and rounded.

"The doctor's coming in just a minute," she said while tinkering with instruments spread out on the metal table. "You have anything you want him to look at?"

Ed didn't answer right away, a wave of weariness shooting through his body. He remembered his blow on the head, the bandage long gone. "Yeah, I think I do. I was hit in the head with a rifle two or three days ago. It was all swelled up and I was out for awhile, but I feel pretty much okay now."

The nurse gazed up with a look of concern. "Let me take a look before he gets here. Which side?"

"Right."

She stepped over and placed fingers on his head, ever so lightly, her touch penetrating into the scalp with some sort of mystical healing power. To Ed, it felt fine. Her dainty in-and-out breathing was near and it sounded caring and seductive at the same time. He didn't say anything, preferring that she remain as long as she wanted.

Too fast, she backed away. "There's a nasty welt and I wouldn't be surprised if you have a bit of a concussion, but there's no major external wound. You're a lucky man."

She turned as if to leave and Ed blurted out, "Say, what's your name? This is unfair; you know mine, but I don't know yours."

"It's Betsy," she said. "Lieutenant Betsy Harris, Army Nurse Corps."

Ed nodded. "Nice to meet you, Lieutenant Harris." He struggled for more words. "Um, where'd you come from, back in the states, I mean?"

"Chicago, Captain. The windy city. How about you?"

"Yuma, Arizona. On the Colorado River across from California."

"That's nice," she mumbled, not showing any interest in continuing the conversation. She stepped around the screen. "The doctor will be here soon," she called.

The physician entered a moment later, gave him a perfunctory examination and a clean bill of health, other than the normal malnourishment and lack of preventative medication seen in men from Bataan. He leaned against the edge of the table making notes on a clipboard.

"She gave you an inoculation, right?" The doctor didn't glance up as he wrote.

"Yep, the one for malaria, or tetanus or something." Ed swiveled his eyes, scanning the doctor and everything else in the room. "She gonna come back?"

The doctor glanced up and shook his head. He had been through this many times before, almost daily. "Let me give you some free advice, Captain Bannon. The nurses here are the only white women on the island. There are thousands of men and every one of them wants to see a nurse in private. Nurse Harris is sick and tired of it.

I know you haven't seen a woman in months, but you're barking up the wrong tree. She's not interested in you or anyone else."

Ed's gaze lowered, as did his voice. "I didn't think I was so obvious."

The doctor smiled and inclined his head. "Everyone around here is starved for female companionship. Don't worry about it. You're one of many."

Frustrated, Ed raised an eyebrow. This was the first time he had shown interest in a woman since Barbara. Lieutenant Harris had stamped out his feelings so quickly that he felt like the snuffed out flame of a candle. "Okay," he muttered, "but one more question."

"Go ahead, ask." The doctor looked down at the clipboard writing the final lines of his report.

"When do you guys have the next meal?"

The doctor finished and looked up. "We have two meals per day on Corregidor; one in the morning and the second in the evening. You missed breakfast, but can you wait until supper?"

"Yeah, I guess so. We just came in on the *Mindanao* and the navy served us one helluva good breakfast. Best I've had in a long time."

The doctor snapped the metal cap on his fountain pen and slid it into a pocket. "All right, Captain," he said. "Your next step is to report to operations and they'll give you something to do. Should be plenty if Bataan is falling."

"Okay," Ed replied as he slipped off the table and onto a chair to lace his boots. "See you later, Doc. Or, should I say I don't want to see you later because I don't want to get hit? Anyway, you know what I mean."

"Yeah, I do. So long, Captain. Good luck."

Ed walked to the long bench and waited for his friends to be examined, which didn't take long, as several physicians were at work. They walked together out to the main tunnel and several laterals over to the operations office and were given duties at Kindley Field, the island's short and often-bombed airstrip. Since both Ed and Gatling were air officers, the assignment made sense and they had no complaints.

They found their duties light, leaving plenty of time to loaf and recuperate from the trials of the past months. For this they were grateful, for once the Japanese consolidated their gains on Bataan, Corregidor would be in for a frightful beating.

The next evening after dinner they hiked to the top of Corregidor's highest peak to gaze at the tremendous explosions taking place across the channel in Mariveles. Several ammunition dumps were located there and engineers had drilled six partially completed tunnels into the solid rock of Mariveles Mountain, stuffed with air corps bombs, torpedo warheads, gasoline, artillery shells, black powder, small arms ammunition, and much more. Warehouses of dynamite also stood nearby.

An odd thing occurred just before the mass destruction was set to begin. A massive earthquake tore through Southern Bataan, causing the ground to shake and rocks to fall. Engineers started exploding the munitions minutes afterward, flames belching into the nighttime sky, transforming Mariveles into a shadowy semblance of hell itself, lighting the sky for miles around. Boulders and loose dirt plunged out of the heavens and explosions continued for hours, making Mariveles a site of pandemonium. Japanese artillery continued to drop random shells, causing everyone to push and shove, with explosions and shouting all around. The climax came when the *USS Canopus* erupted with a thunderous roar, jumping from the water in a sheet of flame and sinking to the bottom.

"It seems like the end of the world," observed Gatling with a grimace as they leaned against a rock outcropping, captivated. Ammunition dumps located near Hospital Number One joined in moments later, sending up the most spectacular fireworks display they had ever seen, with bursting shells and colored lights, painting the black sky with all the colors of the rainbow.

A grimfaced Leuterio stared in silence, sadly swinging his head back and forth, wondering what was to happen. Ed, sitting on a rock nearby, whispered aloud, "It looks like a volcano erupting. Ammo is shooting into the air everywhere I look." He cast his head down and turned away. "History is being made," he announced with disgust. "An unprepared and overconfident America is getting its comeuppance."

Ed rose up and dusted the back of his trousers. The color had drained from his face. "It's a 4th of July hell and I've seen enough," he ripped out in an irritated, distressed voice. "I'm heading back to the airfield."

He trudged away down the steep slope, leaving the two others behind staring at the spectacle in silence. The jagged trail leveled into a fairly easy downward grade after about five minutes and he thrust hands deep into pockets, lost in thought. "Corregidor is in for it next," he mumbled aloud. "We were evacuated from one hellhole to an island that's about to become one. Why oh why did I ever get involved in this?"

Yuma, Arizona

It had been a hard day of work in the Arizona desert, the sun beating down relentlessly, showing no mercy to the men handling picks and shovels. Railroad traffic increased as factories ramped up production and the military services rushed men and equipment to the West Coast, and upgraded trackage was needed to hurry trains along. Everyone worked at full speed, from the lowliest ticket clerk to the district supervisor.

The day had started at an early hour and Marshall Bannon trudged up the concrete sidewalk leading to his house with a slight bend to his frame and muscles aching, the hot April sun having sucked out a good deal of his energy. As he clicked open the front door, Marion sprang from the sofa, where she had been waiting most of the afternoon, twisting and straightening her handkerchief over and over, dabbing at her eyes.

"The mailman brought two letters from Eddy today," she announced in a jagged voice, her red eyes damp with moisture. "I've been waiting so we could read them together."

Stunned, Marshall's eyebrows shot up. He snatched the letters from her hand. Holding them in clammy fingers, he looked for postage marks indicating where they had been sent. "They were both mailed in Darwin, Australia, honey. Maybe he got out of the Philippines."

He reached for a pocketknife and positioned it to rip open the first envelope, but hesitated. "I gotta have a drink of water first." Setting the letters down, he walked into the kitchen and removed a glass container of cold water from the icebox, raising it to his lips. He used a glass when sharing the kitchen with his wife, but when she was out of eyesight, he always drank straight from the two-quart container. Ed did it, too, he thought to himself with a chuckle. He took two big gulps and slid it back into the icebox, wiped his mouth on a sleeve and returned to the living room.

He grinned bravely. "Okay, where were we?" He picked up the letters and opened them. "Let's sit, Marion," he said, beckoning to the sofa. "I'll read the one that's postmarked earlier first." He swung an arm over his wife's shoulders and began to read.

February 28, 1942

Dear Mom and Dad:

We're on the Bataan peninsula at a village called Cabcaben. It's a nice place with swaying palms, native huts, lots of vegetation and plenty to eat. We've built a new airfield here and are expecting reinforcements anytime. We're ready to take the sky back from the Japs once and for all when new planes arrive. You can imagine how excited we are.

Jim Gatling is fine. I know I told you about him many times, and we are good pals. I've become a pretty fair shot with a Springfield rifle, too. That will come into good use when Dad and I go hunting together after I get back. I'm looking forward to it, how much you don't know.

A submarine is taking out this letter tonight, so I better finish up. I don't know how long it will take to reach you, but it's bound to be awhile. We don't get the chance to write home often because there aren't many ships sailing into or out of here.

As you've probably guessed, I still miss Barbara. I saw her in my dreams the other night. She was on one side of a fence and I was on the other, and I couldn't get through to her. Someday I'll find my way through that fence.

Well, Mom and Dad, so long for now. Tell everyone I said hello.

Love,
Ed

Marshall gushed out a long, thoughtful sigh. He squeezed his wife tightly. "Ed still can't get Barbara out of his mind," he muttered in a clipped voice, swinging his head. Then he straightened. "Now I'll read the second one. It's dated about one week later."

March 5, 1942

Dear Mom and Dad:

Hello, everyone, greetings from the sunny Philippines. We continue to hold the Japanese back and seem to be doing a darn good job of it. We get plenty to eat, but I haven't had many milk shakes lately. You can buy me one when I get home. Sorry I haven't written more letters the past few months. We stay pretty busy at the airfield.

Have you read much about Corregidor Island? The place bristles with cannons and tunnels and is impregnable to anything the Japs throw at it. Huge mortars from there fired on the Japs during one of our battles on Bataan and it was sure a sight to see. Blasted them right and left. We can hold out for a long time. People call Corregidor the "Gibraltar of the Pacific."

I was thinking about when we used to live in that boxcar when I was a kid. Remember when Barbara lived with us? I have good memories from those days. Not to take anything away from Yuma, though. That's home and I can't wait to come back. I think I want to finish my last years of college, too.

Well, I have to get this letter posted or it won't get out. I hope to see you soon and, Dad, keep those trains moving, especially the ones headed west!

Love,
Ed

Marshall clenched his teeth and Marion dabbed at her eyes. She turned toward him. "He's not in Australia, is he?" she asked.

"No, he's still in the Philippines, where he's been stuck since the war broke out. I sure hope those reinforcements got through."

"Have you heard anything about it?"

He shook his head. "Oh, the government says they're doing all they can, but I don't know." He cast his eyes up. "Ed says he's become a good shot with a rifle. If they had planes to fly, I doubt he'd be fooling around with a Springfield. Something's got to be wrong over there."

An icy shiver coursed down Marion's spine. She lifted a hand to her cheek. "Oh, my Eddy," she mumbled.

Marshall took pity on his wife, disliking seeing her so sad. "Marion," he said, "the president is a good man—I know he'd send planes to the Philippines if it was possible."

Her eyebrows shot up. "The president's a good man? I thought you didn't like President Roosevelt. You've ranted and raved about him for years."

Marshall's face reddened. "Well, I changed my mind. I was wrong, he was right. I stood with those America-Firsters and Republican isolationists before the war, but I won't have anything to do with 'em anymore. I'm backing this war one hundred percent. Hell, we have a boy in it."

"I guess being able to change your mind is one of the things this war's about." Marion spoke in a soft, distracted voice, for her husband's political beliefs were far from uppermost in her mind. The fate of her son occupied that position. "Honey, do you think there'll be another letter?"

Marshall removed his arm from over her shoulder and straightened, feeling the throbbing effects of the long day of backbreaking labor. "I don't know," he said, "I'd like to think so, but I just don't know."

He moved his shoulder muscles up and down for a moment, then leaned over and kissed his wife, understanding the deep and unique love a mother feels for an only child. "Ed's a good boy. He'll write if he can," he said with a warm smile. He leaned back with an air of forced pleasure. Then he surprised her by quickly leaning forward and brushing a kiss across her forehead. "I love you," he said, "I really do. And I know Ed'll get back, too. We just need to have confidence."

Marion returned the kiss, enchantment touching her lips. Marshall could be a hard, opinionated man, but he was a softhearted teddy bear inside. He'd been drawing closer to her, showing his inner love, more and more all year. Maybe it was the increased tempo of work on the railroad, which required him to spend more hours away than ever before. Or maybe he was trying to prepare for the loss of their son, which she knew would be devastating. He had always been a proud, understanding father, doting on Ed and giving him every opportunity. Saving money to send him to college began the day Ed was born and never stopped, though it slowed considerably during the depression.

But the possibility of their son's not returning was something she didn't care to think about. She put it out of her mind, knowing they would have to take one day at a time. If that bridge had to be crossed, they would do it, but, meanwhile, there was nothing that could be done. The best method of coping was to go on, to think positive.

Marion steeled herself, putting on a cheerful face. "I've got dinner on the stove," she said. "Tonight it's spaghetti and meatballs, rennet custard for dessert."

"That sounds fine, dear. Let's eat. I'm starving!" Marshall rose from the sofa, extending a helping hand to Marion, and stepped toward the kitchen. But before Marion left, she bent down and slipped the letters into the front pocket of her housedress. If this was the closest she could be to her boy, so be it.

"Let's do something together after dinner," she said while walking to the stove. "How about we put the radio on the window sill and listen from out back in the yard. It's a nice evening and we can sit together on the swing while we listen."

Marshall sat at the table, reached for a slice of bread and spread butter on it. "Anything good on the radio tonight?" He bit into the bread and waited for her response.

"There's one program I've been listening to on Monday nights that's pretty good. They do radio versions of movies. We don't get to go out much and this is sort of fun."

Marshall finished off the bread by popping the last corner into his mouth. "What movie are they doing tonight?"

Marion shook her head while carrying a bowlful of spaghetti to the table. The spicy, garlicky aroma of the spaghetti's marinara sauce curled toward the ceiling and filled the room. She made the sauce from homegrown Roma tomatoes she grew and canned herself. "I can't remember the name of it, but I think it's a musical. Something that was out in the last year or two. It might be good."

"Okay," he said. "Dinner and the radio. Not bad." The two commenced piling spaghetti onto their plates. As he reached forward to replace the spoon in the spaghetti bowl, Marshall said in a cheerful voice, "You say tomato and I say tomahto, but we both say spaghetti." He laughed aloud, a lighthearted chuckle that shot through the room.

"That's it!" Marion exclaimed. "They're doing a Fred Astaire movie tonight, with singing and such. That's the one I was trying to think of!"

Marshall was busy winding long strands of spaghetti around a fork and bringing it up to his mouth. He nodded and winked an eye. Marion winked back. Both knew that getting immersed in a light-hearted sixty minute radio drama would help turn their minds from a tragic eventuality neither wished to think about.

Chapter 19

Corregidor Under Siege

April 1942

Bataan surrendered early April 9th after a stubborn blood-soaked defense marked by desperation and immense courage. The angry crack of guns gradually subsided as groups of disheveled, starving men assembled in Mariveles and Cabcaben to begin the long sixty-mile trek to the railhead at San Fernando and from there by rail to the Camp O'Donnell prisoner of war camp.

The Japanese had thrown together a plan for transporting the Americans and Filipinos by truck, but it fell apart quickly, for they had assumed a much smaller body of defenders. Instead, guards at the assembly areas looted prisoners of their valuables and shoved them forward to make the journey on foot. They executed on the spot anyone found with war souvenirs or Japanese money.

Prisoner treatment varied widely, with a minority jammed into motor vehicles for an uncomfortable but safe trip to the railhead. Cruel guards served up harsh brutality and torture to others. Many received no food and little water during the long march, with captives forced to stand for hours in the open with no purpose other than to blast them in the searing tropical sun. Sympathetic Filipinos alongside the road offered food and water from outstretched hands, but if a guard spotted it, the prisoner and the Filipino were frequently beaten or killed.

Some marchers had the water in their canteens poured onto the ground by the Japanese just to be cruel. Guards shot those who lagged behind or lunged toward pools of stagnant water. To conserve ammunition, use of the bayonet was all too common.

Upon reaching the railhead, the exhausted soldiers were forced into boxcars in groups numbering more than one hundred, though the cars had been designed to hold no more than forty. The cars were packed so full that men could not sit. This caused more to die of heat exhaustion and suffocation.

The trek resulted in over 11,000 deaths and became known throughout the world as the "Bataan Death March." When word spread among the American public, the Japanese were widely denounced and the affair became a popular rallying cry. Everyone considered it one of the blackest events in American military history.

Japanese forces wasted little time bringing up artillery to fire at Corregidor. A battery of 75mm cannons moved out in clear view on the side of Mariveles Mountain within hours of the surrender and started banging away at the big guns nearest the Bataan shore. Taking the fire in stride, crews manning 155mm artillery at Corregidor's Battery Kysor took careful aim and opened a devastating return fire. Explosions blossomed upward and, within minutes, silenced the Japanese threat.

But Lieutenant General Jonathon Wainwright, commanding officer of the forces in the Philippines, called a halt to any further counter-battery fire while visiting the artillery's command center. Worried that stray shots would harm friendly troops marching off the peninsula, he ordered firing from Corregidor to cease. Many officers disagreed, often vociferously.

"Sir, this is our best chance to destroy enemy artillery before they dig in," argued Major General George Moore, commander of the local defenses. "If we wait, they'll be able to fire at will, whittling down our ability to hold out."

Wainwright slumped into a wooden chair and rubbed fingers through stubble on his chin. A thirty-five year army veteran who had earned a reputation on Bataan as a hard fighter, he was a lean, taciturn man who believed in leading by personal example. He took pride in caring for his men, blocking out time each day to visit units around the island, even venturing across the channel to Bataan on several occasions. MacArthur had visited Bataan only once.

After pondering a moment, Wainwright shook his head. "I've been a soldier for years," he said, "and I don't like it, but we can't risk harming our own troops. The needs of humanity are above our own."

Moore, standing with a wooden pointer before a map of the Bataan shoreline, sucked in his breath. He chose his next words carefully. "Sir, we've identified precise locations of enemy targets and stand ready to open fire. This is our chance to give the Japs a taste of the hell they deserve." He stared into his eyes. "I urge you to reconsider."

Wainwright, having made up his mind, rose up and gave a quick shake of the head. "No, General, the order stands. Hold your fire for three days. At the end of that time you can give them everything you've got."

"But, General Wainwright . . . ."

"Can it, George, the matter's closed," snapped Wainwright as he walked toward the door. "We'll hold our fire."

The artillery officers in the command center rolled their eyes in disbelief, but remained politely silent until Wainwright turned a corner, out of hearing distance. Then uproar erupted. Eager to tear into the Japanese, they complained loudly, some of the harshest words coming from Colonel Ronald Berman, feisty commander of Fort Frank, one of the bay's smaller fortifications.

"Goddamn it!" he fumed, pounding a fist into his hand. "Now's the time to hit 'em hard, before they get under protection. My Battery Craighill can blow hell out of 'em." Berman paced back and forth, trying to dissipate his fury.

"Haven't the brass hats learned anything?" shouted another. "They've pulled the same boner over and over; waiting too long, being overly cautious, prohibiting us from firing when we should. We now have perfect targets. How are we supposed to win this war?"

General Moore slapped the pointer against the wall and scowled at the men. "Settle down, gentlemen, settle down," he cautioned. "We've no choice but to obey orders, even if we don't like them. Besides, American lives may very well be saved."

"But General," pleaded Berman, "what if we know the *exact* location of enemy batteries? We can't just leave them alone." He crossed his arms and gazed in despair. "It's an open invitation for them to plaster us."

"I'll not argue with anybody. The orders are clear," said Moore, advancing a step. "But I will do this. I'll talk to General Wainwright tonight and clarify what he'll allow us to do. Maybe I can get him to let up a little."

Berman nodded vigorously, his unruly hair flying up and down. "We're counting on you, sir. We've got to fire back!"

Moore nodded, placed the pointer on a desk and walked out, followed by two aides. The group gradually dispersed, some, like Berman, transiting by boat to another island, others reporting to the various batteries dotting Corregidor's rugged shore.

The two generals met together that evening over cigars outside Malinta Tunnel. It took some convincing, but Wainwright finally agreed to permit batteries to fire on definitely located enemy positions, but he refused to allow searching or adjustment fire. He had observed Japanese batteries setting up in ravines and gullies on Bataan and feared the growing threat. Some were locating in landscape folds near Hospital Number Two, thus offering well protected positions immune from the flat trajectories of the majority of Corregidor's twenty-three batteries. Hundreds of helpless American and Filipino hospital patients remained in danger for weeks.

Kindley Field, a 600-foot earth airstrip running at an angle on the tail of the island, had been designed for light observation aircraft. After the siege began, it came in for regular pounding from Japanese artillery and bombers, becoming a gruesome ruin of coughed up dirt and rocks. Aircraft hangers and other structures had been transformed into burned out, twisted skeletons.

As members of the operations staff, Ed and Gatling had been charged with the responsibility of keeping the field operational on nights when aircraft flew in from the south carrying vital messages or medical supplies. Sometimes they carried off government officials or military officers, but other items, like personnel rosters and official records, most often took precedence.

Besides offering few ground facilities, Kindley Field's short airstrip dictated that only light, nimble aircraft could use the field. Heavily armed P-40's were out of the question, since they required a much longer runway. The smaller and lighter P-35's were possible, but unarmed observation or light civilian aircraft were best. Both Ed and Gatling became experts at operating a bulldozer in short order, smoothing out and clearing the churned runway before planes arrived for a brief visit before refueling and again taking to the sky. Air operations occurred only during the darkest night hours and, as the weeks passed, became more and more dangerous, with Japanese artillery zeroed in on the field, ready to fire at a moments notice.

One pilot, a civilian from New Mexico who had flown before the war for an American mining company, made numerous trips in a slow two seat biplane trainer between Cebu and Corregidor, flying in medicines, mostly novocaine, quinine and vitamin concentrates that were running low. Bob Cabral, a leather-faced 28-year-old who grew up around the copper mines of Silver City and Lordsburg, New Mexico, found the journey increasingly dangerous as the siege continued. Japanese combat patrols searched likely air corridors, forcing him to fly roundabout routes at a variety of altitudes through murk and clouds, always in the worst of conditions.

One dark night he circled the island and made a quick landing on Kindley Field, cutting the engine as soon as the plane touched down. Men ran out and pushed it into a nearby revetment, a thick canvas tarp stretched over the top permitting mechanics to use lanterns without detection. They refueled and made adjustments to the engine, preparing it for a safe return flight. The process took about thirty minutes. After handing out candy bars to the ground crew, Cabral drew Ed to a corner, explaining that his shuttle flights were coming to an end.

"I'm living on borrowed time," he said while leaning against a wall massaging muscles in his legs. "The Japs are on to what I'm doing and they're out looking. They'll get me one of these nights."

"You're about our last link to the outside," replied Ed, taking a miniscule bite of a Hershey chocolate bar, intending to make it last as long as possible. "This your last trip or are you gonna try it one more time?"

Cabral pointed toward a container of water on a nearby crate. "Just a second, let me get a drink," he said. After gulping several mouthfuls, he wiped his mouth and answered. "No, I think I'll try it once more, but that'll be it. Like I said, it's too dangerous."

Cabral scanned the scene within the revetment. Under the yellow glow of a gasoline lantern, three mechanics worked on the plane, two fussing over the engine and a third pumping fuel. A shower of shells exploded in the background on the far side of the island, leaving Kindley Field in relative security. The racket prevented Cabral's voice from carrying far and made it a good time for a private conversation. He sidled to Ed's side and spoke into his ear.

"Look, Ed," he whispered, "you've been through hell during this campaign and I'm willing to get you out of here." He raised up and scanned everyone inside the revetment to ensure his words remained absolutely private, for he didn't want it to become common knowledge. Satisfied, he continued. "I'll squeeze you into the plane on my next trip and we'll both get out of here. What do you say?"

Ed couldn't believe his good fortune. The eleven thousand men and women on Corregidor had given up hope of being rescued and escape seemed out of the question. But now, out of everyone, he had been singled out. What luck! His response was immediate.

"Yeah, I'll go," he snapped. "I'd be a crazy fool if I didn't. But the extra weight'll mean you'll never make Cebu." Ed swallowed hard. "Getting out of here would mean everything, but I don't see how you can do it. Besides, if I got out, I'd be arrested as a deserter and thrown behind bars."

Cabral replied with a dismissive wave of a hand. "You won't be a deserter, so don't worry about that. I got it in writing a month ago that I could bring out whoever I wanted on my last trip. That'll be you." Cabral grinned and continued. "As for the actual flight, I've got it all figured. Here's what we do." He proceeded to lay it out. On his next trip, the plane would be refueled as fast as possible before taking off. Ed would climb into the forward flying cockpit, where student pilots once sat, amid canvas sacks of official reports and outgoing mail always stored inside. "We'll fly to Palayan instead of Cebu," Cabral explained. "It's closer and we can land on a dirt strip there. A Filipino buddy told me his family will hide us long enough to get out. All we need is for the Japs to cooperate by not shooting us down on the way."

Ed's brows flickered a little. "Might work," he said softly. Stroking his chin, he was still hardly able to believe his good fortune. "But, Bob, how'd you pick me out of the pack of people on this island? I'm one guy among thousands."

Cabral smiled. "I thought about it a lot," he said. "I didn't want it to be some no-account colonel with political pull, so I had to come up with something. What I decided made me settle on you."

"What was it?"

"You're a pilot and a couple weeks ago you told me about your first plane. Remember? It was a Lincoln Standard." Cabral's lips spread into a grin. "That was my first plane, too, and I've got great memories of hauling passengers and cargo in it. I had to do something to choose one man over another and that's the way I did it. There isn't a rational way to make a decision like this, when you think about it."

Ed's eyebrows shot up. Owning the same plane was pure luck. Little did Cabral know that he had cracked up his Lincoln Standard in 1940, killing his future wife in the process. Something good coming out of that tragedy was almost too much. He remained speechless for a moment but then his face took on an expression of agony. "There's one more thing," he stammered. "It'll be hard to leave my buddies behind. It's almost like we've become members of the same family."

"Well, it's up to you," shrugged Cabral. "You have a couple of days to think it over. If you want to go, be ready. It'll be your only chance. I can always take someone else."

Ed nodded with a taut jerk of the head. "Okay, fair enough." At that moment, the chief mechanic glanced up, wiped his greasy hands on a rag, and shouted that the plane was ready. It was only a matter of time until the Japanese sent a few rounds at the field, so it was prudent to depart as fast as possible. Ed and Cabral shook hands and both sauntered toward the aircraft. Cabral climbed into the rear pilot's seat and pulled on his leather helmet and goggles. "So long," he called to everyone gathered around.

Within minutes, they positioned the aircraft at the end of the strip and he zoomed off, avoiding by a hair a jumble of rocks jutting up from the bay on the far side. Wriggling his wings, he disappeared into the black night almost immediately, the steady throb of the engine vanishing, replaced by the staccato report of artillery and the sound of waves lapping against the rocky shore.

"Come on, let's get that medicine to the hospital," Ed ordered as they watched. "And write your letters over the next day or two. His next trip is the last one."

Japanese bombing and shelling caused light casualties during the siege's first weeks. Most of the pre-war surface buildings had been long abandoned, from the huge two story concrete barracks to the hospital and post exchange. The enemy bombarded the island with an array of over two hundred large artillery pieces, supplemented by multiple daily air attacks, and Corregidor's garrison had moved underground as much as possible. Morale sagged over the weeks, but considering the hopeless situation, spirits remained remarkably high.

Most of the American batteries facing the Bataan shoreline were destroyed by the middle of the month, but accurate antiaircraft fire forced Japanese planes to fly above 24,000 feet, where bombing was less precise. Determined to eliminate the threat, the Japanese high command instructed spotters on the relocated observation balloon, dubbed "Peeping Tom" by the Americans, to pinpoint the location of the antiaircraft positions. The observers performed a fine tooth study of the island and passed along their findings. Japanese artillery opened up and obliterated the antiaircraft batteries, ending the menace for good. Attacking planes now flew lower and lower, ranging up and down the island, strafing, bombing and destroying at will.

A pivotal point came in late April when the Japanese opened up with enormous 240mm howitzers, enabling them to fire huge plunging shells with devastating accuracy from positions safe from American return fire. Many of the soldiers in the Corregidor garrison came to believe they were living on a giant bulls-eye.

Ed, Gatling and Leuterio spent many daylight hours huddling inside Corregidor's cavernous Malinta Tunnel, constructed by Army engineers ten years before. Reinforced with tough concrete beneath a minimum of seventy feet of solid rock, the tunnel offered welcome security, albeit amid a hot, fly infested, foul smelling environment. They debated whether the tunnel would stand up to direct pounding from the five hundred pound shells hurled by the 240mm howitzers, but though the tunnel trembled and rock dust drifted down from the ceiling, it held.

The many soldiers taking shelter there huddled against boxes of food and ammunition stacked along the sides to a height of six feet. Some never left Malinta Tunnel's safety and were treated with contempt by those manning fixed artillery emplacements or beach defenses. A few broke down, becoming furtive, haggard creatures with no military value.

Of the three fugitives from Bataan, Gatling had the most trouble adapting. He found the artillery fire a persistent irritation, one that blasted away at his frazzled nerves, as steady as salt water corroding bare metal. Pauses in the bombardment came less frequently as the siege progressed, with the attacks becoming more or less continuous. Gatling reverted to his normal, jovial self during periods in which the shelling slacked off, but when the attacks resumed, he curled up against a tunnel wall and mumbled to himself, praying with all his might to be almost anywhere else. Within minutes, his eyes bulged and his hair dripped with perspiration.

A favorite activity during the slack times was exploring old buildings in search of abandoned valuables. Late one afternoon, Leuterio and Ed left Malinta Tunnel and wandered to the rubble of the post exchange in search of containers of food passed over by earlier scavengers. As they crossed once heavily wooded, lush terrain that had been transformed into an empty moonscape, they looked up as an aircraft with a peculiar, deep-throated hum droned overhead.

"Plane upstairs!" exclaimed Leuterio as he spied the lumbering craft emerge from a billowy white cloud into clear blue sky. The two raced to the nearest cover, a jagged crater from an artillery shell explosion, stretched out and craned up their necks. The plane flew at a high altitude and did not pose an imminent threat. They rose to a crouch, squinted and gave it closer scrutiny.

"I can't believe it," whispered Ed. He balled his hands into fists and rubbed his eyes, and looked again. "That plane's a B-17 Flying Fortress. There's American insignia on each wing."

They scrambled out of the crater, whooping and hollering. Nearby, other soldiers poked heads out of holes and looked at them with curiosity. "That's an American plane!" Ed hollered through hands cupped around his mouth. The others turned and gawked upward. Leuterio danced a little jig in the open, his happy enthusiasm bubbling over. Ed joined in and the two danced around in circles, hands on their hips, collapsing to the ground some minutes later, laughing wildly. All thoughts of visiting the exchange vanished.

"Let's go back to the tunnel and spread the word," proposed Ed. He picked himself up and ran back, zigzagging around the protective sandbag barricades at the tunnel entrance, on the lookout for Gatling. He spotted him against a wall with several others, crouched over throwing dice, wagering money that couldn't be spent anywhere else. "We saw American planes up there; bombers," Ed said in an excited voice as he pulled Gatling up by the collar. "They're here to blast hell out of the Japs."

Gatling gave off a thin smile. "Sure," he replied.

"No, really. They're American. I spotted them myself."

Gatling shook his head with disgust. "Ed, you must be seeing things. There's been nothing but Jap planes around for weeks. Where the hell would we get bombers?"

"I saw a B-17," said Ed, "flying at about 20,000 feet. It probably came in from Mindanao."

"Yeah, and jackrabbits have antlers." Gatling turned back to the game and spoke through the side of his mouth. "I've got a hot streak going, Ed. I gotta keep playing." He threw the dice, the cubes bouncing against the gray concrete and tumbling over several times before rolling to a halt. One showed five spots and the other two.

"Craps!" exclaimed Gatling, jerking his head to the side. The other players laughed and guffawed, for the score meant Gatling lost all his bets. Shaking his head in disappointment, he spun around. "Eddy boy, no offense, but you're bad luck right now. Why don't you and Leuterio go back outside and look for more planes." He flicked fingers toward the tunnel entrance. "Go on, now." Wearing sheepish expressions, the two left.

It wasn't announced until two days later, but American bombers had indeed flown over Corregidor that day, on their way to Clark Field to bomb Japanese planes. Ten B-25 medium and three B-17 heavy bombers had flown up from Australia and landed at Del Monte Field in Mindanao to bomb enemy shipping and shore facilities. The B-25s concentrated on targets near Mindanao while the B-17s flew the eight hundred mile round trip to Luzon, catching numerous enemy planes asleep on the ground.

Many weeks earlier, American commanders had conceived the plan of using the striking force to create confusion in enemy ranks to allow blockade-runners laden with food and medicine from the supply base at Cebu to run to Bataan. Unfortunately, by the time the raid occurred, both Bataan and the supply base had fallen. Air commanders went ahead with the plan anyway, but it amounted only to a pinprick that proved nothing more than a minor annoyance to the Japanese. No help got through to the beleaguered Corregidor defenders. Submarines and two seaplanes arrived to evacuate nurses and other key personnel a few days later, but nothing occurred to turn matters around.

Chapter 20

Evacuation

Late April-May 2, 1942

April 29th, Emperor Hirohito's birthday, proved the worst day yet. Japanese officers "celebrated" by pummeling Corregidor with thousands of artillery shells at a rate faster than ever before. The pounding began at 7:25 a.m. and averaged hundreds of shells per hour, supplemented by over one hundred tons of aerial bombs in the course of the day. By mid-morning, fires blazed all over the island and smoke plumes towered thousands of feet from gasoline ruptures at Kindley Field. Shells blasted and burned nearly every building remaining above ground, denuded the island of foliage, destroyed barbed wire entanglements, and exploded numerous ammunition dumps.

The three Bataan veterans huddled within the moisture-lined gloom of Malinta Tunnel, listening with nerve-wracking, helpless terror to the pounding, wondering if Malinta Hill would withstand the bombardment. The hours crept by ever so slowly. The strain cut angular lines in everyone's face, but for Gatling, a man plagued with a life-long history of claustrophobia, the drawn out hours proved unadulterated torture.

"We've never been through a pasting like this, hour after hour," gushed Gatling in a shaky, high pitched voice as two heavy shells exploded overhead in rapid succession, the floor heaving while light fixtures rattled in their sockets. Beads of perspiration glistened on his beet red forehead. "You think they'd take a break."

"Yeah," croaked Ed in reply, spread eagled under a wood slat bench. A blurry cloud of dust filled the tunnel, kicked up by the outside firestorm. "The air is so bad I can hardly breathe." He twisted at the waist, spying Leuterio hunkered against a coil of steel cable, hands clasped over his helmeted head. Leuterio also hated being cooped up, preferring to take his chances in the jungle. But Corregidor presented little choice and he had resigned himself to their plight.

With a sigh, Ed settled back to the floor, distracting his thoughts by concentrating on events and places far away. It was not easy, what with the constant shelling sounding like a giant jackhammer at work. The strain was telling on everyone.

He waited a couple minutes and raised his eyes toward Gatling, who had become a source of constant worry. The man didn't look well at all. His bloodshot eyes darted back and forth, his facial complexion had turned ashen in color and buckets of perspiration that dripped down his face revealed the mental tension he was under. The caustic effects of the bombardment were becoming all too apparent and Ed didn't like it. He had to do something to get Gatling's mind onto something else.

"Why don't you get out your playing cards," Ed muttered in the cheeriest voice he could muster. "We've gotta do something to make the time pass."

Gatling let out a disgusted moan and reached into a back pocket. "Here," he said, flinging the greasy, well-used deck on the concrete floor. "Be my guest." Like roaring, deep-throated earthquakes, the explosive nightmare continued without letup.

"What'll we play?" asked Ed.

"I didn't say I would. You're the one who wanted the cards."

"I'm not in the mood for solitaire. Let's you and me play something."

At that moment, a shell exploded with a tremendous, deafening blast, tossing over sandbags at the tunnel entrance and causing the lights to flicker and fail. Darkness slammed down and the lights didn't glimmer back to life for a full thirty seconds. Gatling turned away in fright, curled against a wall, his head throbbing. Sweat poured down his forehead.

Knowing there was nothing to be done about the barrage, Ed leaned forward and nudged a shoulder. "Okay, let's play. I'll deal the cards. What'll we bet?"

Gatling showed no interest. Ed leaned forward and nudged harder. "C'mon, card shark. Let's go."

Outside, the rain of artillery shells continued, the Japanese showing no mercy whatsoever. Every once in awhile a gun from Corregidor fired in reply, but the enemy met such aggressive actions with a shower of incoming rounds, forcing crews to scramble for cover. Only the four 14-inch guns mounted in armored turrets at nearby Fort Drum on tiny El Fraille Island, protected by 20-feet of solid concrete, kept up a steady return fire.

"Ed, there's no way I can play cards. This shell fire is driving me crazy."

"They gotta stop sometime, even if it's just to let their guns cool," replied Ed. The two remained silent for a moment as artillery explosions died down in the immediate area, a low rumble sounding from the far side of the island. It was a welcome respite both knew wouldn't last long.

Ed rubbed his hands together. "Okay, now we can play. C'mon, Jim, I feel lucky."

Gatling refused to move. "I don't want to play," he said in a whisper. "I just want to get out of here. I want to go back to California, to Becky. I can't put up with these conditions. I'm not made out to be a tunnel rat."

All of a sudden, a giant 240mm howitzer shell walloped the hill in a thunderous blast, causing the floor to surge back and forth. He squeezed his eyes shut in abject misery and threw up his hands. "I gotta get out of here!" Gatling cried, choking out the words. "I don't know how much longer I can take it." He began to whimper into a sleeve.

Gray dust, microscopic concrete particles drifting down from the ceiling, swirled up in a dense, choking cloud. The ventilators hadn't operated for hours, it being impossible to run the electric generators during a major artillery barrage. As a result, the air had turned foul and oppressive.

"You go outside and those shells will rip you to pieces." Ed paused to run fingers through stubble under his lower lip. "We have no choice but to take it. I wish we could do something, but we can't."

Gatling's chest heaved and sweat ran freely down his face. His hair hung down as if he had just stepped out of a shower. "That's fine for you, but I'm being tortured. I can't live like this."

"There's still a chance reinforcements will come to save the day." Ed spoke as if encouraging a recalcitrant child with cheerful words having no basis in reality. His faith in the possibility of reinforcement had vanished long ago.

"Ed, you no good liar!" bellowed Gatling, swinging around. This was his first real reaction to anything Ed had to say in the last hour. Ed bit his lower lip to stifle a smile. Gatling raved on. "Reinforcements were goddam lies all along and you know it."

Ed took a long moment to rub a congealed mixture of sweat and dust off his eyebrows before answering. "Yeah, you're right. I suppose they were." Artillery fire again rumbled over the top of Malinta Hill and his eyes swept the ceiling. "But we had to believe in something—defeat is final only when you give up fighting, you know."

Gatling propped himself up with his filthy hands and, with a gasp, rolled back against the wall. Massaging his tightly closed eye sockets, hollowed and darkened by lack of sleep, his head felt as if filled with a bucket of rocks. Ed watched and shook his head. "Come on, Jim. Let's you and me play poker. We can ask Leuterio to be a third. What do you say?"

No reaction from Gatling came in response. Staring vacantly through bloodshot eyes set deep in his grimy face, he remained flat on the floor. With little reserve of energy himself after the unremitting onslaught, Ed gave up.

He felt his anger rise, for his best attempts at reaching out had met with maddening failure. The man wasn't even trying to retain his sanity! Ed opened his mouth to speak, but quickly relented. Give the guy a break, he told himself. Life in the tunnel was a nightmare for everyone.

Ed shook his head and let out an audible gasp, his face clouded with uneasiness. How could I leave behind on Corregidor my best friend and the man who saved my life? What should I do?

Ed chewed his lower lip and took at quick glance at his troubled friend. Assailed by a terrible sense of impotence and bitterness, he reached for the cards and began dealing them on the floor. Solitaire would be the name of the game.

The deluge of explosions continued into the evening but slacked off as the sky darkened. The dazed men raised themselves and brushed away gray powdery dust. Blinking, they groped to the entrance and took deep breaths, filling their lungs with the first fresh air in hours. The ventilators kicked on, exchanging the old, stale air inside the tunnel with cool evening air from outside.

It was time for the men assigned to Kindley Field to go to work, too. No flights had arrived for the past week and, since tonight would be moonless, there was a chance Cabral would bring in his antique biplane. The conditions would give him his best chance.

Ed had a letter to his folks ready to go in his breast pocket and had assembled a small pouch of belongings. Though he fretted about it, he still hadn't brought up the subject to Gatling, just then walking beside him to the airstrip.

As they trudged across the blasted landscape, accompanied by the rumble of artillery a mile away, Ed deliberated. Gatling was a good, faithful friend, not by habit impetuous, but humorous and composed; a man he could count on. Even now, after the brutal strain of a pitiless bombardment, here he was at his side, stoically trudging toward the island's shattered airfield. Here was a man who knew his duty and did it; a true friend. No person could ask for more.

Ed blew out a thin stream of air, deep in thought. The idea of getting away from Corregidor, of leaving this scene of chaos behind, struck the very wellspring of his soul. All men have a fundamental, almost instinctual desire for survival and Ed felt it tugging at his insides. He wanted to leave more than anything. But if he got away, could he live with himself, knowing he had abandoned the closest buddy he had ever had?

Cabral presented Ed with the prospect of escape. His choice was either to accept it or let someone else take his place. If he stayed, he and Gatling would continue on the path on which they had set out, the likely end a grave or a prison compound.

When a chance like this came, you had to either grab it or lose it, for it wouldn't come twice: Especially a matter involving life, death or becoming a prisoner of the Japanese, which might mean death anyway. If the situation were reversed, what would Gatling do?

The Japanese had turned the runway into a serrated mess again, with ragged craters, chunks of shrapnel and churned earth. They checked in with the airfield commander, who rarely left his desk within the navy's tunnel at Monkey Point, and found a familiar face inside—Lieutenant Colonel Dohlman. He wore a freshly laundered uniform and was thinner than when they last saw him at Cabcaben, but, as before, he carried himself with icy superiority, his face stubborn and arrogant. Seated in a straight-back wood chair beside the desk, he swiveled toward them, as surprised as they were.

"Well, it's you two again," he blustered, showing off in front of the airfield commander, who he outranked. "Bannon and Gatling. The two boys that went off to the front and were never seen again. How'd you get to Corregidor?"

Stunned to see him, they had no words for a few moments. Finally, Ed spoke. "We went up to the front in time for the Jap breakthrough. We retreated to the coast and were picked up by the *Mindanao*. We've been here since the first week of April."

Dohlman nodded and ran his tongue over yellowed teeth. "I always wondered if you two had figured some way to escape from Bataan," he said. "Tell me the truth. Did you go up to the front at all?"

Gatling took an angry lunge forward, but Ed reached out a restraining arm. "Hold on, Jim," he muttered. "Cool it."

Snarling, Gatling pulled back and Ed faced the now standing Dohlman, glaring straight into his eyes. "You good-for-nothing," Ed snapped, advancing a step. "You're a pathetic loafer who hides behind a desk. We accomplished more on Bataan than you ever did, including killing more Japs. We came close to getting killed ourselves three or four times."

Ed wanted to say more, but knowing he could easily step over the line, stifled himself after hissing, "One might ask why you're even here. Isn't an officer supposed to stay with his troops? What happened to the rest of the guys at Cabcaben?"

Dohlman's face grew scarlet; his voice inflamed and belligerent. "What happened back there is none of your business. You deserted us, remember?" He pointed an accusing finger, his face a glowering mask of rage. "And don't use that kind of language with me, Bannon, or I'll have you placed under arrest."

"You're no threat," answered Ed, a heavy dose of sarcasm in his voice. "The only people you pick-on are cadets and privates, who can't stand up to your kind. You've been trying to get something on me for years."

Dohlman ignored his words. "General Wainright's staff needs me. I got out on one of the last boats. People like me are putting backbone into the resistance."

Ed rolled his eyes. "Sure you are. You're the guy who said Germans were the ones flying Jap planes. A lot you know. Far as I can see you're just another useless mouth to feed."

They stared at each other in mutual hostility, then Ed shifted his gaze to the airfield commander, who, fascinated, had watched the exchange from the comfort of a padded swivel chair. He had done nothing to stop it. "Sir," Ed said, "Jim and me are going down to the field to smooth it out. Have you got word about planes coming in?"

He roused himself with a thin smile, not yet ready to answer Ed's question. "Seems you men know each other," he chuckled under his breath. Squirming upright, he glanced at each man. "Well, you two keep your arguments outside. I've got better things to do than listen to bickering."

Ed nodded and took a quick look at Dohlman, his eyes filled with contempt he no longer bothered to hide. "Okay, sir," he said to the commander. "But did you get any word on plane activity?"

"Yeah," he replied in a dry, matter of fact tone. "Cabral is coming in tonight. The navy handed me a radio transmission a few minutes ago."

"Good," Ed said, his mouth curling into an unconscious smile. "We'll make sure the runway's ready."

Dohlman, a clever man, had been closely studying Ed's face. The smile aroused his suspicion. "Bannon, what exactly is your interest?" he asked. "You seem pretty eager for a guy who's just gone through a day of non-stop shelling."

Irritated by the mocking tone, Ed gritted his teeth. "Our interest is simply getting that plane in and out of here. The medicine it brings will save American lives."

Dohlman turned toward the airfield commander. "Quite a man, isn't he? Truly dedicated." Dohlman snorted and gave a scornful chuckle.

The airfield commander rose and placed hands atop the desk. "All right, that's enough," he barked, arching his back. "The three of you get out of my office. Captain Bannon, take Lieutenant Gatling with you and get out to the field. Lieutenant Colonel Dohlman, go where you like, but try to be useful. Now, all of you, leave! I've got work to do."

Ed couldn't imagine what work that would be. The airfield's hangers and other structures had been blasted into rubble. No planes had landed in the past week and few over the course of a month. After tonight, there would be no more. Eyebrows raised in amusement, he and Gatling came to attention, nodded and walked out, headed downhill toward Kindley Field's single dirt runway.

* * *

They kept a battered bulldozer stored inside one of the field's deep dirt revetments, safe from all artillery fire other than a direct hit. The sun had descended and the full dark of night had closed around the island. It was safe to begin work. No enlisted soldiers had yet shown up, so Gatling climbed onto the bulldozer, revved up the engine and bucked out onto the field. He drove to the end of the runway and dropped the blade, smoothing the surface of the strip in repeated back and forth runs. As enlisted soldiers drifted in, Ed threw shovels and rakes into their hands and put them to work filling craters that pockmarked the field.

After a few hours, the strip looked to be in decent shape. By prewar standards it was still a wreck, but for Corregidor's condition after nearly six months of combat, it was perfectly acceptable. They drove the bulldozer back into the revetment, covered it carefully with a canvas tarp and waited. It wasn't until later that an excited shout announced the drone of an approaching aircraft.

"Listen!" cried Private Ivan Sota, recognized by everyone for his keen sense of hearing. For some reason, he could make out sounds long before others could. It was a handy skill. "Everybody shut up!"

The men came to a position of stock rigidity, holding their collective breaths. "Yep, it's definitely a plane," whispered Sota. As the buzz increased, others could hear it, too, and they exchanged grins. All had letters ready to go and Cabral would bring along a fresh supply of candy bars for all hands. He always did.

A message was sent to a nearby searchlight and it beamed a brief light on the field, allowing Cabral to line up his approach. A couple minutes later, it bounded down and made a rough landing. Once it slowed to a stop, they ran out and manhandled the plane to the safety of a revetment. Skilled mechanics gave it a quick inspection, made adjustments to the engine and poured aviation fuel into its tank.

Cabral grinned as he pulled into the revetment, hopping out as soon as it came to a stop. As was his custom, he handed out candy bars to everyone, this time outdoing himself, giving two to each man. In return, they thrust out letters and he slid them into the breast pocket of his brown leather jacket.

"You know I'll see to each one, personal," he said. "People call me "Mailman" because I always get the job done; through hell, high water and Japs." He grinned, waved a hand over his head and sauntered toward Ed, standing in a corner. The two greeted each other and shook hands.

Bending forward, Cabral whispered, "Well, what have you decided? Better make it fast. We haven't much time."

"I'm going," Ed answered. "I've got a satchel packed."

Cabral's light hair offered a stark contrast to his deep tan. Nodding, it glinted in the dim yellow lantern-light. "Good. I'll bet you never thought owning a Lincoln Standard would get you out of Corregidor." He laughed and walked back to the aircraft, now in its final stage of inspection. Just then the canvas tarp covering the entrance moved aside and Lieutenant Colonel Dohlman strutted in, dangling a riding crop.

"Carry on, you men," he announced in a brusque voice as he approached Cabral, motioning the enlisted crew away with a wave of his hand. "Me and the pilot need to talk," he said in a gravelly voice. Cabral shrugged and shuffled back to a dirt wall, not far from Ed and Gatling.

The two longtime buddies had drawn together and were engaged in quiet conversation, Ed breaking the news about his escape. Gatling stared forward, his mouth tight and grim, color draining from his face, terrified at the prospect of losing Ed's vital caring and support. As he went on, Gatling felt an icy fear twisting through his insides. What would become of him? Ed's words were leaving him speechless.

A few feet away, Dohlman glared at Cabral, his look accusing and cold. A muscle quivered in his jaw as he spoke. "I know you're leaving in a few minutes, so this has to be fast," he said. "I've got five thousand dollars, cash, in my pocket. The money is yours if you get me out of here. How about it?"

Cabral's lips spread into a thin-lipped smile. "Sorry, Colonel, but I'm full up this trip. Maybe next time."

Dohlman shook his head. “Come on, man, I’ll make it ten thousand. Besides, you know this is your last trip. Corregidor’s about to fall.”

“No, American money’s not much good out here. I hear men are using it to light cigarettes. Once the Japs take over, it’ll be worth nothing.”

“Look, you’ll be a rich man on the outside and nobody has to know why.” On the verge of unconcealed pleading, Dohlman had raised his voice. Ed and Gatling looked over; hearing enough to know an attempt at bribery was being made.

Cabral straightened himself with dignity. “Sorry, no more passengers.” He took a step forward. “Now, if you’ll excuse me . . .”

Dohlman, eyes darkening like angry thunderclouds, grabbed Cabral’s collar and spun him around. “Are you taking passengers? If so, kick them off and put me on.”

Cabral reached up and threw off Dohlman’s hand. He replied in a low voice, taut with exasperation. “Look, whoever you are, you’re not going . . . got it? Now get out of my way.”

His features contorted with anger, knowing this was the last chance of escape, Dohlman drew himself up. “Listen up, everybody!” he hollered. “We’re clearing the revetment. Everyone out—*now*!”

The ground crew, having just completed its work, stared back unbelieving. “What?” asked Private Sota. “We need to get this crate up in the air. Artillery could start up any minute.”

Dohlman gave him an icy stare. “Don’t cross me, boy. I can break you without half trying.” Sota shuddered and retreated to the opposite side of the aircraft.

Ed decided it was time to step in. The men knew and trusted him. “All right, you guys, roll the plane out to the end of the runway and warm it up. We’ll meet you by the time you get it ready.”

The crewmen nodded, moved behind the wings and pushed the old plane out of the revetment, leaving Dohlman behind with Cabral, Gatling and Ed. The four drew together.

“I’m not taking him,” blustered Cabral, jerking an accusatory thumb. “And I don’t want his filthy money.”

"Just settle down," calmed Ed. He turned toward Dohlman. "Colonel Dohlman, you best get back to the commander's office. We've got work to do out here."

Dohlman sputtered, bristling with indignation. "He's got room for a passenger and I intend for it to be me. Which of you bums is hitching a ride? I outrank you, so you'll do as I say."

"What I do with my plane is none of your business," shot back Cabral. "I'm not even in the army, so I don't have to take orders from the likes of you. I'm a civilian volunteer and do what I want." He faced Ed. "Let's go."

Dohlman's eyes grew wide. "So that's it!" he bellowed. "Bannon, you wangled a way out of here. I should have figured. The passenger is you!"

"Here's my bag," said Ed, handing it to Cabral. "Go out to the plane and get ready. Your passenger'll be right there."

Dohlman glared at Cabral. "I'll be the one coming out," he muttered, his face marked with loathing. "Just give me one minute."

He advanced toward Ed, fists bunched at his side. "Bannon," he said, "I've never liked you, but we go a ways back, so I'll give you a chance. Cabral doesn't want it, so you can have the money. Take it, keep your mouth shut and walk back to Monkey Point. Deal?"

Ed's expression held a note of mockery. He considered the proposition for five or six seconds, casting a brief, appraising glance at Gatling. He began to blurt an answer, hesitated and again glanced at his friend, then continued. "Okay," he muttered slowly. "Let's see the money."

Dohlman's lips spread into a surly smile and he reached down into the front pocket of his trousers. He pulled out a huge wad of bills and held it up. "Here it is, Bannon. You're a smart man," he said, licking his cracked lips. "Ten thousand bucks is a lot of money."

Gatling stared in disbelief. Was Ed giving up his ticket off Corregidor? Why stay behind for money he could never use?

Ed fixed his eyes on Dohlman. "Not so fast. Lemme count it first. I want everything above board."

Suspicious, Dohlman hesitated and said, "We'll count it together."

"Sure," Ed replied. Moving like a flash, he reached forward and grabbed the wad of bills out of Dohlman's hand. He tossed it to Gatling, who, surprised, trapped it against his chest.

"Heh!" hollered Dohlman, lifting a fist to strike Ed. He aimed at the chin, but Ed ducked and gave him a swift uppercut with his left, followed by a roundabout punch to Dohlman's left cheek. He dropped to the floor, out cold.

Breathless, Ed faced Gatling. "Take the bills and get on the plane," he stammered. "That money's a gift for you and Becky. Do something good with it."

Gatling's mouth dropped in astonishment. Five minutes ago Ed was about to leave and he felt himself slipping into depression. What happened?

"Ed," he stammered, weighing his friend with a critical squint. "Do you know what you're doing? You struck a superior officer, robbed him and gave up getting out of here. What the hell's going on?"

"Don't worry about me. Just get on the plane. You and Becky have your lives in front of you. Mine ended when Barbara died. Only one of us can leave and you're it. I'm a poker player, too, and know a good bet when I see it—you and Becky are that bet."

Gatling's chest heaved up and down, but he knew time was short. He could hear the plane warming up. "Thank you, buddy, thank you," he said, wrapping two hands around one of Ed's. "Becky thanks you, I thank you."

Ed smiled back. "I know you're grateful, but you better leave. And don't forget the letter to my folks." He handed it over.

"I'll guard it with my life." Gatling took a step toward the entrance then swiveled back. "I'll never forget you, Ed. You're the best friend I ever had and ever will have. Don't worry about your letter. I'll deliver it myself."

"Bye, Jim. Take care of yourself." Gatling tried to say something but Ed pushed him toward the entrance. He turned and dashed out, waving an exultant hand over his head. The plane waited at the end of the airstrip, propeller humming, ready for takeoff. Gatling crawled into the forward seat, having nothing with him other than the clothes on his back and what Ed had stowed in the bag. He settled himself between mailbags and the plane rumbled forward along the uneven surface until jumping into the air and ascending toward the clouds. The men left behind on the runway watched until it vanished from sight.

Ed remained, leaning against the side of the revetment, tossing around what he had done. The last five minutes had zipped by at an astonishing pace, with no time to stop and ponder the ramifications. He had acted almost on instinct.

Never in his life had he stolen money, but, minutes ago, he had clipped a superior officer for thousands of dollars, then given it away! Ed shook his head, hardly believing it.

Then there was the matter of striking down Dohlman. Now stretched out on the oily revetment floor, once he woke and cleared his head, Dohlman would tell the airfield commander what happened in lurid detail, most likely adding a few creative twists. Assuming no action resulted, a likely scenario since the airfield commander wasn't exactly a ball of fire, he would run to the military police. But they had more important things to do. Besides, the airfield commander would back Ed's story since they had known each other for weeks. Dohlman was nothing more than a pushy newcomer.

Ed's mind moved to another pressing issue—his place on the plane. Giving up escape was in a far different category from everything else. He desperately wanted to get off Corregidor, had decided to do so, but quickly relented.

The reason was Jim Gatling, his best friend in the world. The pressure of the siege had caused him to fade fast, on a one-way journey to the deep end. It was a painful process to watch. They had shared tents, food and nearly everything for months. Gatling had even saved his life. After living through hell in the aftermath of Barbara's death, how could he go on in peace knowing he had escaped at Gatling's expense?

No, giving up the seat was right. It meant Gatling now had decades of life to look forward to with Becky and an extra ten thousand dollars to make it even better.

Artillery fire picked up and shells thumped into Malinta Hill. Ed swiveled around and saw explosions erupt along the crest like geysers of fire. Soldiers cowered in that dark, dank tunnel right now. He took satisfaction knowing Gatling would no longer have to be among them.

After watching for half a minute, he took a last glance at Dohlman's prostrate body. The man had not moved an inch. Ed sidled away and reached into a shirt pocket, pulling out a Big Hunk candy bar delivered by Cabral. Absent mindedly, he ripped off the wrapper and took a bite, chewing in silence.

Better get up to Monkey Point and make my report before Dohlman wakes up, he told himself. Why would anyone in authority believe that man anyway? He's a blowhard who tried to buy his way onto the last plane leaving Corregidor. A worthless disgrace to the uniform, he said to himself, shaking his head.

CHAPTER 21

CORREGIDOR'S DEATH THROES

May 2-6, 1942

Despite Lieutenant Colonel Dohlman's blustering roars, nobody believed him. He invented explanations, attempted to use his superior rank to force others to act, and badly overplayed his hand. His intention to bully his way out at any expense became obvious. The affair was quickly forgotten. Dohlman burrowed into the depths of Malinta Tunnel, hunkering there for the remainder of the campaign.

Corregidor, with most of its batteries silenced and its beaches denuded of barbed wire, invited attack. General Wainwright, reporting by radio to military superiors in Washington, D.C., estimated the island's chances for repelling an assault at "a little less than fifty percent."

Incredible as it may seem, Japanese artillery fire intensified with the new month. Over one five hour stretch, they rained a total of 3600 shells on Corregidor—one shell every five seconds; enough to fill six hundred trucks.

The Japanese fire, though slacking off at night in the early weeks of the siege to allow hardworking gunners a few hours rest, continued around the clock by May 3rd, offering no respite to Corregidor's garrison. Life within the tunnels became unbearable, with soaring heat, clouds of dust, foul air, and near constant humidity. Tempers flared and some broke under the constant tension.

Many developed vicious earaches and headaches. In the hospital, jars crashed to the floor from shelves and nurses covered the faces of patients with wet gauze to filter out the choking dust. A constant stream of blood-spattered soldiers depleted the island's stock of medical supplies, with stocks of ether, novocain and other painkillers especially short. When electrical generators failed, as they often did, medics shined flashlights to permit surgical procedures to continue.

With air operations at Kindley Field impossible, Ed squatted within the squalor of Malinta Tunnel waiting out the never-ending, violent firestorm. There was nothing to do but suffer in silence, though the sensation of terror was almost palpable. For everyone, there was no longer a clean dividing line between periods of sleep and wakefulness; it was almost as if time had stopped.

Ed's head ached monstrously and he kept his eyes shut tight, praying for the barrage to slacken, hoping against hope for the B-17's to return from Australia. Sleep came in spurts, but never for long and never deep. He spent hours crouched against the damp concrete tunnel wall, head between his knees, beset with a thick, boundless terror that froze the air in his lungs.

Late May 4th, the Japanese barrage shifted from Corregidor's artillery batteries and command centers to the beach defenses, concentrating on those closest to Bataan. They blasted away, riddling the dug-in defenders with heavy doses of shrapnel and high explosives, intending to break their morale and ability to resist. Many were out in the open huddled in deep foxholes, manning positions over which they knew the Japanese would come. Because of the heavy fire, trucks carrying meals were unable to make deliveries, leaving the men hungry and weak. Field kitchens had long ago been blasted away.

Both Ed and Leuterio sensed the change in the barrage minutes after it came about. They turned toward the tunnel entrance and listened, noting that the main barrage had moved off. They looked at each other and rose, regarding the dust thickly covering their uniforms. Leaning against a stack of metal pipes, they stretched their legs, grateful that a break in the long ordeal had arrived.

But others also took advantage of the lull. Stretcher-bearers began carrying litters of wounded soldiers into the tunnel, racing toward the hospital. Ed and Leuterio sidled back to allow them to pass, soberly gazing without expression upon the prostrate wounded. They saw every conceivable type of injury, from blown off legs and arms to grotesque facial wounds. Some unfortunates screamed in misery. Both found the sight stomach turning.

"Let's get out of here," snapped Ed, tightening the helmet's leather strap under his chin. "Let's go see what Kindley looks like then head to Monkey Point. We can shelter in the navy tunnels there."

Leuterio grabbed his Springfield leaning against the wall. He had covered it with the scrap of a blanket as protection from the constant shower of dust. "Let's go," he said, kicking a blackened piece of wood with the toe of a shoe. "I've had enough of this place."

The two moved down Malinta Hill toward Kindley Field, discovering it had been as thoroughly turned as any plowed farmer's field. Japanese artillery fire and bombs had dug craters that now overlapped each other, making the airstrip a ragged expanse of destruction. The hangers, pounded down to their foundations, were barely recognizable as once standing buildings.

They stopped on a rise overlooking the field and, after gazing upon it with disapproving squints, continued toward Monkey Point, flinging open a door and entering the airfield commander's office within the navy tunnel. Cabinets hung open, emptied of their contents, once important papers scattered across the floor. Five enlisted soldiers assigned to the airfield crowded in a circle against the far wall, engaged in shooting dice while the barrage picked up outside. They exchanged greetings with the newcomers and continued playing.

The two Bataan veterans placed their rifles on the surface of the empty desk and sat down in chairs, resting their feet and making themselves at home. Bored deep into a ridge, the office was a safe, uncrowded place to hole up. They determined to wait there until the Japanese made their move.

* * *

Early the next evening, after a full day of shelling, two thousand heavily laden Japanese infantrymen clambered aboard landing barges and began the jolting journey across Manila Bay's choppy waters to Corregidor. At the same time, artillerymen turned the landing areas into giant sheets of flame, with plumes of gritty dust and dark smoke curling above. Red lights within Malinta Tunnel blinked on, the signal for soldiers assigned to beach defenses to report to their positions.

The Japanese landed before midnight, taking heavy losses while approaching. Two American 75mm artillery pieces that had never fired during the campaign opened an accurate and devastating fire, sending in round after shattering round, turning numerous barges into slaughter pens. Machine guns and small arms blazed away, sinking half the barges and slicing down men wading toward the sloping shore. The remaining big guns on Corregidor and the other fortified islands fired as rapidly as possible in accordance with defense plans drawn up weeks earlier, adding to the deadly mayhem. The Japanese, who had expected an easy landing, were shocked.

Ed lay perched at the ragged edge of a shell crater atop a rise on Kindley Field's western fringe, firing his Springfield at hundreds of Japanese troops struggling through the surf. Illuminated by flaming barges, the shadowy figures appeared as ghostly smudges in the dark night.

An American searchlight snapped on for the briefest of moments before being shot out, but not before illuminating the enemy heading toward shore. Leuterio, at Ed's side, fired his rifle over and over, pausing only to toss an occasional hand grenade when groups approached the cliff face below. Streams of bright tracer machine gun rounds sliced through the sky, guiding their aim.

"My gun's kicking like a mule," shouted Ed as he worked the bolt on his Springfield.

Leuterio barely glanced up, ramming clip after clip into his rifle, firing at the invaders gathering below. "Their strength is building," he shouted. "It's time to use the fragmentation bombs."

Ed nodded, emptied his rifle and edged toward the lip of the ridge. A dozen other Americans nearby madly worked the bolts of their Springfields, the enemy return fire increasing as more Japanese struggled ashore. A barge landed virtually unopposed about two hundred yards to the right, resisted by a few riflemen in foxholes among rocks behind the flat beach. They were far too few in number and he could see Americans advancing across Kindley Field to reinforce them. Armed only with small arms and grenades, with nothing heavier to fire, it looked like a chancy undertaking, given the number of Japanese, who were already pushing the riflemen aside and advancing onto the airstrip.

There was no time to waste; Ed edged back and got down to business. With few planes to service in the course of the campaign, the stockpile of 25 lb. fragmentation bombs had been barely touched. Marines assigned to beach defense had figured out how to make profitable use of them and had scattered caches of the bombs along the cliffs. They instructed defenders to use chutes constructed from wood planks to plunge the deadly projectiles on the enemy below.

Ed and Leuterio lugged a chute and two crates of bombs to just below the top of the ridge. Three others rushed over to help, bringing forward additional bombs.

Ed wedged the chute into position and hollered, "Okay, boys, let's give it to 'em."

Leuterio positioned the first bomb and another tipped the chute frontward. It slid forward in the "V" created by the two planks, gathered speed, and plunged out of sight into the darkness. In a split second the night lit up with a flash of orange flame and a satisfying, roaring explosion. They grinned at each other. After weeks of being on the receiving end, it was a nice feeling to dish it out.

"Let's give 'em one more then move over ten yards," shouted Ed. Leuterio grabbed another bomb and let her rip down the chute. Another detonation occurred. It felt great.

They continued hurling bombs down on the Japanese invaders all along the ridge, emptying ten crates in the process. They must have killed and wounded dozens, though intermittent return fire continued. Suddenly, something whistled past Ed's head, plowing into churned up brown dirt. He threw himself down.

It was a Japanese sniper firing from the far right—one from the lightly opposed barge that landed earlier. The American counter-attack had sputtered out and Japanese were advancing across the northern edge of the strip, though resistance continued. Two machine guns held them up for awhile, but the Japanese, alternately crawling and rushing forward, put the guns out of action and forced a retreat all the way back to Monkey Point.

"We're getting outflanked," whispered Ed under his breath. He swung around and watched the Filipino and American defenders along the ridgeline firing their rifles and tossing grenades. They had put up a stout defense for the two hours, not allowing the Japanese beyond the beach, exacting a huge casualty toll. But despite their stubborn resistance, the enemy now had a firm foothold on Corregidor and threatened to go farther.

Leuterio crawled up, enemy small arms fire bursting around him. "Sir, there've been several hits from the crossfire. We have to do something."

Ed scrunched up his mouth and ran a hand over his forehead. He looked down in disgust. "I know," he said. Ed paused, reflecting on their suddenly exposed position. "We've got two choices; attack and be forced to fall back later or retire now while we have a chance. As soon as daylight comes, they'll send over reinforcements."

Ed twisted around to gaze with profound sympathy upon the men scattered along the ridge. They had been through hell, enduring months of steady retreat, empty promises, starvation, and near-constant bombardment. Their resistance was a testament to their grit and determination, but he knew the effort was futile. Since the opening day of the war, the writing had been on the wall. The forces in the Philippines had become nothing more than symbols of resistance.

Ed rose up, his jaw set and eyes blazing fire. "Armando," he said in the clipped voice of authority, "pass the word to fall back. We'll reform at Monkey Point."

Leuterio took in a quick, sharp breath, staring back in astonishment. “Fall back, sir?”

Ed had not undergone formal training as an infantry officer, but the last three months of on-the-job experience were of a great deal more consequence. The self-doubt that once existed had vanished. “Yeah, that’s what I said, Armando. We’re falling back.”

“But, sir, if we move forward we might be able to drive them off.”

Ed shook his head, frowning. “Not with twenty men, we can’t.” He lowered himself down the ridge a few feet and looked at the Japanese advancing across Kindley Field in ever increasing numbers. The formerly black sky was now becoming gray. Pinkish streaks glinted up from the horizon. The Japanese had set up several machine guns in shell craters and were hammering the American line at Monkey Point. Mortars they had carried ashore opened up seconds later, thudding explosions blossoming upward. “We better get moving or we’re gonna get cut off,” he said.

Leuterio nodded and scampered along the ridge, patting each man on the shoulder and giving him the news. Having exhausted the supply of 25 lb. bombs, they picked up their remaining hand grenades and gathered at the base of the ridge. A short time later they ran a zigzag course toward Monkey Point, skirting the field, keeping behind hills and in depressions as much as possible. Upon reaching the point as the glow of dawn cast gray shadows, they joined a ragged line of about one hundred and fifty American and Filipino defenders. Most were armed with Springfields, but a few water-cooled .30 caliber machine guns and Browning Automatic Rifles stiffened resistance. Gun crews fired them in short chattering bursts whenever an enthusiastic Japanese soldier raised his head or attempted to advance. The fire slowed momentum a great deal.

Ed trudged down the line observing the state of the defenses and seeking out the ranking officer, Major Zachary Byrd. He found him on the far right, seeming in a state of perpetual motion, running between his headquarters and the defense line, plugging holes and making sure supplies got to where they were needed. Communications with officers coordinating the Corregidor defense back in Malinta Tunnel were completely out and he was forced to use runners to send messages. It made for a chaotic situation.

"Captain Bannon, reporting," said Ed, throwing a salute. Byrd, just then immersed in reloading his .45 caliber pistol, was happy for the distraction and looked up. His facial skin was pulled taut over the irregular ridge of his cheekbones and drops of moisture clung to his forehead. Ed spoke in a low, composed voice. "I brought back twenty men and they're in line on the far left. Anything in particular you want us to do?"

Byrd gave a hint of a smile, glad for the additional help. "Good job, Captain. Just leave your men there. Do they have grenades? We need'em."

"Yes, sir, we have two or three per man." Ed's eyes drew downward in a frown as he glanced down the slope. A curtain of artillery fire from Bataan was striking the American line, forcing the machine gunners down in their holes. When the fire let up, mortar shells fired by the approaching Japanese erupted up and down the line. A solitary Stokes trench mortar, a relic from World War I, fired in reply but stopped after six rounds due to lack of ammunition. Ed shook his head in disbelief; the odds were certainly against them. "Have you taken many casualties?" he asked.

His expression tight with strain, Byrd answered that a number had been wounded, but few stretcher-bearers were available. Many casualties remained where they fell, in great danger. "Why don't you go back to the navy tunnel and see about getting some stretcher-bearers up here. Take a look around for some grenades, too."

"All right," replied Ed. "I'll be back as soon as I can."

Ed headed south toward the navy tunnel, a miniature version of the army's cavernous Malinta Tunnel. The navy had housed sensitive code-breaking equipment within the tunnel in the years before the war, but had destroyed it in recent days to prevent its capture. Eavesdropping on Japanese communications, highly trained specialists on Corregidor relayed choice tidbits of information on Japanese intentions to Hawaii, even collaborating to deduce future enemy fleet movements. Many intercepted messages in the latter weeks of April centered on the central Pacific, in the Midway Island area, a region that had not yet fallen under Japanese control.

As Ed zigzagged around sandbag baffles protecting the tunnel entrance and walked inside, he came across hundreds of terrified, cowering men, two or three times more than the number manning the feeble defense line. Most were office workers who formerly handled reams of paperwork, now out of a job. Untrained to fight as infantry, demoralized and shell-shocked, they hadn't ventured beyond the safety of the tunnel in days.

Ed stepped onto a wooden crate and placed hands on his hips. "I'm Captain Bannon," he announced, "and we need help out there." He jerked a thumb over a shoulder. "Now's your chance to fight back and give the Japs some of their own medicine."

Hollow eyes met his words, most not even looking up. The faces were grim, haggard, covered with whiskers and dirt. Intent on waiting for the inevitable, the sailors had been thoroughly crushed.

Ed scanned the empty faces and tried again, this time lowering his voice. "Look, if you don't want to use a gun, you can carry a stretcher. We need stretcher-bearers bad. There's lots of wounded."

A couple men looked up, but only a few. Ed gazed down and nudged the nearest man with a foot. No response. Puzzled, he flung his hands out in despair. Why were these men refusing to lift a finger?

He shook his head and hollered in a loud, raking voice. "We have wounded men lying in foxholes who need a doctor. If you won't help, you'll have blood on your hands." He drove a fist hard into an open palm. "When we get out of here, some people may even call you cowards!"

A chief petty officer twenty feet away shot to his feet as if propelled by an explosive force. "We ain't cowards!" he shouted, his expression mocking and resentful. He pointed an accusing finger. "We'll surrender within hours and you know it. If we go out there, we'll die for nothing."

"No," responded Ed, wagging his head, "you're wrong. I'm just asking for stretcher-bearers to carry back men who can't help themselves. If you're any kind of a person, you'll help."

The sailor waved his hand to the side in a gesture of derision. "Don't give us that kind of hogwash. We're through listening to officers. People like you led us down the primrose path and look where it got us. Do yourself a favor and get out."

Ed felt his face color. He clamped his lips together, hands formed into fists at his side. "We have men fighting and dying out there," he bellowed. "They're fighting for you, they're fighting for me. They need our help."

The man cast a withering eye at Ed and sat back down. "You're full of shit," he mocked. In a sharp voice he added, "You army officers better stay out of here."

An awkward silence descended for a moment, a series of artillery shells exploding on Monkey Point seconds later, sending a rumbling roar through the tunnel. As dust drifted down and relative silence returned, a thin voice called out. Ed swerved around.

"We'll help," announced a man rising from a crouched position against the wall. "There are four men in my section and we'll all go." He raised his voice and addressed everyone within hearing distance. "We might as well do one thing to fight the Japs before going to prison camp!"

Several turned to each other and shrugged their shoulders. Why not? They were nothing better than caged rats anyway. Within a minute, eight more stood and volunteered. Ed inclined his head toward them and muttered, "Thank you, men. We'll leave in just a second."

He turned toward Leuterio, who had remained silent during the exchange, amazed and disgusted to see how far discipline and good order had deteriorated. "Go find some grenades, will you? Check that arms room back there."

Leuterio nodded and ran to a locked steel door about twenty yards inside the tunnel, hoping it hadn't already been cleaned out. It hadn't. A sailor came over and unlocked it and, within seconds, Leuterio emerged lugging two wood cases of hand grenades. Two sailors came forward to grab more.

They gathered at the tunnel entrance and made a run for it, Ed and Leuterio leading the way. Little puffs of dirt kicked up around their feet as the group of volunteers hightailed it toward the line's command post, the fire coming from Japanese infiltrators who had pierced through undetected. Leuterio pulled the pins on a couple grenades and tossed them in the direction of likely hiding places and continued on, barely missing a step.

The new supply of grenades was helpful, but far from enough to tip the balance in favor of the Americans. The confrontation fast developed into a stalemate, the Japanese unable to move forward and the Americans unable to drive them off. The two sides exchanged volleys, raked each other with machine gun fire, took casualties, and pushed back and forth, but nothing of a material nature took place to change things. Dive-bombers swooped down on the Americans five times over the next two hours, forcing them into their foxholes, causing more casualties. Artillery fire from Bataan was almost continual. Stretcher-bearers kept busy shuttling back and forth to the tunnel, dodging artillery and rifle fire on the way. Many more sailors had volunteered to help.

About 11 a.m., word spread that General Wainwright had decided to surrender. Though the Japanese were being temporarily held at Kindley Field, additional barges were landing reinforcements and equipment. Several armored tanks clanked toward Malinta Tunnel, resisted by a single last-ditch line of defenders armed with rifles, grenades and mortars, wishing against hope for antitank weapons. All personnel reserves had been called into the fight and none remained.

Earlier, Wainwright had reported to Washington, D.C., that the situation "was fast becoming desperate." When he learned of the Japanese tanks and visualized the slaughter that could take place within Malinta Tunnel, he contemplated a few minutes and threw in the towel. He ordered all defenders on the island to destroy their equipment and surrender.

Major Byrd passed the word that resistance would end at noon. Some began bashing rifles against boulders and tossing firing pins into the sea. Others leaned back, not quite believing the enormity of what was about to happen. Tears welled up in many eyes. Japanese forces had emerged victorious from nearly every confrontation they had faced in the Pacific since the beginning of the war, no matter who the defender; British, Dutch, American, or Australian. The world, it seemed, was changing before their eyes.

Ed watched with an air of curiosity, able to do nothing to lessen the pain. But there was one thing he *could* do. Something his father taught him as a young boy in the empty desert outside Yuma. It involved rusty tin cans and the single-shot .22 rifle he kept stored in the back of a closet. He narrowed his eyes, tightened the helmet strap under his chin and raised himself to just over the top of the hole.

For some time, the past ten minutes, he had kept an eye on a Japanese soldier circling wide around their position to sneak behind the American line. Dodging behind hills and crawling through ravines, going at a slow, careful pace to avoid detection, he thought he was fooling the defenders, but Ed had no intention of letting him get away with it. The enemy soldier was just about in range and now was the time to nail him. Ten minutes remained before Wainwright's order went into effect.

He raised the Springfield and snugged it against his shoulder. Taking a deep breath, he sighted down the barrel. "This is for you, Dad," he muttered.

Studying his target, he took his time, waiting until the man was in the clear and the shot couldn't miss. Slowly, he sucked in his breath and tightened his finger on the trigger. Crack! The Japanese soldier pitched back, his rifle tumbling to the ground.

Ed lowered the rifle, tipped back the brim of his helmet and turned toward his men. Through hollow, sad eyes peering out from a battle hardened, blackened face, he spoke. "All right," he barked in a gravelly, cheerless voice. "The game's up. We fought the good fight and lost. Run up the white flag, then sit here and wait. Let's see how honorable our captors'll be. If you have any food, eat it. Let's not leave anything for the Japs."

Ed leaned to the side and placed a hand on Leuterio's shoulder, nudging it while managing a small, tentative smile. Leuterio wore a glum look and gazed back through eyes that were clouding over. Ed nudged him again. "It'll be all right," he said in a gentle voice. "Let's you and me stick together."

The two had become committed friends and Ed valued his judgment. He would need Leuterio, a resourceful man who knew the country and the techniques of survival, during the captivity Ed knew to be in the offing.

They sat in their hole the next ten minutes, artillery shells continuing to burst, machine gun fire still directed at them from the Japanese line. The closing moments of the long ordeal were at hand. Or was a new ordeal, one they could hardly imagine, about to begin?

Each man became lost in private thoughts; thinking of home, reflecting on loved ones. Some prayed, mumbling to themselves. Little discussion took place. No one had gone through a situation like this before. Until the war began, if anyone had predicted the Japanese army would place American soldiers in a catastrophic mess like this, he or she would have been laughed off the face of the planet.

Some five minutes later, two sailors wearing torn, disheveled dungarees ran up from the tunnel lugging a battered crate of C-rations. Grinning, they ripped off the top and began tossing cans to grateful men who reached out to catch them.

"Eat up," they called. "There're more back in the tunnel. We can at least surrender with full stomachs."

Ed grabbed a can rolling on the ground and knocked down another flying overhead. He tossed one to Leuterio and, after cutting through the lids, the two enjoyed their first canned fruit in weeks. It tasted sweet on the tongue and slipped smooth down the throat. Heavenly! The sweet flavor reminded Ed of those early, more hopeful days back at Cabcaben.

Leuterio ventured out of the foxhole three or four minutes later and, hunched over, ran back to the tunnel and returned with a sackful of canned goods, gleefully dumping them into the foxhole.

"The arms room is stacked full of C-rations," he said. "There must be fifty cases. People are ransacking the place."

Ed shook his head, reached for the two nearest cans and opened them with a pocketknife. One contained pork and beans and the other corned beef hash. The two ate half, then exchanged cans with the other.

They continued eating for the next hour, taking their time, no longer firing, as white flags fluttered all over the island and Morse code messages announcing the surrender were broadcast over and over from Malinta. Ed lined up the empty cans along the edge of the foxhole and stared at them, patting his belly, satisfied for the first time in weeks. Now there was nothing to do but wait.

A variety of white flags fluttered; bed sheets, shirts, old rags, anything white they could find. Sooner or later the enemy would get the message. The battle for Corregidor, and the Philippines, was over.

After Jim Gatling and Ron Cabral climbed away from Kindley Field and disappeared into low hanging clouds, they could make out little more than the steady metallic roar of the aircraft's piston engine and the dull explosions of artillery shells. After a very few minutes, the sound died away and the aircraft settled into a slow even flight toward the island of Palayan, some two hundred miles distant and a world apart from the nightmare of Corregidor.

Still staggered by Ed's offer of escape, Gatling had no previous inkling of what was about to happen. One moment he was living a terrible dream, the next he was being pushed toward a plane and told to get on board. It was too fast!

He blinked his bloodshot eyes over and over, realizing he was being transported inside the thin skin of an airplane, leaving Corregidor farther and farther behind. He reached down to a pocket on the front of his trousers and fingered a hefty bulge caused by the huge wad of bills Ed had tossed.

What had happened was almost unbelievable. Shaking his head, he knew he now would see Becky again. Together, their life would go on. Yesterday he wasn't so sure.

Gatling raised himself up and stuck out his head over the top of the fuselage, looking back. Located behind the engine forward of the pilot's seat, he found himself staring straight at Cabral, just then displaying a wide grin. He released a hand from the controls and lifted up the cone-shaped metal end of a speaking tube, indicating he wanted to talk through it by waving it up and down.

Gatling lowered himself into the compartment and came back up with the shiny end of the tube against his mouth. "Okay, I'm ready," he shouted. "Can you hear me?"

Holding the tube against his ear, Cabral gave an exaggerated up and down movement of his head. He moved it down to his mouth. "You know where we're going?" he called through the tube.

Gatling wagged his head. "I don't know. Cebu, I guess."

"No, Cebu's been captured. Besides, we wouldn't have even have enough fuel to make it there. We're heading for Palayan. We'll set down on a short strip—nothing more than a wide road."

"We gonna refuel and move on?"

Cabral shook his head. "Palayan's our final stop. We'll wait until we can find a way out. Might take a while, but we'll do it."

Gatling brought up a hand and rubbed rough knuckles over his mouth, contemplating the situation. "I guess Palayan's a helluva lot better than Corregidor. But then practically anywhere is."

Cabral chuckled. "Yeah, I guess so." He glanced at the compass on the instrument panel, noticed they were slightly off course, and corrected by banking to the left. He leveled off and resumed his previous speed. "I know where to go on Palayan and we'll be taken care of. Maybe we can catch a submarine."

Gatling took in a breath of cool nighttime air. It felt crisp, clean. He liked it. "Okay," he said. "I'm grateful for everything. Lead on; I'll follow."

Cabral winked an eye. "I guess that wad of bills helps, too. A fella can do a lot with that kind of money."

"Yeah, you're right on that. I'm married and I can tell you my wife and me are going to do something really good. Maybe buy a house."

Cabral nodded in a distracted sort of way and continued flying. Several minutes passed without any conversation, then he brought up a delicate subject that had been on the top of his mind since leaving. "Why do you think Ed Bannon gave up his seat?" he asked. "It's hard to figure why a guy would do that. He was ready to go; even gave me his bag. Now he's stuck on Corregidor, with no hope of escape."

"Doesn't make much sense," observed Gatling, scowling, unsure of the answer. There had always been a mysterious, thoughtful side of Ed's personality he didn't understand. The man could be pushy and unreasonable, like when he regained consciousness on Bataan, but Ed was normally an even-tempered, nice guy. He spent a great deal of time by himself, more than most, reading or just thinking, and he held his own skeptical thoughts on things.

Finally, Gatling stammered, "Ed and I were best friends. We did everything together and, let me tell you, we went through a lot. Bataan was no picnic."

"Yeah, I heard stories," remarked Cabral. He snapped his gaze forward. "What happened in the revetment? His giving his place to you was pretty fast."

Propelled by the swift velocity of the passing wind, Gatling's rumpled hair flew wildly over his head. A thick knot of it fastened itself over an eye. He twisted slightly and the wind swept it away. He snarled into the speaking tube.

"Ed hated Lieutenant Colonel Dohlman. Thought he was a pompous idiot. Ed blew his top and knocked him to the ground."

He paused as Cabral spoke. "Should have done it myself," he said. "Imagine, trying to buy your way out. Some officer he is."

Gatling nodded. "But there's one other thing, something Ed told me one time. His fiancé died when the two of them cracked up in a plane a couple years ago. He was pretty broken up and never got over it. Said he didn't have anything to live for and I did."

"Huh. That's too bad," grunted Cabral. He paused a moment. "The plane wasn't a Lincoln Standard, was it?"

Gatling shrugged. "I don't rightly know," he said. "It could've been. He said he owned one once."

"Well I guess we won't know until after the war."

The clouds were thinning and stars appeared in the sky like shimmering diamonds. Cabral gunned the engine and swooped down low to the water, flying no more than twenty feet above the waves. They seemed to be clipping right along. "We'll stay low like this all the way to Palayan," he said. "We'll be hard to spot and can go wide around any enemy ships. Lights will give them away and we'll see'em from a long way off."

Absorbed in flying, Cabral tossed the speaking tube aside and focused his thoughts on the job, keeping a sharp lookout ahead. Gatling felt a wave of exhaustion pass through his body and decided to lie back against mail pouches piled against the fuselage and get some sleep. But the question of the Lincoln-Standard pressed at his mind. Why did Cabral ask such a foolish thing? He waved a hand in the air, signaling Cabral to pick up his end of the speaking tube.

"What's the big deal with the Lincoln Standard?" Gatling demanded. "What the hell does that have to do with anything?" He spat out the words in a sharp, jagged voice.

Cabral cast a quick glance, a corner of his mouth turned up, easily visible. "As far as you're concerned," he said, "the Lincoln Standard was the best plane ever built. Someday you'll know why."

Gatling scrunched up his mouth. "What are you talking about?"

Cabral's lips settled into a full smile. "It was my first plane, but that's only half the story. Like I said, someday you'll figure the rest out."

Shaking his head, figuring Cabral wouldn't give a straight answer and that it didn't matter anyway, Gatling lowered himself and rearranged the mailbags, intending to catch some shut eye. He was in no mood for figuring out silly riddles. Getting out was enough.

It was comfortable against the sacks and within seconds he fell into a heavy, drug-like sleep, not waking until the plane touched down on Palayan's short palm-lined airstrip. Several men ran toward the plane to maneuver it into the jungle and, as they did, Gatling raised his head outside the cockpit. A faint glow of red shined over the horizon, birds squawked and chirped overhead, and monkeys chattered in the verdant, unspoiled jungle. No explosions, no smoke, no booms. Just the refreshing sound of nature. The day seemed promising indeed.

Chapter 22

Home in Arizona

Yuma, Arizona, December 3, 1942

The Southern Pacific train *Argonaut* hurtled through the tiny community of Niland, California, near the southern tip of the inland Salton Sea, and headed southeast into a vast expanse of barren desert, skirting hundreds of miles of wide, drifting sand dunes resembling those of Africa's Sahara Desert. Becky Gatling, head resting on her husband's warm shoulder, sat in a passenger coach enjoying his closeness, dozing in and out. She had longed for this for many months and his return seemed almost miraculous.

She had received a Western Union telegram two months before from Darwin, Australia, sent the morning he stepped off the submarine *Sea Tiger*, sick with a case of malaria. Whisked off to a hospital, he was pumped full of quinine and sentenced to bed rest in a sunny room for three weeks. Nurses then bundled him up and sent him home on a cargo ship bound for San Francisco, arriving in late November.

Barely able to hold down her excitement, Becky waited to greet him at Fort Mason, and never a more wonderful sight did she see. Gaunt and hardened from the long ordeal of avoiding Japanese forces that occupied Palayan and his bout with malaria, she found he hadn't really changed. His sense of humor, his easygoing personality; all were there.

The homecoming was magical. Since Jim Gatling now had plenty of money, they spent four nights in a palatial suite at the Mark Hopkins Hotel atop San Francisco's Nob Hill, hardly stepping outside the first two days, ordering room service meals and going through bottle after bottle of champagne. They later ventured into the city, riding cable cars through foggy streets, eating cracked crab and fresh sourdough bread at Fisherman's Wharf, and riding a ferry across the bay to Sausalito for lunch overlooking the water.

On the final morning, they took a cab to the Southern Pacific Depot on Townsend Street and purchased two round trip tickets for Yuma, Arizona, to visit Ed's parents. Gatling had guarded the letter ever since that fateful night on Corregidor. To Gatling, what Ed had done was the most remarkable, most unexpected event in his life. Visiting Yuma had become a burning necessity.

Gatling stared out the train window, gazing at the passing brown countryside punctuated with scraggly underbrush, reflecting on that night at Kindley Field. Ed had given the greatest gift any man can bestow, life, with the full knowledge that remaining in the Philippines would be unpleasant at best, terrifying at worst. Ed had conquered man's all-consuming primal urge for self-preservation; his strongest desire.

Becoming a prisoner of the Japanese would be nasty and could very well result in death, for Gatling knew the cruelty soldiers of the imperial army could exact. Starvation, beatings and constant work would be the day-to-day regimen in a Japanese prisoner of war camp. But at least Ed would be alive with the prospect of returning.

As for other possibilities, Gatling loathed even considering them. There had been no way to determine what had occurred during Corregidor's final days. Ed would have been on the beaches fighting when the Japanese came ashore, he was sure of that, and may have taken a bullet, or even a bayonet. Who knows?

Gatling took a deep breath and turned toward Becky, tightening the arm around her shoulders and drawing her close. Looking down on her delicate features, he realized what a lucky, fortunate man he was. Her face was well-modeled and feminine, lips curled with a soft, pink radiance. He inclined his head and brushed a soft kiss against her forehead, remembering the days when her presence, her touch, were only the stuff of dreams, a yearned for but distant memory.

He cradled her for the next five minutes, then the train slowed and clattered across a steel bridge over the blue Colorado River, the adobe-colored Yuma train depot on the right just beyond. Coming into view, its concrete platforms were crowded with travelers and local members of the Quechan Indian Tribe selling trinkets spread out on blankets.

"We're coming into Yuma," he whispered to Becky, still half-sleeping in his arms. "Ed's mother and father will be waiting. You only have a minute or two to freshen up."

She smiled, a coy, sweet curving of her lips, and brushed a hand over her forehead. "Okay, honey," she said, rising up. "But the train makes a thirty minute stop here. I checked the timetable. I'll be ready in five." She picked up a case at her feet and walked to the end of the car, clicking the door of the woman's restroom behind.

Gatling pressed his face against the window and looked out. He spotted a man and woman outside, looking as if they were waiting for someone. The two were dressed formally, the middle-aged man sporting an out-of-date brown derby and smoking a pipe. The woman wore a gray hat with a white veil descending half way down her face. It must be them, he told himself.

Rising up, he reached for two suitcases on the metal rack near the ceiling and squeezed his way to the rear of the car. The aisle was crowded with people stretching their legs. As he passed the women's restroom, he called out his wife's name and she peeked through the door, calmly brushing her hair. "I'm going outside to meet the Bannons," he said. "We'll wait for you." She nodded and clicked the door shut.

Gatling shrugged and walked outside, a brakeman helping him down with the bags. The man and woman still waited, looking up and down the platform as they held hands. Gatling took a big swallow and walked up. "Are you Mr. and Mrs. Marshall Bannon?"

The two looked at him. The man removed the pipe from his mouth. "You must be Jim Gatling," he said. Smiling, he extended a hand and the two shook. Marshall's hand was muscular and calloused, exactly as you'd expect of a railroad worker.

"That's quite a handshake you've got," grinned Gatling.

"Yeah, you work on the railroad for twenty years and you'll get one just like it."

Gatling released his grip and turned to Marion. She reached up and placed both arms around his shoulders, hugging him tight. "You're Eddie's best friend," she said in a broken whisper. "He told us about you so many times."

Surprised, Gatling leaned forward, allowing her to draw him close. She obviously needed the nearness and he was the closest thing available to her son. He stood there for a moment and she started to cry. Stepping back, she slipped a handkerchief from her purse and dabbed at tears streaking her cheeks.

"My makeup's going to be ruined," she said with a bland half-smile.

Marshall put an arm around Marion and stepped forward. "Where's Becky" he said, "your lovely wife? We've heard about her, too."

"Oh, she's back on the train. She'll be out in a second."

Just then, Becky emerged down the steps leading from the car. She looked like she had just come out of a beauty salon, with all her hair in place and makeup perfect. At least that's the way Jim Gatling assessed it.

"There she is now," he said, strolling forward and taking her hand. Turning toward the Bannons, he said, "Honey, I'd like you to meet Marshall and Marion Bannon. The parents of the best guy I ever met."

"It's nice to meet you," she said, shaking Marshall's hand and giving a quick hug to Marion. "We've both been looking forward to visiting."

Marshall nodded, took an inward breath through his pipe and spoke. "Marion's got a light meal all made up at home, so why don't we get going. Lemonade in the icebox and everything. We can take my car."

"Sounds good," replied Gatling. "I've got some things for you, too."

Marshall and Marion exchanged glances and descended the concrete stairs toward the dirt parking lot. "We want to hear all about what you and Ed did back on Bataan," Marshall said over his shoulder.

They drove the few blocks to the Bannon house and pulled up in the driveway, got out and walked inside. As if on a mission, Marion headed straight for the kitchen where she slid trays of cheeses and meats from the icebox and spread them out on the table in the dining room next to fragrant white rolls baked early that morning. On a second trip she retrieved a pitcher of lemonade and a quart bottle of fresh milk. Everything looked ready.

Marshall winked at his wife. "Well, let's dig in," he announced, moving toward the table.

Both women hung back and allowed the men to go first, slowly retreating toward two straight back chairs against the wall. The two men assembled huge sandwiches, made up of layers of meats, cheese and garden vegetables piled between two slices of bun.

"Boy, we never once had a meal like this the whole time we were on Bataan," Gatling said with a touch of sadness. "We never had enough food."

"I thought as much," said Marshall, shaking his head. "We got a few letters from Ed and he never mentioned the shortages. We read between the lines and got the point."

"He said you fought in World War I." Gatling took a huge bite of the sandwich, chewed rapidly and gulped it down, following with a smile. "Did you go to France?"

"Yeah, I did, but I don't make a habit of talking about it. I only opened up to Ed about it once—when trying to get him to stay out of the army. Didn't do any good, as he joined anyway." He shrugged. "Combat, as you now know, is a horrible thing. I still wake up nights thinking about it."

Gatling drew his eyebrows together. "Yeah," he said, nodding as he spoke. "I never wanted to be a foot soldier and will never do it again."

Marshall took a bite of his sandwich and chewed in silence, taking a moment before swallowing. He washed it down with a gulp of lemonade and then set the sandwich and glass on the table. He walked to an upholstered easy chair and settled into it. He beckoned Gatling to sit across from him on the sofa. Leaning back, he clasped hands together.

"Okay," he said, "I gotta ask you a favor, Jim."

"You got it," he replied. "Just ask."

"This is it. I'm going to ask you lots of questions about Ed. I want you to answer them with complete honesty. Don't gloss over anything or leave things out to pretty them up. All I want is the truth."

Gatling answered with a quiet, polite nod. "Go ahead," he said in a serious voice. "Ed is my best friend in the world and you're his parents. You're entitled to know everything."

"Good." He reached toward the coffee table and lifted a pipe from a pipe stand, tamped tobacco into it and placed it in his mouth. He lit it with a match and breathed in and out through the stem. Soon, the smoldering tobacco glowed red and a thin stream of fragrant gray smoke drifted toward the ceiling. He settled back. "Tell me," he said, "when was it you started running out of planes? Ed wrote that he shot down a Jap, but how many did you and he get? You must've had plenty of targets." He clamped the pipe firmly between his teeth and fixed his eyes on Gatling.

Cheeks reddening, Gatling was embarrassed at the answer to that question. He glanced across the room at Becky through wide eyes before turning back. "Mr. Bannon, it was a lot worse than you know," he answered slowly. "Both of us went down when the Japs first attacked and never flew again."

"What?" Marshall pulled the pipe from his mouth and jerked forward. "The first day?" He shook his head in disbelief. "Why, there must have been other planes or, at least, other pilots to spell. What the hell went on over there?"

Gatling squirmed. "Sir, I don't know what the newspapers said over here, but we lost most of our air force the first day. The Japs got most of our planes on the ground or when they were almost out of fuel. They caught us with our pants down."

Angry, Marshall banged himself into the back of the chair. "I can't believe it," he roared. "Those self-important generals strutting about in their fancy uniforms acting like they know everything didn't do their jobs, did they?" He scrunched up his mouth in bitterness. "It's exactly what I learned back in the Great War; never trust the big brass. They'll sell you down the river to save their own skins."

"Well, sir," said Gatling, raising his right brow, "I met a few good ones over there, but I met another who fits the bill about right. Douglas MacArthur. We called him 'Dugout Doug.'"

Marshall looked up. "He got out of there before the end, didn't he? The papers say he left on a torpedo boat. Quite an escape, they say."

Gatling straightened. "Yeah, he ran out, leaving all his men to die. Plus, he lied throughout the campaign. Kept saying reinforcements were around the corner when they weren't. That pompous jerk was responsible for the lousy supply situation and screwing up the first day of the war."

"How did he do that?" asked Marshall. "News reports make him out to be quite the military man."

"MacArthur's nothing but smoke and mirrors. He took credit for every success and made up others. During the last weeks of peace, he held back our planes from reconnoitering Jap air bases on Formosa because he said it would be 'provocative,' while they reconnoitered the hell out of us. The Japs had detailed maps of everything by the time the war started."

Gatling stopped, disgusted, and took a deep breath. "I tell you," he declared, "I have no respect for that man and will never serve under him again."

Marion approached from the dining room, not liking the scene before her. The men were getting riled up and she wanted to hear more about her son, not Douglas MacArthur. "Jim," she interjected,

"Becky told me you brought along a bag of things from Ed. Will you give them to me?"

"Sure, ma'am," he replied, grateful for the distraction. He walked outside to the car, removed Ed's bag from a suitcase and carried it back. He handed it to Marion.

"Here it is, Mrs. Bannon. I went through it back on Palayan and had to use a few things, but it's basically all there. Not much, really."

Marion drew the bag open and emptied its contents. There were socks and underwear, a .45 caliber pistol and a few rounds of ammunition, some letters from home, a paperback novel, an engraved Zippo cigarette lighter, spare shirt, and a photograph of Barbara in a brass frame.

Marion took the photograph into her hands, gazed at it and brought it up to her breast, a soft gasp catching in her throat. Ed had pasted a photo of himself on the glass so that the cheek of each person touched the other. It was as if he wanted to be at Barbara's side at all times, though she had been gone for over two years.

Marion lifted the picture away and held it out to Marshall. The two looked at each other, raw hurt glimmering in their eyes. A muscle quivering in his jaw, Marshall turned toward Gatling.

"Jim, I suppose he told you about Barbara. She's buried a few blocks from here."

"One of the things I want to do while I'm in Yuma is go out to the grave."

Marshall nodded. He pressed his lips together, leaned back and closed his eyes. He sat very still for several minutes. During this time, Gatling reflected on getting out of Corregidor. He remembered something the pilot, Cabral, told him while flying away from the island. It seemed a cryptic, meaningless comment at the time. He said that the Lincoln Standard was the best plane ever made. Why did he say that? The Lincoln Standard was no slouch of an aircraft, but it was far from a landmark of aviation development. Maybe it had something to do with Ed. Perhaps now was the time to ask.

"Mr. Bannon, after Ed learned to fly before the war, what was the plane he owned?"

"Oh gosh, I'm not sure. It was pretty outmoded by then. I think it was called a Lincoln. Something like that. It was a biplane, though."

"I see," Gatling nodded. "If you don't mind me asking, was that the plane he and Barbara crashed in?"

Marshall gave him a quizzical look. "Yeah, it was. Why are you asking?"

"Well, the pilot who flew me out of Corregidor had some good things to say about Lincoln Standards. Seemed like it related to Ed somehow, but I never figured out why. He said I would know someday." Gatling scowled. "Can't figure out how I can do that."

It sounded far-fetched to Marshall, too. Paying it no mind, he leaned back into the soft cushion of the chair, suppressing a sigh. This was not proving to be a good afternoon. The uncertainty of Ed's loss held him in its grip and waves of nausea tore at his insides. He wanted to talk more to Jim Gatling, to learn more about Ed, but the time didn't seem right for some reason.

Disturbed by his inner confusion, he blinked, feeling lightheaded. "Jim, Becky, I'm sorry we're not better company." He took a deep, unsteady breath. "This hasn't been a good year for us. Not with what's happened to Ed and all."

He straightened and rose from the easy chair. "Look," he said with a sad face, "you two move your bags into Ed's old room at the top of the stairs and stay there tonight. You can sit down here and eat all you want. Maybe listen to the radio or something. We'll walk over to Barbara's grave in the morning. That sound okay?"

"Sure, if it's no bother."

"It's no bother; we're glad you're here," chimed in Marion. "I'll make us a nice hot breakfast, too."

Gatling rose, knowing this was a difficult, emotional time. He cleared his throat and spoke in a calm, forthright voice. "That sounds fine, Mrs. Bannon." He took a step toward Marshall and stopped in front of him, slipping a letter out of his breast pocket. He handed it over. "This here is a letter Ed gave me as I was leaving Corregidor. I'll tell you how it happened tomorrow, but I promised him I would deliver it personal. So, here it is. I never opened it."

Stunned, Marshall gazed upon the letter as if manna from heaven. There had been no letters from Ed since the two back in March. He looked up at Marion, his lips trembling. She quickly glanced at Gatling. "We'll read it in our room," she said. "I think we need some privacy."

Marshall stepped toward his wife, grasped her forearm and walked side-by-side to the stairs. He seemed to have aged five years in the last five minutes, thought Gatling as they walked away.

Swiveling around at the base of the stairs, Marshall spoke, his voice cracking. "I pray you two never have to deal with something like this. It isn't right for parents to bury their own children. It's supposed to be the other way around." He turned and the two vanished up the stairs.

Both Jim and Becky knew the situation would be awkward, but had to be done. In silence, Becky returned to the dining room to assemble a sandwich, and the two sat across from each other, eating and talking in subdued tones. Later, they cleaned up and put everything away, sat on the porch for a while, and walked up to Ed's old room. They shared the narrow bed and listened to the radio before drifting off. They never did hear any sound issue from the master bedroom.

May 2, 1942

Dear Mom and Dad:

I'm on Corregidor and we're taking a pasting from the Japs, but our artillery pieces are dishing it right back. We're still hoping for that reinforcement convoy and plan to hold out until it comes in.

Jim Gatling and I had quite a series of adventures back on Bataan. A navy ship rescued us just before it fell. That's how we got to Corregidor.

This is quite a place. There are miles of tunnels and an entire underground hospital. General MacArthur isn't around anymore, but we don't miss him. "Skinny"

Wainwright is in charge now and I've already met him twice. He tours gun positions and makes a point of *visiting people everyday. I'm told MacArthur rarely did that.*

I might be able to get out of here by plane in a few days, but it may or may not happen. If I get out, you'll know before you get this letter anyway. But get this—the pilot agreed to take me because we both used to own a Lincoln Standard! That's the criteria he used to select me from everyone else. Sounds crazy, but that's good luck for me.

Mom, Dad, I want you to know you are the best parents anyone could ask for. Remember that advice you gave me about not joining the army? You were right and I was wrong. I should have listened. But what kid listens to his parents, anyway? (That was a joke.) Anyway, I just want you to know that I appreciate everything you did for me. Whether I get back or whether I don't, you're tops in my book.

The idea of dying doesn't really scare me. I suppose I know inside that Barbara is waiting. Sometimes at night I dream that she has her arms out, beckoning to me. It may seem funny, but that makes me feel better. The thought that we'll be together again doesn't sound so bad.

Well, I guess I better go. This letter was tougher to write than I thought. I crumpled up three pieces of paper. Oh yeah, Dad, keep those trains moving! Maybe some of that freight is bound for the Philippines.

Love,
Ed

After a breakfast of bacon, fried eggs and toast, the four walked to the cemetery behind Immaculate Conception Church. For a reason he never explained at breakfast, Gatling wore his full dress military uniform, complete with decorations and silver-colored bars signifying his new rank, captain.

The red brick church was only a short distance away and Marshall led them directly to Barbara's smooth granite headstone, a place he obviously frequented. A few weeds edged their spindly heads through a narrow crack in the headstone's concrete base and he made short work of them. Marshall reached down in his pocket for a knife and sliced them at ground level, taking the opportunity to manicure the grass to an even height all around.

The four stood in polite reverence for a few moments, when Gatling retrieved a small green case from his front pocket. He snapped it open, a green ribbon with a shiny brass medal affixed to it inside. A grinning colonel from General MacArthur's staff had presented it to him, the army's Distinguished Service Cross, at his hospital bed in Australia in front of two newspaper photographers, for his service on Bataan and Corregidor. He accepted the medal in silence, feeling inside that Ed was the one who truly deserved it.

Removing the medal from the box, his face shining with steadfast, serene peace, he took two steps forward and draped it over the corner of Barbara's headstone. Taking a step to the rear, he thrust back his shoulders, came to full attention and saluted, holding the position for a prolonged series of seconds. The others watched from behind, silent and respectful, straightening themselves with dignity.

Gatling finally snapped his hand, concluding the salute, and lowered it to his side. Biting his lower lip, he did a quick about face and returned to the others. He swallowed hard and squared his shoulders. "Barbara was the closest person to Ed in the whole world. She deserves this medal more than me. Until Ed comes home, this is where it stays."

He kept his expression under firm restraint. "I'm going back to the house," he stammered. "Stay here as long as you want. I'll be on the porch."

Becky stepped forward and extended a hand. "I'm coming with you," she said, gazing at him with pride. "You're not going anyplace by yourself." She reached up and kissed his cheek. "If Barbara was here, that's what she'd do, too."

The Gatling's stayed in Yuma the remainder of the day and returned to northern California the following morning. The two men spent most of the day talking, Jim Gatling describing his escape and the times he and Ed spent together on Bataan and Corregidor. The story was a great deal different, and much more depressing, than what military authorities had allowed newspapers to disseminate to the American public.

When the train pulled away from the station, it left Marshall and Marion behind at the depot grieving over their son, praying he remained alive. They watched the train vanish around a curve after crossing the Colorado River and, having nothing better to do, ambled across the street to the Del Sol Hotel. They walked into the lobby and made an immediate right into the hotel coffee shop, where they sat at an out of the way corner table and shared a pot of black tea. Neither spoke, not knowing what to say to comfort the other, the fate of their son uppermost in their minds.

They raised cups to their lips and sipped the hot liquid, staring through a streaked window overlooking the street at passersby clutching holiday gifts wrapped in shiny green, gold and red or hurrying toward the train depot with stuffed suitcases. Everyone seemed so happy; red-tinged faces filled with the merriment and anticipation of the season. Marshall and Marion exchanged pained looks of resignation, finished their tea, got up and left for home.

It was a cheerless, cold holiday in the desert, the first Christmas they faced since food rationing went into effect throughout the country. The complicated system made it more difficult to purchase meat products, gasoline for the car and much else, but the forced frugality mattered little during the 1942 holiday season, since neither felt much like celebrating.

Two days after Christmas, before the New Year, the postman delivered a plain white postcard from the International Red Cross. In cold, bureaucratic language, the card stated that Ed was a prisoner of war at Camp O'Donnell, on the island of Luzon.

Each looked at each other in astonishment and together they broke into wide, grateful grins. No Christmas gift could have been better or meant more. For the first time in over a year, they knew, for certain, that their son was alive.

—The End—

www.ingramcontent.com/pod-product-compliance
Lightning Source LLC
LaVergne TN
LVHW041322300426
837719LV00005B/78